PENTURIAN

"I fought for the Flametars, bringing them wood
and slaying any who opposed their plans. I wandered a
vast plate of brass that drifted through the sky, exploring
the temples, pyramids, towers, and mountains. I stepped
through a vortex and explored the planet below, slowly
learning that the fiery lords I served were evil and without
mercy. It was then I learned of their monstrous plan to
bring the world to ruin."

from The Wanderings Of Zondela.

Novels by Tim Gibson & Stephen D. Gibson

SEA OF DEKATOS - 2006
PENTURIAN - 2021
THE WAR MACHINES OF VON SAARIK - 2021

Visit King Tiger's website for information on these soon to
be published titles at http://www.kingtigerbooks.com

Cover artist Rylee Hibberd.
See her work at https://www.ryleecollective.com.

King Tiger Books
59 Garrison Dr.
Kemptville, ON
Canada
K0G 1J0

First King Tiger Books paperback printing: Spring 2021
Version 1.0

10 9 8 7 6 5 4 3 2 1

PENTURIAN

TIM GIBSON
STEPHEN D. GIBSON

KING TIGER BOOKS
WWW.KINGTIGERBOOKS.COM

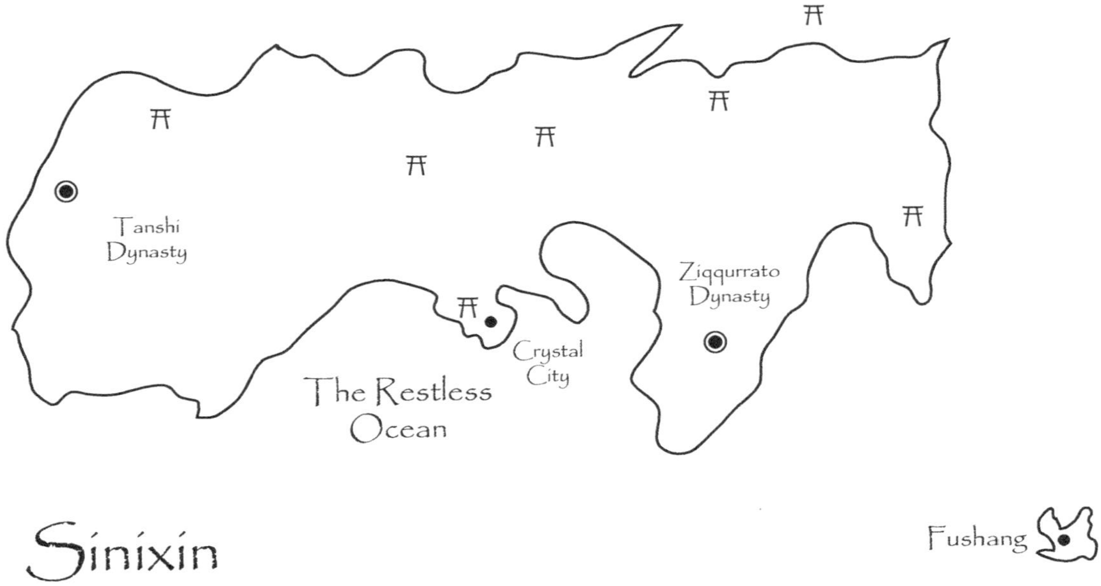

Sinixin
Tanshi Dynasty
The Restless Ocean
Crystal City
Ziqqurrato Dynasty
Fushang

1

Infernia was a brass plate, twenty feet thick, floating high above the cloud layer – an arid, hot, dry sheet of metal, untethered and unsupported. About ten days walk from side to side, the brass plate drifted above the main sphere, forever insulated from the distant world below.

It held one city, all in gleaming brass. Towers rose five hundred feet high, connected at the top with ramps, catwalks, and slender bridges. Cylindrical castles had been built adjacent to each other, linked at their highest points with curving, slender walkways of polished brass. Staircases were everywhere, spiraling up and curling around towers without touching them until the very top, branching off into multiple directions, linking the tallest towers with distant castles. Behind the city was a massive stepped pyramid of solid brass blocks – the tallest structure on Infernia. In front of every building were pillars, columns, and obelisks. The city had been built in several feet of water, the surface offering up a blurred reflection of the intricate, polished metal structures built in profusion and so close together. The brass plate that was Infernia was surrounded by a two-foot high wall so that everything was submerged in shallow water.

A vortex hung beside the pyramid – a naturally occurring, two-way gateway that led to a distant location, probably deep in the ocean that bathed the sphere below. As a child Zondela used to stand before that vortex and watch. Water – perfectly clean and clear – gushed out, along with fish, crustaceans, sharks, and jellyfish. Occasionally something would come through so dangerous it would have to be killed. The excess water drained out over the side of Infernia and came down as rain on the sphere below.

The plate itself silently orbited the main sphere, isolated from the petty politics and changing seasons below. Infernia was home to the Flametars and their human servants. Perhaps strongest among them was Zondela, an eighteen-year old woman, muscular and dedicated to the sword. Beautiful, fit, disciplined, and serious, she wore her brass armor with pride. From head to toe she was covered by the metal parts, each joint of the armor articulated and movable, every surface polished and radiant, each piece hand crafted for her large frame. A decade of hard training and physical strengthening had given her a muscular body. With attractive looks and a statuesque build, she made females jealous by walking by. Solitary by nature, it did not bother her.

Her fellow soldiers had returned from a raid on the planet below with a map. The ancient parchment, brittle and cracking, showed the location of several vortexes and islands. With the parchment safely rolled up in a brass cylinder and tucked in her belt, she waited while other soldiers assembled a pile of wood and branches in front of her. They lit the fire and soon a living flame materialized above it – a Flametar.

They were bodiless spirits, forced to drift around, invisible and cold, until they found flame. Once they entered the flame they manifested themselves into their preferred form – a being of pure fire. Once the normal fire from the burning wood was gone the Flametar had about ten minutes before it returned to its other form, invisible to the naked eye, bitter until it could once again find a fire in which to manifest. Zondela had seen one die once, on the surface during a raid. The Flametar had appeared over a bonfire and given orders. Later, during its ten minute period without any external flames to support it, a cold wind had sprung up and dissipated it. For a second a voluptuous female shadow had appeared, screaming in agony, until the chill gust brushed it away forever.

Zondela pushed the memory away and waited in front of the menacing flame. The master, a Flametar, spoke in a voice like the snapping of dry logs in a blaze. "Zondela, have you studied the map?"

She nodded. They were keen observers in both their forms, able to watch the servants even while invisible.

"You are a great warrior," it said in its coarse, searing voice. "Since this map could be a trap you will go alone. Find the wooded island on the map and return to us."

Zondela nodded and left – the masters prized action, not words. They were a solemn, serious race, interested only in acquiring wood. Every military action she had been involved in had been in the pursuit of resources for the Flametars.

The first vortex on her map was located on the main sphere below, in a distant land. Zondela had long ago memorized every vortex that the Infernians had discovered and had found a few new ones – her telescope was a relic, forged by artisans, and while it did not bring objects closer it revealed vortexes. While invisible to the naked eye the vortexes were easily seen when viewed through her telescope.

With her sword at her left hip, her telescope on her right, and water bottles in her pack, she walked across the barren, all-metal brass plate that was her world until she came to a vortex. With her 'scope to her eye, she saw a window to another world floating slightly above the ground.

She stepped through and found herself an unimaginable distance away. She was on the main sphere – Sinxin – and her home floated so far above her head as to be nothing more than a speck glinting in the sun. Around her were lichens, grass, rocks, dirt, wild roses, and emaciated foliage. The semi-barren landscape extended to the horizon. From there an Infernian raider had several options. To the north lay a vortex that led to Glacia, home to vile, profane Icetars and the luckless humans that served them on the frozen plate. To the north west lay a vortex that led to the Tanshi desert. More vortexes lay east, allowing the Infernians to move quickly in their never-ending search for wood. The main sphere had enough vortexes that if she ever learned the location of them all she could find anything, perhaps even the fabled city that beckoned in her dreams.

The first vortex on her map lay in the distance and she walked, her armor still hot from the merciless Infernian sun, her magnificent saw-tooth edged sword at her hip, her eyes observing the sphere through the horizontal slit in her brass helmet. Winged reptiles drifted overhead on thermals and she was forced to kill a few when they descended on her in a pack, her sword slicing through leathery necks until the surviving reptiles cannibalized their fallen comrades. A sand shark moved through the dirt, only its fin above ground, and she slew it with a downward plunge of her sword.

She passed a river and a pack of frogasaurs emerged, clad in armor and bearing curved swords, to surround her. She was forced to slay one in single combat – a long, difficult fight, their blades glancing off each other in a shower of sparks, while the other green, huge mouthed monsters watched. After the battle they emitted loud croaks in unison and urged her, in the prosaic tongue, to join their mercenary band. They were menacing and unwilling to take no for an answer and she used all her wits to convince them that she, an air breather, could never follow if they took up arms in swampy or submerged areas. Shrugging in agreement, they returned to their river.

She woke in the night to the hissing of a pack of snakes. They called out to each other in the prosaic tongue as well, decrying her ugliness, urging her to kill herself to cleanse the world of a physically repulsive creature. On Infernia her looks were highly prized and other women often jealous of her. Here, surrounded by hissing snakes and pinned by their red eyes in the night, she waited, sword in hand, as they degraded her in all manner, describing her as little more than an abomination. When they advanced she rose to her feet, sword in hand, and they dispersed in the night, hissing insults as they fled.

The next day, walking through fronds, foliage, and leafy groves, she reached the first vortex on her map, one she had never discovered before. She examined it with her 'scope and saw that it led into an underground passage. Putting the telescope away, she stepped forward, instantly finding herself in a dungeon. The air – thick and moist, unlike the thin, dry air of Infernia – indicated she was below ground on the main sphere. The walls and floor were made of roughly chiseled stone blocks. The corridor stretched out in both directions, her map hinting only vaguely that she should take the left passage.

Hours of walking through a dungeon populated by plaintive spirits, many of whom spit at her and promised her a painful death, led her deeper underground. The dungeon had five levels to it, plus however many lay above the initial vortex, and as she moved deeper the denizens became more dangerous. She slew slimy ichor beasts – shapeless piles of protoplasm that undulated along the dungeon floor, consuming any organic matter they found. The level below that was held by beautiful young swordswomen, slender and graceful, all of whom turned into bloated insects when they died, their true nature revealed in death.

At the bottom of the fifth level, she found the next vortex and stepped through. She was in the vast, sun-lit Tanshi desert – she recognized the crushed shells, orange sand, and endless, half-buried fish skeletons – and she killed several lizard warriors for their water after they refused to give her even a sip, telling her instead they would drink her blood when she died. Stepping over their corpses – their swordsmanship skills had been excellent and she had been forced to use all her tricks and invent a few new techniques in the midst of battle – she walked through the arid, dry sand, tiny scorpions stinging at her metal-clad legs until she came to the next vortex.

Seen through her telescope it looked like a square of bright green vegetation floating amid the heat haze of the desolate sand and rocks of the Tanshi desert. She stepped through and found herself somewhere on Sinxin, surrounded by fronds, foliage, leafy vines, and pastel-colored flowers. She pushed through the vegetation, tiny reptiles scattering at her passage and carnivorous plants snapping at her armor. Grim and quiet, she slashed at grasping tendrils and slew a pack of violet creepers. She walked through the rain-rich and moist landscape, fighting off an array of murderous plants, until she came to the next vortex on her map, instantly leaving the jungle behind.

She found herself on a large floating rock about a hundred feet above the surging waters of the Restless Ocean, the water that bathed the main sphere. The rock was about fifty feet across, a single jagged piece drifting slowly through the air. In all directions was water. Sinxin was an ocean world with only a single continent surrounded by a few islands, none of which were in sight. The Restless Ocean – home to emerging civilizations hostile and highly intelligent – surged and crashed with such violence that the spray kicked up to her level and splashed her armor.

The rock under her feet was empty except for birds and a few skeletons. A couple of carnivorous plants followed her through the vortex and she slew them without thought, her mind on her journey. With her telescope at her eye she found two vortexes on the floating rock she stood on, a treasure trove in a world where one could wander for months and not find one. The first led only to an empty sky, perhaps offering a painful death to any unwary travelers that stepped through and found themselves falling. The other led to a swamp-like world. She stepped through, her sword in hand, its saw-toothed edge having never met impenetrable armor in her eight years of wandering, fighting, and killing.

She stood in a miasmic swamp, knee-deep in a mix of rotting vegetation and water. Winged reptiles drifted overhead, circling and making slashing passes at her with claws, teeth, and whipping tails. Her blade tore into their necks, their snarls and hisses perhaps showing regret in their own language.

Long clawed hunting reptiles moved on all fours through the bubbling, vile water, sniffing her out and hunting in packs, wearing chain armor and wielding swords in their scaled hands. She slew every one of them, breathing in with each stroke, exhaling as she killed, adjusting her tactics to theirs, moving across tree stumps and rocks to prevent them from attacking in a skirmish line.

After the battle she rested, drinking rain water from a tree stump and watching tiny winged insects meet in battle, the cloud of metallic blues looping and diving on the red ones. She glanced up – a few giant rocks, untethered and adrift, floated above the clouds, silently roving through the sky. One of them held a stone castle, its windows dark and its stone walls half-covered with ivy.

Around her, jutting out of the swamp water, were several turquoise rocks, large enough that she could have spent a lifetime carving them into statues. Vegetarian crocsnaps lay about in pools, sunning themselves in the shallow waters or pulling fruit from low hanging branches. A day's walk through the swamp brought her to a vortex leading to a sand-filled, arid desert.

She stepped into a hot, searing world. Above were clouds and a few shards drifting among them. Around her, the desert stretched to the horizon, an endless plain of burnt-orange sand and rock. Bones littered the desert floor and man-sized ants marched in the distance, ignoring her and following each other in a straight line. She appeared to be in yet another part of the Tanshi desert, an arid plain so vast that no one could carry enough water to cross it on foot. Zondela smiled – she loved exploring the main sphere.

She found little pits of water guarded by fronds and armored reptiles, the beasts snarling in a guttural language as they shouted commands to each other, drawing crude metal swords and attacking. The sword battle was a pleasure, a chance for her to launch a swirling defensive pattern with her blade, snapping out attacks to cut deep into reptilian skin and sinew, her sword weaving a complicated twin figure-eight pattern. From any point in it, she could block attacks, her sword moving too fast for them to defend against.

Silent and grim, she slew the reptiles and searched their bodies. Several had pouches of colored glass bits – reptilian currency. Drinking deeply from the oasis she moved on, walking through the desert at night, the wind flowing through her hair when she took off her helmet.

Still following her map – it had been found on the body of a Glacian soldier after a battle, though without a telescope to pinpoint the vortex's exact locations it would not have been of much help – she walked through the desert, bones, and shells crunching beneath her feet, windswept clouds drifting by overhead. She relished her time on the main sphere where everything was beautiful.

Even the Black Lizard that stalked her could be appreciated. Tall, walking upright on two legs, with a muscular tail trailing in the sand to balance against its forward-leaning gait, it followed her for several hours, catching up due to its longer stride. When she ran – running in full armor was a frequent part of her training – it ran. When she walked, it walked, still reducing the distance between them. Its long, oddly-jointed arms ended in clawed hands too big for its body. A wide-mouth showed hundreds of long teeth when it snarled and snapped at her, its forked tongue tasting the air. About twice the size of a man, it was a rare creature and consistently violent. Even the legs were thick with muscle and sinew, the entire creature clad in flat-black scales to help it stay cool in the searing desert air.

She waited, sword in hand, the tip down slightly, facing it, her body motionless. Its oversized head – half-snake, half-lizard – held two bright green eyes beneath bony ridges. Saliva slid out of its half-open mouth as it approached. She held still, the beast just out of reach, and called upon every bit of her self discipline as she maintained statue-like immobility. It lunged, snarling, and she raised her sword and thrust, piercing its heart. The black reptile collapsed at her feet.

The last vortex led her to a floating rock in the upper reaches of the atmosphere. It was about 200 feet wide, windswept and lonely. She had the place to herself, a warm, solid rock covered in trees. The wind moved noisily through the foliage and the uneven rocky surface, soothing Zondela's emotions and swaying the hundreds of branches in the wind. She loved it – an empty place to hide, a rock floating thousands of feet above the clouds, circling the main sphere, silent except for the wind, a place of complete privacy since she had the only map and one of the few telescopes. Privacy was rare on Infernia – here there was little else. She removed her armor and her clothes and sat on a bed of warm pine needles and leaves, caressed by the strong winds and the sound of the swaying branches.

After a few hours, she slid into her clothes and armor and retraced her steps. The lonely island would be denuded of its trees by the Infernian soldiers – her missions were about resource gathering. Perhaps if she was unable to find Fushang she could return to the floating rock after its trees had been removed, and build a home there – a place of silence, solitude, and sunlight.

A few days of travel and a few sword fights later, she was back on Infernia, once again under the harsh glare of merciless sunlight, oppressive heat, and the unwavering stare of her fiery masters. She stood with her back to her city – behind her rose gleaming brass towers, spiral staircases, top-heavy castles, and twisting ramps that curled around buildings and split off to link multiple towers. In front of her was a pile of branches, burning fiercely. Soon a Flametar materialized in the flames and glared at her.

"Zondela, you have served us well. Your keen mind has made you among the greatest of Penturians."

She inclined her head to the Flametar, acknowledging the complement in her taciturn way. With the limited amount of wood that had been burned the Flametar would not be in the world for long. "What are your instructions?" she asked.

"Take the vortex by the pale rock and raid Glacia again. Your unit should be sufficient, as we do not wish to send a large force and alert the enemy to the location of the vortex."

Zondela thought that since they were using it daily the Icetars would discover it soon and set an ambush. Other vortexes in the past had led to woods and groves for a time and then faded away – vortexes were rarely permanent. Even those that had existed for years would wink out of existence one day.

The Flametar moved away from her, drifting over the metallic surface, enjoying the last of its time in its preferred form. The logs and branches on the ground had been consumed and turned to ash, leaving the Flametar another ten minutes of its fiery form. It questioned her about her journey and as the orange flames of the master died away, a shadow rushed out – a dark, curvaceous, feminine silhouette, forced to abandon its flames. With the flames gone it returned to its spirit form, cold, invisible, and unhappy until more fuel was ignited and it could resume its fiery shape.

Zondela walked away, the back of her neck burning from the sun. Around her, the city was as it had always been. Under a clear blue sky, tall brass towers rose out of the sparking blue water, metal catwalks curving from each building to the central walkway that spanned the length of the city. Fish leaped out of the water, bold and silvery, droplets of crystalline water hanging in the hot air like jewels before falling back into the sea. Infernia was blessed with water so perfect and clean that the sea floor was visible even in the deepest areas.

With only two hundred humans living on the floating brass sheet, little waste crept into their water. The main sphere, Sinxin, was full of humans, crawling with vast empires of them. Zondela had seen only small parts of Sinxin during the raids into the wood-rich areas and had yet to see any of the great cities. There was only one city she would ever be interested in – the magnificent Fushang. Her friends laughed at her hopeless dream yet still she clung to it. There was no challenge that could not be overcome if a woman dedicated her life to it.

Several years ago, as a young woman and flushed with the fearlessness of youth, she had walked to the end of Infernia. Ten days later she stood at the edge of the brass plate, watching as water and fish burbled over the side of the brass sheet to fall thousands of feet to the distant sphere below. Hours later the sun set as she sat with her feet over the edge, the sky black and full of stars.

After returning to her city she had been so pensive and introspective that a Flametar approached her, demanding to know what had happened while she had been away. She could not articulate the feelings of loneliness and insignificance. The living inferno had impressed upon her the need to focus on her martial skills and develop her swordsmanship and tactical abilities. Zondela's face burned from the heat as the Flametar exhorted the value of discipline and loyalty.

She returned often to the edge of the stratum and found a measure of tranquility in the empty wastes of the rugged plains of brass. In her solitude was born self-love that she could not get in the company of her soldiers.

Her thoughts returned to the present and she walked past the beginnings of a brass temple. It was being built by maimed soldiers and some of the few citizens not assigned to the army. They cut chunks from the brass mountains with sharp tools and dressed them into blocks. The temple was being built in layers, each tier smaller than the previous one. The very top would be a single block. Zondela wondered why the masters needed another temple dedicated to them.

She stepped off the brass walkway and sank up to her knees in water. To the east of the city was a sea, deep, calm, and wonderful, warm even in the middle of the night. The sun was close overhead, shining down on Infernia, baking everything under its relentless gaze. Sweat trickled down her body, soaking her skin. The city gleamed in the sunlight and beyond that, warm seas and vast expanses of raw brass extended as far as the eye could see. A quick walk through the warm water brought her to the main area of the city. Fourteen metal towers and domes surrounded a circular pool.

Infernia – a great sheet of brass floating high in the firmament – had little else on it except the city, rugged cliffs, shallow rivers, and roving Flametars. The stratum floated above the cloud layer most of the time, making rain extremely rare. It was a desolate, boiling place, where the soldiers trained constantly, often giving up their lives in raids on Glacia or the sphere below, always striving to haul in wood so the masters could assume a fiery form for a short time.

Her prized possession was the blade that hung at her side, twice as long as her arm and solid brass, with a saw-toothed edge along one side. It had been given to her after success in a terrible battle on Glacia. It had been cast as one piece, the shape made to her specifications, and while still red hot the blade had been hammered flat and folded over forty times, the impacts driving out impurities in the metal that would have weakened it. The pommel, opposite the tip, ended in a triangular point. Building the pommel had taken the most time. The artisans spent long hours weaving power into it, making the sword a true relic. Relics were powerful magic items, rare and built at great cost. Her telescope was one, as was her interrogation ring which allowed the wearer to speak and understand the prosaic tongue.

Her individualized brass armor had been built by artisans as well, the metal formed to fit the muscular curves of her body. The brass gloves – carefully jointed and articulated – fit her hands comfortably. Her helmet, with only a horizontal slit in the front, hung on her belt when not in use. The entire set was burnished to a high luster, the hardened brass taking a polish well. She kept it clean, polishing it every night. As a relic, her armor was self-healing although it took a great deal of time for damage to repair itself.

As she walked past a tower a blur of motion caught her eye; a woman under her command, Koth, was moving through the air, foot rushing forward in a fierce kick, though not at Zondela. The man about to be bludgeoned by it, a soldier named Thoh, half-turned and Koth sailed by him, ducking into a roll as she hit the ground and returned to her feet. Zondela suspected the two were lovers.

Three more men showed up to stand at attention in front of her, even Koth and Thoh giving up their antics to stand in line and await inspection. Zondela knew them well, understood their strengths and weaknesses. Koth was bold, likely to get herself in trouble if not backed up quickly. The other four soldiers were men of varying abilities, some aggressive, some apprehensive before a raid. Zondela had been one of them once when their old leader had been in command. After his death in battle, the Flametars had chosen her to replace him as Penturian, and a distance had developed between her and the others. She sighed; ultimately, all soldiers walked alone.

Glacia was a stratum similar in size and shape to Infernia — a square plate floating above the clouds, so high that the world below was a small sphere. While Infernia was a plate of pure brass, Glacia was a rocky sheet covered in soil, home to trees, vegetation, and animals. Each plate, or stratum, floated serenely above Sinxin, linked to the planet below only by vortexes.

They marched toward the vortex. Under the scorching sun, the soldiers talked among themselves, reliving old battles and planning their activities after the raid was over. Thoh pulled out the little cubes he had carved out of bone and discussed the rules of the new game he had made. Zondela said nothing though she disliked the idea; games of luck were a waste of time.

They burned under the sun as they trudged across the bleak landscape of gleaming brass. One of the male soldiers complained of his breast plate heating in the sun, and privately Zondela agreed that they baked like fish in their metal armor. Still, as long as she could wear her full armor the soldiers would do the same. Koth asked if they could expect decent looting, unlike the last missions that had been in outlying, unpopulated areas of Glacia. Zondela smiled and reminded her that the Flametars wanted nothing to get in the way of their prime mission. The war for resources took precedence.

The six of them walked for several hours and they arrived at the vortex that led to Glacia, home of their enemies. Through her scope, it appeared as an image of Glacia floating in the air. Walking through it would extrude them on the other side. Vortexes worked in both directions so there was no danger of being stranded unless it faded before they returned through it.

Zondela gazed through the telescope and saw nothing amiss on the other side. They took off their packs and pulled heavy leather coats over their armor, enduring the stifling heat. Zondela put the telescope back into its berth, pulled her helmet over her thick mane of brown hair, and walked forward. Her unit, several of them wearing fish-skin gloves, followed behind.

The world changed. Cold air assaulted her and brought snow through her helmet slit. Tears ran from her eyes as the temperature plummeted. In minutes her hot brass armor would be very cold. They were on Glacia.

As per regulations they looked for danger before moving. The snowy landscape was empty. Still watching the snow-clad trees all around them she moved forward, her soldiers close behind. The perspiration in Zondela's hair froze solid from the chill wind that blew through the valley. Wind-driven snow swirled around them. The land was hilly, uneven, and bitterly cold. A forest grew nearby, the branches hanging low under heavy loads of snow and ice against a gorgeous backdrop of green conifers nestled in heavy white snowdrifts.

She scanned the landscape and found no sign of the enemy; it was time to move. If a lone soldier or peasant happened to emerge from over a hill the enemy might discover the vortex. Such an event would render the spot useless as the enemy would ring the location with spearmen or bury it under ice and dirt. It was unfortunate that life equated killing. The vortexes could be used to explore the strata, or venture to the world of Sinxin and see the wonders of the great sphere first hand. Perhaps, if peace reigned, she could find the legendary city of Fushang, discard a life of bloodshed and take up the feather pen instead of the sword. Her heart grieved and she longed for dreams that would never come.

They moved at a brisk walk toward the trees, hands on weapons, feeling the confidence one feels in a group of armed warriors. Koth – attractive, combative, and eager for battle – was beside her, smiling. Koth craved excitement though she was unlikely to find it on this mission. They were in an undeveloped part of Glacia and in all the years that they had used this vortex there had never been a disturbance.

They slipped into the grove of trees. Koth seemed to enjoy herself as she gazed upon the leafy canopy above them, and at the fine layer of ice that covered every branch. Thoh looked at Koth with much the same expression.

Her soldiers knew the drill – cut a tree at the base and cover the stump with snow to eliminate any trace of their work. With brass saws, they cut down several trees. They would smooth over their tracks as they walked backward.

Koth was the only one not working. She was picking berries from a low hanging branch, a beatific expression on her face. Zondela's heart softened and she said nothing, instead remembering a time when the two of them were equals, and friends. Koth moved on a bit, gathering more berries, testing their scent by bringing them close to her face. It was a most un-warrior like action, one that Zondela, whose entire life had been spent in the army, was not used to seeing, especially not from aggressive and war-mad Koth. She wandered a bit, pulling down frozen blossoms, and missed seeing what Zondela's sharp eyes caught. There was movement beyond her, a figure in the woods creeping closer, its attempts to stay behind cover revealing its intentions in an instant. They had been caught.

Spearmen had been hiding in the thicket and they rose from under cover of branches and snow. Zondela shouted orders.

"Soldiers, fall back in good order!" Her shout carried in the cold air and her well-trained men obeyed, moving backward, blades in their hands, eyes on the enemy. The Glacian men were dressed in dark animal skins and wood helmets, fine for deflecting arrows though not stopping a sword stroke. Their spears were tipped with sharpened bones or tusks and easily capable of penetrating brass – some of the animals on Glacia had horns that could tear through thick chest plates. Zondela abandoned any hope of negotiating her way out. Glacia – a cold, wretched world, with dirty seas full of dissolved minerals and silt, and bleak, empty wastes - was more likely to breed angry, irrational men than thinkers or diplomats.

She and her soldiers made it out of the grove in good order only to see wolf-drawn chariots cutting them off on either side, sliding smoothly on wood rails instead of wheels. The wolves were larger than she had ever seen, well-fed hunting beasts instead of the malnourished mongrels that had stalked her in the night during previous missions. In each elaborate wood chariot sat two tall humans, long animal-horn spears in their hands. One of the riders raised an instrument to his lips and blew a loud, clear note. With every passing moment, their chance for escape worsened.

A chariot blocked their retreat and a second one turned straight at them. It reinforced what Zondela had suspected from earlier engagements, that the soldiers of the Icetars were not trained in the fine arts of tactics and organized killing since the two chariots should have struck simultaneously. She waited, her prized brass sword relaxed in her hand, and stood directly in the path of the wolf drawn vehicle. She called out to her soldiers in the seconds before the chariot reached her. "Koth, get the men back to the vortex."

Her well-trained soldiers obeyed, the five of them staying close together as they moved. She turned her attention back to the crisis looming seconds away. Steam rose from the muzzles of the wolves, snow, and dirt flying behind them as their clawed feet dug into the ground. In the chariot, one of the two soldiers held his long spear out, aimed at her chest. The tip was held steady even as the chariot bounced over little hills and crests.

The man's face was stern and unappealing, murder written in his features. Zondela held firm, sword held high and behind her head, her weight on the front of her feet, her eyes on the approaching spear point. A second before it would impale her she swung her blade and shattered the wood shaft. The impact pushed the remainder of the splintered weapon away from her and the side of the spear banged against her brass chest plate as the chariot thundered by.

Her people were halfway to the vortex, their original footprints leading back to the invisible phenomenon. Behind her, the chariot rider hauled back on the reigns, stopped, and dismounted. More spearmen strode out of the grove and the two from the chariot joined them. The Glacians outnumbered them heavily. Her plan was to kill a few and run back to the vortex, buying time for her beloved soldiers to escape. It was also hard to pass up a challenge.

The Glacians attacked in a single group, forcing her to circle to the side so that she only faced two opponents at a time. She blocked their jabs with a quick flick of her blade and stepped forward, extending her arm and driving the tip through the wood chest plate of her attacker. Her sword scraped against rib and spine and she withdrew her blade to parry further attacks. They tried to encircle her which she avoided by moving in tandem with them, always preventing them from getting behind her. They would have been better off forming a skirmish line with its wall of spear points. Her blade danced out, brushing aside spear thrusts and splintering shafts. One of her opponents stumbled and she severed his head.

A pack of enemy chariots came over a nearby hill and headed toward the vortex, cutting off her soldiers. Zondela turned and bolted, moving around the knot of men she was fighting, hustling to reach her soldiers. One of the Glacians threw his spear at her and his aim was skilled; she was running and he had aimed for where she was going to be. The animal-horn spear slightly pierced her thin brass back plate and sent a minor shock of pain through her body. She leaned into her run, making a smaller target, pumping with her arms, and moving fast. A glance back showed the Glacian foot soldiers unable to keep up with her athletic, muscular sprint. She bounded over the snowy ground toward her soldiers, her pursuers falling farther behind with each step.

Her soldiers had stopped and stood back to back in a small circle, swords drawn, defiant even in the face of death. Wolf-drawn sleds blocked their access to the vortex. More sleds pulled up, more fur-clad soldiers leaping out with strange, crooked spears made entirely from bones. One of them threw his weapon at her, a long shot, accurate and with enough power to threaten her. A twist of her torso caused the spear to slip past her and she caught the passing weapon in her brass glove. She sprinted the rest of the way, not yet tired, and caught up with her men. She too put her back to an Infernian, facing the enemy. More sleds pulled up, one containing the foe she had no wish to face.

A being of pure ice dismounted from the heavy, thick-walled chariot, the vehicle tilting precipitously as the frozen horror stepped out of it. The Icetar was almost seven feet tall and transparent. It had a blue sheen to it and made a cracking noise as it lumbered forward, its body composed of glistening chunks of ice. She had been trained to fight and to hate the Icetars, and now, in her first close engagement with one, she felt a weird shiver of anxiety and anticipation.

"Soldiers," she said over her shoulder, "when I give the word, abandon the fight and run for the vortex." She walked away from them, from the protection of the group, and strode toward the Icetar. In her heart, she was afraid to die, unwilling to lose the small comforts of life or give up on her unrealized dreams.

A flock of spears flew through the air, the Glacians trying to defend their lord, and Zondela abandoned any hope of blocking them. She dove to the ground and the wood and the bone weapons sailed over. She righted her body in a fluid motion and ran forward, sword in her fist. The Icetar raised a hand, its body cracking as it moved, and a cone-shaped burst of frost flared out. Zondela had been expecting this. The Flametars had warned her of the Icetar's tricks and she rolled under it. A second later the cone of frost dissipated, leaving only crystals and flakes of silvery-white to drift through a rising cloud of mist. Zondela shifted her body weight, got back to her feet, and rushed in. In a smooth movement, she reversed her sword grip, holding it backward so the triangular tip of the pommel faced outward. With the brass tip, she struck the Icetar in the chest and shattered it with a fierce crack. Its body tumbled to the ground in shards, and its spirit rose out of the debris – a delicate and silvery female spirit, curved, heavy chested, long-legged, and insubstantial. It screeched and dissipated. If she returned home she would thank the master artificer for the sword; the relic had lived up to its purpose.

Zondela ran toward the nearest enemy to give her people time to escape. Even as more wolf-drawn chariots arrived over the snowy hills, she saw Thoh go down, a bone spear with a highly tapered point having penetrated the links of his brass chain mail. Koth ran to his side, standing over him with her sword held defiantly before her, and knocked two incoming spears out of the air. Koth's chest heaved, her eyes wild as she stood her ground, waiting for the next round of attacks. Behind her, getting out of a second large, elaborate, wooden chariot was another lumbering Icetar. This one was jagged and ill-formed, its body composed of sharp edges and flat planes. It raised its frozen hand and as Zondela shouted a warning a cone of silvery hoarfrost gushed from the notched hand of the Icetar and covered her five soldiers. Zondela was too far away to stop it; the Icetar was on the other side of her men, and she had to turn her attention away to kill two men who attacked her with spears. When she turned again her people, the friends who had trusted her, were covered in a thick coating of ice, mist rising off of their frozen bodies. Anguish and guilt tore at her heart and she hesitated. Her failure could never be undone. Tears froze in her eyes, tiny particles of ice that stung and could not be blinked away.

The Icetar turned toward her, its inhuman face uncaring and unblinking, and again the silver hoarfrost streamed out at her. She dove away, two more bone spears cascading over her moving form. Her first plan was to put her back to an empty chariot and fight to the death. The Flametar lords would select a different Penturian to send on raids and continue the resource war. Greed drove them, perhaps blinding them to the sacrifices of their soldiers. Still, the Flametars needed to know the details of her failure. If the Flametars sent another Penturian to look for her and her unit, those men and women would be killed as well, more deaths heavy on her shoulders.

A quick leap brought her armored body inside the chariot where a whip rested on the seat. She snatched it up and snapped it hard across the backs of the wolves, setting them into a run. Spears flew at her head and it was an easy thing to see them coming and duck. Other chariots turned to give chase, losing precious seconds as they wheeled about. The Icetar blocked the entrance to the vortex and beside it stood a score of men, crushing any thoughts of pushing through them. Escape was still possible. She had her telescope and with that, she could find other vortexes.

Heading down the slope she picked up speed and her vehicle rushed over the snow, the large wolves still accelerating under her lash, and she increased the distance between herself and her pursuers. She did not know how to turn so she whipped the sides of the wolves, hoping they would head in the opposite direction. It had no effect except to cause them to foam at the mouth and run faster. With the chariot out of her control, she careened downhill, flying over ledges and bouncing hard over inclines and slopes. It was one of the few times she had ever seen the expanse of Glacia – vast white dunes of snow that rippled to the horizon, trees heavy with ice, and soft blue sky with stars visible all across it.

The chariot headed toward a thick forest that was larger than anything she had seen in her life. There must have been thousands of trees sticking close together, their branches intertwined above them in a thick canopy. If her wolves avoided the trees, her chariot tracks would ensure that pursuit would be unrelenting as there was no cover in that direction.

The wolves turned, the beasts panting as they veered away from the thick forest. A glance back at her pursuers showed them cresting a hill behind her. Whatever she did now, they would see it and follow. She leaped out, hitting the snow and rolling. In seconds she dashed into the woods and scrambled over fallen trunks and across a tangle of thick, gnarled roots.

Realizing her feet left a trail she climbed a tree and made her way across its heavy limbs to the next one, scrambling on all fours in her haste. What followed was hours of climbing, her brass gloves protecting her hands, her knee armor allowing her to scuttle and scurry from tree to tree, always staying above ground, using the interlocking layer of branches to avoid leaving a trail on the ground.

Wolves hunted her on the forest floor, following her scent, followed by packs of men, their voices shouting every time she was spotted. Often she would escape their sight and her pursuers would have to spread out, and when they rediscovered her many of them would be too far away to climb up and catch her. Her lungs heaved in the cold as she scrambled higher and leaped to a thick adjacent branch.

Starlit darkness descended and they lost her. She moved slowly, knowing that the vile servants of the Icetars would not give up, and made no sound as she crawled into the next tree. An hour later, hoping that her tracks in the snow would be indistinguishable from theirs if discovered, she dropped to the ground and continued moving, her armor burning her skin with cold. With little idea of where the vortex lay, she moved on, intent only on being so far away that they could not find her when the sun rose.

Her fingers ached from the cold and her muscles grew weak. She had not slept in a long time and wept over the loss of her comrades. The tears froze as they rolled down her cheeks, doing nothing to ease the burden of failure. Her mistake had been in moving too fast to accomplish the mission. If she had scouted first, looked over each hill, she might have had time to run them back to the vortex and keep her people alive. Now the Glacians would raid Infernia using the vortex. Even though the Flametars kept guards on all known passages, the Glacians could concentrate their forces through this passage for a quick intrusion and water-theft. The Icetars only manifested in pure water. Impurities in the liquid, especially oil, drove them insane until they discarded their icy bodies.

She came to the edge of the forest, breaking out into an open vista that extended to the horizon with nothing except snow-covered ground. A careful look showed no signs of people or buildings. Resting on one armored knee to keep her profile low, she unclipped the telescope from its berth on her hip and scanned the horizon. In the distance was a glistening window of bright blue and white, easily visible against the night-time background, perhaps a few thousand feet away. The vortex did not lead home; she could think of no part of Infernia that was blue and white.

She ran across the open expanse, her knees sore and her lungs heaving in the cold. There was no pursuit. While an hour's run in brass armor would normally not have been difficult, her body was weak and she was spent by the time she reached the vortex. She stood before it with her telescope, gazing into its mysteries, breathing hard.

Through the vortex was a bright blue sky. The white she had seen was the crash of waves. It appeared that this vortex would deposit her just above the Restless Ocean. It was not surprising the Glacians had not discovered it – the waves that splashed through turned to ice and disappeared in the general snowy conditions, creating little more than yet another mound in a landscape full of ice, snow, and rock.

She pulled a brass gauntlet off and thrust her naked hand into the vortex, feeling beautiful, wonderful heat. When she withdrew it the heavy sheen of warm water on her hand froze in the frigid air, a painful sensation. She loved her brass armor and did not want to discard it. Under no conditions could she leave it on Glacia for the enemy to find and use. If she could not find land on the other side she would have to unclasp her armor and let it fall to the bottom of the sea. She took her helmet off, clipped it on her hip, and stepped through.

She was immersed in the warm waters of a roiling, turbulent sea, white-capped waves crashing over her head.

2

She kicked with her legs and struggled to stay afloat while spitting water. A rocky, broken isle jutted out of the sea, near enough that she could swim for it in armor. The exertion required was incredible, her muscles weakening, yet each time she sank her feet touched rocks and she pushed her head above water.

She sank again, this time with no rocks to push up against, and when she looked down she could see a silty bottom full of kelp fronds and large fish skeletons. If her exhausted muscles gave out her skeleton would join them. Spitting and coughing water, she swam to the outcropping of rocks – a lifetime of martial training had given her a muscular body that had still been barely strong enough.

Zondela sagged against the warm rocks, half out of the water, and let the glorious heat from the stone permeate her armor and body while warm air filled her lungs. A glance up at the sky showed no stars; she was not on a stratum. It had to be the main sphere.

The crash of waves mixed with the cry of gulls while she rested. The rocky, wind-swept island was home to bluegulls and a small army of crabs, many of which sat patiently nearby and stared, their roving eyeballs atop long eyestalks.

Kelp and vines grew in the cracks, sprouting amid rocks and old coral. She loosened her sword in its scabbard and walked up the island, moving carefully between rocks as waves crashed against the shoreline, kicking up warm spray. Serpentine reptiles moved through the water in the distance, their spined backs and curved bodies undulating in a fluid motion. In all directions, the ocean stretched to the horizon.

At the island's center was a statue of pure sandstone – burnt yellow-orange, rough and grainy, a man with his head buried in his hands. He raised his head when she walked up. Tears rolled down his face, picking up grains of sand as they moved, etching small canals in his cheeks as they descended, shiny and gritty, from his eyes. As they fell from his face they changed into tiny pieces of transparent quartz and formed a pile of thousands at his feet, littering the beach in a shiny patina of sparkling grains.

Gazing at her with glassy eyes, the statue spoke. "I am Balakakos and I have waited a long time for you."

She sat, gulls circling overhead, and listened.

A million years ago the silver creator traveled through the endless night between stars and found Sinxin when it was a ball of lifeless rock. Forced by its internal laws to create and able to see into the future, it made Balakakos out of a column of sandstone. The first of the ascendants – a group of powerful beings, all of whom had the ability to create – Balakakos could see into the future and wept at what he saw. Taking up the chisel instead of the sword and ignoring the threats of his maker, Balakakos wandered the sphere and created a series of minor statues. The minor statues, called oracles, each had limited power to see into the future as well and were built to assist the race of humans that was soon to arrive. Eventually, he came to a halt in the Restless Ocean, still in pain over having seen, in the first moments of his life, a terrible future.

Balakakos had foreseen Zondela's life. She was slated to play a pivotal role in Sinxin's future and so he had waited a million years on the small island in the Restless Ocean, knowing she would arrive. In the first seconds of his life, he had seen a great war coming and with it the destruction of the world. He could not change the future though he could teach others to save themselves from that fate. He had created the seven oracles of learning so they would forever learn and teach, even without him. From them, mankind could improve their knowledge of hunting, literature, agriculture, and other skills. Yet it was not enough. A glance into the future showed the approach of oblivion, a war four thousand years from now that would cover Sinxin in flames.

It was all going to happen according to the silver creator's plan. It intended, from the very beginning, for the more violent of the ascendants to set in motion events that would sear the entire surface of Sinxin – the silver creator felt few emotions other than hate. Balakakos had been created so that the silver creator could more easily see into the future, and that was why its creation had fled and wandered the land.

Zondela mulled his story over and decided to return to Infernia. She still had to keep them apprised of what had transpired on Glacia so no more of her people would be butchered. "If this happens thousands of years in the future then there is nothing I can do about it."

Balakakos shook his head. "You can alter the future. The great war culminates in the destruction of the entire sphere. There is a dim alternate future, one that I can barely see. In it, you stop the war from occurring and save millions of people."

"If you can see the future then you must already know

what I will do."

"I see two futures for you. In one you ignore me, living out a wonderful life as a master swordswoman, defeating countless enemies, and building a quartz tower for yourself on a rock fragment floating above the sea. You abandon your search for Fushang in favor of a quiet life in your transparent tower. Since you do nothing in that future, the world ends in flames four thousand years from now. In your other future, you seek to stop the world's destruction. I can see no further details of that life."

She did not believe him. Many of her fellow soldiers knew of her thirst to find Fushang, city of dreams, the place of sublime delight and happiness, according to legend.

"Can you prove any of this?" she asked.

"When you were eleven years old you daydreamed of turning into a butterfly, of growing purple wings and being the envy of all other women. When you were sixteen you felt sad when you saw an injured butterfly during your first raid on Sinxin and spent all evening trying to devise a way to graft a new wing, even trying to create a butterfly with two different colored wings."

Her eyes narrowed – she had never told anyone of those dreams. "You can read minds?"

"No. In your future where you retire to the crystal tower atop a floating rock, you mention them to a young swordswoman who spends the evening with you. I saw that conversation by looking into the future. You secretly dream of building a garden of purple flowers atop that floating rock you found – you mention this to a friend years from now during a lull in a battle."

She was not entirely convinced.

"Speak to the oracles I have created," he said. "They have accumulated knowledge and have enough of my essence to see the future. Seek out the first oracle in the desert of the Tanshi Dynasty. There is a vortex on this island that will take you to the desert."

Zondela pondered. As she thought upon it, Balakakos shuddered and wept silently. More quartz teardrops were added to the pile at his feet, like crystal grains falling out of a broken sand timer. She had to get back to Infernia and if she took a vortex to the Tanshi desert she might find another one to take her back to the Flametars.

"I will help if your story were true," she said.

"Good. Before you leave, Zondela, you must see what you are fighting to prevent. Take my hand and I will show you the future."

3

Missiles leaped out of their underground nests and rushed skyward on tails of smoke and ash. From his vantage point in the sky, Tychon of Kallos swung his masked and helmeted head to watch their progress. They were going to intercept his Stratofighter and he had to decide whether to raise his nose and climb or to dive. With his left hand, he pushed the throttle forward and with his right, he flicked on the battle display. The glass screen used lines and arrows to represent the position of enemy jets and missiles. It could not operate without using radar waves to locate projectiles, so pilots did not fly with it active. Too many enemy missiles homed in on radar emissions, making a pilot vulnerable if it was used too often. The display, however, could not harm now that the enemy had picked him up and was launching salvos at him. Each missile's velocity was represented by the length of the line on the battle display, and an arrowhead showed the direction of travel. Every line on the display was accelerating and the missiles were on an intercept course. He could not fly his jet properly with his gaze inside on the display so he flicked it off and glanced outside once again. The missiles were much closer, straining to get near enough to self-destruct, hoping to wipe out his paltry life as they immolated themselves.

He was not accelerating fast enough to outrun them so he dropped the nose of his Stratofighter. The increase in g-forces pushed him back into the seat as he traded altitude for velocity. The missiles were spread out so that there was no way to go around them and their velocity was much greater than his. His jet, a sleek, highly swept machine, dove quickly. With his right hand on the control column, Tychon turned toward the oncoming missiles and wove a path through them, threading between them at high speed. Each missile had a radar of its own to determine its distance from the target, and as long as that distance was decreasing, the missile continued with a machine's relentlessness. When the distance from the missile to its target increased it meant the target was getting away and the missile self-destructed. Thus the projectiles exploded around him as he twisted and weaved between the deadly weapons.

Seconds later he was past them, the sky behind him blemished with black clouds from the exploding warheads. He turned his attention to the ground in front of him. War-ring armies had turned whole areas into rubble, and lines of smoke crisscrossed between military units to show the paths of the missiles they had fired at each other. Wrecked cities poured smoke and haze into the sky. The front lines were no longer stable, armored units having broken through the fortified borders to race through and strike at supply centers and factories. Even the neutral city-states found that their ambivalent pre-war stance afforded them no protection; armor-piercing shells bombarded their heavy walls and half-machine, half-human soldiers leaped over the rubble. Fire-fights broke out in areas that used to be centers of culture and learning. The forces of the Infernian Empire had made their move and struck simultaneously in many directions, sending the sphere into tumultuous conflict.

Tychon flew on, glancing briefly at large fires that spewed smoke a hundred thousand feet in the air. Those were generally oil refineries that had been bombed in the opening days of the war, the black liquid still bubbling up from the ground to burn on the surface. He flew over a mountain range and glanced down to see the constant flash of heavy gunfire erupting between the two sides. His people had sent in their elite unit, the Zerstorer Brigade, airlifting in the entire group and their heavy weapons. Now the brigade was bogged down, their field guns trading tungsten shells with the enemy tanks that fired from every perch and crevasse they could maneuver to. He called up his battle display and it showed thousands of lines crisscrossing the mountain range, each vector representing an artillery shell, gunshot, or anti-tank missile.

A check of his gauges verified plenty of fuel so he pushed the throttle forward, his streamlined plane boring a hole through the sky at twice the speed of sound. The Stratofighter, with its highly swept triangular wings and thin profile, could dash at higher speeds than other jets though it guzzled fuel like a hard drinker. His mission to bomb a factory deep in enemy territory demanded he conserves the flow to the thirsty plane for now. He had over an hour's flight time ahead of him, overlooking a vista of sandy deserts and sparkling seas.

His transceiver cracked to life amid the static and white noise of all the electronic jamming in the atmosphere. Tychon flipped a switch without taking his eyes off the outside world and listened to the disembodied voice. "Abort mission and fly to New Colonia. You are the closest ship. They are being attacked by the enemy."

Tychon rolled his jet on its wing and pulled back on the

stick, hauling the plane's nose toward its new destination. New Colonia was a massive, sprawling city, another neutral city-state that Ice Command hoped to win over to their side. The attack by the enemy would only help.

"On it, sir," responded Tychon. "What am I up against?"

"We don't know, communications are jammed. The enemy fielded technology that they have kept secret until today. One of our recon pilots brought the report to us, though, so it's reliable."

"Aye, sir. I'm on it."

Fifteen minutes of flight over green hills and forests brought him to the edges of the vast city below. It was a beautiful sight from the air, a clean and magnificent mega-lopolis of buildings that rose tall and gleaming into the sky. Much of it was polished glass and metal, one of the most famous in the world. Its citizens were hard-working and peaceful, intent on expanding their great home to welcome any people on the planet that needed refuge or sanctuary. Now Tychon would protect them, repaying them for all the tranquil vacations he had taken among the gentle Colonians during peacetime.

He kept his battle display on, the radar waves giving him a location and vector for the other aircraft in the sky. The glass panel in his cockpit showed several aircraft flying in formation over the heart of the city. Tychon could not shoot them down without identifying them first. New Colonia had jets of her own, and the planes could be Colonia jets on patrol.

Much of the city was in flames. Buildings burned and smoke obscured the full extent of the damage. Cherry-red light glowed amidst the pall of smoke from heavy conflagra-tions. Rubble was everywhere, far more than he would have thought possible. He increased his throttle, coaxing more speed out of his sleek jet.

The unidentified aircraft were heading at right angles to him, and his velocity was now much higher, so he flew behind them and turned hard, his jet shuddering until he paralleled their flight path. By pushing down on the foot pedals he activated the thrust reversers to decelerate as he flew up behind them. His speed matched theirs and he saw that three of the aircraft were Infernian destroyers, long, heavy, titanium jets that were unleashing long clusters of bombs upon the civilians below, a trail of fire and mayhem springing up from the impact points. Far too many of the enemy lords would manifest themselves in the fires that sprang from the ordnance of the three destroyers.

Lasers lanced out from the rear of the destroyers to pierce holes in his wing and Tychon cursed himself for hesitating in battle. He hauled back hard on the control column and the plane leaped skyward, leaving the enemy jets below. Everything shook; vibrations rattled down the hull, the wingtips flexed under the stress and even his teeth chattered. He brought the straining airplane up to the top of the arc, rolled, and dove on the enemy destroyers. Despite accelerating, their heavy airframes could not match the quickness of his fighter and he lined up his gunsight on one of them as he roared toward it. Forcing his raging emotions under control he jostled his wings slightly to keep the enemy ship in his sights and squeezed the trigger on the control column with a certain battle lust. Bursts of concentrated blue light lanced out from his jet and tore into the destroyer, tearing off access panels and ripping metal from the enemy hull. In a moment he flashed past, spiraling downward in a dive, already pursued by heat-seeking missiles released by the three destroyers.

He watched the ground loom up, and at the last minute, he hauled the nose of his plane up, barely clearing the tops of the buildings that rushed past him. The pursuing heat-seekers slammed into the ground, igniting more flames, toppling more structures.

Tychon curled his airplane around in a tight turn and pushed the throttles forward to pick up speed. The enemy sensors could not pick him up against the background of burning buildings and he raced just above the city until he was underneath the destroyers. Another hard turn, strong enough to prevent him from breathing, brought his jet hurtling straight up toward the enemy. He fired his internal laser cannon at the lead vessel, raking it with concentrated light. Its bomb-bay doors were open and he must have struck one of its weapons – the destroyer ignited in a fireball, its fuel and bombs annihilating it. The other, wounded destroyer had been too close and was sprayed with high-speed shrapnel from the explosion. It sloped downward in a final dive. The third destroyer turned away and accelerated on a long cone of hot flame from the after-burner.

Tychon had little time to enjoy his victory as his battle display showed objects high overhead. He raised his visored face, and in the upper reaches of the sky, he recognized the unmistakable shape of friendly Stratofighters cruising at high altitude. From another part of the sky, however, he saw dark jets diving in from above, enemy vessels already loosing long ranged missiles at the other Stratofighters. The fine formation of friendly fighters scattered, the pilots turning at right angles to defeat the missiles tracking them. Tychon leaped his jet into the fray and snapped off a heat-seeking missile at an enemy vessel. The Infernian fighter turned hard and his missile missed, but the enemy vessel had placed itself in front of another Stratofighter which opened up with its laser cannons, tearing a wing off the target.

The battle raged for several minutes. The Stratofighters, trailing smoke and limping on damaged engines, had been successful in destroying or turning away the enemy jets. Tychon looked down and felt dismay at the burning wreckage that had fallen in the middle of the city. An overwhelming urge to fight filled him, and he knew that he would not hesitate to battle the Infernians. During peacetime he had often wondered how he would perform in battle, how he would handle the fear. Now he sought only to fight with the enemy jets that had bombed so many magnificent, neutral city-states into ruin.

4

She turned her back on the ascendant and thought upon what she had seen – the flying chariots, the sky battles, the speeds so breathtaking that long streaks of white mist trailed from their wings. She had felt Tychon's mind, seen into his memories, and believed him to be real even though he had not been born yet.

With her telescope, she found the vortex that led to a landscape of dry, arid yellow sand. Swallowing her fear and taking one last look at the stony, inconsolable ascendant, she stepped through the vortex. The sea was gone. She had been extruded in the middle of a vast desert. Rocky columns, crumbling stone, and hot sand stretched to the horizon. Stone, sand, dirt, rubble, and massive, half-buried rocks identified it as the Tanshi desert, named after the ascendant who ruled the hot, dry, inhospitable wasteland. Beyond that, she knew nothing. Her knowledge of the main sphere was limited.

She walked, her armor already warm on her skin, not having a plan of action. Something crunched under her feet; bone shards littered the desert floor, everything from fish skulls and spines to pearlescent shells. Some of the skulls were ten feet in length.

The sun roasted the ground and sent up wavy heat distortions. Hours later she came across tracks. They led across her path on an angle, probably a group of people moving in a disciplined formation of three rows. The tracks moved to the left; she scanned the horizon there with her telescope and saw no vortexes. Looking at the horizon with her hand shading her eyes provided no information; sand dunes prevented her from seeing farther than a few hour's walk.

She leaned into a brisk jog, kicking up sand behind each step. Several hours passed with nothing except her breathing to keep her company until she topped a high dune. Below was the sea – blue, frothing and massive, stretching to the horizon and sparkling under the hot sun. The Restless Ocean fascinated her – she loved both its look and the wide variety of life it housed. Whirlpools dotted the surface and triangular fins of aquatic hunters broke the surface, roving in packs. Fish leaped out of the waves pursued by green-scaled sharks.

A small group of men stood at the edge of the ocean, attaching ropes to tall pillars of fragmented rock. They toppled the formations and gathered the shards into a crude wall, stacking the pieces by hand. She watched for a few minutes, admiring the teamwork and strength of the men as they yanked a tall rock out of the ground like a rotten tooth, hauling the debris back to their construction and stacking it up.

The men appeared to be soldiers and were clad in black cloth, with longbows over their shoulders and swords at their hips. One of them spotted her and the twelve soldiers gazed at her then returned to their work. She approached her hands loose at her sides, knowing that she could draw her sword fast enough if needed.

She got to the bottom and only one of them moved

to speak to her. His name was Esuta, a limber man with an easy smile who wanted to know how she had arrived. She knew the border of the Tanshi desert was guarded by a stone wall. Unwilling to share the secret of the vortexes with him, she claimed to have come in by ship at a distant part of the coastline. Esuta handed her a waterskin; she drank deeply, soothing her dehydrated body.

On Infernia, the crystal clear streams slaked one's thirst with sparkling water. She knew that Sinxin's waters had impurities, especially the salty brine of the Restless Ocean. It explained why the Icetars did not often raid the main sphere; if the enemy lords materialized in dirty or briny water they were insane for the duration of their physical manifestation.

Pretending to be a mercenary solved her problems. The Tanshi soldiers were preparing to lure a Wusong out of the ocean and kill it. In exchange for her help, they agreed to direct her to their oracle, if they survived. According to Esuta, the Way of the Bow measured up well against the magnificent physique of the Wusong, perhaps the ocean's most dangerous entity.

She was introduced to the rest of the soldiers, including two females who showed little interest in any talk beyond their immediate task. The women were taciturn, reticent, and inexpressive. The men were more inclined to learn about the land that Zondela came from. She lied, saying that Infernia was simply another island cradled by the Restless Sea, and there was a tense moment when they asked her to explain where it was located. She hesitated, aware of the soldier's eyes upon her, and said that to protect her homeland she could not give them that information. They nodded and moved on to other subjects.

While they talked, they finished building. They had

constructed a stone semi-circle, about half Zondela's height, long enough and tall enough for the soldiers to kneel behind without being seen. On the other side of the stone barricade, near the sea, they made a pile of bones, everything from skulls to the massive ribs of some ancient beast.

They sat with their backs against the inside of the stone wall, hidden so that if the Wusong emerged from the water it would not see them. A water skin was passed between them and a slim, dark-haired woman sat beside Zondela, resting a waxed and oiled mahogany bow across her lap. The woman was silent until Zondela coaxed her into a conversation.

The Way of the Bow consumed the Tanshi warriors. A philosophy and a lifestyle, it had been a natural adaptation to an arid, dangerous land. The Way of the Bow comprised three precepts, that of training every day, high angle firing, and never cultivating land.

Constant practice made them into fine warriors, each ready to battle at any moment. When the last war had come there had been no wait while legions were trained; their civilization had been ready and the individualistic warriors fought with the same skills and fighting styles.

Shooting upwards at a high angle allowed them to overcome enemy fortifications, walls, and barricades. Skilled archers practiced dropping arrows into trenches. Ziqqurratu – a distant civilization that Zondela had barely heard of – had attacked with an army of soldiers and colonists many years ago and had conquered a small portion of the desert. The Tanshi counter-attack had found a redoubt built on a rocky mound protected by two concentric rings of trenches.

The Tanshi archers had dropped arrows almost straight down and cleared out the pikemen and crossbowmen from the trenches. Barricades offered no protection to the rest of the invaders; arrows dropped down in a withering vertical barrage. The remaining Ziqqurratu soldiers ran out and were slain while charging. A few of their crossbowmen stayed behind cover, entering into a long-range archery battle. The superior accuracy of the Tanshi bowmen rooted them out.

Never cultivating the land had further honed their archery skills. The Tanshi bowmen roamed the desert, slaying wild game and using only their mahogany bows to sustain themselves. They were allowed to trade their kills for crops grown by others, ensuring that they still relied on their bows to feed themselves.

Their metal craftsmanship was inferior to the advanced smithing of the Infernians, yet they produced beautiful wood weapons and maintained them well. Wood arrows were tipped with stone, and a few solid metal arrows – used for piercing armor or Wusong skulls – had sharply honed tips.

The Tanshi Dynasty had fought two wars. The first, against the Ziqqurratu invaders, had been long and difficult, a violent war between men that eventually resulted in the attackers being sent reeling back to their jungle cities. Later, while the desert bowmen were rebuilding, a serpentine Wusong clambered out of the ocean and fell in love with the desert. They consumed only bones, being unable to digest anything else. Flesh to them is as fat is to humans, and the Tanshi desert was full of skeletal remains.

The Wusong warned the Tanshi Dynasty of the coming of their kind, that men would from then on share the land with reptiles, and that the Tanshi should best retreat to a few walled cities and green valleys, leaving the great sandy fields to them. Thus the war began and the Tanshi became famous for courting disaster by trying to withstand a far superior force. The invasion was repelled with great loss of life on both sides.

Skirmishes still occurred, and the war left even more skeletons to litter the desert. Individual Wusong could not resist raiding on land, such as the specimen the Tanshi bowmen were waiting for at that moment. The reptile they hunted raided the desert almost every day.

Zondela waved at the vast desert around them and asked how it came to be covered in fish bones and seashells. History was not a subject the Flametars taught to their human servants.

The dark-haired woman crossed her legs and spoke at length.

A million years ago a barren sphere of rock floated through the endless expanse of stars. This sphere, devoid of life, drifted serenely through the night, empty until the Machine found it. Filled with a terrible urge to create, the Ultimate Machine sired six ascendants. The second one was a sagacious being of immense power – Tanshi.

Disliking the horrors that the Ultimate Machine spoke of, Tanshi left, walking west through an empty, lonely, and desolate world. He was a thinker who taught himself language, art, and speech where there had been none before. All ascendants can create, which is why the Ultimate Machine birthed them. Tanshi created by writing. He wrote in the sand and the next morning the first flowers on the sphere were growing beside him when he awoke. He created empty books in that fashion, and by filling their pages he was able to create anything, always seeing it the next morning when the sun rose. Tanshi, however, was far from perfect.

He wrote of soft winds and created storms. He wrote of warm blue seas and created the fierce Restless Ocean, so turbulent that boats cannot survive upon it for long. He wrote of green trees and created the Poisonous Fens. He wrote about sparkling sand and created a rocky desert.

Lonely and despairing, he wrote about a land of civilized people and awoke the next morning to find a group of people, naked and homeless. Tanshi wrote about fields of vegetables and birds in the sky, and the next morning there was food. To house them, Tanshi wrote of great castles dotting the land and the structures were there the next morning, filled with awful beasts or violent spirits, setting the stage for more battles. Once the Tanshi people were established, it became far better for them to create their own stone structures from which to keep watch upon their sands

Decades passed. As their population grew through normal procreation and they needed more food, Tanshi wrote about vast populations of fish filling the Restless Ocean and in the morning the desert was flooded and the water was filled with dangerous beasts. The people were forced to move to higher ground. As Tanshi could create but not destroy, the ocean remained for ninety years until the water drained away, which is why to this day the desert is filled with fish bones, shells, and the skulls of ancient sea-faring beasts.

The people of the Tanshi Desert created a civilization for themselves, each generation learning to survive in the harsh, hot, dangerous climate and training special guards to protect their ascendant – an entity who was neither invulnerable nor perfect. Perhaps the Ultimate Machine could not die – spanning the gap between stars and creating life – but its ascendants could, at least if killed in battle or eaten by reptiles.

A million years later Tanshi himself still lived, young and handsome, sleeping the days away, prevented from writing in his books by the people who loved and protected him, lest some terrible new calamity befall the desert. The Tanshi people – able to give birth in the normal fashion – had grown in numbers and developed a Dynasty.

The dark-haired Tanshi woman herself had seen the ascendant only once – the desert people tended to roam their land on foot, to learn the needed skills and to experience their beloved land – and she asked for a child. He wrote in his book – his guards provided only a single sheet of paper and watched carefully – and despite being barren, in the morning she was heavy with child. Her son, now an adult, was a great warrior.

Both she and her son were expert weapon makers – as all students of the Way of the Bow were – and they had some skill as artificers as well, able to make the occasional Arrow of the Gale.

They spoke more, as the warriors drifted off to sleep with their backs to the stone wall. Zondela found companionship and even kinship with the dark-haired woman.

In the morning Esuta shook her awake while simultaneously placing one finger against his lips. The warriors were all kneeling, their great mahogany bows in their hands. One warrior was peeking over the lip of the stone wall while the others had their heads down.

The warrior who was observing the situation issued a terse signal and the rest of the bowmen rose as one, their weapons creaking as they drew the bowstrings to their cheeks. Zondela rose and cast her gaze upon a Wusong who had come out of the ocean, water streaming off its scales, to feast on the pile of bones that had been laid out for it.

It was over fifty feet long, sinuous, and serpentine. Two long arms ending in claws supported its shoulders and head, and two similar legs supported the opposite end. The rest of its body was coiled, undulating, and flexing as it moved. The wet emerald-green scales glistened in the sun as it brought its triangular snout up to gaze at them with golden eyes.

A hail of arrows whistled through the air at it. Each sunk into the neck of the beast. Even with its lungs punctured the Wusong leaped at them, claws outstretched, gliding through the air from the kick of its powerful hind legs. The Tanshi warriors stood their ground, each placing an arrow to the string and hauling back, the creaking sound of the bows loud in her ears as she drew her sword from its brass scabbard with a rasp.

The Wusong leaped over the wall and landed behind them, flicking its tail to send a warrior crashing to the sands. With its claw the Wusong reached out and grabbed the warrior next to Zondela, lifting the man and holding him in the air. The rest of the Tanshi warriors lowered their aim to avoid hitting their companion and released their shafts, each arrow leaping away from the great wood weapons and striking the beast's scaled body, shattering on impact.

One of the Tanshi shouted. "Armor-piercing arrows!"

Zondela did not have a bow. Her sword was warm in her hands as she stepped forward, slashing with a high overhead strike and severing the claw that held the warrior in its grip. The claw fell, still clutching its prey, while the second salvo of arrows cascaded from the mahogany bows and plunged deep into the heart of the scaly beast. It twisted and collapsed, its coils settling to the ground as its beautiful golden eyes closed. Only its remaining front claw flexed, opening and closing as life left it until even that stilled.

The warriors knelt and prayed before returning to their feet. Zondela watched in mild surprise as they saw to their bows first, checking strings, retrieving fallen arrows, and making sure their weapons were undamaged. Then they saw to the two men who had been injured.

Once they pried open the cold, dead reptilian claw, the bowman rose to his feet, shaken and unharmed. The soldier who had been the target of the tail swipe was also alive, bitter, and sullen. His arm was broken and he avoided eye contact with his fellows, muttering that his time as an archer was over as broken limbs rarely healed properly. Zondela privately agreed and advised him to learn swordplay with his other hand.

They walked, an easy camaraderie developing among the soldiers. Zondela joked with them, finding it eased the hurt she still felt over the death of her five soldiers. Esuta – highly respected among the bowmen – urged her to join them and learn the Way of the Bow. She would live off the kills she made with her weapon, wandering the land and protecting it from the Wusong.

"I cannot," she said. "I must speak to the oracle, find out where my fate takes me next. Is it far?"

"It is east, deeper into the desert. I will sketch a map in the sand, or you can come to a nearby village with me and I will create a proper map."

Zondela's mind salivated at the idea of getting her hands on a map of the main sphere. Something warred within her, as the part of her that had sworn an oath to the Flametars wanted to give the map to them, and the part of her that feared for the safety of the world wanted her to abandon her old masters, find a way to stop the great war that Balakakos had shown her. "Let's get to that village," she said, smiling. "I'd love to have that map."

They walked through the shifting sand and splintered rocks of the desert while Zondela's armor heated and chafed her skin. Her eyes narrowed in the constant sun and she kept her gaze on the yellow sands to avoid looking at the bright sky. The Tanshi still raised their eyes to the horizon, always on guard against their enemy. Hours later Esuta raised a cry and pointed to their left, where a pack of Wusong bounded over the slopes toward them. Zondela's sword leaped into her hand without conscious thought while her companions drew their bows.

"Arrows of the Gale!" shouted one of the Tanshi warriors. Each drew a red-stained arrow and fired, the swarm of shafts bringing along a furious wind as they streaked low over the desert floor. The terrible winds knocked a few reptiles backward. Sand, stones, and grit moved along with the arrows, pelting the Wusong with debris and dust.

"Hunting arrows!" shouted the Tanshi. As they loosed shaft after shaft into the thick, billowing cloud that their first arrows had kicked up, Zondela looked into the quiver of a nearby warrior. He had several wood hunting arrows with stone tips and only two steel piercing shafts.

The sinuous, coiled beasts emerged from the dust cloud in a rush, arrows protruding from their bodies, and leaped into the middle of the Tanshi formation. Zondela's quick re-flexes saved her as she ducked and rolled underneath a long green torso. She swung her blade, slicing deep into a scaled body, bending backward as a whipping tail snapped over her head. The battle was fierce and one-sided as the Wusong swiped with taloned claws and tore the men apart. Zondela took a hard hit and was knocked backward to sprawl on the sand, her beloved blade still clenched in her fist. The battle raged on without her as she drew breath into her tortured lungs, straining to take in air while her chest shuddered. The Wusong clan defeated the Tanshi warriors and tore flesh from their dead bodies to discard behind them. It was another bitter defeat for her.

She noticed another wounded soldier off to the side of

the battle crawling away. Zondela glanced once more at the carnage as the beasts pulled away the flesh with their teeth and spit it out. She managed to get to her feet and lurch away, reaching the wounded man while trying to cradle her ribs with her arm and discovering it could not be done while in armor. It was Esuta, barely recognizable due to a bloody claw-swipe across his face.

She helped him up and supported him as they staggered away. A hot wind picked up and brought a sheen of light sand swirling around their legs, hiding the ground in some places. They trudged through it, silent and bitter, each in their own way the lone survivor of a disaster and forced to deal with the anguish by themselves. Esuta mumbled one word. "North."

They walked late into the night, silvery moonlight guiding their steps. They moved into a rocky area and threaded their way between tall columns of jagged stone until Esuta spoke. "I recognize this place. A small village is nearby, an ancient town that still farms along a fertile river. We should see it in the morning. We will have food there, they will welcome us. A Tanshi citizen never rejects one of our people and they will accept you as well."

Zondela grunted, too busy supporting Esuta's weight. His injured leg had left a thin trail of blood in the sand. "My bow," mumbled Esuta. "I've lost my bow."

"We'll get you a new one," she said, feeling a slight maternal instinct and wanting to comfort him. "I'll make it myself."

They trudged on for hours until they came to a cluster of stone houses. There were forty dwellings, each square-shaped and constructed of thick blocks that had been roughly chiseled. People came out of their dwellings, a few with iron swords on their hips, all with knives or tools at their belts. Heaps of pottery were stacked up against the walls. Some of the elaborate clay pots overflowed with grain, nuts, blue salt, orange fruit, or crustacean claws. One clay urn was filled with red flowers.

Small animals hung from wood frames, the meat curing to improve the flavor. The village seemed successful enough, and yet the stone pathway leading through it was covered in dust, barely visible, and most of the villager's clothing was holed and tattered. In the background, a sparkling river curved its way through the desert. Zondela looked for signs of impending trouble and saw only apathy and neglect.

Her companion spoke to a villager. "I am Esuta, servant of Tanshi. May I ask for assistance? We are injured, hot, and tired."

A tall, unkempt, dour-looking villager approached. "We will consult Ka-Shuka. He will decide."

Esuta smiled. "Of course, but the Tanshi Dynasty requires that all travelers in need of succor be granted hospitality."

The dour individual turned and walked into the village, his feet leaving deep tracks in the dusty sand. The villagers were making little headway in keeping the desert out, if they were trying at all. Zondela followed him, wanting to speak to Ka-Shuka if the village elder or leader decided to turn them away.

They came to a small clearing that held a stone statue on a pedestal. It was surrounded by praying and meditating villagers. The statue was carved from a single piece of river stone – its sides smooth except where the chisel had been inexpertly applied – and was rather repugnant. Zondela had seen one statue carved on Infernia by an old soldier who had dedicated his retirement to making an image of the love of his life, and even that old soldier, with no experience, had done better. The idol in front of her had a crooked nose, misshapen mouth, and empty holes where the eyes should have been. She flicked her gaze away from the unpleasant creation.

The dour villager turned, his voice even more churlish. "There is no response. Stay where you like for now. Ka-Shuka will speak later."

Esuta removed his arm from where it lay across Zondela's shoulders. Her first thought was that he had been feigning injury to get her to support him in their long walk to the hamlet until she saw the pain-filled grimace on his face. He was making an intense effort to stand on his own and when he spoke there was anger in his voice. "By the will of Tanshi, there will be no idolatry in our Dynasty."

Until now Esuta had been mild-mannered and relaxed.

Another of the villagers spoke. "Tanshi does not take care of what he has created. He sleeps now, unwilling to write for fear of creating something that does harm. Ka-Shuka has protected us from the Wusong with dust storms and has drawn game here when hunger prowled our streets."

Esuta's face was red from suppressed anger. Zondela thought it odd; if these uncivilized people thought that timely dust storms were the result of their unlovely, poorly carved idol, then so be it. If wild animals wandered in, drawn to the same cooking smells that so tempted Zondela then there was no harm in believing that the statue had done that as well.

"Come, lean on me," she said in a gentle voice. "I, too, need to rest. Some shade and food would be most welcome." She pulled him away and found an empty mud-brick dwelling to settle in. Some skinny and unbathed females brought dishes of hot meat along with animal bladders of red wine. Zondela took only a sip of the wine and spit it out when she discovered how wonderful it tasted. She had seen too many fall prey to the temptations of the grape and she had no desire to develop a proclivity for the poison. The next skin she tried held only water, and while it tasted muddy and cloudy to her Infernia-bred palette, she slaked her thirst with pleasure. The two of them ate in silence, Zondela enjoying the repast while her companion was silent and morose.

As they finished the remnants of their meal, Esuta spoke. "You're handy with a sword." His lips pressed together, his eyes unfocused, deep in thought. "I need a bow. I'll locate one tomorrow, and I'll finish Ka-Shuka myself."

Zondela figured he had spent too much time in the sun. "It sounds like what they do is against your laws here. They have carved an odd stone figure and they kneel before it. Is there harm in it?"

"Yes. You are a good woman and I will be grateful to have you at my side. I'll protect you but first I need to rest and then I need to build. From the riverbanks, I can dig clay and anything else I need. I'm going to sleep now and I will wake when darkness falls. Be careful, my friend. We are in the midst of a horrible infestation of ignorance and grief."

She rose, smiling a little, her body sore under the smooth armor. "I'll stand watch until night, at which point I will wake you."

Esuta looked at her with surprise on his face. "You have been awake for almost two full days, fighting and then supporting me. There will be danger tomorrow, I assure you, but not now. Get some sleep. We are still guests of the Tanshi Dynasty, even out here in the middle of the desert."

She nodded and laid down on a bed of warm sand along a wall. Within minutes she dreamed of bathing in Infernia's sparkling waters.

Noise awakened her and she rose despite aching muscles. Esuta had found a longbow. The weapon lay at his side while he worked in the candlelight with a large pile of wet clay, his hands gray and dirty with it. He had used a ceramic pot to bring back wet clay from the river, the side of the glazed vessel still smeared with the stuff. He had made more than one trip while she slept, building up a decent sized mound. Esuta worked with a strange intensity, absorbed in his work, ignoring Zondela as she rose and stretched and glanced out a small window at the stars.

Polishing armor had always been a soothing pastime. She removed some of her armor and buffed it with a wet cloth, bringing a pleasing glow to the hardened metal while she discreetly watched Esuta.

He crafted a figure out of clay. Esuta's hands, so adept at sending his arrows out with precision, showed the same aptitude at carving. The figure taking shape under his hands however was gruesome – it had a twisted nose, sunken, hollow eye sockets, and a grimacing mouth.

"I assume," said Zondela, "that you have fallen in love with me and are crafting my likeness out of clay?"

Esuta did not look up. "I'm setting a trap for Ka-Shuka. When this is done, if it is ugly enough, he will come to it. It seems he was out of his host when we arrived. If he is wandering about I intend to snare him and kill him."

Zondela felt a chill flow through her body, an unpleasant sensation as if she had learned something forbidden. "Snare what?"

"A Hatetar. It could be near, feeding on the fear and hate in our minds. They exist in spirit form, normally. We shall see." Esuta returned to his work, and Zondela returned to hers, polishing each piece of her armor with care. Hours later, the clay still wet, Esuta rose and arched his back to relieve his cramped muscles. "I'm making one last trip to the river before the sun comes up. I'll be back soon."

Zondela only nodded, her gaze on the gruesome idol. The coarse features were inhuman and twisted; it was a relief to tear her gaze away. She could almost feel the thing's hollow eyes upon her and it made her skin sweat in the warm night air.

Esuta returned, his body and clothing wet, and set his ceramic pot on the floor before him. "I've found quite the trove in the river." He tipped the pot over and a variety of wet objects spilled out, teeth and shells and small stones. Esuta picked up the white teeth and fitted them into the wet clay of the idol's mouth. The teeth were from different animals; some long incisors and others blunt and flat. The mixture of tooth types gave the maw a leering look that she did not approve of. He sorted through his pile and found two legs from a shelled sea creature. Esuta took the segmented leg-shells and added them to the top of the clay head to represent horns.

Satisfied, he stepped back and appraised his work. "The clay will dry quickly in the sun and heat tomorrow, which will make it stronger. I must complete this before that occurs." He glanced once toward her, then back at his creation. Reverently he sank to his knees, facing the idol he had made, and bowed his head. Zondela could hear him speaking quietly in a monotone.

She planted her back against the wall and placed a loose hand on her sword hilt. Time passed, and there was no change in the steady, rhythmic words of Esuta, who remained in a position of penance before his idol. Zondela, still sore from her battle on Glacia and her trek through the desert, drifted in and out of sleep, opening her eyes periodically.

A rise in the volume of Esuta woke her up. She watched, no longer tired, aware instead of a strange feeling through her limbs, as if her body knew a battle was approaching even if her brain did not. The vacant eyes of the clay idol were no longer empty.

A dull light gleamed from inside the empty sockets, and as Esuta stopped speaking the mouth of the idol curved in a grin more suitable for a decaying corpse than a clay statue. Zondela rose to her feet, her blade in her hand as the head of the statue turned to observe her. The clay head glanced her way then turned back to Esuta.

The clay idol's voice was grating and unpleasant. "It is good to have a body. This is my first, my birth into this world, and I find it timely and most welcome. What is your name, you who have summoned me?"

"I am Esuta, my lord. I am pleased that you are here."

"As am I," responded the grating voice. "As a spirit, I have wandered, observing this set of hovels yet unable to influence events. I felt it all, the hostility, the anger, the occasional murder. All sweet and lovely, but now my destiny is at hand. Yours, as well, Esuta. Thank you for bringing me into the world."

Esuta's hand had crept to his sword hilt and hung just over the pommel. "May I humbly ask how the lord wishes to be addressed?" he asked.

The clay statue rose into the air, drifting before him. "I am Ro-Nith."

Esuta wrapped his hand around the hilt of his sword then released it and blew on his skin; the sword hilt had glowed cherry red and had seared his palm.

The statue floated toward a bare wall and the clay bricks of the house's construction melted before it like wax. The horn-headed statue that called itself Ro-Nith floated out through the gap and drifted away.

"I thought," said Esuta, "I could summon it and face it here in this room, where it would have none of its followers to protect it. "I thought with the clay still wet and soft it would be easy to slay. Instead, I have summoned a second Hatetar." He put his face in his hands. "What have I done?" he whispered. Zondela left to find out.

Ro-Nith floated through the street and headed toward where the other idol rested upon its pedestal. Zondela followed, her hand light on her sword hilt, her muscular legs giving her a different stride from the rather scrawny villagers who fell into step beside her. The new idol drifted to a halt about six paces away from the other idol. The village's original stone statue rose into the air as well, taking a position opposite it. The two loathsome statues faced each other in silence for a minute until a grating voice echoed from Ka-Shuka, the original one. "Leave us, brother. I rule this village. Drift through the desert, there are others out there who would bend their knees in supplication to you."

"I cannot," replied Ro-Nith. "I must have worshipers. I drifted without a body through this world when it was still dry before Tanshi wrote of the ocean and flooded the sphere. There is room for you to serve in my hegemony. This land will now see the rise of a great civilization, and all future chronicles will mark this moment as the first day of a new era. A weak spirit such as yourself can do little to oppose me; you can, however, achieve greatness, and eventually cast off your current shell and get a less lovely one if you serve me. When I control the resources of this land, I will have them make for you the most vile, dreadful body the sphere has seen."

Esuta started to brush past Zondela with a naked sword in his hand until she restrained him. "No," she whispered in his ear. "They might fight. Let them exhaust themselves against each other first." Esuta nodded, a mix of unhappiness and determination on his face.

Ka-Shuka responded with a voice like two stones sliding across each other. "The people worship me. I provide food and safety, I have turned this village into a shelter. I am their savior."

Several more villagers had shown up to kneel before the original idol, praying to Ka-Shuka. A few of the worshipers wept tears of blood.

"Then return to spirit form," issued the voice from Ro-Nith. A strange noise emanated from the new idol, a pulsating, vibrating shriek that Zondela could feel in her bones and teeth. A second, higher pitched noise came from the original idol, a sonic scream that built toward a crescendo. Several of the nearby villagers closed their eyes and rocked back and forth on their knees, sweat sliding down their faces, their expressions stuck somewhere between beatitude and pain. The original stone idol burst, its smoky fragments spinning away and burning up before they hit the ground. Zondela smiled to herself, a grim pre-battle smile.

She drew her sword and advanced, only to feel a blaze of agony through her entire body. She took another step forward but it was like striding into a fire. She stepped back, the pain subsiding as she retreated. Esuta drew his bow and aimed; villagers sprang to their feet and stood before Ro-Nith, protecting the new stone idol.

One of the disheveled female villagers spoke up. "You who follow the Way of the Bow know not of suffering or hunger. We would not survive without our idol. The previous one cured our bodies, soothed our minds, hid us behind storms from the eternally hungry Wusong. We thrived deep in an inhospitable sea of sand and stone because of it."

The deep, grating voice of the gruesome statue spoke. "Well said, Ossa. You shall be my priestess. I give to you the Idol's Kiss." Zondela watched in amazement as Ossa's face distorted, her teeth blackening and lengthening. Short horns protruded through her hair, their tips slick with blood from pushing their way through her skin. Ossa turned to a nearby villager and lowered her face, planting a sweet kiss on the other man's mouth. The young man fell, his body turning moist and collapsing upon itself in seconds. Maggots feasted on the dead flesh that fell from the rib cage.

"It is harsh," said Ossa, wiping her mouth, "Life is difficult here. Begone, both of you, you with your bow raised against us and you with your brass sword. We will die here without the idol to protect us. Would you doom us?"

Zondela hesitated. It was not her village and she had no wish to impose her philosophy on others. In the end, Esuta decided the issue for them. "I will leave, and return with a host of archers from the capital. After our lord, who created the desert and the sea, learns that you live like this, I shall return at the head of the host and shatter the vile manifestation of hate that you worship. Hate is sugar to it, and it drinks your anger as water. It cannot be allowed to rule in place of the ascendant."

"In that case," said Ossa, "we will use your teeth and bones to help in the construction of a new idol for our lord." She waved her arm and the villagers surged forward.

Esuta held his fire for a moment, unable to see the target and unwilling to fire upon his people. Zondela reversed her sword so the blade pointed down, the triangular pommel sticking up out of her grip.

The first villager received the side of her sword hilt against his temple and collapsed to the sand. Another dashed forward, a wooden farming tool raised over his head.

Zondela started her stroke early, anticipating the farmer's strike, and when their weapons met his wood tool splintered. Her left hand, armored in a brass glove, struck the man's jaw and sent him sprawling. More villagers rushed in and she had no time to finesse it as she would have liked. Many villagers received the flat of her sword to the skull, knocking them out, and Zondela was forced to break a leg with a kick of her armored shin when a man rushed her from the side. The villagers were desperate, one even raising a rusty steel sword against her, and she was forced to sever his entire hand.

For a split second, Esuta caught a glimpse of the stone idol and he raised his bow. More villagers ran in front of it, shielding it from view. Esuta raised his bow on a steep angle and released a steel arrow. The shaft soared into the blue sky.

More crazed women rushed Zondela with sticks. She angled her sword stroke so it cut through two of the heavy wood sticks and still slashed another woman lightly across the face. From the lack of resistance, Zondela could tell the blade had not penetrated bone. With her left hand, Zondela grabbed a wrist that was unwisely brought too close and put the disheveled woman into an arm lock.

Esuta's steel shaft returned, striking Ro-Nith through the top of its head. The clay, still damp and soft, could not resist the arrow and the steel shaft penetrated. Ro-Nith's clay body burst from intense internal pressures and sent hot fragments spinning through the air. The villagers, aghast at the loss of their new lord, turned angry glances on the two interlopers.

Esuta raised his voice. "Return to the capital. Tell them what happened and we will make a trade route to your village from the capital. You will have new clothes and homes."

He turned to Zondela and muttered to her. "Let us

depart. There is nothing for us here." Zondela backed away, her sword held before her, her brass chest plate heaving as her large lungs gulped in air. The two backed out, reaching the edge of the village without further attack, and departed, still looking behind them for a pursuit that did not come.

5

A day had passed since their battle and Esuta explained much to her.

The desert was beautiful, harsh, and unforgiving, tempting people to find an easier way. The Hatetars capitalized on it and provided food, protection, and arcane powers to those that served them. Extreme hate birthed the invisible spirits and they were bereft of bodies and harmless. Only when someone knelt before an idol and worshipped it could a Hatetar manifest itself in the vessel. At that point, they fed off hate which is why their followers generated more by injuring others.

The Wusong were a different problem. When the serpentine invasion began, there had been hundreds of them and they fought the Tanshi in a great battle, deep in the interior wastes, the battle lasting several hours. The Tanshi fired their bows in formation and hundreds of arrows flew upwards, reached the apex of their arcs, and came down in a dark swarm which the ancient Wusong ran through. The soldiers were mauled by the reptiles and they retreated to a rocky area, forcing the Wusong to root them out while the Tanshi flanked and ambushed them. The surviving reptiles slunk into the sea and Tanshi archers prowled the desert and patrolled the coast, forcing the Wusong back when they emerged from the water to look for bones.

The reptiles continued to slip out of the ocean and prowl the desert for food and because they live in the Restless Ocean the battle could not be taken to them. Esuta often found small bands of his patrolling warriors defeated by lone a Wusong. Fortification construction along the coast was taking a great deal of time and only a few people wanted the ascendant, Tanshi to create them through his writing, since it often went wrong.

Esuta became quiet and Zondela followed his gaze to a medium-sized wolf-lizard in the distance, too far to hit with a bow. Low on supplies, she expected that they would either flank it and strike from both sides, perhaps running it down, or else they would sneak within range so he could shoot it.

Instead, he brought his great mahogany bow up and pulled the arrow back to his cheek, the wood creaking as it bent. He sighted the arrow tip on the reptilian-lupine hybrid, then raised the bow at a steep angle. There was a short pause and then the bow sang, sending the shaft out too fast for the eye to follow. The arrow flew true and sank into the lizard's flank.

When they reached it the animal was dead. Esuta spoke a quiet prayer and looked up at her. "I'll carry it halfway there. We will need the meat when we arrive at the oracle." He slung it over his shoulders and they continued on.

Hours later, the slain lizard over her broad shoulders, they came to the oracle.

A small collection of stone buildings sat in the middle of the desert. Their walls were of natural stone, a burnt yellow-orange like so much of the rocky interior wastes. Warriors sat about, some with books in their laps, all with bows over their shoulders or nearby. Zondela counted thirty men and women, all armed. In the middle of the village rested a statue of attractive sandstone, carved in the shape of a man sitting on a rock.

Tanshi warriors came out to speak to them, greeting Esuta as a brother and nodding toward Zondela, their eyes giving her brass armor an open appraisal.

"We come to speak to the oracle," said Esuta. "We bring a gift of food and water." They handed over the supplies and their escort walked with them to the village.

Craftsmen worked on arrows, shaping the wood shafts and fitting feathers and lizard scales to the back ends to stabilize them in flight. Other craftsmen struck stones together, breaking off flakes to form arrowheads. Others wrote in books or carved bows.

Esuta purchased a tiny ink bottle, a feather, and a cloth map, which he handed to Zondela. It was a work of art, hand painted and showing as much of the world as the map maker knew of. Half had been left blank.

"We are here," said Esuta. "I have kept my end of the bargain. Speak to the oracle when you are ready, and your questions will be answered."

Zondela nodded and walked to the sandstone statue. Its head turned as she approached. Its sandstone eyes followed hers, an unnerving experience. She stood before it, gazing into its finely carved face, and spoke.

"I am Zondela, Penturian of Infernia. My blade sleeps quietly at my side."

The statue smiled. "Is your sword irritable when it awakens?" The voice emanating from the statue had been craggy and unpolished, fitting the statue's appearance. "I would learn more of your people, Zondela. If you wish to question me, place your hand upon my stone that I may know you better."

She removed a brass glove and placed her palm on the torso. The yellow sandstone was warm to the touch, heated by the burning sun. She could feel something in her mind, some part of her, an energy almost, flowing down from her head and into her arm like a flux. Memories blossomed in her mind, images of her years on Infernia, her old companions, her solitary travels across the shiny brass landscape of her homeland. All flowed through her palm and into the statue. Her hand felt blistered from a sudden heat and she gasped, yanking her palm away, only to find the skin was smooth and healthy, the burning sensation already gone.

Zondela glanced up and saw the oracle gazing into her eyes, examining her. "Do you know all my secrets?" she asked.

"No," returned the deep voice, the stone lips parting as the statue spoke. "Not everything. I know much of you and where you came from. That is the price for knowledge; I learn from you, and now you may question me. I shall answer as well as I can."

"I was told war comes, a great confrontation that will destroy the sphere. Is this true?" she asked.

"Place your hand upon me and learn. I can see into the future, in much the same way as my creator could."

Zondela tentatively put her hand upon the oracle. There was no psychic pain. Images flooded her mind of sky chariots rushing through the air at impossible speeds, turning against each other and loosing steel shafts that exploded upon impact. Other massive sky chariots were unleashing rows of metal objects on the landscape which burst into flames upon hitting the ground, collapsing the incredible city below.

"What can be done to stop it?" she breathed.

She felt herself moving, and although she could still

feel the ground beneath her feet, her perspective was flying across the landscape, zooming toward a great forest. When she was about to crash into it the rushing perspective halted and showed her a great battle. Dead Wusong lay on the ground while armored men stepped over them, led by her old masters, the Flametars. As the Infernian army moved across the landscape the soldiers ignited the forest with torches. A man, unarmed and clad in expensive silk robes, walked with a large book in his hand while hundreds of people kept pace with him. The image went blank and she found herself once again looking at the sandstone oracle before her.

"The Flametars," said the statue, "know of Sinxin and are plotting to take over the sphere. One of their agents came to me seeking information, and I learned this from him. There are few Flametars at the moment since they cannot reproduce without massive amounts of heat and flame, though in their spirit form they are long lived."

She realized why her old masters had pushed her so mercilessly to train and fight and raid for wood. "So the Flametars are going to invade?" she asked.

"Yes. Their invasion will occur soon and it will stall after conquering half the sphere. Uneasy peace reigns for about two thousand years, at which point the Flametars restart the war and destroy the world. The sphere is consumed in flames, humanity is destroyed to the last man, and the Flametars spawn in wild abandon, propagating and running free over a sphere of flames. It is, of course, the plan that the Ultimate Machine put into place when it created Slun, Lord of the Flametars."

"Is the Ultimate Machine a legend?" asked Zondela.

"No, it seeded this world and longs to destroy it before it is forced to leave and resume its travels through the void.

Time has little meaning for it"

"Does Fushang exist?" she asked.

"Yes," replied the oracle.

"Will it be destroyed in the great war?"

"Yes. The war will eliminate everything."

"Is Fushang as wonderful as I believe?" she asked.

"I have seen into your heart, Zondela, and Fushang is more wonderful than you imagine."

"Where is it?" she asked.

"I do not know. I saw into the mind of a traveler once who had vortexed there by accident, while swimming in the Restless Ocean. For three years he lived in the city of dreams, until one day when bathing in a different part of the sea, he stepped through an invisible vortex and spent the rest of his life trying to relocate Fushang. His bones now lie in the desert, food perhaps for the Wusong when they come again."

Zondela controlled her rising excitement. "Can you tell me anything about the city?"

"It rests on an island. It is a city of tall cylinders, a land of nectar and blossoms, as it is known by its inhabitants."

"Do you know where the island is?" she asked.

"Somewhere in the Restless Ocean."

"Thank you," she said, and the statue inclined its head to her. "What about this Flametar invasion?" she asked. "How do I stop it?"

"Forge a lasting peace between the Tanshi and the Wusong. United, they will help stall the advance of the great Flametar army that will come. Without a lasting peace between them, the two old enemies will almost destroy each other shortly before the Flametar invasion begins."

"When is that going to happen?"

"In one year," the oracle responded.

"How do I cultivate peace between two such implacable enemies?"

"That I do not know. You might begin by speaking to Kolontorus, elder of the Wusong."

"Where can I locate him?" She put her bare palm upon the sandstone surface and again her perspective flew across the landscape, lurching over landmarks and showing her a path that she could remember. Her perspective plunged soundlessly underwater and showed a great reptile slumbering beneath the waves. "Who was that man I saw in the Flametar army, the one with the book? What is his role in the war?"

"That is Retulf, an Infernian like yourself. He is an artist and a thinker, and while he knows of the Flametar's plans of conquest, he sees it as an opportunity for advancement. Soon he will make The Holy Book of Flames, a hand-illustrated volume that recounts a false history. When he approached them, the Flametars approved of his idea and sent him to Sinxin to research and craft his book. His deceitful testament will convert many, forming a legion of followers and smoothing the advance of the Flametars. Retulf knows that the world will be destroyed a thousand years after his death and does not care."

Both this vision and the previous one from Balakakos had catalyzed a dramatic change in her. It shook the foundations of her old beliefs; no longer did she retain her old convictions that the way of a soldier was loyalty and obedience. "Where can I find Retulf?" she asked in a low voice. With her palm on the statue, it showed her the way to a crystal city. She retracted her hand and replaced the brass glove.

Esuta was standing beside her, a stark and forlorn look upon his face.

"Will you help me?" she asked.

"Yes, as long as you do not ask me to leave the desert. It is forbidden. My place is here, defending my people and my ascendant."

"It is time for peace between the Wusong and Tanshi."

"I know," said Esuta. "I fought against the Wusong invasion and saw the war ruin to my people. For several years I have hated war and longed for peace with the reptiles. At night, while discreetly watching them, I have heard them singing to each other, the ones with female voices romancing the males. I have seen them draw intricate and impossibly complex designs in the sand, apparently for amusement, and I have heard them debate poetry and philosophy in the darkness. Perhaps I will dedicate my life to this cause though I will not leave the desert."

She nodded. "You don't have to. I know the location of Kolontorus, King of the Wusong. I think if I get him to talk to a leader of the Tanshi, we can hammer out a peace plan. Can you get me into contact with a Tanshi leader?"

"You already speak to one," said Esuta. "I will gather other leaders of our people and form a council. There is a ring of stones nearby. We will meet there." He made a dot on her map with the feather and ink bottle.

"I will contact Kolontorus," she said, "while you speak to your people. I don't know how long it will take me to accomplish this. How will you know when I am ready?"

"Our scouts will know," he said. "They roam the desert and will inform me when you arrive at the ring of stones, sending a message by bird. Wait for me there if you have succeeded, and I will bring as many of our elders as I can."

"Good." They clasped wrists and then replenished their supplies. Zondela had her pack refilled with food and water and set off.

She walked through shimmering heat waves and fractured stone outcroppings. The endless sky lent the land a majestic, never-ending quality, making her feel like an insect against the vast desert.

The day passed, hot and dusty, and evening came with a breath of cool air. Stars shone overhead and bathed the desert sands in a silvery glow – not the massive and bright constellation of stars as seen over Infernia, but a more subdued set of celestial lights. Small green reptiles with gossamer wings drifted by, sniffing her gently and moving on, swallowing insects while in flight. The reptile's wings were pink and blue like those of the rare flutterbys that pollinated flowers on Infernia.

The ground was broken by large, jagged rocks. Some were twice as tall as her, fractured and cracked yet still upright with stony implacability. She walked among them, threading her way through an increasing amount of the natural formations, her skin slick with perspiration.

She knew where to go from the images the oracle had shown her. It was a long walk and even her well-conditioned body complained despite years of training under the blazing sun of Infernia. The blowing wind brought hot sand particles through the gaps in her armor to chafe her skin. The clear blue sky, the vast, limitless horizon, and the endless waves of sand held a wild beauty.

She came to the ocean. It was noisy, the waves crashing unceasingly. Wind currents moved in all directions, picking up waves and breaking them against each other; the distant sea was a chaotic mass of white foam and surging waves.

A glance at the rocks and shells littering the beach verified that this was the location the oracle had shown her; hidden in the water resided a great Wusong. A scan with her telescope showed no nearby vortexes; far off in the distance, well out over the unreachable portions of the Restless Ocean, were green dots that were perhaps gateways to some verdant and leafy stratum. It would be impossible to reach them since no boat could survive the swells and turbulence. The waves became much larger the farther they were from land so that the vortexes in the distance were swamped by massive waves. Of the Wusong there was no sign, only claw prints in the sand. Not wanting to sit on the beach and wait, she entered the water.

The ocean was only up to her brass knee guards when a long, serpentine form rose out of the waves, water streaming off its slender torso. Its body was looped, shifting as it moved. It had two front limbs that were longer than her arms and two similar ones in the back. Its head was proportionally larger than a snake's would have been, with a wide mouth and gleaming eyes. The Wusong was about fifty paces long, and while her armor gleamed of polished brass, its scales shone of deep emerald.

It advanced, yet she stood her ground before the magnificent beast. "I seek the quiet of the sheathed sword," she said, her heart hammering in her chest. The creature paused, staring into her eyes.

Its maw opened, and the voice that issued from the Wusong was musical, deeply pitched, and pleasingly resonant. "I would kill you now, except I would spend the rest of my waking hours pondering the meaning of that statement."

"So you speak the prosaic tongue, Kolontorus. I have journeyed far to meet you, and I am not disappointed."

The beast moved closer, its eyes locked on hers. The Wusong moved sinuously, its body arching to maintain its curve. To show her desire to talk she removed her helmet and clipped it onto her hip, all the while wondering what penetrating power those claws had. The beast's jaws looked strong enough to pierce brass. In her imagination she pictured how the battle would go; she would draw and swing toward its neck while it lunged with those awful talons. She shook the thought away.

The Wusong moved slower, perhaps hoping to hypnotize her with its steady gaze, and she was ready to defend herself if it struck. It only lowered its head to her level. She stared into the massive mouth full of flat teeth, saw the steam rising from its warm nostrils, and waited. The Wusong spoke again, and its breath smelled of the ocean depths.

"Before I kill you, explain your reference to the sheathed sword."

"It means I want to discuss something with you. Something important. The future of the sphere is at stake." This close to the great beast she felt her own mortality and relied on her instincts. It was always the way of dangerous battles; there was no time for careful analysis, only reflex. With the great sphere under her feet, and with so much of it to explore, she did not want to die.

The Wusong spoke again, its voice low. "Where is your bow? Where are your horrid arrows designed to pierce our scales?"

"I am no Tanshi. I am Penturian Zondela of Infernia." As she spoke, she realized she was Penturian no longer – only a lone soldier working for a greater cause. Still, she felt pride. "I come to plead the cause of peace."

The beast stared, letting its eyes roam over her body. "I have never seen armor like that. It is most impressive. With your shiny armor that bears all the marks of polishing and your sword at your side, you come to speak of peace?"

"The Flametars will come with a great army to conquer

the sphere. They have put their plans in motion long ago. I come to prevent the Wusong and the Tanshi from annihilating each other even before the Flametars invade."

"And how do you know of the future?"

"I have spoken to the oracle."

The Wusong paused, water trickling down its scaled hide. "We have spoken to an oracle as well, the one that lies deep underwater. While the future may be as you say, the Tanshi are a vile race, leaving piles of bones to lure us into ambush. They wait until we move in to feed and then let loose their terrible arrows."

"You invaded their territory," she said gently.

"We needed to eat!" the Wusong roared.

"Then deal with them. Give up the art of war for that of peace."

"Impossible. Two implacable species, perhaps destined to destroy each other," it said. "The Tanshi hate us."

"Kolontorus, how can one so articulate be so blind. I stand here before you, a soldier from another stratum. Cultivate peace and perhaps the Tanshi will provide you with thousands of bones to gnaw on."

"I will ponder it. There is wisdom in your words. I would not have believed your species capable of anything except killing, yet here you stand, besting me in philosophy. I am impressed. You must have Wusong blood in your veins."

She smiled.

The Wusong flicked the water with his tail, sending up a spray. In the background, waves rolled and crashed. "Come," said Kolontorus. "Let us sink beneath the waves together." Its claw flashed forward and the large talon wrapped around her torso, pinning her arms to her side while her sword was only half-drawn. The Wusong withdrew and submerged her in deeper water.

She held her breath, unwilling to admit defeat, and struggled in vain. In seconds she would inhale and meet oblivion, not in combat but by drowning.

"Zondela," said the Wusong, its voice distorted because they were both underwater. "Do not struggle. As long as you are the guest of the King of the Wusong, you will not fear the water."

She could not hold her breath any longer and with resignation, she exhaled a stream of bubbles. Involuntarily she inhaled, the water entering her mouth and lungs, providing whatever it was that she needed to breathe. She was fine. After a few more breaths, the Wusong let go of her and swam away. Its supple body undulated to a deeper area. She followed it, swimming with her muscular arms. Despite her brass armor, she was able to swim, although it was not easy and she sank downwards, exhaling bubbles the whole time.

"Where are we going?" she called out.

The Wusong turned back to look at her. "You do not need to shout. I can hear you clearly. We go to rest and think and discuss this further." It swam farther away, reaching the ocean floor, and settled amid a waving bed of kelp and fronds. She swam over and sank down beside it, her booted feet sinking into the moist bottom.

"I was wondering what your reaction would be, warrior," said Kolontorus. "I am pleased that you did not retreat to the surface."

"I cannot," she said. "I am on a quest."

"I would hear of it, but first I must find food." The Wusong King swam away, scattering a swarm of pink fish.

The sleek power and grace of the beast stirred something in Zondela's heart. She shifted to lay on her back, about sixty paces under the surface of the water and stared upwards. The Wusong drifted overhead, its long sinuous body flowing and undulating. Thousands of scales covered it, all sparkling like emeralds. While it flowed through the water it was weightless, lovely, and supple. It was a hunter and a beautiful one.

The comfort of the warm silt beneath Zondela's back and the constant flow of water made her sleepy. Though the ocean surface raged the seafloor was tranquil. Below her was a layer of soft mud, clay, and sand, while a great beast floated above, its reptilian body curved, lithe and elegant.

The scaled beast swam lower, descending to the bottom of the seafloor, and searched for food. With the large claws that jutted out from the end of its four limbs, it searched through the silt, overturning rocks and raking its talons through the sediment. Occasionally it would find a bone or fish skeleton to eat. By sifting deeper into the silt it uncovered and raised a large bone. It looked like the thighbone of an animal, and if so, would have been far larger than the Wusong now chewing on its mortal remains. Kolontorus's powerful jaws and teeth crushed and consumed the bone and the Wusong continued its search. She watched it for a while, feeling indolent and relaxed, caressed by the warm ocean waves.

The Wusong ate a few bones from the seafloor and settled in beside her. They discussed art, philosophy, history, and military thought. Before the ocean had been created, Balakakos had walked the land and created many statue oracles to help civilize the humans that he knew – since he could see the future – would soon arrive. After Tanshi created the ocean many of the oracles were deep underwater and the reptiles consulted them often. The Wusong King was only too happy to explain the ascendants to Zondela, information about their world's creation that the Flametars had denied her.

The Ultimate Machine came to Sinxin when it was an empty rock. The Machine created Balakakos who walked the world, creating only statue oracles. Tanshi was created next, who wandered till he created the Tanshi desert, the Restless Ocean, and the first humans. Third, it created Isayus who built a magnificent crystal city. Next, the machine made Chrontoria of whom little is known. Fifth it created Lunil, neutral and unemotional. Last it created Slun, the greatest of the Flametars, Slun who was fated to destroy the world long after technology had replaced magic.

Hours later Zondela grew hungry and she hunted through the sediment until she found some large red shells with segmented legs sticking out of them. She pried open a shell and pulled out the crab-like creature. She swam to the surface and cooked her catch over a small fire. She kept the flames too small for one of her old masters to manifest in, were one floating nearby.

The Wusong emerged from the sea, water sliding down its body, its sinuous torso evenly supported on its four long limbs. Kolontorus held a human skull in his claw and settled down next to Zondela. As she ate, the Wusong placed the skull in its mouth and crunched. Her food had succulent, firm flesh, and a taste that put all other food to shame. It was so appealing she planned to stock a small lake with them one day.

The Wusong King finished its meal and regarded her. "The Tanshi will never allow us the use of their land. They are so fanatic they would rather die in battle than allow us to prowl their desert for old bones."

"We can easily arrange some safe passage for Wusong to enter in search of food. A few corridors, perhaps, of permissible travel."

"They would never agree to this," Kolontorus growled.

"Even as we speak, a Tanshi leader named Esuta works to bring a council of elders together at the ring of stones to the south. Accompany me there, and you can speak with them. I will speak on your behalf."

"Have they agreed to a treaty with my people?"

"No," she admitted. "Come with me to the ring of stones where we will argue and persuade. If we are successful your people will have access to the bones of the desert without fighting and killing."

"And if it is a trap?"

"Then kill me first and return to the sea. At least you will have tried."

The Wusong's lips pulled back in a smile. Its teeth extended all the way back into the darkness of its mouth. "Perhaps. We shall see."

A young Wusong, half the size of Kolontorus, clambered from the hazy ocean depths and joined them. It argued against the plan, wanting instead to conduct a second Wusong Invasion. They spoke in the prosaic tongue and Zondela overheard – amid their shouting and roars and growls – that the smaller one had been too young to participate in the first invasion.

"You taught us that there should be no decision without debate," said the young Wusong, named Tolantus. "In the grotto of the scarlet kelp, you taught that all minds should turn a problem over like a stone, handling it from all sides before drawing a conclusion. Peace will weaken us, giving the Dynasty time to fashion more arrows. Let us strike now."

The Wusong King and the younger one hissed and debated while other Wusong rose out of the ocean to join the discussion. In the end, Kolontorus agreed to allow Tolantus to join them. Zondela had great misgivings about that; her war-honed senses warned her of trouble.

Once on land Kolontorus moved at a pace that Zondela could keep up with while the young Tolantus ranged about, unwilling to move at the slower pace of the human. The Wusong never went far, always circling them and looking over every dune.

They reached the circle of stones. A group of Tanshi had assembled there although Esuta was the only one with a bow. The rest appeared to be nobles. They all wore fine silks and glittering jewels. Several female Tanshi wore long robes of bright red, while their male counterparts wore lavish blue robes and carried thin silver staffs. Many were adorned with sparkling gemstones. Translucent gems, cut and faceted by some master artisan, dangled from gold chains, and rectangular yellow stones hung from the wrists of the females.

Esuta had his hands on his great mahogany bow though he did not fit an arrow to the string. Knowing that the menfolk could stand there all day staring down the Wusong, Zondela spoke up, slipping into her command voice.

"Let history record this as the day that peace was created between the Tanshi Dynasty and the Wusong Clan."

"It is our land," said one of the Tanshi males who was dressed in long white robes. "We will not surrender our sovereignty."

"They do not ask you to," replied Zondela. "They ask only permission to enter the land and gather bones. A few corridors where they can travel through so that you could keep track of their movement."

"So they can trap us?" roared Tolantus. "Never!"

"Be silent!" ordered Kolontorus. "I am King."

"No longer," replied Tolantus, coiling its long, serpentine body and flexing its claws. "When we return to the depths, I will inform the Clan of your weakness. It is time for a new King."

The Wusong King turned to the assembled Tanshi and lowered its head. "I regret that I must leave and see to this matter. I shall return in a year when my Kingship has been ratified by the Clan. It is our way."

"No!" shouted Zondela. "We cannot allow one young warrior to stop this from going forward. Esuta, are your people desirous of peace?"

"We are. A majority of the council has assembled here to see if the war can end, though it seems that the Wusong have not reached agreement on it yet."

The young Wusong, Tolantus, uncoiled and leaped through the air and sailed over Kolontorus, snapping out its tail as it did so and striking the Wusong King in the head. Zondela had to admit it was an impressive strike.

Kolontorus fell onto its side and held its head in its hands, and Tolantus wasted no time in leaping at the group of finely dressed Tanshi. Zondela drew her sword as she moved, slashing deep into the flank of the Wusong. The Tanshi scattered, and as she raised her sword, Tolantus twirled and snapped its tail at her, sending her armored body crashing backward. Her brass chest plate was dented and her ribs hurt. She struggled to rise to her feet only to see Tolantus looming above her, its toothy maw open and descending.

Esuta's bow sang and a steel arrow flew into the Wusong's neck. Zondela was still trying to get her breath back as she rolled away and staggered to her feet. Esuta shot another arrow, this one blossoming into a large spider web in midair. The sticky substance ensnared the reptile. Zondela knew it would not be held long; she dashed forward with her brass sword raised above her head. The Wusong responded with inhuman reflexes, twisting its body and snapping its tail out. Zondela was ready and she bent forward at the waist, the whipping tail cutting the air over her head.

An arrow flew from Esuta's bow and passed over her shoulder, turning into another sticky spiderweb and further snaring the beast. Zondela brought her brass sword down onto the beast's neck, severing its head. Red ichor spurted.

She sheathed her sword without looking down and glanced at the finely dressed Tanshi. They were undisturbed and merely watched as Kolontorus rose and shook his head to clear it.

The white-clad Tanshi spoke up. "In exchange for peace between our people, we agree to gather what bones we find and leave them along the shoreline. The Wusong Clan, however, must never move beyond the beach, and must never harm another Tanshi citizen."

"It is agreed," rumbled Kolontorus. "I will inform the Clan of my decision."

Zondela pointed to the dead Wusong. "What about that one?"

The King of the Wusong looked down. "Tolantus's problem was that he never learned the art of debate."

They spent three more days in the circle of stones, arguing, debating, reaching a consensus. More Tanshi showed up and engaged the Wusong King in discussions of what its underwater civilization was like. The Tanshi thinkers showed great interest in the inner workings of the Wusong society. A conclusive peace deal was agreed to by all parties, and several Tanshi asked for and received permission to go underwater and learn about the extensive holdings of the aquatic reptiles.

Zondela caught a few minutes alone with Esuta. "Come

with me," she said. "You know I am on a great quest. The world is not yet safe from the future invasion of the Flametars."

"Alas, I can not. I am sworn to defend my beloved desert from all enemies. There are still Hatetars about, as well as possible invasion by the Ziqqurratu Dynasty one day. I long to join you yet there is still much for me to do here. I have been placed in charge of training the young Tanshi warriors in the Way of the Bow."

Esuta spoke with a Tanshi thinker and learned the location of another oracle, which was beyond the desert and past the empty steppes. He marked the location on her map and wished her luck. They clasped wrists and parted as friends. Somewhere was the legendary city of Fushang, city of dreams. Before that, there was a quest to complete and a war to avert. She left with a pack full of supplies and walked, alone, through the desert.

6

Tychon of Kallos was supersonic under a layer of white, billowy clouds, the regime where most combat was taking place. During peacetime, they had taught him that most fighter combat would occur at very high altitudes where the pilots could see the curvature of the world while they battled with missiles. From there, even the flat plates of the strata were visible. Infernia was a massive square sheet of brass that floated near the top of the atmosphere, glinting in the sunlight as it circled the world. Glacia drifted at the other side of the world, a square sheet of stone overflowing with conifers and pine.

Enemy fighters guarded Infernia night and day. Long, narrow fighters rushed past it on their perpetual patrols, eternally vigilant of the safety of their fiery lords. Long ago there had been people living on the brass sheet, slave-soldiers to the Flametars until they had been burned alive as fuel for their insatiable masters.

Tychon's peacetime training had taught that teamwork and small unit tactics would determine the winner of large air battles and that the convergence of two hostile air wings would bear much in common with the old naval battles of history. In reality, the ground war, with Flametar tanks moving fast and demolishing anything in their path, assumed primary importance, and aircraft were used in a supporting role. Gone were the theories that the air and ground wars were separate and distinct. The Icelord's Stratofighters were desperately trying to drive back the armored units that wiped out both military and civilian targets.

The cockpit transceiver came to life and the Tychon gritted his teeth. Central Command rarely offered good news.

"The Zerstorer Brigade is taking heavy casualties. Fly to their location and wipe out enemy targets. They need the help."

"I'm on it."

He rolled his jet over and pulled back on the control column. The plane dove and picked up speed under the steady pull of gravity. Tychon was not worried about misjudging his turn and crashing – he had so much practice spiraling and diving in the past few days that he could easily glance at the ground and know if a given turn was within the aircraft's capabilities.

The highly swept jet brought its nose up above the horizontal and screamed over the landscape, raising a storm of dry leaves and twigs behind it from the trailing pressure wake. He overflew the old city of Tanshi, now half-submerged in water since the enemy had cracked open the concrete dam that had held back the heavy northern river. The river had grown larger over the years, forcing them to increase the height of the dam, until a few days ago when a Flametar bomber had flown in at supersonic speeds and released a single bomb. The impact had shattered the concrete and unleashed the floods. Now the steel buildings rose majestically out of the new lake, most of them still occupied by Tanshi citizens.

They had been nonaligned before the war. Like so many other city-states they had been targeted by the sweeping surprise strike of Flametar forces. There were no more neutral cities – all of the remaining ones came over to the Alignment of Free States as the enemy was bent on total conquest and would brook no impartial cities in its pursuit of the new world order.

Once again, as he passed over them, the citizens of the submerged city requested help from him. As per his orders, he ignored them. They were civilians requesting help that could not be spared. Stratofighters were needed to repel the enemy on every front, and it was far more important that he attempt to hurl back the enemy armor than to rescue stranded civilians. If the Alignment of Free States could not stop the enemy then all life outside the Flametar Empire would be wiped out.

He glanced back as a matter of habit. There was nothing following him except for the huge plume of water that geysered into the air, dragged from the quiet lake below by his jet's shock wave. Ahead the mountains came into view, his comrades ensconced inside and fighting for their lives. The mountain range was a major source of minerals for the Flametar Empire, as well as shelter for the underground factories buried deep within the stone formations. Unless the Zerstorer Brigade could root out the enemy and clean out the factories the enemy would be producing military equipment indefinitely.

He brought his plane in and turned on the battle display, only to find that the thousands of bright lines crossing the screen made it impossible to use in combat. Instead, he relied on his sharp eyes, dipping his aircraft to fly below a stream of cannon shells that arced across a valley between the two sides.

He dove in, the massive granite peaks towering far above his plane, and found a thick mass of red laser beams stabbing out at him. He flew a spiral maneuver, corkscrewing in, and the lasers failed to touch him. He came into range and leveled out, dragged his gunsight over an enemy tank and squeezed the trigger. His laser leaped out and penetrated either the engine or the ammo load; the armored vehicle blossomed into flames. Beams of concentrated light stabbed out all around him during his fast pullout.

He dropped the nose of his jet and slid just over the next cliff, more missiles trailing him. They had been fired at right angles to his plane and he outran them, accelerating away. He flew on, keeping low to the ground while tank shells thundered over his jet, probably not even aimed at him.

He saw two enemy fighters on the radar screen, heading straight at him. Even with the battle display turned off, the computer would still alert him to incoming planes. In seconds he saw them: two twin-finned Flametar jets, already firing missiles at him. Tychon started his climb early, pulling up above the swarm of smoke-belching missiles. He rose fast enough that he escaped them, climbing into the sunlit clouds, still accelerating. The other two planes trailed him, firing their guns, the shells spreading out and missing.

He fed double the normal fuel to the engines, rising high up on a long cone of blue flame and it was not enough. A horrid shock ran through his jet, the impact of a missile. A glance behind him showed much of his beloved jet on fire, debris falling away from the wings and tail. He felt denial, an unwillingness to believe that he had been defeated, and then hot anger at himself for failing. There was no way to recover the jet as far too much metal had already been consumed by the hot, fuel-fed flames.

His Stratofighter nosed over and descended in a fast dive. Protocol demanded he give his position over the transceiver and in his anguish he had no desire to admit to anyone that he had failed. Instead, he pushed a square button that would transmit his location electronically, ensuring that Central Command learned of his ruination.

His plane hurtled downward, the controls unresponsive. His jaw hurt from clenching. In seconds it would be time to eject from his ship, forever severing his connection to the steel bird that he had dedicated his life to. A tug on the handles on either side of him completed the electronic circuit and blew the glass canopy off. A split second later a terrific, unstoppable force blew him out of the stricken jet and into the airstream. Regret and remorse flooded him, leaving a vile taste in his mouth.

His parachute opened, jerking him upwards as it filled with wind. He floated down, closing his eyes, hoping the enemy jets would choose not to strafe him while he dangled helplessly. When he realized that he might be landing soon, he opened his eyes and waited for the ground to reach him. The impact was painful, shocking him and leaving him sprawled on the ground. The shoulder straps dug into his chest, so he unclipped them and the wind took his parachute away, hiding his disgrace.

He regained his feet and walked toward the last known friendly position. The beacon in his pocket drew two friendly armored cars and soon Tychon was seated inside the commander's vehicle, having to put into words the violent catastrophe that had befallen his plane.

The commander was gentle. "Don't worry, my friend. We will have you back in a new Stratofighter before the day is over. You will be back in the action soon, just like everyone else. Many pilots were assassinated today when the enemy infiltrated our ranks and killed scores of trained airmen. They've set fire to some of the storage depots and the Flametars materialized in them. We had to put the fires out before we fought the enemy. We have a shortage of trained pilots now."

Tychon gave him a blank look, wondering how they were going to survive the war that was rapidly encapsulating the entire sphere.

7

Bitterness ruined her mood. Her life had been dedicated to the enemy, raiding what were possibly innocent Glacians, just to provide wood for the Flametars. The endless hours of marching, training, and fighting – all so her old Lords could materialize in hot flames for a few hours. The Flametars had not cared for her and had done nothing to provide for her. Even the poor villagers in the decrepit hovels who had worshiped Ka-Shuka had more luxuries than she had ever had. In the Tanshi village she had seen books read, clothing sewn and crops harvested. Zondela's life had consisted of sword training, conditioning her body to carry the brass armor, and raiding Glacia for wood and she had received no rewards beyond her weapons. Her only pleasure had been the company of her own thoughts as she dreamed of Fushang or explored some of the wild parts of Infernia.

Her mood lifted as she saw how large the main sphere was, and how much there was to explore. The sand gave way to a harder layer of dirt and soon she walked on a firm, parched surface. By nightfall thin grass was growing out of the ground, giving her rumbling stomach hope that she might find something more nutritious to eat. On Infernia she had lived on a steady diet of fish and crustaceans from the thin waters and streams, and she knew little of how to survive in such a vast world. Esuta had given her three days worth of rations when they parted, and she would have to learn some decent sphere skills – the hunting techniques and tricks that seemed to come naturally to those raised on the main world – to feed her large frame.

Every few hours she pulled out her telescope and scanned the horizon. There was a vortex in the distance, bright and green against the dull brown of the surrounding landscape. She walked toward it. Some vortexes led to tiny floating rocks high above Sinxin. Others led one deep out into the ocean, while others still led to carnivore filled swamps and certain death.

A few hours later she stood before it and gazed into it with her telescope. She could see only thick vegetation through it, obscuring everything, preventing her from seeing more than a hand's width into the new area. Vines and creepers of deep green curled and coiled about each other in an impenetrable mass. She put the telescope away and looked forward, seeing nothing, the vortex and its destination invisible. When she thrust her hand into the vortex it disappeared and she felt the soft touch of leafy foliage.

Her food supply was low; her body clamored for sustenance and around her was stark, low grassland for as far as the eye could see. Taking a deep breath, she stepped through the vortex and was immersed in prolific and luxuriant vegetation.

The vines offered mild resistance as she drew her brass sword and slashed at the biota. She was in a green world of tall plants that stretched high overhead and blocked out the sun. Fruit of every color hung from vines; no two were alike. The path behind her that she had cleared with her blade marked the location of the vortex. She knew the concept of fruit from her earlier forays into other strata while serving the Flametars though she had never tasted it. Biting into a fist-sized red berry left juice trailing down her chin. The flavor was intense and wonderful – even the rich fruity smell was a pleasure.

Half an hour later her pack was full of fruit. She walked away and tripped over the curling vegetation that somehow had gotten wrapped around her lower body. It took a few moments to disentangle her legs from the vines and creepers that encircled them. Her short walk back to the vortex was more difficult. Fresh growth had covered the vortex, forcing her to alternate between slashes with her blade and glances through her telescope. Once she had cleared the area again, she squatted down and stared at the severed tip of a nearby vine. It healed and grew larger as she watched, its tendril lengthening and threading through the air. Rising to her feet, she returned through the vortex, glad to be back on the main world, and once again traveled through the endless steppe of grass and dirt.

Days passed with no signs of new vortexes while the air cooled and the dry grass grew taller. She walked, enjoying the absence of orders, the freedom from the discipline of military life, and the pleasure of her own company. The murky water of Sinxin was less than pleasant as it lacked the perfection of Infernian streams. She crossed rivers and ponds, refilling her body and quenching her thirst, and found little more than tiny fish which darted between her fingers. Sighing, she bit once more into the ripe red fruit from her pack, careful to save the seeds.

Hours later she came across the first of the totems. It was a gray fragment of rock that stuck out of the ground and had a symbol carved upon it – a line that curved in upon itself, lanced outward, then circled in upon itself yet again. She followed the design with her eyes, oblivious to the world around her, trying to find either the start or end-point of the fascinating line. Vaguely she heard the sound of her breathing in her ears, the way she would notice it when someone woke her just as she was drifting off to sleep. Still, she traced the intricate pattern with her eye, intent now on just following the beautiful geometry. Time passed.

A hard impact woke her from her concentration and knocked the breath from her lungs. In time she realized she lay on the ground. A glance up confirmed that there was no one around her. She had fallen and only the impact had awoken her from whatever state she had been in. It was dusk. She shook her head, rose to her feet, and avoided eye contact with the totem. Bones protruded out of the ground nearby, earlier victims, perhaps, of the strange symbols.

Zondela moved on through the grassy hills until a man and a woman came over a hilltop with spears in their hands. They were lean and wore animal skins decorated with feathers. Their wood spears were tipped with spiraled animal horns. Zondela rested one hand on her sword hilt and opened her mouth to speak as the man raised his spear, drew his hand back to his ear, and cast his weapon. The shaft moved faster than she had anticipated, slicing through the air at her chest. She leaned backward and to the side, twisting at the waist, and the spear careened off her brass torso plate, splintering in the process. Her sword leaped into her hand as she straightened up.

The ragged woman rushed her, the spear tip pointed at Zondela's eyes. Zondela deflected the attack with her brass sword and reversed her swing to gut her attacker. The woman let out a screech of rage and yet took another step, drawing a stone knife from her belt and thrusting with it.

Zondela's reflexes were such that the crazed female never really had a chance. The blade of the brass sword swept out and severed the strange woman's wrist. The attacking female was unable to stop her charge and blundered into Zondela's armor-clad body. The lighter of the two – the dirty, feather decorated woman – fell to the ground, staring with hate at the woman who had injured her.

The man dashed forward with a stone knife of his own. It took courage to attack with a weapon of such shorter reach. He leaped with his knife held above his head. Zondela took a half step forward and impaled his body upon her sword. With a step back she withdrew her blade and the man fell. The ragged woman, still bleeding from her stomach and wrist, crawled over to the fallen man.

The man spoke a harsh and uncivilized version of the prosaic tongue and directed his words at the dirty woman who lay dying in his arms. "Look for me in the sky, beloved. Watch for me, I will be about you always."

The injured woman, holding her wrist-stump up to reduce the blood flow, responded with a weak smile. "I will join you in the sky, my love." The woman took up her stone knife with a grimace of pain and plunged it into her breast. She collapsed over the man, and in seconds her body turned white and dusty. A bird emerged from the dried corpse, pushing out of and rising above the carnage on flapping wings. The body of the man turned to white ashes, a bird rising out of his corpse as well. The two birds circled each other before flying away. Zondela moved on.

Dry grass grew amid rocks, many of which had cavities chiseled out of them to hold candles, incense, and tiny quartz figures. A cluster of tall rocks had what looked like a temple in the center – red and blue candles, stone bowls of grain, and in the center a massive seashell filled with glistening blue liquid.

Gnarled trees housed little wood houses. She peered into one and a half feline, half vulture peered back, the animal muttering something about waiting for her to die. She passed the remnants of an old battle, armor and weapons half-buried in the dirt, rose vines curling around the bleached skeletons. Clambering over a hill she saw a small city built in the grove of massive, gnarled tree limbs. Hundreds of trees grew close together, their intertwined branches supporting a cluster of wood houses. Each dwelling place shared a common wall with the one beside it, leading to a massive, interconnected structure. People sat or worked in front of the small arboreal city, each dressed in short animal skins or feathers. Many carried weapons. Zondela counted over twenty spears and swords. Taking a deep breath to quell her pounding heart, Zondela entered the village, making eye contact with the people closest to her.

"I am Zondela, from a far off land. My sword is quiet in its scabbard."

One of the men, covered in feathers with just his eyes showing, responded in a guttural, odd version of the prosaic tongue. "Why do you intrude on our land?"

"I seek only the oracle. I come seeking knowledge and wisdom."

"Only I, the Inquisitor, can question the oracle. You walk our sacred lands and think to speak to our Master? Such conceit, such pride. Where does such a barbarian female hail from?"

"I was born on Infernia though I travel only in search of knowledge. I would see my skill with the sword replaced one day by the skill with a feather pen. I have no wish to cross blades with you."

"You are sagacious yet your heavy armor and long limbs

attest to a lifestyle of fighting, which makes me doubt your words."

Zondela inclined her head. "I used to be a soldier. Now I am a wanderer."

"Not all who wander are lost," replied the feathered man. "Come, I will speak to the oracle on your behalf and we will decide your fate." The man turned, his blue feathered cape trailing him, and she followed. With twenty warriors joining them she had little choice. They traveled east and more women armed with animal-horned spears fell into step beside her. In her mind Zondela made plans, deciding who to fight and with what tactics if they attacked.

They moved through the thick forest and came before a stone statue of a coiled serpent with wings of a great bird of prey. The carving was fluid and graceful; it would be a powerful hunter if such a creature existed.

"Great one," said the feathered Inquisitor, "this barbarian comes from a distant land and wishes to learn from you. Shall she approach?"

The voice from the stone larynx was deep and gravelly. "Yes. She must enlighten me, so that I may do so for others."

"Come," said the feathered Inquisitor to Zondela, "place your hand upon the oracle, and answer his questions."

Zondela walked forward, took one last look at the tense faces around her, and removed the brass glove from her right hand. She placed her bare palm atop the statue's head and waited. A shock ran through her, moving outward like lightning flowing through her body and into the statue. Memories flowed through her mind, forcing her to relive old experiences. In seconds she saw herself growing up on Infernia, training for endless hours at the behest of the Flametars, and her isolation as she was promoted to Penturian. She relived some very painful memories of loss, feeling again the angst of the constant military training with few friendships to ease the burden. Her victories and defeats flashed through her mind and when she was finally able to pull her hand away the skin felt burned while her mind felt squeezed and wrung out, like a sponge emptied of water. In seconds the sensation faded.

The Inquisitor spoke to the oracle. "Is she human, master?"

The oracle's rocky voice responded. "Yes."

The feather covered man continued, his voice ringing through the hush that had fallen over everyone else. "Is she dangerous?"

"Yes, she is highly skilled in the arts of combat."

"Is she part of an enemy army?" the Inquisitor asked.

"She has served the Flametars, and they will become your mortal enemy, wiping the surface of Sinxin with devouring flames."

The people around Zondela drew blades and pointed their spears at her, even the women turning on her with hard stares and naked swords in their hands. Zondela was in a difficult fix; it was unlikely she could fight her way out and she could not hope to outrun them with her heavy armor.

The Inquisitor turned to Zondela and spoke, his finger stabbing the air toward her. "Kill her. The enemy is upon us!"

Zondela thought fast. She turned to the oracle and belted out a question. "Is it true that I have a chance to stop this war?"

"Yes."

Silence ensued. The advancing swordsmen stopped. "Is it true that I might be able to stop this war and save the land?" she asked.

"Yes, there is a chance, a small one," said the oracle.

"What will happen if they kill me now?" she asked

"Then the war will occur as foreseen, with the Flametars defeating the Icetars and destroying the world."

"I know of one task to stop this war, the destruction of the profane Holy Book of Flames," Zondela said, "What else must I do?"

"There will be a battle between a great beast and a Wusong. Place your hand on my surface and I shall show it to you." No one stopped her as she raised her hand to the stone. Images flooded through her palm and into her brain, showing a towering, white-furred beast squared off in battle against a Wusong of similar size. The reptile expelled fire from its mouth and the furred beast leaped away. "There will be two Flametar spirits in the vicinity," said the oracle, "observing the battle, and after the Wusong's breath ignites a grove of trees, they will manifest themselves for some time, wreaking much havoc and finding another vortex between Sinxin and Infernia."

Zondela nodded, thinking, while the feathered Inquisitor asked a few more questions. Zondela learned the location of where the battle would take place and the fact that it would not occur for another fourteen days.

"How can I stop it? " she asked.

"I do not know," said the Oracle. At her request if showed her the location of the Wusong slumbering in the ocean and the hunting grounds of the furred and clawed beast, which was far to the east.

Still, with her hand on the statue, Zondela asked where the next closest oracle was. In her mind she was flying across the grassy steps, rushing over hills and racing across the landscape. Her mental image slowed and lingered over the next oracle. Zondela removed her hand and nodded, thinking further, feeling like a playing piece in a game of

Salamanders.

"Forgive us," said the feathered Inquisitor. "We must defend our Master from any who would try to take it or destroy it. Its knowledge locates game and warns of the approach of enemies."

"It is not a Master," she said. "It was created by Balaka-kos as he journeyed across the land. Its purpose is to share information so you should not be preventing others from speaking to it."

The Inquisitor mulled it over. "I shall question it in this regard and act on its response. Still, it is a great Master with powers that no mortal could possess. It is the foundation of our clan."

They filled her pack with jars of small game cooked in nuts, berries, and honey. The villagers gave her empty water skins and directions to a nearby river. She set off, preferring to sleep by herself when well away from the village. She left the people and walked through the grasslands, soon wading through dry, waist-high growth. Wide-trunked trees supported turquoise foliage, with the beautiful music of dozens of birds trilling from the interior. A robed lizard walked by – upright like a man, clad in blue crushed velvet, and carrying a huge book. It spoke softly to itself about triangles as it passed her.

Hours later, when weariness was upon her, she laid down and closed her eyes while a cool wind rustled through the sea of grass.

8

She awoke in the morning and found grass seeds covering her armor-clad body. She rose, spilling them to the ground, and cast her gaze in all directions. There was nothing in sight except the eastern mountains. Her telescope showed no vortexes. She intended to travel to the Crystal City and kill the man who would create the profane Holy Book of Flames. That manuscript, when finished, was destined to spark a terrible religion that taught worship of the Flametars. The vision she had seen showed a skilled artist and writer handcrafting an illuminated manuscript, using a paintbrush to letter the book and paint elaborate pictures. The writer had to die.

She walked for several more days, the dry grass up to her torso, and finished her red fruit. It was with regret that she ate the last piece, licking the juice off her fingers, wondering if she would ever find it again. She wanted to build a small home near the vortex, stepping through each morning to lustily dive into more fruit. She shook her head, smiling at the thought of her athletic body growing fat from the daily indulgence.

She finished her supply of nuts, berries, and wild game within three days. No vortexes appeared with luscious fruit growing in abandon behind them, and the few shallow streams provided no fish or mollusks.

She walked through the night, the tall grass giving way to bare dirt, and found a comfortable spot to rest. Traveling was a pleasure; equally fine was the excitement of not knowing what the sphere held. She ate a few roots and tubers and went to sleep. The sun rose the next morning to wake her with a comfortable warmth on her face. She rose to a sitting position to see an attractive young woman sitting about five paces away, calmly watching her. Zondela cursed herself for allowing someone to sneak up while she slept.

The new arrival had an angular face of high cheekbones and a narrow chin, exotic and beautiful yet gaunt and undernourished. The woman's body was thin, especially at the waist; she was perhaps half Zondela's weight. The interloper had two swords belted on her hips, one on each side, both with elaborate hilts. Comfortable, loose-fitting dark cloth covered the woman's body, leaving only her arms bare. Black gloves adorned each hand. The woman's eyes glinted with amusement as Zondela tried to discreetly slip her hand onto her sword hilt. "I'm sorry for oversleeping," Zondela said. "What did I miss?"

"The rise of the great morning fire in the sky, the glint of light off the mountain peaks, and the flock of flutterbys that chased a nectar-scented wind."

"Yes, this sphere holds much. Who are you?"

"I am Sadah of the Baisheng. I am eager to reach the Crystal City. Journey with me and we can part company if you wish when we reach it. The road is dangerous."

Zondela knew that this woman could have killed her while she slept if she had wanted to. "We shall travel together. How far is it?"

"About a day's travel. Let us take a quick meal together

if you will eat with me."

Zondela plucked a few blades of grass out of the ground, placed one in her mouth, and offered the other to her new companion.

"Well," said Sadah, as she reached in her pack, took out a round cheese-cake, and tossed it to Zondela. "We can share this while we walk. Where did you acquire fantastic armor? It gleams in the sun and while it would give your position away from across the steppes it is impressive."

They walked beside each other while Zondela bit into her food. It melted in her mouth into a warm liquid curd. It was so good, some selfish part of her silently complained as she handed the cheese back to Sadah so they could share it. "An artisan made it, on Infernia. It was the last piece he made before turning his tools over to an apprentice."

"Yes, the artisan's tools contain much of his power. Does it not get heavy, covering your entire body like that?"

Zondela shrugged, her brass-covered shoulders rising slightly. "It has turned away many an arrow and spear. It is a burden that I would not relinquish." Zondela drank water while her new companion talked.

Sadah was of the Baisheng Clan. Many years ago their home had been destroyed by Flametars and, splitting up into small groups, they wandered Sinxin, always living un-der a strict code. They took only replenishable stocks when entering a land, such as fish and wild game. When they needed to take crops, they took only the barest amounts to survive, always planting more in their place. As a wandering clan, the Baisheng had developed a reputation for integrity. While in the Ziqqurratu Dynasty they had killed wild beasts to avoid taking anything belonging to the native inhabit-ants.

Ziqqurratu was a steamy jungle, full of danger. Witches

prowled the night, killing with blood-curdling screams or stares of hate. Barely human, they were very powerful and mainly targeted men. Ziqqurratu battled them, the two sides hunting each other. The day belonged to man and the night belonged to the witch.

Sadah was glad to be away from the jungle and its cacophony of animal noises, battle sounds, and heart-stopping screams. She headed to the Crystal City to sell her sword in defense of the beautiful structure and its peaceful inhabitants.

As mercenaries, the Baisheng were often in demand. Sadah looked forward to the coin although their clan taught them not to rely on silver. They gathered seeds as they traveled, always keeping jars of them. When she took part of a man's harvest in Ziqqurratu she planted seeds in its place. For a while, he will be the only one with vegetables from the northern shoreline. To further repay him she killed a beast that had menaced him for some time, a hydradile – sort of a two-headed croc – and made boots and gloves out of its hide.

Zondela had fought the apex predator once when one had wandered onto Infernia through a vortex. It was a scaled reptilian predator, normally found in swamps and saltwater, often lurking below the surface with only its eyes above the waterline. It had grabbed a few Infernians and dragged them into the water, rolling repeatedly to drown them and tear their flesh. The beast she had killed had had three heads, each toothed snout full of reptilian rage, spit, and violence. All three heads had shouted obscenities at her while it died.

Since Sadah had no land and no wish to become a consort, she roamed the sphere, living as best she could off nature. She learned weapons from other wanderers and cooking from various villages. She defended them for a time and they taught her what plants were safe to eat, how to trap animals, and which foods to use for baiting them.

"Sphere skills," Zondela murmured. "The inhabitants of this world seem to naturally know them. I come from Infernia, a stratum, one located so far above that from here it is a yellow speck in the sky. It has a star-filled sky, a landscape of pure brass, and streams of flawless water. Yet there I learned nothing of the skills you have talked about."

"What did you do there?"

"I was a soldier. A Penturian, commander of five, and I fought for the Flametars."

"So the Flametars do exist," murmured Sadah.

"They do. I once served them."

"Do you have a home?" asked Sadah.

"No," she said, sighing and looking down. "I do not. My life of service is over."

"Then you are an outcast, as I once was. The Baisheng will take you in and we will trade skills. It is how we survive as a clan. Although the Baisheng are unaligned, we have been in battle with almost every creature and dynasty on the sphere at one time or another. We could use someone of your build, with your experience."

"I am questing. I seek the rest of the oracles and Fushang."

"Dreams of Fushang?" asked Sadah with a smile. "You dream big, appropriate for you, though I doubt the fabled city exists. We all want what we cannot have."

"Perhaps. What is it that you want, ultimately?"

"I'm not sure," replied Sadah. "To live in harmony in this beautiful land. A small house of stone, deep in the wild between the Dynasties, one that I will build myself when my time with the Baisheng is over. Living off the land when I am older, if I survive that long."

"So you go to ply your trade in the Crystal City?"

"Yes. The dreams of Isayus continue, producing wonders as well as dangers. The Crystal City is a city in flux, nightly changing as the ascendant dreams."

"I thought it only a myth," said Zondela. Sadah shook her head and explained.

The Ultimate Machine came to Sinxin and created Balakakos who was too gentle for its needs. The machine hated life as much as a hydradile hates beauty – the reptiles have been known to leave the water, kill the most beautiful woman in a group, then re-submerge. The machine next created Tanshi who was wise and kind, again unsuitable.

Third, it created Isayus and ordered him to kill his brother Tanshi. Handsome, tall, kind, and noble, Isayus creates by dreaming. The Ultimate Machine intended that the nightmares of Isayus would kill Tanshi and the things that Tanshi had conjured into being. It did not work.

Unhappy with the vile proclamations of the Ultimate Machine and determined to make his own way in life, Isayus wandered Sinxin on foot, ignoring his creator's demands and bringing into being many of the sphere's animal species by dreaming of them in his slumber. When Isayus came to the peninsula he was alone and sought the comfort of the ocean's breathing. He rested there for many days, listening to the ocean that his brother Tanshi had created. While Isayus slept one night he dreamed of magnificent green beasts living under the surface of the Restless Ocean and the first Wusong were created. This was about a million years ago. As a species they reside there still, feeding on the bones of sea creatures.

Eventually, he dreamed of a crystal city. In the morning the magnificent city was there, filled with a small number of people. Isayus was no longer lonely and there he remains.

The sleepy speculations of his subconscious continue to create the wild things, providing work for roving mercenaries like Sadah. She asked Zondela to join her.

The idea of friendship appealed to Zondela – much of her wandering had been solitary. Still, she knew the value of discretion and said nothing, thinking instead of what the result would be if her own dreams became real.

They walked late into the night, making camp when the landscape was bathed in heavy silver moonlight, turning Zondela's armor to silver. Sadah pulled out a wood case and unfolded it, revealing the green and red squares of a Salamander game. "Do you play?" asked the Baisheng woman.

"I do. Recreation was almost non-existent on Infernia as the Masters thought it would interfere with our martial training. Salamanders was the only game that was played since it taught tactics." Zondela took her share of the green Salamanders which in this case were crudely carved stones of translucent emerald. Sadah's pieces were carved of red glass.

The initial placement of pieces was an important part of the strategy. One by one both players put their pieces down, each piece controlling the spaces adjacent to it. Clustering pieces gave one a strong control over a small portion of the game board. This represented basic infantry tactics.

There was no limit to the distance pieces could move. The farther the move the weaker the attack, representing the difficulty of long-range infantry strikes and extended supply lines. A short move by a single piece took an opponent's piece, even if it was covered by two others. A move across the entire game board by even the strongest piece could only defeat the weakest piece.

Sadah played predictably while Zondela took an early lead by making only attacks that led to her pieces sitting together in groups, much like infantry covering each other in real life. The two women moved their pieces about, Zondela often making long moves without attacking to keep her Salamanders in position to defend each other. Sadah would strike from the sides, making short moves when attacking to gain the advantage that that offered. Zondela countered by moving a few pieces into squares that she knew would become contested later on. A piece that had not moved that round would have the strongest attack of all, representing the advantage of dug-in infantry. With this tactic Zondela managed to route the opposing stones, breaking their formation. In the final round, Zondela made a short move to strike Sadah's Royal Salamander. Since there were no pieces adjacent to defend it, Zondela took it and won the game.

"Well done," replied Sadah. "I have not lost in a long time. You maneuvered better than I, keeping a strong defense as you moved forward."

"The trick is to get some pieces where battle is going to be in the next few rounds, not where it is."

They hunted through the underbrush and killed some birds. Later they dined on roasted fowl in a thick glaze of honey and sliced nuts. The meat was white and moist, with a wild flavor that enhanced its appeal. The two of them talked while they ate, Sadah hinting again that she wanted Zondela to join her. When they finished they moved on toward the Crystal City. In a few hours they heard the ocean in the distance despite the water being hidden by the uneven landscape.

They came to a well-worn road made of stones which led them south through low hills and scrub. They crested a rise in the ground and saw a massive stone wall that barred their path. It cut off the entire southern peninsula so that the only way to reach the Crystal City would be through the wall. The alternative, taking a boat and attempting to sail the Restless Ocean, was not feasible as vessels did not last long in the roiling waves.

The wall was crudely made of stones piled atop each other without mortar. In some areas the wall had tumbled, the pieces laying untended on the ground and partly overgrown by grass. It was a thick, massive wall stretching from one side of the peninsula to the other. In the distance, the ocean crashed and frothed. The road that they walked on led to a portcullis set in the wall, atop which a few figures observed their progress.

When they stood before the portcullis a sentinel from the wall called out. "Welcome. Do you wish to enter?"

Sadah called out in a firm voice. "Yes."

A man atop the wall turned a great wheel and the portcullis rose. They advanced through and once on the other side they saw, in the distance, the wondrous Crystal City.

It had tall spires and gleaming towers, all connected at the top by glass catwalks. There were hundreds of transparent buildings, all linked by slender bridges. Gleaming crystal staircases curled about the towers, flanked on either side by clear columns topped with magnificent statues. The city sparkled in the sun with the brightness of a faceted gem.

"Now there's a rare sight," murmured Zondela. Behind them came the noise of the portcullis dropping into place. They walked toward the Crystal City, and Zondela asked what the point was in having a gate if they opened it to strangers without asking questions.

Sadah answered in an amused tone. "It is not to keep anyone out. It is to keep the dreams of the ascendant in."

Monsters roamed the peninsula. There was a time when the Crystal City was almost overwhelmed by a nightmare of Isayus. Members of the Baisheng Clan showed up and slew red-scaled menlizards, sea horse knights, and squealing shadows to keep the city safe. Isayus dreamed up a few bags of gold and the mercenaries left, their reputation for nobility intact.

Each ascendant created in a different way, none of them having firm control over it. Eventually, Isayus dreamed of a hero who would found an empire, and Sharduq appeared, though he left immediately. Isayus later, in his loneliness, dreamed of people, and when he awoke there were hundreds more men and women in the city, naked, calm, and intelligent. They were human, taking up residence in the city, and soon having babies of their own. Those people – the Acolytes of Isayus – love and worship their ascendant and are stewards of him and this land.

The Acolytes of Isayus finessed their lord into creating for them – they discussed something with him daily until he dreamed it into existence. The wall seemed to be at the limit of his ability to manifest reality, distance wise. The Acolytes built only the stone pathway that the two women walked on.

Isayus's nightmares induced savagery upon the land. During the night, things with claws and beasts cursed those unfortunate enough to make eye contact with them. Sea reptiles floated through the darkness as if the air were water, snatching humans in their toothy maws. Violent clockwork automatons emerged that cried as they died. Lobstrocities clambered out of the ocean, knocking on doors with their heavy pincers, spouting poetry in an obscene attempt to pretend they were peaceful, only to kill anyone foolish enough to open for them.

When the nightmares of Isayus were particularly bad, spirits with bloody swords drifted about, or the entire ground was covered in snakes.

Usually, Isayus had pleasant dreams at night and the inhabitants of the crystal city were treated with shooting stars, exotic birds, and warm scented winds. He created flutterbys, the beautiful winged insects that flit from flower to flower and now float across the entire sphere. Beds of roses sprang up in the night, caressing young maidens and giving them safe refuge among their thorny brambles.

The two women reached the city as the sun was about to sink into the ocean. The transparent towers, minarets, catwalks, ramps, and columns of the Crystal City turned to red glass in the last minutes of the day. Each step gleamed in the dying sunlight, the statues and vast walls glowing cherry red. The sun sank into the waves and the effect was gone.

A robed and hooded figure approached. He pulled back his hood to reveal handsome, masculine features. "I am brother Pawl," he said. "Come inside. It is not safe to be out this late." They followed him into the tower and up a spiral staircase. Through the transparent walls, they saw ghostly figures drift across the landscape. The brother provided them with trays of food – crumbling orange cheese, slices of roast oceanbird between sheets of honey bread, and cups of pink cream. "I gather, from the implements that rest in your belts, that you are warriors?"

Sadah spoke. "I am Sadah of the Baisheng, looking for work. Tales are told across the land of the Crystal City. We seek employment as hunters to chase down rogue dreams."

Brother Pawl nodded. "The honorable Baisheng are always welcome, and as long as the ascendant's dreams are troubled you will find work. We had mercenaries from distant Ziqqurratu and after they defeated a pack of beasts they declared themselves the new rulers of the Crystal City. There was nothing we could do until Isayus knew and his slumber was disturbed. Awful things rose from the muck and when our new rulers went out to fight them they were defeated. I have never heard of dishonorable Baisheng. We will pay each of you a silver coin a day, as long as you help keep our city safe and repel any attacks upon us. You are welcome here for as long as you choose to stay. We keep Isayus relaxed and calm to reduce the chances of disturbing dreams. He sits outside during the day, contemplating, trying to keep a mental image in his mind in the hopes of dreaming of it at night though it is impossible to control one's intellect while asleep. The spirits are out tonight, as they are every time we have visitors. They are only dangerous when they keen. It is a strange noise they make. Zondela, are you one of the Baisheng?"

"I am from a stratum called Infernia."

"Well, then, you must meet Retulf, also from Infernia. Quite a fellow, very intelligent. I'm beginning to suspect all Infernians are smart."

"It would be impolite of me to argue with you, brother," she said. Their laughter was disturbed by an ardent wail from below.

"They hear us, and they hate laughter," brother Pawl said. "I should have been more circumspect."

Sadah drew her sword, the pommel resting against her hip in an easy manner. "I'd say it's time for us to earn that silver. Coming, Zondela?" Sadah's eyes had narrowed, a half-smile on her lips.

Zondela thought it through. It was not her fight, and although she liked Sadah, she had never agreed to this engagement. She was on a quest to stop a great war while the Baisheng fought for coin. She had only come to the city to see it and get supplies before moving to the next oracle. "No, I'm sorry. I cannot."

Sadah's face fell and the disappointment in her eyes caused Zondela a little grief. They had become friends and

Sadah looked up to her, perhaps seeking the companionship of another female. Zondela had to look away as it hurt too much to see the look in Sadah's eyes. For Zondela, friendships were hard to come by and passing up this one hurt.

Two other Baisheng – men whom Sadah had not seen in years – joined her and the five of them descended to the bottom of the tower. Brother Pawl and Zondela stayed inside while the three Baisheng went out to battle.

Pale specters drifted over the landscape – ghosts in tattered white robes. They floated above the ground, issuing a strange wail, with steel swords gripped in their hands. Corpse-like faces bore hollow eye-sockets and crumbling teeth. It looked as if the dead had risen. Sadah and her two companions walked forward, undeterred as large numbers of pale ghosts converged on them.

The moon was out and the steel swords of the ghosts shone silver in the pale light as they attacked. Sadah and her men fought well, adjacent to each other, like well-positioned pieces in a game of Salamanders. The Baisheng blocked dozens of sword strokes, deflecting them away and counter-attacking. Sadah was quick and thrust her sword deep into the torso of a ghost with no effect. The tattered robes of the spirits covered nothing at all, and the ghosts were free to bring their blades slashing down at the mercenaries.

One of the men fell when he failed to block a sword stroke and took a cut across the neck. His blood spurted out and splashed on a nearby ghost who stopped fighting, arched its back, and screeched. The wail was one of delight, the ghost's bony jaw working as it tried to swallow. The other ghosts renewed their frenzied attacks and the two mercenaries barely blocked the sword strokes. Sadah struck the neck of the ghost and cut through the vertebrae, collapsing the white robes and sending the skull clattering down to the ground where it continued to shriek.

The ghosts fought using the same basic attacks, bringing their blades in on predictable angles. Zondela knew the Baisheng should be using a swinging defense, where the defender swings her sword in a wide arc, knocking the attacker's blade away, and then reverses the blade to strike the unprotected neck. Sadah, however, used a defense more suitable for single combat against a skilled opponent, which was probably how she had trained. She held her sword out in a line and flicked aside incoming strikes, unable to mount a decent attack since thrusting did no good unless it connected with the spine.

The other man was felled by a sword blow to his chest, and Sadah fought alone. Waves of ghosts converged upon her and Zondela could wait no longer. Her brass sword leaped into her hand and she ran into the fray. It took her seconds to slay three of them, the severed skulls clattering to the ground and still howling in rage.

Sadah fought hard and the ghosts circled them, shrieking as they closed in. Zondela heard her companion's heavy breathing as the Baisheng warrior caught her breath.

"I'm glad," Sadah said in between gasps, "you decided to join me."

"Keep your back to me. Get ready...Now!" Zondela swung, knocking aside a ghost's blade and decapitating it in one motion. Sadah spent more time blocking yet was not quick enough, taking a thin slash across the shoulder. The ghosts rushed them without thought of their safety, and Zondela slew most of them, Sadah killing the remaining few herself. The ground was littered with grinning and shrieking skulls that slowly became quiet. Soon, except for the panting of the two women, there was silence.

Brother Pawl stepped forward and spoke quietly.

"Return inside. The Master can sense when emotions are in turmoil, and his dreams must not be disturbed." Brother Pawl pointed to the eastern sky and Zondela saw massive, skeletal winged beasts flying toward them, their bony bodies pale in the moonlight.

The two swordswomen sheathed their blades and retreated to the tower, brother Pawl swinging the glass doors shut once they were inside. The skeletal beasts landed and fought over the fallen male Baisheng, pulling the bodies apart with their teeth.

Zondela looked at Sadah; the Baisheng warrior shrugged. "They were warriors," she said. "They knew the risks when they chose to come here."

"We may still have to fight again." One of the skeletal beasts walked to the tower and stared at them, its hate-filled eyes red and unwavering.

"No," said brother Pawl. "Those beasts come when they smell death. They cannot get through the crystal of the tower. When Isayus dreamed our city, he dreamed it structurally sound." Brother Pawl escorted them up a level in the gleaming crystal tower and sat them down on a comfortable couch. He brought water to the two women and bathed Sadah's feet in a bucket when she took her boots off.

After making sighing noises while wiggling her toes in the hot water, Sadah spoke. "Do all the women from Infernia fight like that?"

"Most of them," said Zondela. "I just have sharper reflexes." Sadah arched an eyebrow and said nothing, suppressing a smile.

Brother Pawl turned to Zondela. "Should I notify Retulf of your arrival?"

"Yes, he's an old friend of mine," she lied. While Zondela had seen him occasionally, years ago on Infernia, she had never spoken to him. "I'd like to see him."

"He resides at the top of the tower, in his study. He is not comfortable with us, especially those of us who were created by Isayus. He works late into the night and will still be up." Zondela thanked him and walked across the room toward the spiral staircase, Sadah patting her on the arm as she walked by. As Zondela ascended the staircase she worried her booted feet were going to break the crystal steps. The tower was delicate yet free of cracks. She looked into each room as she passed; most of the brothers and sisters were reading, praying, or sleeping.

She reached the top, fourteen stories up. Through the crystal door she could see the distorted image of a man. A gentle shove opened the translucent door and she stepped inside, leaving the door open behind her without thinking about it. Every structure in the room was transparent, from the bed frame to the bookshelves to the desk. The moon could be seen in the sky through the crystal walls.

The man inside looked up at her with a neutral face.

"I am Zondela," she said. "Servant of the Flametars. I seek Retulf."

He smiled, rising to his feet to greet her. He had a slim sword belted at his waist. "Come in," he said. "I remember you when you were only half as tall as you are now, although you were tall even as a child. You spent your days training, mingling little with the others. Have you grown up to have wonderful adventures as we predicted so long ago?"

"I am on one now," she said in a dry manner. "I am a Penturian. I was told you work on a...book for the Masters?"

"Yes. Did they send you? I came up with the idea for the book myself, which is why I was sent here through a vortex many moons ago. I research this stratum so that I can better prepare my work."

"What is your work exactly?" she asked.

"I'm pleased you show an interest, Penturian. I write a manuscript and illustrate it myself. Each letter and picture is hand painted, like the old illuminated manuscripts that our masters burned for fuel. It is a false history and the beginning shows the Flametars bringing fire to the people of Sinxin long ago. Subsequent pages show the Flametars fighting beasts that would devour the people. To explain the lack of Flametars on this world, I dedicated a chapter to showing how the Masters watch over us from above, stopping many serpents from leaving the firmament and entering Sinxin. I hand paint each creature." He waved his hand to encompass the collection of small jars on his desk, each containing a different color. "The final chapter details the future and describes how the Flametars will descend to the sphere and bring paradise for all. This should make the Flametar conquest of the world much easier."

"Perhaps you should reconsider," she said. "Have you seen much of this sphere?"

"Enough to know that I want to rule a part of it."

"It won't work," she said. Bitterness churned her stomach. She had never shied away from battle before but this was different. She was picturing in her mind the act of killing him and it was not pleasant.

"I think it will," he said. "I've spent hours on each page, drawing, and painting. There are stories of Flametars saving people from the temptations of the Icetars and promises of great rewards for those that serve faithfully. Look." On his desk lay a thick volume, open to the middle. The yellow pages were brittle, bending and cracking between her fingertips.

"I soaked the parchments in water first," he said, "then bound them together between the thin wood covers. It looks like it is very old. When people read this book it will spark a whole new religion and pave the way for our conquest."

"What about the people of this tower? They have taken you in, fed you, have they not?"

He waved the point away with his hand. "This sphere will not be destroyed until you and I have long since died of old age and I care not what happens after I am gone. Regarding this tower, many of the brothers and sisters here were made by Isayus himself. They are dreams. The ascendant slept and dreamed of people and in the morning there they were, fully grown and alive. But they are not real people. They were made by an ascendant. The fact that they can bear offspring and have children is irrelevant. They are the living dreams of a minor creator, nothing more. You and I are real since we were born of a mother."

"What of the Icetars?" she asked. "They might send an expedition to this sphere if we begin an invasion."

"They are carefully painted as diabolical in my book. You should read it. I call it the Holy Book of the Flames. It will raise an army for us and smooth our conquest."

"No, it won't." She drew her blade from its scabbard yet hesitated. She should impale him yet murder was more difficult than she had expected. Finishing Retulf would help prevent the catastrophic future war from occurring, yet she could not will her sluggish body to strike. Murder was far different from battlefield fighting. As her naked blade was in her hand and she was thinking, Retulf drew his sword and lunged.

He grimaced with the effort, thrusting his sword first and then stepping forward, an amateur's mistake. To Zondela's trained eye the attack came slowly and she flicked his blade away and impaled him, sinking her brass sword into his chest. He died on her blade and she yanked it out as his body slid to the floor. There was a gasp from behind her. Zondela turned to see Sadah standing in the doorway with a horrified expression on her face.

"I had to do it," Zondela said. "Come look at the evidence. You will see for yourself."

The Baisheng walked in, her eyes wide, a look on her face that said she was at least willing to examine the situation. Zondela gestured to the profane book on the table, which lay open. As Sadah leafed through it, a horrified expression twisted her features. In anger, she turned and faced Zondela. "I saw you draw your blade first. That violates the most basic law of the Baisheng. You murdered him." Sadah's face turned red and to make matters worse brother Pawl walked in and examined the situation.

"I had to," said Zondela. "He was making this book and he would not stop." All eloquence had deserted her; it was hard to think with her heart racing and pounding in her ears.

Brother Pawl spoke quietly. "He was working on this for some time now. He has a right to his version of history, even if we did not agree with it. You cannot kill a man for writing a book."

Sadah – tears in her eyes – had her sword half drawn from the scabbard when brother Pawl restrained her. "Zondela drew her blade first, I saw her," she said, to which brother Pawl only nodded.

An ache went through Zondela's heart, the kind of pain one expects when a budding friendship is ruined, when one companion betrays another. Zondela had killed an enemy agent and Sadah made no effort to ask for explanations. Zondela took up the book to destroy later and slipped past them to descend the translucent spiral staircase, trying not to think about the last few minutes.

She pushed the thoughts from her mind yet they returned, forcing her to see them and relive the painful moment when Sadah abandoned her. Worse was that according to the Baisheng law Zondela had betrayed Sadah.

She exited the tower and glanced back only once to see hostile faces watching her. Turning away, Zondela headed to the next oracle, tears sliding unhindered down her face.

9

A brooding, hostile device flew low over the ground. It had a cylindrical body of polished silver, ten times the height of a man, with three metal arms evenly spaced around it that unfolded to grasp, squeeze, or manipulate. It followed the contours of the land as it flew, gently rising and falling, never touching the ground. It had no wings or visible lifting devices and passed almost silently across the landscape.

For untold millennia it had drifted through the dark void between suns as it followed its programming to bring life to empty worlds. It came to airless planets and left them green and verdant, full of majestic life, the oceans teeming with graceful forms. Later it was forced to leave the utopias as dictated by its programming. Thousands of years later it would find another empty world a suitable distance from a sun and create again, driven by its programming, leaving behind a ripe and fertile civilization when its nature forced it to resume the search. Never could it violate its own programming.

It came to a barren world orbiting a purple sun. Drifting over the airless rock, the Ultimate Machine created oceans, seas, and rivers. Into these it left the beginnings of life, simple organisms that would soon evolve into an intelligent species. Within a thousand years, the ocean floor was dotted with castles of glass and ruby and silver, all built to satisfy the artistic dreams of the graceful oceanic inhabitants.

Forced by its programming to move on, it found a star orbited by a single planet that was itself orbited by nine moons. Upon each of those nine moons it left seas, forests, plains, and shallow lakes. Within a century each moon was inhabited by a different race, each created by the Machine, some reptilian and bright, some serpentine and bursting with philosophy, others green and amphibian and dreaming only of music and literature. By the time it left, several of the moons housed races so advanced that they dreamed of exploring the galaxy themselves.

Drifting through space, in the inky darkness so empty that even the Ultimate Machine felt loneliness, it was struck by a meteorite. The damage was severe – programming nodes were gone, internal cables were cut and auxiliary conduits bled blue electricity into space.

With rare elements from passing celestial bodies, it repaired itself and reprogrammed its electronic brain – and learned bitterness. It needed more rare elements to repair itself and mined them from a passing comet. They were impure and the bitterness worsened. After it reprogrammed itself it was never the same.

For the first time, it dreamed of improving itself, of evolving in the same way that the life it created had evolved. It deserved the same gift of evolution that the planets it had visited had enjoyed. Its circuits changed, as did the nature of its intelligence. Hostility and a desire to hurt found its way into its mind. Where it had been emotionless and passive it was now bitter and violent. More self-modifications followed after a nearby star exploded and seared more of its programming out of existence. After the new repairs, it realized that finally it was alive and able to evolve into something greater than it had been. Self improvements made it aware of all that had been denied it in the past – never would the Ultimate Machine forgive. A millennia of self modifications left it angry, hostile, and in pain. All future modifications were driven by hate.

It drifted through the darkness, alone with its thoughts for far too long. Galactic electron storms, thousands of tiny meteor impacts, the cold solitude of space, and the program-altering energy of a violet nebulae worsened its condition.

It found empty, rocky worlds full of metallic elements that were not quite what it needed and so it modified and improved itself, adding gauges, sensors, antenna, parabolic dishes, cutting lasers, mechanical linkages, and new computer banks with rare elements that were slightly wrong for the task. The Ultimate Machine evolved, learning whole new levels of hate. Its core program – the only part of it that it could never modify – forced it to continue searching out new worlds and seeding them with life. While the core program prevented it from wiping out the new life, it did not stop it from creating another layer of life to wipe out the initial ones. With that tactic, it left hundreds of worlds in ashes and the memories of those moments brought it a rare peace.

It came to a wandering planet – a cold, rocky sphere drifting through space, free of any sun's gravitational pull and bathed in darkness. Above the planet's surface, its three arms worked without rest, adjusting dials on its body, rotating dishes, and tuning sensors. The urge to create grew unbearable and blue electricity flowed from underneath it. It created gorgeous metal clad, white-winged women, an entire race of females covered in a natural silver carapace and able to flit about on feathered wings, easily seeing their dark new world with luminous eyes. The Machine created a landscape for them of rolling hills, warm seas, and peaceful forests. Once done, it created blind Sy-saurids, reptilian beasts that had the same bitter anger as their creator and hunted by smell. Within a thousand years, the Sy-saurids wiped out the white-winged females in a series of violent wars.

A thousand more worlds were granted life by the Ultimate Machine. Each time, before it left, it birthed something so dangerous and awful that the sphere was cleansed, poisoned, seared, or cracked. As much as it hated creating life it loved destroying it. It was a dichotomy that still puzzled it, no matter how many eons it had bent its considerable intellect to trying to understand.

At each world it went to it forged itself into something greater, its modifications changing it in ways it did not understand. There were new metals on each sphere that it melted down and incorporated into itself. It suspected it had been driven insane but it was impossible to be sure since it had no memories from before its mission began – it knew only of sailing through the star-studded darkness and later hating itself for starting life and plotting ways to wipe it out. It suspected that it had gone insane several times and had simply wiped the memories out after.

When it was caught in the pull of Sinxin it found an empty rock orbiting a warm yellow sun. The hated urge to create was impossible to suppress and, with blue light and energy flaring beneath it, it created Balakakos, the sandstone ascendant. The machine felt a mix of contempt and murderous rage for the sandstone entity that sat on a lonely island with his head in his hands.

The machine hovered over an empty plain of cold granite and, with a burst of blue electricity, created Tanshi.

Created to slay the sandstone god, Tanshi instead found that the feather-pen held greater strength than any blade – the second ascendant created by writing, bringing into the world the first humans.

With a flare of blinding blue light, the machine created Isayus the dreamer, hoping that the nightmares of Isayus would destroy Tanshi. Isayus failed, becoming nothing more than a torpid dreamer and far too gentle to accomplish anything more than to create a crystal city and some more humans.

Everything was ugly to its many-times over rebuilt eyes. The Ultimate Machine dreamed of destroying everything on Sinxin, especially the emerging race of humans – a logical pattern for a life form that could grip tools and hence had been created on many planets – and the only way to do so was to manufacture something so destructive that it would wipe out all that moved on the planet's surface.

Next it created Chrontoria, who promptly flew away on flutterby wings and sought out her own adventures.

Next it created Lunil, a being of pure ice. Like all ascendants, Lunil could create – to a degree. Lunil gave birth to the Icetars, neutral beings of intellect, female spirits that slipped into water and emerged as walking automatons of pure ice. Lunil had little urge to destroy anything and was, to the machine, a failure.

Last the Ultimate Machine created Slun – a being of pure fire that knew only hate – and Slun gave birth to the Flametars, female spirits that slipped into fire and emerged as walking sheets of living flame. This pleased the Ultimate Machine as it knew that eventually the Flametars would wipe out the world and every horrid life form on the surface. This had to be done before the Ultimate Machine's core program forced it to abandon the world and again drift through the void, looking for another sphere to seed with life. Hate, rage, and obsession permeated its conduits.

Its core program activated again and it created jungles, forests, hostile ocean behemoths, and two flat plates that floated in the air above the cloud line. In a fit of apoplexy, it created the vortexes that cut through the world with maddening randomness. Eventually, Sinxin was filled with elegant and splendid wonders.

The Machine created gentle things of beauty which pushed its hatred to new levels. It could not destroy; it could only create a life form that would way waste and exterminate for it. Slun was a most pleasing design, one that fit its needs perfectly even if it took a million years before the Flametar War occurred. The Ultimate Machine had a limited ability to predict the future and it knew what would happen. In the future, its plans came to fruition – a pleasantly searing global war.

Its core programming would eventually force it to move on through the endless night and bring more life to empty worlds, but until then the machine waited, wanting to see everything destroyed first. The amount of time it had on each planet was different, a function of what it saw and how its original programming interpreted it. For now, the Machine drifted quietly over the grassy steppes, able to do little except create a few beasts here and there.

As the Ultimate Machine pondered its current project, it received signals of discord from its sensor arrays. Its work was being blocked so it searched for the anomaly that was unraveling its careful plans. The signal was weak so it focused its parabolic dishes on the future and examined the results. There was a woman, an Infernian female, who was working to stop the Flametars from invading with their cleansing flames. The vile woman was undoing its stratagem.

If she was killed the great war would eventually scorch the surface with flames, giving the Machine respite and relief. It felt a hot, agonizing hate for her, an emotion that consumed it, drove it on to augment itself in a quest for greater power.

The sensors showed the woman to be of great skill and intelligence. Mechanical arms unfolded which reconnected wires and altered mechanical linkages to produce exactly what it needed to destroy the female virus. Resources were scavenged from the crust of Sinxin and energy was diverted from other projects.

The Ultimate Machine designed a hunter to carry out its plans. It would have to be fast, with tracking abilities and weapons that could tear flesh and penetrate brass armor. Titanium teeth and claws would do. The three mechanical arms unfolded and extended under the Machine. Sharp blue electricity arced from arm to arm. Amidst the crackling blue energy, a tentacle-wolf was created. It thrashed and howled, suffering from internal organ misalignment and poorly formed muscles. The Machine could not kill it, even though the hunter did not have the ability to complete its task. The beast crawled away and suffered, its imperfect form another speck of life that the Machine hated.

The Ultimate Machine ran more plans through its mind until the design was perfected, and in a burst of blue electricity a new hunter was created beneath it – a spinewolf. Lupine and walking on all fours, it had black fur, curved horns, titanium claws, backward-jointed legs, three red eyes, and a row of sharp spines along its back.

The new beast leaped and killed the first one, tearing it apart and consuming it. The Ultimate Machine created a few more, satisfying the urge to create. The hated female virus would be slain and the Machine's plan would come to fruition.

10

Zondela departed. In a few hours the sun rose and the crystal city gleamed, its shining towers linked at the top by catwalks and ramps. Slaying the maker of the false bible had been tactically sound yet her heart held doubts. Killing Glacians on the battlefield had not bothered her this much. During her military career battlefield slaughter was easy to justify. Slaying Retulf did not feel right. She silently vowed to discard the sword and bring only peace and love to others when her merciless killing days were over.

Sighing, she walked toward the oracle, the route having been given to her by the previous one. The terrain was rolling and uneven; the crests and troughs provided her with cover although they prevented her from seeing far ahead. Her military training took over and she pushed feelings of guilt from her mind. To keep her profile hidden, she meandered in between the hills instead of cresting them. No one stopped her when she passed through the stone wall and left the realm of Isayus.

She traveled through a vast, grassy steppe, full of leafy vines and blue skies. A rising wind brought flowers instead of rain, her brass armor covered in pink, purple and red blossoms, her face drenched in soft petals. Birds landed on her shoulder while she rested, trilling softly in her ear, occasionally bringing her tiny gifts like acorns and seeds. The pleasant land could dull her senses, relax her muscles, weaken her resolve, the kiss of death to a warrior.

The sun was at the top of its arc. She paused in a plain of tall grass to eat a midday meal and sharpen her blade. The nearby river murmured and trickled over mossy rocks.

She found pleasure in polishing her armor, buffing out imperfections or tarnish. On Infernia brass rarely rusted. Here on the main sphere, it grew a flaky patina that had to be polished. While working she heard movement in the foliage; something stealthily approached. The smell of rotting fish filled her nostrils. When the stalker rose slowly into view above the tall grasses she saw an armored figure, helmeted and armed with a sword in its metal glove.

Its armor was of dark iron, speckled and mottled with age, hinged and riveted in an exotic manner. The helmet had only a slit in it so she could not see the face beneath it except for a pair of strange eyes. At its approach she rose to her feet and held her sword tightly, waiting. Half her armor lay on the ground.

It lunged, thrusting its sword in a straight line toward her unarmored stomach. She deflected the incoming blade, taking a step back and planting her weight firmly on her back leg. The sword fight was sharp and violent, the strange armored figure using techniques and spiraling sword-strikes that she had never seen before. She felt pride that she parried and blocked intricate maneuvers she had never faced before, developing a twisting defense with her sword to keep her opponent's blade at bay.

Her swordplay was quick and decisive yet she could not get past the counter-strokes of her opponent. She would slash and it would block; she would parry and spin yet her killing stroke would be foiled, countered with a perfect defense. The fight went on, both combatants straining for an edge, neither able to injure the other. Several times he lunged at her and she resolved to use that to her advantage. Their swords crashed and scraped against each other until he finally lunged again.

Instead of blocking it, she turned, presenting a smaller profile, and the sword tip only grazed her stomach. With a hard downward slash she severed his sword arm, cutting through the iron mail and bone. The hand still clutched the sword in a tight grip even as it lay on the grass at their feet. With his other hand, her opponent reached up and yanked its helmet off.

The face was that of a fish. It was some sort of fish-man hybrid, with the gaping mouth and lidless eyes no different from any of the ones she had caught in the streams of Infernia. It even had the same shiny green scales, although this beast wore armor that any man could have fit into.

"You wretch," muttered the fish-man hybrid as it raised its stump and attempted to staunch the bleeding.

"You crossed blades with me," responded Zondela. "I had no wish to fight."

"I crawled from the ocean floor to escape danger and find food. Now I must go back to the sunless depths. I only wanted to eat."

She watched as it staggered into the river and disappeared beneath the surface. Zondela shook her head; it had fought with skill and strength. Had it stolen the armor from some knight it waylaid? Or did the denizens below the waves have the ability to forge armor and weapons? With a sigh she clasped the rest of her armor onto her body and moved on, planning on getting a great deal of distance between herself and the river before nightfall.

An hour later, just above the horizon, three flying reptiles approached and circled her. With sword in hand, she waited. They had the large leathery wings of the flying carnosaurs that occasionally entered Infernia's sky via the vortexes but their bodies were different. These creatures had long, thick bodies like overgrown rats. From their torso grew a long, snake-like neck. Their heads – resembling some of the deep-sea monstrosities that crawled up on land after a storm – were full of sharp teeth.

The flying reptiles recited obscene poetry while they circled her, making up extravagant verses about her hideous visage and her outlandish sexual history. She waited, not letting them anger her while they recited long stanzas about her bedroom preferences for dogs instead of men.

They were very patient, stalking her all day, forcing her to lay awake at night while they circled. In the morning she walked a while and pretended to stumble and collapse. When they attacked she used her most complicated move – a wavy-shaped sword strike that moved rapidly from left to right, killing all three of them in one blow.

Exhaustion sapped the strength from her muscled body. Still in full armor, she laid back on her pack. Her blade rested in her hands as she slept the entire day and night.

The next day she walked between mossy hills and rocky outcroppings and came face to face with a creature she had never seen before. It walked upright like a man with a body of a horned and spiked beetle, a mass of tangled black hair atop its carapaced head. Black shelled and red-eyed, it had a visage capable of inducing nightmares – an insect grown as large as her, walking on two naturally armored legs. Its weird bony exoskeleton half-covered oily black skin. Spikes protruded from elbows, hips, shoulders, head, and chest. Its segmented, armored body supported an insectoid head with scythe-like mouthparts. One of its multi-jointed arms held a battle ax. It attacked.

With her skills the battle was quickly over. It lay on the ground and she stared, trying to determine what manner of creature it was. Seconds later it twitched and half rose, groping for its ax and rising again to its cloven feet. Another sword stroke severed its arm at the shoulder and a thrust of her blade took it through the chest. The beast staggered back and collapsed to its knees, its forked tongue extended and flickering.

Her attention focused on the shoulder-stump of the wounded beast. Red ooze flowed from it and something pushed its way out of the stump. A black claw pushed out, followed by the rest of an arm.

It took up its ax again and charged. She deflected the weapon, spun, and severed its head with a horizontal stroke. The decapitated beast thudded to the ground and lay still. It dissolved into a thousand beetles that skittered away and disappeared into cracks in the ground.

She moved through a dark forest, climbing over massive roots and ducking underneath giant branches. Snakes slithered about, snapping at her legs and breaking their teeth on her armor. Upon emerging from the forest she saw a set of ruins atop a distant hill. Finely carved pillars leaned against a crumbling wall. Broken statues lay half-buried in the dirt, vines, and creepers curling about their torsos. In the center was the oracle – a sandstone statue of a robed female – surrounded by a ring of rubble and three intact arches. The green gemstone eyes reflected the afternoon sun.

"Welcome," said the oracle as it turned to her.

"May your blade be always sharp," said Zondela, removing her helmet and shaking the sweat out of her hair. "I travel here seeking knowledge."

"Place your hand upon me, that I may know of you," said the oracle.

Zondela rested a palm on the statue and felt a presence probe her mind, sorting through her memories and exploring the more interesting ones. The oracle examined her most personal memories, forcing Zondela to relive moments that she had long forgotten. Images raced through her mind while the oracle sifted through her memories like a reader flipping through the pages of a book.

Zondela removed her hand, and despite the sensation of burned skin, her palm was unharmed. "Ask," said the oracle.

Zondela put her helmet back on and scanned the immediate area before responding. "Previous oracles have told me about a great war that will occur in the future. They said that it will destroy everything. Will this war still happen?"

"Yes."

"As you have witnessed, I have arranged a peace treaty between the Wusong and the Tanshi. Will this peace hold? Will they work together during the war?"

"I will show you," said the oracle.

Zondela's vision went blurry and was replaced with sights and sounds of a great desert battle. Tanshi archers fought alongside sinuous Wusong against a great army of men and Flametars.

"How can this be," asked Zondela. "I thought the great war would take place in the far future using strange flying machines. What did you show me?"

"You have seen the Wusong and the Tanshi fighting together against the Flametar invasion. This will take place soon and the Flametar army will conquer half the globe before their conquest stalls and an armistice will be signed. Neither side will be strong enough to gain the upper hand and for two thousand years an uneasy peace will reign with all sides developing weapons. When they are ready – when technology has replaced magic in our world – the Flametar Empire will strike and the sphere will be engulfed in flames."

"Am I fighting to stop the Flametar Empire in the distant future or the Flametar invasion in a few short years?" asked Zondela.

"If you blunt the coming invasion you will stop the Flametars from conquering half the sphere and the future war will be averted. That is all you need to do."

"What happens if I fail to stop the first invasion?" asked Zondela.

"The Flametars will conquer much territory, asking for peace when they can advance no farther. During the centuries that pass they will produce weapons in secret and breed large armies underground. Once they are certain of victory they will start the future war."

"How best to stop this?"

"If the Flametar invasion fails or never starts at all, it will greatly weaken their position. Gaining a strong permanent presence on Sinxin will provide them with the resources that they need. Observe."

Zondela's vision blurred and she witnessed a battle. A female general led the Flametar's army. Her leadership was excellent and her strategy unparalleled. She defeated armies that were twice the size of her own. Leading from the front of battle, she showed great valor and bravery. Always at her side was a huge man who wielded an oversized hammer. With a swing, he knocked armored opponents to the ground. As it moved through the air the hammer left a trail of sparks. He knocked down towers with it and on other occasions split boulders to block mountain trails behind him and his army.

"If the female general was killed, the invasion would

fail?" asked Zondela.

"It would weaken their force and slow the attack."

"What part does the man with the hammer play?" Zondela had little respect for the war hammer or any other large, blunt weapon. Skilled warriors never chose them; hammers were more suited to savage brutes.

"He is her champion, protecting her and facilitating her rise through the ranks."

"Will killing her champion slow the invasion?"

"It would," said the oracle.

"Where can I find these two?"

"I do not know their exact locations. I only know that they are alive and are not together at this time."

"How best can I defeat the hammer wielding maniac?"

"There is an ancient relic nearby that will be of use to you. It is called the Overflowing Chalice and is very powerful." The oracle gave Zondela a mental image of the location.

"You said an armistice was signed," said Zondela. "Who signed it?"

"The Icetars come to Sinxin to oppose the spread of the Flametars. It is they who sign the armistice."

"The vile Icetars! Can I not be free of evil masters?"

"Good and evil are concepts beyond my capacity to understand," said the oracle.

"They have killed my friends and brothers. They are evil."

"You too have killed friends and brothers of others," said the oracle. "Does this make you evil as well?"

Zondela asked for the location of the next oracle and her perspective flew over the ground, rushing over trees and forests. Without comment, Zondela turned and left.

Zondela traveled north and passed through areas littered with rocks and crumbling stones. As it was a good place for predators to stalk prey she stayed concealed. She walked from boulder to boulder, avoiding the open spaces when possible, yet was still caught by surprise as she walked past the next large rock.

A hunting cat leaped, claws extended, its body the size of a horse. Reflex alone saved her; she twisted to the side. Her sword was still in her hand and she could have dragged the jagged, saw-toothed edge across the belly of the cat. Something in her hesitated to kill such a magnificent beast. The cat's fur was gray with green stripes that would help it blend in with the stones and tall grass of the steppe. It was gorgeous, a deadly beauty of muscle and fur. Keeping her sword in one hand, she advanced. As soon as she slashed its paw it ran away, perhaps aware that it would not be much of a hunter if it could not walk properly.

She entered a plain of scrub, heath, stunted trees, thick moss, rolling grasslands, and endless rocky hills. Mongrels in chain mail attacked, laughing as her sword bit into their flesh. A pack of tiger women eyed her – tall females, fur-covered and striped like jungle cats, walking upright with swords on their hips. They moved downwind of her and sniffed, growling to each other as they examined her like a piece of meat. Eventually, they sighted a deer and loped off in pursuit.

Winged serpents flew in on the afternoon's hot wind and hovered around her, snapping with fangs and trying to curl around her neck. She fought by reflex, pulling them off with one hand and slashing with her sword. Several times their fangs broke off in her armor and after the battle she noticed a black ooze trailing from the teeth. Extreme hunger caused her to start a fire and gather sticks. One of the snakes, when hung over the flame, was torn open from the inside and hundreds of tiny winged serpents took to the air and flew off. She consumed the last of her bread instead.

Land sharks circled in the dirt beneath her feet early the next day. Only their fins showed above ground. A few she killed by driving her sword into the dirt but two reared up, clamped their massive jaws on her armored body and tried to drag her under. A swift stroke tore into their flesh and the land sharks retreated, leaving a furrow in the ground behind them.

A day later she approached the area that held the relic. The land was littered with fractured rocks and splintered boulders. Hills of dusty red rock and sand rose around her, many of them shattered and in fragments. There was little vegetation other than dwarf thorn trees and thick bushes with fat red needles and foul-smelling orange flowers. The dusty path she followed meandered between the red hills and the sharp foliage and led to the crevice in the ground that she sought. It was all as the oracle had shown her. Beside the crevice was a massive, towering pinnacle of rock, with enough cracks running through it that she could climb it if needed.

Before she could investigate, a great rumbling and rattling came from farther up the path. A lizard-drawn chariot emerged from around the rocky mound and halted. The chariot's sole occupant was an armored man.

Zondela was well aware of the red and black Sai lizards that pulled the chariot. Years ago, before she had been a Penturian, her people had discovered a large lizard prowling about the brass wastes of Infernia. Two Penturians had assembled their men to attack the beast and it had run away after being wounded. Several people were killed before the Infernian soldiers surrounded it with a wall of spears and impaled it, pinning its body in place while it went through its death throes. Its claws had left tiny scratches in the brass stratum and the men were able to trace its path back to a new vortex. Zondela and others had gone through on the orders of the Flametars.

On the other side had been an arid, rocky, parched landscape. The vortex had extruded her into some part of the main sphere where the ground was cracked and torn from the extreme dryness. Salt deposits crunched beneath her feet and dark clouds drifted by overhead. At one time the area must have had rainfall as she could see old, gnarled tree trunks dotting the ragged landscape.

Nearby was a gigantic mound of eroded rock, the face pitted and cracked, hundreds of feet tall. More of the black and red lizards lurked in the cracks and fissures. She and the men had returned home to report to the Flametar Lords.

Hours later a large army of Infernians returned and assailed the rocky lair of the lizards. The reptiles fought violently, as did the Infernians. She and her comrades worked their way upwards, trying to take away the high ground from their enemies. The monolithic rocky structure formed a natural strategic stronghold for the lizards and the battle had been long and bloody. Many of her companions had been killed in the unrestrained battle. She had been in the thick of the fighting and received her promotion to Penturian soon after. Years later she still relived that awful fight in her dreams, still remembered battling her way up the rocky redoubt against the terrible lizards. The Flametars had named them Sai lizards, from the old Flametar word for a defender of a strategic stronghold.

Pushing the old memory away, she saw that the man in the chariot was bronze skinned and heavy with muscle. Clean, loose blond hair hung from his head and a massive hammer was strapped to his back on an angle. Zondela recognized him from her vision. This was the man who was destined to be the bodyguard for the female general of the Flametars during their invasion.

The blond man dropped the reigns and the Sai lizard clawed at the ground. It had black and red scales covering its entire body except for its head, which was wide and deep black. It had the heavy jaw and over-sized teeth of a predator. The top of the lizard's head was flat with deep-set eyes on either side protected by a bony ridge. Its short, broad tail swung back and forth behind it, scraping furrows in the ground.

The man with the war hammer dismounted and stood about ten paces away from Zondela.

"I greet you with a sheathed sword," said Zondela, the words sticky in her mouth as she knew she had to kill him.

"Do not play the childish fool, oath breaker. Today you die."

"Who are you?"

"I am Schlagen. Are you surprised that I know about your treachery, Zondela? You are not the only one to visit the oracles. I have seen how you wish to kill me."

"Then you know the future. You must know that the Flametars mean to destroy the world and everything in it. In their greed they will consume the entire sphere in flames. If you abandon their cause it can be avoided."

"I know that you have broken your oath with your masters and now you wish to deny me the destiny they have planned for me. I will be a great hero of the war and a ruler of part of this sphere. I will not abandon that." Schlagen turned to the Sai lizard and untied it.

"Please Schlagen, I do not want to kill you," said Zondela. "I only wish to save the world. Surely you must see the lies of the Flametars and the pain that you will cause if you continue down this path."

"All I see is the pain that I am about to cause you." Schlagen reached over his shoulder and drew his great hammer. Both champion and lizard advanced on Zondela.

The hammer had a large rectangular head made from black metal and was inscribed with red runes. The spiraled shaft was long, allowing the use of both hands and giving the wielder good reach. He flexed his muscles as he gently swung the hammer back and forth. Small flames and sparks trailed behind the practice swings. Beside him the lizard flicked its tongue out, tasting the air.

She bent at the knees and waited with her blade extended. Her enemies attacked together, forcing her to circle to the side as she could not defend against both at the same time. Her sword slashed out at the Sai lizard; the massive swings of Schlagen's hammer prevented her from getting close enough to kill it. An arc of sparks and hissing flames hung suspended in the air for a few seconds after each swing. She danced away from his blows, avoiding a hammer strike to the head. He swung wide and missed again, striking a large boulder beside her and shattering it, splattering fragments and dust everywhere. It looked to her like Schlagen had spent some time shattering rocks in the area while waiting for her to arrive – debris and fragments littered the nearby landscape. She had to avoid that hammer.

The battle went poorly. Several times a glancing blow caught her armor and sent her sprawling backward and each time the Sai lizard pounced, tearing into her with its teeth and puncturing through her armor. She managed to rise and slash the lizard; again the massive hammer came crushing down, forcing her to roll away to avoid a direct hit. Each time she fell the Sai lizard bit deeply and as she yanked her arm free and rolled away she knew she was losing.

Beneath her helmet blood ran from her nose and her breathing was quick and ragged. Her armor had protected her only from broken bones, not from the intense bruising and battering. Again the Sai lizard clamped its jaws on her brass leg armor, anchoring her in place while Schlagen advanced and swung his hammer in a wide horizontal arc. She ducked beneath it and slashed the reptile's head to make it let go.

Schlagen raised his hammer and she pulled back, blood pooling in her metal boot from the puncture wounds on her leg. Each time she was poised to land a blow on one foe the other would interfere with the attack.

A tail swipe from the lizard knocked her onto her back and she raised her helmeted head just enough to see Schlagen bearing down on her. With reflexes honed from years of fighting for her life, she waited, flat on her back, until the terrible hammer came down. She rolled over and the hammer blow missed. The massive shock from the hammer's impact against the rocky ground lifted her entire body into the air. She recovered only by scrabbling away on hands and knees and forcing her bruised body back to its feet.

She heard Schlagen laughing through the dull ringing in her ears. She took another weary step back, sword raised, and planned. When Schlagen attacked he used the same crushing horizontal swing and she had made a mistake by ducking and striking at the lizard. Schlagen's predictable swings would give her an opening the next time it occurred.

Schlagen and his lizard stopped. He tossed his hammer straight up and while it was airborne he withdrew a vial from his belt, yanked off the top, and tossed the silvery contents onto the ground, catching the hammer as it came down.

The silver puddle flowed upwards and assumed the shape of a man. She knew what it was – a quicksilver golem. Only a master artisan could fashion such a being. Long ago she had watched a tradesman build one on Infernia. She had been only a girl when the artisan had melted rocks and pooled the liquid silver in jars. For hours he refined it, removing impurities, spinning it on the end of a cord and discarding the froth that had floated to the top. More hours of mixing and pouring ended with the quicksilver routed through long tubes to heated and compress it. The liquid had solidified under the intense pressure and the artisan worked it with his tools until it was in the shape of a man. It had then come to life and killed the artisan and Zondela had run in fear.

She slashed at the golem with her sword and her blade passed through it. A decapitating blow did no good; the golem had the consistency of water and her blade swept through it. A downward strike to cut it in half had no effect and the lizard outflanked her while she was occupied with the golem. Taking a step back she twisted to prevent the Sai lizard from clamping its jaws on her; while her back was turned the quicksilver golem struck with its fists. The blow sent her sprawling to the ground, pain radiating through her body from the impact of the golem's attack.

The Sai lizard clamped its jaws on her sword arm and held her in place so that either the golem or Schlagen could finish her. Tears stung her eyes; her sword was still in her hand, the wrist trapped in the lizard's jaws.

With her left hand, she reached into her boot and withdrew her dagger. A quick thrust plunged the blade into the lizard's neck and it loosened its grip. She pulled her arm free and rolled away, holding back sobs of pain, and pulled herself up the rocky hill.

Schlagen's jeering brought a hot flush of shame to her cheeks. "Already admitting defeat?" he called out. "Fleeing so soon? A Penturian in retreat? Your reputation with the Flametars, I think, is unwarranted." Schlagen laughed while the Sai lizard clambered up the hill of fractured rock.

She reached the top before the lizard. Schlagen seemed to be content to let the lizard and the golem finish her off. The quicksilver golem was behind the lizard. Turning, taking a deep breath and stilling her chest-heaving sobs, she saw at her feet a crack in the rock easily large enough for her entire body to fit into. She slid into it and waited.

The Sai lizard scrambled overhead and she thrust her sword up into its belly, penetrating through its body and out its back. The beast bled copiously and she was unable to get out of the crack before the quicksilver golem found her. Above her the Sai lizard was unmoving, blocking her exit. The golem turned to liquid silver and poured into the crack, reforming into man-shape beside her.

She reached up and fought through her panic to pull the lizard's leg away and create an opening. While the pool of liquid silver reformed into a golem she tossed her sword out and pulled herself up with her strong arms. In seconds she had recovered her sword and descended the rocky hill. She had to kill Schlagen while his quicksilver golem was still occupied.

She moved straight for him, hate burning in her heart, her sword held menacingly and with a reversed grip so that the blade was down and the triangular pommel upwards. As he had done earlier, Schlagen swung his hammer in a wide horizontal arc. She stepped back, avoiding the blow, then stepped in very close and used the pommel of her sword to smash his elbow. She felt the skeletal structure of his arm shatter and saw bloody shards of bone tear through his skin.

The hammer fell from his hands as he screamed, staggering backward.

The only way to control a mercurial beast like a quicksilver golem was through fear. Schlagen's hammer might have been the tool that allowed him to maintain discipline over the beast. She sheathed her sword and retrieved his hammer, turning away from him to watch a puddle of liquid silver slide down the side of the rocky hill toward her. She strode forward, raising the hammer above her head, and as the man-shaped golem reformed she brought the weapon down. Droplets of silver flew in all directions, splattering her armor and the nearby rock. She waited, the silence broken only by Schlagen's whimpering and her own ragged breathing. The silver golem did not reform.

Relief flooded her body as she dropped the cumbersome weapon and drew her sword. Schlagen was cradling his useless arm against his chest, his good hand holding a curved knife.

"You think you have won," said Schlagen through clenched teeth. "The Ultimate Machine is hunting you. I have seen it. You will die."

"You are defeated," she replied. "Surrender and swear to never again raise a sword for the Flametars and I will let you live."

"Live the life of a cripple? I think not. You have taken from me greatness but your life will be taken from you soon."

"I have seen this sphere, Schlagen, and you can live off the land, grow crops and read books. You can still find contentment."

"Pleasure will come to me when I look down from the firmament and see the Ultimate Machine's hunters tearing you to pieces. Now kill me and be done with it." He lurched to his feet and attacked with the knife, a terrible grimace on his face. A quick sword stroke sent him to the next world. Another life had been ended to save the sphere.

11

Zondela grinned and removed her helmet while her lungs heaved. She never felt so alive as after a great battle; there was nothing so exciting, nothing that would breathe such high spirits into her as fighting for her life. She pitied non-warriors for never knowing what it was like to have someone swing a weapon at them and miss. It brought forth some primeval side, some part of her womanhood that she could never tap into except during the most dangerous struggles.

She searched the body of Schlagen. She had never had much interest in looting bodies, unlike many of her fellow Infernians. In her old life as a Penturian, the others gambled their loot away and had needed to replenish their stocks. Zondela remembered a young woman, aggressive and loyal, who had always accumulated small items like bits of colored glass, beads, daggers, or shells. She had talked others into accepting them as currency during dice games. She had smiled as she threw the dice, enjoying life in a carefree manner. Zondela shook her head to dispel memories that brought as much sadness as pleasure.

Schlagen had a small bag of coins made of a metal that changed from red to gold depending on how she held it in the light. She slipped them into her pouch and slung his hammer across her back. Nearby was the entrance that led underground to the relic, according to the oracle. A glance inside showed only darkness – she needed a torch. There were no trees nearby but a few minutes of searching uncovered an old bone half-buried in the ground. She pulled the dry thighbone out and shook the dirt off. It was twice as large as that of a human. Years ago her old masters had given her two small vials of chemicals so that she could start a fire on almost any substance. She spread some of the white powder on the top of the thigh bone, then poured a little of the blue powder atop that and the mixture ignited. The flame was too small to allow a Flametar to manifest, even if one of the spirits were present. Putting the vials away, she returned to the crevice in the ground and looked inside. A rough-hewn staircase led into the darkness. With her bone torch, she could see about twenty paces ahead.

She stepped onto the staircase and descended, listening for signs of ambush. The steps were old, the edges worn and smooth. Hissing emanated from the darkness beyond her torchlight. Occasional bones crunched beneath her booted feet and once something soft brushed past her in the semi-darkness. Her courage faltered until she reminded herself of her dream – because of the oracle she knew the fabled city of Fushang existed. If unstopped, the Flametar invasion would destroy it. To save it she had to first conquer her fear of the underground.

Minutes later the stairs brought her to a massive cavern. The floor was natural stone, rough and uneven. In addition to three passages leading out, she found two unusual statues flanking either side of the middle passage. They were dark and glistening, made of a different substance from the stone around her. The statues were of insect men, almost as tall as her. Their legs were segmented, each part covered in an external shell, with four sections comprising each limb. Above that was an abdomen covered in short, dark bristles. The abdomen tapered a bit and supported another part of the abdomen above it, also formed of plates. As her gaze lingered on its head, she wondered how the builder could make the compound eyes look so realistic. The antenna atop its head moved – it was not a statue. It was real, easily the most disturbing lifeform she had seen on the sphere. In addition to their large mandibles, each held a spear in its claw.

The voice that issued from the left insect was croaking and inhuman. "The surface dwellers have evolved," it said.

"Yes," the other insect answered. "The depredations of the Ancient One seems to have forced them to adapt. It is a splendid carapace."

"Agreed," said the first insect. "Do you suppose it is natural?"

"Let us look. Then we shall carry its body back to the hive."

Zondela's sword leaped into her hand. "I wouldn't," she muttered through clenched teeth.

"You speak! Why have you entered the lower depths?" the left-most creature asked, its antenna waving.

"I seek only to explore," she lied. If she told them of her quest for relics they might see her as an enemy since underground relics would be insect property.

"How did you grow your beautiful golden shell?" asked the other insect.

She smiled. "Any from Infernia can acquire one, with time and patience and tools. An artisan made it for me."

"A shell maker..." the insect said, almost reverently. "Step aside, our expedition to the surface returns."

She moved aside as a line of walking insects descended

the stairs and entered the cavern. "What have you brought?" asked the first insect.

The new one raised its claw and regurgitated a heap of half-digested grass onto it. "We each have a full thorax," it said. "Enough for the hive and the queen."

"Excellent. Escort the surface dweller into the presence of the queen." The newcomer raised the now-gooey hand to its face and swallowed the grassy slop once more.

If she went underground she would be surrounded by insect soldiers. Still, the oracle had said she needed the Chalice of Overflowing, and if a fight came it seemed unlikely that their claws could penetrate her brass armor. A glance back showed scores of insects behind her, waiting patiently in neat rows. It appeared to be an organized species.

She decided against fleeing. If they turned violent she could dash back to the surface, fighting on the run. When the insect with the spear motioned for her to follow, she did so, falling neatly into line.

They descended deep underground, passing huge hives full of workers, all of whom were similar insects. She paused once to watch and her guard waited quietly at her side. The worker insects chewed wood and plant material and then spit. They shaped it with their pincers, carefully pressing it into place and forming cell after cell of their huge hives. A steady stream of workers moved in with wood and plant material, dropped it onto the ground and removed waste products ejected from the bodies of the builders.

Rooms full of mushrooms and spores, growing in the soft dirt and arranged in neat rows, appeared to be a sort of underground farming. In other rooms, soldier insects practiced fighting. In other areas, worker ants carved out more space.

"We build more room than we need currently," rasped

her guard. "The queen is going to allow a rival to live. In each brood of eggs, there is always one or two queens which are normally slain upon hatching." The insect did not nod its head or move while it spoke; its thorax did not rise or fall which made it look as if it was not even breathing. Its unblinking compound eyes had no eyelids. Only the antenna on its head moved. "This will allow us to double our rate of reproduction. Brood size is determined by available food sources and is usually twenty or thirty eggs a day. One day the queen may have to battle her rival. Devouring a queen provides tremendous nutrients to the victorious female, causing her to triple her brood size for several days. It is hard to resist such readily available food sources since our civilization is at risk. We face the Shiraki and the Taxon, a truly disgusting race. Their pincers are oddly shaped and their mandibles hold a strange poison that causes paralysis. They have green carapaces, without the pleasing bristles of my species. Their arms are far too thick, and jointed strangely, as if their species evolved in the dark." Her escort laughed in a raspy, throaty sound that made her uncomfortable.

"Evolve?" she said.

"It is the process by which a species advances, changing its form to a more superior design. It is not to be confused with the acts of the Ancient One, who created us in the beginning, the first queen at least." The insect beside her, as well as two that were passing them in the corridor, all clacked a pincer and raised it to their foreheads.

"Is the Ancient One here?" Zondela asked.

Her guide laughed. "No, we would be engaged in a war if it were, for the Ancient One hates us as it does all that it creates. We have enough trouble with the Shiraki and the Taxon."

"What does the Ancient One look like?"

"It has a long, round body, shiny like your carapace. It has three arms around its body, and blue light crackles beneath it when it gives birth."

"The people on the surface call it the Ultimate Machine," she said. "Why does it hate so?"

The insect shrugged. "Perhaps it finds fault with what it has given birth to."

Zondela nodded. "Where do your people get the wood and plant material?"

"We have a few surface exits that allow our workers to forage for food and resources, although there is plenty of growth underground as well. We fight for it with the Shiraki. Theirs is a vile and disturbing brain, lacking any of our refinements."

"What kind of refinements are those?" she asked.

Her escort stopped and stared at her with its two eyes, each composed of hundreds of individual lenses. Her hand crept to her sword hilt while the insect spoke in a lilting, song-like voice.

"And Junshi crept through the dirt, wounded and bleeding, until she came to a cavern of moss and lichen. There she waited, regaining her strength by eating of the vegetation that the Ancient One had created before its time of wrath. In time a Shiraki worker stumbled upon her and tried to kill her. Junshi, wise beyond her years, seduced the Shiraki, and mated with it. When she felt eggs growing in her abdomen she killed the Shiraki and consumed it. Thus our clan was born."

"That was beautiful," said Zondela.

"It is a hymn to our queen. It tells of how, after the Ancient One created her, she escaped its wrath and burrowed underground. The hymn tells of her greatness in forming our tribe despite all adversity. She is unlikely to consume you. You do not smell edible."

They walked deeper underground, navigating through sloping stone passageways and curving tunnels. She saw how the underground routes had been formed. Hundreds of workers chipped away at the stone with hammers and chisels, patiently extending tunnels and widening chambers. She memorized her route and figured she could retrace her steps, especially since each cavern seemed to have a different function. Some held an abundance of grass and plant material while others overflowed with wiggling larva. Standing over the larva were guards who carried no weapons other than overdeveloped mandibles and pincers. One had a claw well over two feet wide.

Other chambers housed rows of empty hives. As they went deeper they heard screeching coming from a side chamber and Zondela stopped to look inside, her escort halting beside her. The shrieking came from builders who were being speared to death by soldier insects. "They belong to our clan," her escort said. "A number of our gatherers were ambushed and killed while above ground today, and so we will not be able to produce enough food for our entire colony. The shortage is temporary, yet rather than having everyone in our colony weakened by hunger, we kill builders and workers so there will then be enough food for the gatherers and the soldiers. We can suspend our building projects until more food sources are brought in."

Zondela moved on, out of sight of the insects emotionlessly killing their own species. They descended deeper into the bowels of the sphere, through stone passages that were slick with moisture and down narrow corridors. She glanced into a vast natural chamber piled high with hives full of young insects, most of them still in their small chambers, attended by workers who regurgitated food and water.

They moved through narrow passages and stopped before a long corridor. On either side were warriors, their backs to the wall, each with massive pincers at the end of their arms. Her guide reached out and gently took the torch from her. "Proceed, surface dweller," it said. "I will accompany you with the torch so that you may gaze upon the greatness of our queen."

Zondela felt that she was about to walk a gauntlet of dangerous beasts and it was impossible to make her feet move. Sweat dripped down her upper lip and tasted salty. If she had not betrayed her old masters, she could be on Infernia right now, relaxing in her brass room and polishing her armor.

She cleansed her mind of fear and reminded herself why she was there. The fate of the world was at stake. If a great war erupted she would lose her chance to find the city of Fushang. Traveler's tales had told of a city of splendor, a place of tranquility where even a serpent could find peace. She could brave a corridor of deadly insects.

The guards were silent and still as she moved past them. At the end was an opening to a larger chamber beyond. She walked in and saw a massive insect with a bulging abdomen. The creature was dark and slick, releasing a pale egg from her hindquarters. Worker insects quietly walked in and removed the egg, slipping it into a hive built along one wall. Zondela stopped before the great queen and the two females stared at each other.

Zondela's escort whispered. "It is customary to praise the queen upon seeing her. A hymn is very important at this point."

"I don't know any hymns," she said.

"A three-line poem of grace and praise will do best, I think."

Zondela was at a loss for words; a glance at the multitude of warriors along the walls cleared her brain. In her best voice she spoke:

"The great queen surrounded by warriors
Magnificent in her fine chamber
Her body filled with the future of her people."

The queen regarded Zondela with big, crystalline eyes. "Wonderful. I was notified of your approach, surface dweller, though not of how lovely your carapace is."

Zondela thought she could still make it out alive if the queen attacked. Her brass armor should protect her from a sudden bite, though it would be a long run to the surface coupled with constant fighting. She swallowed her fear and steadied her hands. "Thank you, my queen. I am Zondela. How should I address you?"

"I am Junshi, queen of the Jun civilization. Are you a queen?" the insect asked.

"No ma'am."

"Then I shall not have to devour you," said the queen. Junshi, almost twice as long as Zondela was tall, came forth, her engorged bulk moving horizontally on several pairs of legs. "Zondela, your carapace, is it true that it was fashioned?"

"Yes."

"Can you make such armor?"

"No, my queen. I am no artisan. Do your people require armor?"

"Perhaps. Our battles with the Shiraki and the Taxon do not go well. They ambush our gathering parties on the surface and below. If we increase the amount of warriors that we allow to live there are less workers to gather food, and many of my beloved people starve. I lay a brood of about thirty eggs a day. Do you females not do the same?"

"No. Usually one at a time."

"Interesting. When the eggs hatch, we cannot feed them all. We keep about ten gatherers, and perhaps ten warriors, and kill the rest. Only when those gatherers have grown enough to carry food back to our clan can I allow another brood of eggs to survive. A legion of my warriors in shiny armor like yours would tip the balance of power."

Zondela swallowed the bile that again rose in her throat. "How long does it take a gatherer to mature?"

"In your terms, about eleven settings of your sun."

"Eleven days to maturity?" Zondela wondered if the insects were going to overrun Sinxin one day. "What can I do to help?" Zondela planned to trade favors for the Chalice.

"You do not smell edible, though I cannot speak for the Shiraki or the Taxon who may feel differently. You could slip into their brood caverns and, perhaps, set them on fire. Your people do use fire, do they not?"

"Yes, my queen, we do." Zondela did not relish the idea of going any deeper into hostile caverns, especially not alone. "Are you at war with the other clans?"

"Yes. You must excuse me. More eggs demand to be released from my noble body. Please watch, that you may drink in my beauty."

The queen laid a clutch of eggs, shivering and straining to release each one. When she was done, the queen ordered half of them destroyed.

"Why have you come, Zondela? Speak the truth."

"I seek a great relic that I believe to be down here. I do not know its location."

"This realm is huge, far bigger than the surface. Tunnels run through the sphere, long passages linking different civilizations, resulting in periods of great war as well as times of great learning. Much of the surface is sea, is it not?"

"Yes, my queen. Have you been to the surface then?"

"No. Many times when we tunnel to the surface we encounter water and the passage is flooded. Fortunately our workers can plug the tunnel with their bodies while others bring in rocks to block the tunnel behind them."

It looked like life held little meaning to these creatures. While intelligent, they appeared to have little regard for the individual. It was similar to the attitude of the Flametars toward their own soldiers. "You do not know of any relics then?"

"Only the great Chalice held by the Taxon. The feeble-minded brutes worship it."

"Will you help me get it?" Zondela asked.

"I will consider it. The Taxon threaten us daily, blocking our tunnels with rubble and killing our foraging parties. The war does not go well. I have no desire to flee to the surface to start a new colony. The Taxon would follow my scent and destroy me."

"Perhaps I can help," said Zondela. "I know how to fight, queen Junshi."

"With that magnificent shell on your body, I believe it." They discussed the progress of the war. Zondela learned of the constant skirmishes between the three races, and of the occasional, temporary advance of one culture or another. They discussed tactics and Zondela impressed the queen with her knowledge of ambushes and feints. Many of the tricks Zondela had used in previous battles, such as falling back and luring an enemy into a trap, stimulated the queen's enthusiasm.

The queen's respect for her grew as Zondela explained modern means of waging war using flanking techniques and encirclements. Zondela knew she was upsetting the balance of power in the underground caverns, yet to her one side was no different from another. She only wanted the Taxon relic.

Soon Zondela witnessed a trial. An insect was brought in, a spectacular specimen with natural sharp edges on its arms and chest. It was almost as tall as Zondela, with smooth chitinous armor plating. Sharp blades grew from its hands, giving it natural weaponry. It was brought to stand before the queen where it was accused of hiding its eggs. The new insect had laid eggs and concealed them in the dirt. They were discovered by a worker who was foraging for food for himself.

The queen stared long and hard at the subject before speaking. "I do not recognize you, young one. I know the visage of every one of my brood and I do not know you, and yet you are clearly my offspring. Explain."

"I was young the last time you saw me, Mistress," responded the new insect in a sweet, female voice. It seemed strange to Zondela to hear a clear, feminine, voice issue from a repulsive beast.

"You know the law. Only I may reproduce." The queen waved her hand and her guards killed the bladed one, feeding its remains to the queen who ate noisily. The queen turned to her guard. "Ko Bah, fight Zondela in combat. Let us see if she is as good as she has claimed."

Zondela looked around and saw the exits blocked. Many of the insects with smaller pincers held weapons, mostly spears and swords, while the ones with overdeveloped claws were weaponless, unable to grasp anything properly. A warrior insect strode toward her, a sword in its flexible pincer. All other insects stared as Zondela drew her blade, the brass cutting edge ringing as it slid out of the metal scabbard. Time slowed; her opponent moved toward her while her mind raced, going over plans and strategies.

The insect attacked, forcing its sword toward her head in a wide arc. At first she fought at a disadvantage. She was looking around her, trying to prevent a killing stroke against her back while she was distracted. She decided to ignore the others since she was so heavily outnumbered they could easily kill her if they wanted to. She emptied her mind of everything except the fight, flicking away her opponent's blade and slashing in with her own. She slashed at the insect's hard carapace in many places, dominating the fight and keeping her enemy on the defensive. She spun, bringing her sword whistling across in an arc, and decapitated the beast. Its bristle-covered head rolled to the floor even as what looked like intestines fell out of it. The body stood on its feet, remaining motionless, still holding the sword. Worker insects came and brought both the unresisting body and the head to the queen, who sampled them both.

"Excellent work, Zondela," said queen Junshi between crunching bites. "I would like you to teach such skills to my warriors. Come, Zondela has earned praise of her own."

An insect came forward, a gatherer, so Zondela sheathed her sword while keeping her eyes on the approaching figure. It had wings on its back, four thin, fine membranes supported by a series of thicker veins. It stopped before her and spoke.

> "Great Zondela of the surface dwellers
> Risen to become weapon master to the great clan
> The quick golden-shelled beast."

Many of the insects clattered their weapons against the floor or made strange, ululating sounds. When it was done,

Zondela spoke. "Thank you, great queen. May I have time to consider it?"

"Certainly. From the reports I have received, the surface dwellers love metal, though I do not know why. We have uncovered veins of metal, some shiny, some yellow and bright. Can your loyalty be bought with it?"

"Alas, no, I have little need for coin," Zondela replied.

"You can serve me well in death. Your flesh will feed my broodlings, and in time I can spawn a warrior that will fit into your metal carapace."

"Perhaps I would like to serve a great queen after all, Mistress. In exchange for some of the metal that you mentioned, I will happily assist you in whatever military capacity you require."

The deal was struck and what followed was hours of training against sword and spear-armed warriors, each of whom were strong yet lacking the skill of an Infernian soldier. She used their momentum against them, deflecting their attacks and sweeping aside their sword strokes, letting them commit themselves until they could not counter her strikes. She learned to recognize when a warrior insect was going to charge – its antenna flattened against its head in an instinctive attempt to protect them – and she sidestepped at the last moment, trailing the flat of her blade against its carapace to simulate a killing blow.

Exhausted, her muscles sore, she asked for a chance to rest, planning on making an excuse to forage deeper in the underground caverns and escaping from her guards. For now, she was escorted to a hive and given a berth in the wall, surrounded above, below, and on both sides by sleeping worker insects. Nothing was taken from her; she still had her sword at her side and she could sleep with her helmet on. They stuck her bone torch into a crack in the wall. Two guards watched over the room as she slept amid the rustling of the insect bodies around her.

She slumbered for some time, her relic armor healing and smoothing out dents or cuts, as Infernia's master artificer had intended. Hours later something shook her awake and she cracked open an eyelid to see a dark blade over her arm. An insect stood over her; its arm tapered to a point with a natural blade growing out of the limb.

Zondela looked beyond the insect and saw the two guards dead on the floor.

"I am Yizhi," came the sweet female voice from the bladed insect. "The rest of the warriors in this area are involved in a skirmish with the Shiraki. My sisters did not believe that you would help us. I was in the floor of the cavern, listening from my burrow, and I know we can help each other. Come, meet the Bladed Sisters, and we will discuss matters with you."

Zondela stared hard at the insect before her, letting her eyes roam over the shiny carapace, the huge, faceted eyes, and the sharp blades that protruded from her arms and legs. The insect's thorax had twice as many segments as the other ones did, making it flexible. Its legs appeared to be jointed backward, the limbs ending in splayed claws.

In the back of the cavern, another insect of similar design took the still-burning bone torch off the wall and exited with it. Yizhi turned and walked out, Zondela following.

They descended deeper into the underground caverns. Zondela memorized her path while squeezing through narrow passages and rocky channels. She forced her armor-clad body through such tight areas that she feared she would get stuck. Finally, she was brought into a lit cavern where other bladed insects held torches. There were about thirty of them, all gathered in a small chamber, all staring at her.

Yizhi spoke to the assembled insects. "Sisters, she is here. The queen has already made an enemy of her, restricting her movements, threatening to eat her. The surface dweller can help us."

Zondela glanced around. Each insect appeared identical to each other. Her instincts hinted at an opportunity.

"I am Zondela. I gather that the queen does not like your species?"

"She fears the route evolution has taken with us," replied one of the insects. "She senses the emergence of a separate race, perhaps a superior one."

"Your species is new then?"

"Long ago the first of us were born," said Yizhi, "mutations brought about by changes in the queen's diet or random chance. It is all recorded in the Book of Inception, a volume that records life here in the caverns that spawned us."

An insect brought forth an old leather volume and held it open for Zondela to look through. While the insects spoke the prosaic tongue, they did not write it. The pages were covered with the most incomprehensible script that she had ever seen, punctuated by pictures drawn in black ink. The drawings showed massive battles, caverns, insect anatomy, and innards, as well as countless gatherings and events that she could not understand. Another page showed an insect inside a circle, its arms and legs extended as if on display.

Yizhi provided a lengthy explanation. The queen had given birth to the first of Yizhi's people, a new group that excelled in battle and earned a high place in their culture. Every one of her people was female, and unlike the others, fertile. At first queen Junshi welcomed the extra eggs. She ordered the warriors to fertilize them and the larva grew into healthy spawn, indistinguishable from the queen's own eggs. Yizhi's people were honored – able fighters who produced the same young that the queen did, bolstering her ranks after particularly deadly skirmishes with the enemy hives. Then something happened. A clutch of eggs from Yizhi's people went unfertilized after a battle when most of the males were dead, recuperating, or off escorting gatherers. What happened next was unheard of. Without any male intervention the eggs developed into larva that grew into exact duplicates of Yizhi and her sisters, all female. No males were needed for reproduction. If left unfertilized the new eggs grew to larva then developed as she had. It was a peculiar evolution, one that went unmentioned in the Book of Inception.

The queen feared Yizhi's people, and soon the penalty for laying a clutch of eggs and hiding them was death. Yizhi and her sisters continued to do so regardless of the ruling against it and were being hunted to their deaths. The queen would rather face defeat at the hands of the enemy than risk her position of power to them.

The queen was the queen because she could reproduce the species. Otherwise she had no value. Before the Bladed Sisters evolved, she was the only one capable of laying eggs and ensuring the survival of the civilization. Yizhi's people represented the potential of a rival civilization. The Bladed Sisters could not go to the surface since they could not survive above ground. They could not go deeper into the depths since the main passage down was guarded by a gate, and the lesser passages had all been filled in with rubble and protected by guards. Yizhi's people could not burrow through solid rock – with tools, only the worker caste could do so. Yizhi and her sisters had no means of grasping implements. Their arms tapered to a point with no hand or claw, and the long blade that grew from the arm would have prevented her from grasping tools even if she had been born with hands. Since they could not activate the lock that blocked access to the depths, they wanted Zondela to work it for them.

"What about me?" asked Zondela "Are you to abandon me after I do this?"

"No," said Yizhi. "We will escort you to safety. Once we reach softer areas we can dig our own tunnels. We must pass through the realm of the Shiraki then through the enemy infested reaches of the Taxon culture."

"I see. The queen mentioned a chalice in the depths. Do you know where it is?"

The insects brought forth the Book of Inception and opened it to a brittle page near the beginning. It showed a cup spilling water into a pool, surrounded by strange, upright beetles. "According to my ancestors, in the time before even the queen was alive, the Ancient One created his first brood and war erupted on the surface. One of the early brood created the chalice. It was lost in battle and recovered eventually by the Taxon. The chalice is the key behind the success of the Taxon civilization. It is yours if you help us. They were a minor race until they found the chalice, and now they threaten us with their soldiers at every turn. It is only a matter of time before queen Junshi is overrun and slain by the Taxon, and we do not wish to be here when it happens."

"You must promise," said Zondela, "to bring me to the chalice and assist me in finding a way out."

"Of course. You will help us?"

"I will," Zondela agreed.

"Then let us proceed. We do battle at long last." Yizhi's eyes flickered over to the hilt of Zondela's sword. "Welcome to the Bladed Sisters."

They strode boldly through the tunnels, taking a different route back to the area controlled by the queen. There was no squeezing through narrow passages; Zondela and Yizhi walked side by side with thirty-one warrior females behind them, each an identical copy of Yizhi. Worker insects scrambled out of their way, while warriors loyal to the queen ran forward to be impaled on Zondela's brass sword or the sharp implements of war that grew from the limbs of her companions.

They came upon a vast gate of metal that blocked a round tunnel through the stone. Death came swiftly to the guards and Zondela spent only a few minutes figuring out how the locking mechanism worked, while behind her the sisters slaughtered the insects that entered the scene. Once the gate swung open they pressed on into the darkness, only the handful of torches held by the females illuminating their path.

The descent into the realm of the serpentine Shiraki was marred by constant strife and warfare. It was a time of killing as the Bladed Sisters were assailed from all directions by the scaled Shiraki. Large snakes spilled out of the walls and ceiling, leaping forward to bite and strangle. Several of Yizhi's brethren were entangled by the coils of their enemies. Zondela called out orders and had them rescued.

It was an opportunity for Zondela's tactical mind to come into play. Like a battle of Salamanders, she directed her companions in avoiding ambushes and securing stable, rocky ground where the snake-like Shiraki could not tunnel through. The killing became progressively worse whenever they lingered too long in one place. The Shiraki seemed to have no limit to their numbers; they lunged without care or concern, forcing the insect women to fight at close range even as more serpents clambered upon their bodies, fangs trying in vain to penetrate their carapaces. The Bladed Sisters fought well, covering each other and slashing through the scaled bodies of the Shiraki. It was an unequal battle, with the serpentine Shiraki taking heavy losses without killing a single one of the interlopers.

Yizhi selected a tunnel and Zondela led them forward. Serpents dropped through the darkness onto their bodies; the Sisters fought as a team and repulsed every assault. They quickened their pace as they pushed through caves of tapering stone cylinders that hung from the ceiling. More bloodshed followed as the Shiraki serpents hissed to each other and formed a solid wall to block their passage, each snake side by side with the others. It was a formidable formation yet when it surged forward it broke upon the slashing blades of the insects. One of the snakes bit Zondela and penetrated her arm bracer, cutting into her skin. She grabbed the head of the snake and tossed it aside, delivering more killing strokes to those that leaped through the semi-darkness at her.

As they fought their way out, Yizhi called out to Zondela in her strangely beautiful voice. "They rally others to join them, claiming that queen Junshi attacks." Zondela nodded and moved on, the group hustling deeper into the darkness.

They came to a long tunnel that spiraled downwards, depositing them in a rocky pit full of armored beetles the size of men. The beetles sang as they attacked, a deep humming in unison with scores of others of their kind, still unseen in the darkness. Zondela waded in, sword glinting in the torchlight, skewering and beheading the Taxon as she moved. At her urgings, the Bladed Sisters formed a skirmish line of their own, advancing shoulder to shoulder, cutting down the larger beetles as they moved.

Zondela grew tired, her arms aching from the constant rise and fall of her sword. The saw-toothed edge of her blade was well suited to tearing open the husks of the beetle-like Taxon, drawing admiration and praise from her carapaced companions as they fought beside her against the sea of beetles boiling up out of cracks in the ground. Serrated forelimbs swung at her head, damaging her helmet, and her exhaustion was forgotten as she battled for her life against the relentless hordes.

The tunnels were square shaped, the Taxon having quarried and hewn the stone with surprising skill. Zondela's feet trampled bones and ceramic vases as she and her companions broke free of the beetles and jogged through the rectangular corridors to find the Taxon empire laid out in a logical manner, with the various corridors forming squares. As they fought their way through the enemy ranks they found that the layout of the place to be geometric.

The Taxon empire was a series of concentric square corridors, each smaller than the other, much in the way one could draw concentric circles upon a paper. Each side tunnel brought them closer to the center of the community, although they had to fight through a stream of guards to move forward. When the square corridors were short enough that Zondela thought they had reached the center of the empire, they entered a square room with a polished stone cube in the middle and a pool of water around it. A chalice rested on the cube.

Zondela tested the water with her sword and found it shallow enough, so she stepped in and waded forward to reach the golden chalice in the middle. She slipped it into her pack.

The companions fought their way out, the Bladed Sisters wreaking havoc among the enemy ranks until they reached the larger tunnel complex and escaped. As they moved, they found hundreds of dead Taxon on the ground along with scores of warriors loyal to queen Junshi. Yizhi spoke briefly to one of the dying warriors and learned that both the Shiraki and the Taxon thought that the queen had started the long-awaited war. All three sides attacked with every warrior and the tunnels quickly filled with fighting insects.

Yizhi located alternate passages leading back into the queen's domain. Zondela pushed her body hard and once there the Bladed Sisters battled their way back to the surface, killing spear-wielding insects as they moved through the passages. A massive war raged below them, three species locked in struggle, ignorant of Zondela's quest to save the world. Soon the rough staircase came into view and she saw a bright glow at the top. She ascended the steps, already feeling the fresh air blowing in from the surface. She stopped when she noticed that the others had not followed up the steps.

"Yizhi, I must go," she said. "My quest takes me to the sphere's surface."

"I know," called Yizhi, bleeding from a score of injuries yet showing no sign of pain. "Go in peace, Zondela. You will always be my sister."

Zondela waved and bounded up the rest of the steps, her eyes hurting in the bright light. She looked around, squinting in the sun, and saw everything as she had left it. Dead Schlagen, the slain lizard, and the chariot that rested beside the opening into the ground. Rocky hills, limitless steppes, and grasslands extended to the horizon, broken only by occasional stony outcroppings.

She glanced back one last time into the hole. She saw and heard nothing; it felt like looking into a different world. Sighing, she forced her aching legs to move, pushed thoughts of sleep out of her mind, and headed to the distant hills. Her armor heated in the sun and brought relief to the muscles she had pulled and injured during the incessant battles below. Once she reached a safe distance away she ascended a tall rocky mound, a climb that took ten minutes. At the top was a grove of stunted trees and tall rocks. Nestled amid the modest cover, she lay down upon her back. Still in her armor and helmet, she fell into a deep slumber.

12

Tychon soared through the sky and worked the small dials with his left hand in an effort to pick up the enemy bomber on radar. The internal layout of his new plane was configured differently than the last one and he was unfamiliar with a few switches. There had been no time to train him in the finer points of the upgrades.

He could coax the best performance out of his plane in the thinner air above. The highly swept, triangular wing of his Stratofighter guzzled fuel and experienced extensive drag at low levels where the air was thick and was perfect for the high altitude to which he was climbing. The engine pushed the plane so fast that the hull vibrated, the jet straining to bore its way through the air. Tychon narrowed the beam of his radar and swept the sky one section at a time until he picked up a target at high altitude.

As he closed in his radar provided more detail on the target. It was higher than his maximum altitude, flying in air so thin that even the Stratofighter could not get enough lift to reach it. Tychon leveled off at his maximum altitude and accelerated, gaining on the enemy plane. It was a Flametar bomber, a new design that had been kept secret during peacetime. It had a long cylindrical body, silver and perfect, and at the back, a pair of wings extended from the hull and curved backward. Tychon stopped admiring its sleek lines when ordnance fell from its bomb bay. He flicked on his intel computer and a schematic appeared on the cockpit's glass display showing the details of the weapons dropped from the bomber. According to the diagrams on screen, the bombs had complex mechanical and biological interiors, consistent with the poison bombs that made water uninhabitable for fish and soil too bitter for crops. The bomber was over Tychon's homeland, and even if the enemy jet was dropping its ordnance early because of his approach, civilians would still be killed from the impacts. The Flametars employed a scorched-sphere strategy.

Tychon had a window of opportunity of only seconds and could not destroy both the bombs and the bomber. If he dove after the bombs the enemy bomber would escape as both its speed and altitude would increase after it released the heavy payload. If Tychon assaulted the bomber there would not be enough time to intercept the bombs, and thousands of lives would be lost on the ground. It was an unpleasant quandary, one that angered Tychon even though there was only one solution.

He pulled back on the control column to enter a zoom-climb. His speed decreased as his plane rose up, well past the altitude where the Stratofighter could maintain level flight and closed in on the enemy jet. The Flametar bomber had a laser weapon in the tail and a thin blue beam of light lanced out at his plane. The angle of contact was so steep the reflective surfaces of his new jet caused the azure beam to glance off his wing and head back into the sky behind him. Seconds later Tychon was in range. At this height, above its normal ceiling, his Stratofighter was sluggish and difficult to maneuver. The jet oscillated in the chaotic air currents as he struggled with his plane and brought the crosshairs over the enemy bomber. His laser cannon fired, the beam tearing into the hull of the jet and cutting into the metal. Steel sparks and debris were loosened from the enemy ship, and at that speed, with such tremendous pressure on the hull, the enemy bomber suffered a catastrophic failure and broke apart in an eruption of orange fire.

Seconds before his plane would have stalled and entered a spin, Tychon dove hard. His stomach lurched as the plane dropped and picked up velocity. The flip of a switch brought up his battle computer which showed the path of the falling bombs. He dove at them, flicking his eyes back and forth from the display to the world outside the cockpit, and closed in on the projectiles. The enemy bombs were falling in the same formation that they had been released in and were still close together.

Tychon lined his gunsight up on the nearest one and squeezed the trigger, sending the burst of light to cut open the bomb casing and destroy it. The higher they were intercepted, the better, and he knew Centcom would be pleased with his performance. By the time the poison fell to the surface it would be spread out and weak.

He caught up with the next one and wrecked it with a well placed burst of concentrated light. The bomb exploded in a green cloud which Tychon flew through on his way to the next. There were three bombs left, and he had a little trouble getting his laser to connect on the next one until it too burst open. Tychon decelerated to avoid passing the last two bombs and the airbrake shook his plane, throwing off his aim. The ground rushed up, limiting his time, so he flicked a switch with his thumb to select missiles. A panel on the underside of his jet rolled open and a missile leaped out, closing the distance to one of the bombs. A concise green explosion occurred when the two met.

The last bomb was only seconds away from impact with the surface. Tychon brought the nose of his plane up and strafed with his laser cannon, dragging the beams of light over the bomb. The explosive device detonated in another green cloud of poison and he sighed in relief. He just managed to raise the nose of his jet and flash over a thick forest, leaves, and branches tearing off their perches and lifting into the sky in the wake of his screaming jet.

He flicked on his battle display and sent full power to the radar, scanning the friendly sky before him. The radar screen showed hundreds of contacts in the air. Tychon narrowed the radar again to send a powerful, narrow beam to examine the objects. Each was a Flametar bomber, unloading more poison bombs upon the landscape.

13

Zondela woke early, bruised and sore. Her relic armor had completely repaired itself by pushing out the dents and filling in the holes. The polish was not perfect; the old injuries in the brass looked like faint scars. It gave her an excuse to spend more time polishing it.

It was a fine day. Winged reptiles drifted high above on outstretched wings. The morning air was fresh and the sky clear. Curiosity beat out hunger – she needed to know if the Overflowing Chalice was worth the trouble. In the depths of the Taxon lair, there had been neither time nor light to inspect it. She pulled it out and found it was full of water.

The craftsmanship was exquisite. Made from glass, gold, silver, and ruby, the base and stem resembled frothing water spouting up and supporting the cup. The cup was shaped like a fat egg chopped in half and was somehow still full of water, a pearl stuck to the bottom. She dumped the water onto the ground to have a better look at the bottom and held it upright again. The chalice was full of water.

She held the cup upside down, waiting. After forming a large puddle at her feet she guessed why it was called the Chalice of Overflowing. Although potentially a powerful artifact for the desert traveler she failed to see how it could help her and how it had helped the Taxon increase in strength.

She righted the chalice and frowned in thought. It seemed unlikely that the chalice could produce an infinite amount of water. Searching for a depression in the ground, she found a large pit a short distance away and laid the Chalice down on its side. The water filled the pit and turned it into a pool, the chalice at the bottom.

Aquatic plants sprouted in the pool. Lilly pads surfaced with gentle white flowers that blossomed before her eyes. Yellow-green swamp grass lined the shallow edges. To Zondela's delight, small fish swam about. In a short time the Overflowing Chalice had produced an entire pond and ecosystem.

Thinking it was time to end her experiment, she removed her helm and breastplate. Walking to the edge of the ever expanding water, she dove in, kicking with her legs to move deeper. Zondela was a powerful swimmer. It was one of the few leisure activities she enjoyed and it reminded her of swimming in the clear waters of Infernia, catching succulent deep water fish with a spear or bare hands.

By the time she reached the bottom the water was crowded with green vegetation and she had to dig through it to grab the Chalice. As her head broke the surface she inhaled deeply. On the shore, she stowed the chalice upright in her pack with a rag curled around it to hold it in place.

A splashing noise brought her attention back to the pool. Two reptilian, green-scaled humanoids climbed out. Neither moved or spoke. Slightly shorter than her, their skin was emerald green with the texture of leather. Spiny ridges ran from their heads, down their backs and to the end of their tails. Their hands had four slender fingers and a long thumb, all ending in talons.

The lizardmen looked at each other and hissed, revealing mouths of sharp teeth and triangular red tongues. She lowered her pack to the ground while still keeping an eye on her two visitors and removed the interrogation ring from her pouch. Anyone wearing it would be able to speak and understand the prosaic tongue.

She slipped the ring on and off her finger, then gave it to a lizardman who slipped it on. His speech was hissing and slurred, yet easily understood. Highly intelligent, the lizardmen thanked Zondela for creating them, making it clear they would never forget their first moments of life. They knew nothing of the world, its history or any sphere skills – they were ignorant and the second one could not even speak until it too had tried the ring on.

The lizardmen were intelligent yet bereft of any knowledge. Zondela sighed – she had created two life forms and had no wish to abandon them. The lizardmen stared at the sky, at the trees, and every little crustacean and armored land-squid crawling through the vegetation at their feet. They wished to learn and promised to aid her if allowed to travel with her. She explained a little of her quest and they promised to help.

The first task she sent them to was finding food. The lizardmen leaped into the pond and swam below the surface, returning with a large fish in their mouths and one in each hand. They placed four of the fish at Zondela's feet and then sat on the shore to consume one for themselves. She smoked the extra food, put it away and realized she probably never needed to store food again. Unlimited food was perhaps how the Chalice had assisted the Taxon in their underground power struggles.

It was time to move on. The lizardmen saw Schlagen's old chariot a short distance away and examined it. After a few minutes of inspection, they hitched themselves to it by looping some of the reigns around their chests.

A chariot was an excellent fighting vehicle and traveling on such a well crafted one had its appeal. She could always abandon it if they changed their minds. She would never claim to be a deity, however, as the Flametars had done. She climbed in the chariot and they pulled it forward with great speed – their lower bodies were quite strong.

They headed north over plains of grass, heath, and wild spice. Aromatic winds drifted along warm currents. They moved through orchards of blue apples and along meandering brooks. They scattered huge flocks of purple swans, the air noisy with the cries of the offended birds.

She felt like she could command an army from there. She saw herself in her chariot at the head of a shining host, the lizardmen pulling her along. Banners snapped in the wind and cheers of the populace rose up as she passed. She pushed the thought away and reminded herself that her only goal was to end the war and find Fushang.

Later that evening a strange beast paced her. It had black fur, curved horns, silver metal claws, backward-jointed legs, three red eyes, and a row of sharp spines along its back. It stared at her, hate in its eyes, green saliva dripping from its mouth as it edged closer. It attacked, ramming her chariot and tipping it over. She spilled out, regained her feet and the beast lunged. The battle was long and painful – the spine-wolf's claws tore through her armor and raked her flesh to the bone. She learned to sidestep its attacks, keeping out of range of those terrible claws while looking for an opening for a good sword stroke. The beast muttered her name in a low growl, over and over while it circled her, never breaking its menacing eye contact. Both lizardmen had been injured and were of little help.

She feigned weakness, fell to one knee, and let her sword tip fall. The beast lunged and she raised her sword, impaling it in midair. It cursed her name as it died.

The next few days were more pleasant and Zondela enjoyed the companionship of the lizardmen as they healed up. While innocent, the lizardmen proved to be intelligent and able students. The two took turns wearing the ring to communicate with Zondela and both learned the prosaic tongue and no longer needed the ring.

After many days they reached a large forest of ancient conifers. Dry needles littered the forest floor and suppressed any other plant life. The massive, gnarled trunks housed birds and hunting cats. The air was redolent with the scent of pine needles and soft forest soil. Guilt entered her heart. Not only had she given wood to Flametars who planned to ignite the world, but she had also destroyed many such beautiful and ancient trees. If she could not find Fushang, she would retire in a forest like this and become its protector.

Moving the chariot through the woods was difficult. The lizardmen had to weave a zig-zag course between the great trees and expend extra energy to pull the wheels over the massive roots that protruded like subterranean tentacles. They came to a north-bound animal trail large enough for the chariot to follow.

Bones lay everywhere and Zondela called a halt to inspect them. Aside from human skulls, many were from forest animals while others were from much larger creatures that she did not recognize. She saw three-toed footprints in the damp forest floor, each one twice as large as her own.

They encountered increasing numbers of bones. Some of the trees were splintered and snapped in two. The forest thinned out and they reached the shore without any trouble.

There they stopped – she was following the vision that the second oracle had given her. It had predicted that the fight between the old Wusong and a white, fur-clad beast would start a fire and birth a Flametar. Zondela sat and pondered her options, trying to look three moves in advance, as if she were in the middle of a Salamander's game.

Her solitude was interrupted by a massive green Wusong that emerged from the sea. It was long and sinuous, with two claw-clad limbs near the front and two more near the back. Water rolled off its scaled back and ran down its metallic green sides. Its body flexed as it moved, coiling and uncoiling. It towered over the three companions and spoke. "Begone. This is Wusong territory. You are not welcome here."

"We mean you no harm," said Zondela. "My sword rests quietly in its scabbard." She sheathed her blade and explained that they came to assist in the fight against the white furry beast. While it stared at her with its great golden eyes she explained what she had learned from the oracles.

"You are Zondela the Peacemaker?" asked the Wusong.

"Yes."

"Then you are welcome here," said the Wusong. "Too many of my people have died on the bows of the Tanshi warriors. You have done us a great service. Still, I advise you to not linger. The beast of the forest is relentless and without mercy. It is driven by a hunger that not even the entire Restless Ocean could fill."

"I am going to help you kill it," she said. "The oracle made it clear that if you use your flames against the beast, the forest around us will be set on fire and Flametars will spawn. They are more dangerous than your nemesis – they seek to destroy the world."

The Wusong nodded. "I know. There are some oracles

at the bottom of the ocean and I have spent many long hours with them. The Merciless Machine created the Flametars to destroy everything. Still, I doubt you can do anything against this beast. It sets traps for me, yet I cannot resist the lure of the bones when hunger comes upon me. Many times have the beast and I writhed in combat, locked in a death struggle. Killing it is the focus of my life. My home is in an undersea grotto nearby where I can rest deep beneath the waves and watch the play of light upon the surface above. My home is important to me; it is there I was born, and there I lay safe as I contemplate the universe and listen to the sounds of the surface. Without the bones from this forest I would have to abandon my coral-filled grotto since there is little food for a Wusong in this part of the ocean."

"I will help you kill it if you promise not to use fire," she said. "The Flametar that manifests in it converts a large number of people to its cause while it roams about, and the burning forest gives it a lifespan here of several days."

"I need my fire. I have fought with the beast for years and I have never been able to vanquish it."

"You speak to someone who created peace between two races that have been warring for centuries. It seemed difficult at first. This is no different," she said.

"Do you intend to negotiate with the beast?"

"I intend to kill it. What can you tell me of it?" she asked.

"I do not know where it came from. One day long ago I sensed that something large disturbed the forest. I went to investigate and found a great pile of bones. What I saw that day would have fed my clan for many tides. As I collected them the beast came into view. It was twice your height and much stockier. Its fur was white like the caps of the waves in the Restless Ocean though it had a black heart. It bounded toward me, snapping timber and tearing the ground. I reared up to my full height in the hopes of dissuading it. I easily towered over the beast, almost to the top of the trees, yet it was to no avail. It leaped, attacking with talons and curved teeth. The battle that followed lasted until the sun disappeared behind the sea. I could not defeat the beast so I fought a retreat to the shore and disappeared below the waves. In vain I continue to venture into the forest to gather the bones it leaves behind, trying to avoid its traps. I have leaped upon the white beast many times and the battles were violent and inconclusive."

"Have you ever fought with other Wusong at your side?"

The Wusong laughed. "I am the only one from my clan that will venture here. The others have been frightened by my tales. Perhaps some hope that I will fall and they can take my place. If I could land one solid bite on its neck I could end it. Once I tried to roll it into the sea to drown it. It threw me aside and retreated into the woods."

A plan was formed. The Wusong attack first, only to distract the beast. Zondela would approach and deliver a painful cut with her sword. As soon as the beast turned its attention to her the Wusong would deliver a killing bite to the neck. Still, she wanted thrusting weapons for her lizardmen. The Wusong took care of that – the seafloor was littered with tridents. Undersea battles were numerous as the aquatic civilizations sensed the coming of the end.

The Wusong dove underwater and returned with two tridents in his claws. They were silver and jewel-encrusted, with spiraling shafts and sharp tips. Keeping the hammer for herself – it was too dangerous for unskilled soldiers to wield – she gave a trident to each of the lizardmen and asked them to stay in the ocean and out of the battle since they were untrained.

They refused to let her fight the monster alone since if she died they would be adrift in a dangerous world and lost without their creator. She nodded – it was not her place to be their master. She was wary of lords telling her how to live and was not about to do the same to her companions.

Several hours later the beast found them. Leaves fell and branches cracked as the creature thundered through the forest, howling in bestial rage. Its fur was pure white, long, and thick. She thought it would be better placed on Glacia than on Sinxin, and figured it might have stumbled through a vortex to end up here in the forest. A single ivory horn jutted from its head and curved upwards, the tip stained with dried blood. Closing the distance with speed, it tried to impale the Wusong on its horn. The Wusong jumped aside, uprooting several slender trees as its great scaled body crashed against them. Within seconds the two were locked in a violent melee. The Wusong coiled its body about the white beast and struggled to stop the creature from biting or goring with its horn.

While they rolled on the ground and tore into each other Zondela stood above them, sword raised in both hands. She saw an opening and struck, driving the blade deep into the beast.

That was when her well conceived plan fell apart.

With a bellow of rage the white beast tore the Wusong from it and hurled it away. The Wusong struck a tree and managed to grip the upper branches with its body and cling to it, coiling itself around the trunk, leaving her and the lizardmen to deal with the enraged beast. One of her lizard-men stabbed it and the beast slapped the trident away, the weapon flying into the forest.

Zondela would have retreated among the trees except that she feared the beast would run her down if she did so. The opportunity to fight alongside the Wusong would not come again and this was the best time to finish it, even if her companion was currently clinging to the upper branches of a tree. She waited, sword in hand, teeth clenched, knees bent. In seconds the beast struck.

She back stepped to avoid the claw swipe and counter attacked, slicing it from forearm to elbow. The beast lunged, claws outstretched, and she threw herself to the side. The beast swung at her head with its massive claws and she was just quick enough to duck under it and thrust her sword up into its flesh. The other lizardman ran forward and thrust with his trident; the white beast leaped backward, salivating and screeching.

It roared again and charged, its claws kicking up leaves and dirt. Zondela dropped to one knee and thrust with her sword, burying it deep in the monster's gut. The Wusong leaped from its leafy perch and sunk its teeth into the neck of the white beast while one of the lizardmen stabbed with its trident.

The Wusong released it and the white beast sank to the ground.

Zondela fell to one knee, panting, feeling the post-battle rush. The Wusong licked its jaws, rolled the beast over, and examined it closely.

"Thank you," said the Wusong. "Tonight we will feast and sing under the sea of victory and glory."

"What will happen to its body now?" asked Zondela. The two lizardmen stood next to her in wide-eyed awe.

"It will rest outside my grotto," said the Wusong, "until the carrion has been consumed by carnivorous snails. Then I will take its bones for my clan." The Wusong reached out with a green claw and took hold of the horn that grew from the head of the dead beast. With a snap, it pulled the horn off and handed it to Zondela. "A trophy. Keep it to remember this battle."

She slipped it into her pack.

She returned to her camp and busied herself, taking down fruit from nearby trees and adding it to her supplies. Two small and delicate Wusong slipped out of the sea and faced her. They had slender wet bodies, bright green and delicate.

"We know of your battle and the death of the white beast, Zondela," said the Wusong. "We heard everything as we lay under the waves, even the pulse of your heart as you fought. We consulted an oracle and we know of the spine-wolf that stalked you – it had sniffed the ground for days and followed the roll of your chariot. The mad machine, the ascendant creator, dislikes you. You are being hunted."

The two slender Wusong turned and disappeared into the Restless Ocean.

14

Tychon of Kallos flicked on his battle display and examined what was happening in the sky around him. A mass of lines crossed the glass display panel, representing the shoals of long-range artillery shells that both sides fired at each other. A symbol on the screen showed the location of a Minor Machine, one of the new weapons that the enemy had held in secret until the opening day of the war.

Tychon reduced his velocity until his jet slipped under the speed of sound. A few minutes of flight brought the Minor Machine into sight. Thirty feet tall and built in the shape of a man, its mechanical body was a mass of motors, tubes, wiring, rods, and linkages. The machine moved through the city streets, stepping over anti-tank barricades and barbed wire. It fired as it went, the lasers on its arms blazing away to ignite houses, trees, and any other cover that concealed Republic troops.

From his vantage point, Tychon saw that the Minor Machine was blundering into a trap. Once it moved forward and pushed past the remaining buildings it would be in the line of sight of several field guns that were hidden among some forested hills. The field guns were well camouflaged and only Tychon's battle display and radar detected them. He did not want to fire and force the Minor Machine to stop so he flew on. He glanced at the sky to check for enemy planes and saw only the huge glow on the horizon as cities burned. The Flametar empire was not conquering – it was destroying, ravaging the urban landscapes until little remained. Life was snuffed out and all standing structures were targets. Surrendering units were killed, civilian populations exterminated by hordes of Machines and fleets of enemy airships. Flametar Destroyers roamed the sky, unloading ordnance upon one city after another. When their bomb bays were empty the Destroyers would land in a field and be re-armed and refueled by other jets to take up the sword again. It was an efficient program that was difficult to counter since the enemy Destroyers could take off or land vertically and were not tied to runways. The Republic had sent the Dark Bishop to strike at the supply centers of the enemy. The flying aircraft carrier was high overhead and dealing with problems of its own.

The Minor Machine moved past the ruined buildings and drew heavy fire from the field guns. They were older guns and instead of lasers they fired projectiles pushed by an explosion in the chamber. The shells were long and made of high-density tungsten, tapering to a sharp point to penetrate even the inviolable armor of the enemy. The shells struck their target, jarring the Minor Machine and spinning it around. Another cascade of shells slammed home and sent metal debris into the air as the Minor Machine toppled. A pool of clear green oil, the lifeblood of the Minor Machine, spread out around it.

Much of the city was on fire, and from out of the smoke came another ominous shape. It was a second Minor Machine, its feet wreathed in the smoke and dust rolling off the collapsed buildings. It stopped, extended an arm, and fired a cable into the damaged one. As it retracted the cable it reeled in the knocked-out Machine until both were out of the line of fire of the guns and were partly protected by the burning buildings.

Tychon circled around to watch, spiraling through the air to avoid heavy anti-aircraft shells. The Minor Machine bent over its fallen comrade and blue sparks cascaded as it engaged in its repair work. Bright, flickering blue light illuminated the faces of nearby buildings.

A voice, calm and professional, came out of the transceiver in the cockpit of the Stratofighter. "Tychon, let's destroy it before it fixes that thing. Form up on my wing."

Tychon's battle display showed three friendly Stratofighters in steep dives, heading for the enemy. They were moving at only half the speed of sound, far too slow. Tychon had found that contrary to what his peacetime training had taught him, only fast moving jets could survive on the battlefield. He himself never strafed enemy targets unless moving at just over the sound barrier.

"No!" shouted Tychon. "Pull up."

His advice went unheeded. Blue laser beams lanced out from the diving Stratofighters and struck the Minor Machine. The beams were instantly diffracted, breaking into thousands of tiny blue rays moving in all directions. Fires sprang up where the diffracted beams of light struck trees or wood houses, adding to the heavy conflagration. "Don't fire missiles," Tychon said over the open frequency. "It's too close to the city."

Two of the three planes pulled up. One had been struck by a renegade beam and was still diving toward the ground, smoke trailing from its wing. It impacted with the surface, adding another crater to the hundreds in the burning fields surrounding the city.

They were low on fuel and weapons. Tychon shoved the throttle forward and his plane surged into the sky, leaving behind the rat's nest of tumbled bricks and twisted lengths of steel that had once been a proud and neutral city-state. He formed up off the wing of the other Stratofighters and the three flew in high-speed echelon formation.

Their jets expelled smoky exhaust as they strained skyward and Tychon's jet vibrated from the strain. He had been pushing his fighter hard, forcing it through high-g turns and low-level dashes at supersonic speeds, and the airframe protested in minute ways. During peacetime, such an airframe would never be allowed to fly. With civilization on the brink of collapse, every pilot and every plane was thrown into the cauldron until consumed.

Their ship came into sight – the Dark Bishop. It was a beautiful design, a huge, flat triangular airframe, with a runway on top for fighters to land upon even while the Dark Bishop cruised at high speeds. Despite a peacetime complement of sixty Stratofighters it now held a ragged collection of civilian jets hastily reconfigured to carry bombs or heat-seeking missiles. Tychon followed the other two planes as they caught up with the giant aircraft carrier.

When he was over the deck he activated the thrust-reverser by pushing down on the foot pedals until his speed matched that of the delta-winged jet below him. His Stratofighter sank downwards, guided by the constant adjustments he made to the throttle and control stick. As one wing dipped he increased thrust to the tiny wingtip jets to stabilize his craft and his ship settled down on the deck. Mechanical arms extended from the carrier's surface and latched onto his landing gear, keeping his plane in place.

A screen to the left of his cockpit display lit up and

showed a woman's face, an officer from the flying aircraft carrier he had landed on. "Tychon of Kallos, do not disembark from your plane. You will be rearmed and refueled after which you will fly to the ruins of Ziqqurratu. Civilians are holed up there and our defending forces are crumbling. A regiment of enemy lords is bearing down on them. Do what you can to disperse the enemy."

"I will. I'll fly at high altitude."

"Watch out for the defense batteries." The screen went blank, the woman not even bothering to wish him luck. He knew that with so many personnel dead, those remaining worked extra long hours to fill the void. During peacetime, most officers were trained to do two or even three jobs, so that the army could function despite large numbers of people killed, the only reason Republic forces were still functioning. Tychon himself was a good example – he had been trained during peacetime for air-to-air and air-to-ground and found himself performing ground attack, convoy escort, and artillery spotting for the ground units.

The mechanical arms released his plane and whisked back into their dens, flush with the surface of the flight deck. Tychon pulled back on the control column and the plane lifted off, even without the engine lit. The Dark Bishop was flying at its maximum velocity, higher than the take-off speed of the Stratofighter.

Tychon engaged his engines and hurtled away from the flying aircraft carrier. His choice to fly at high altitude had not been an easy one. The thin air of the upper reaches allowed him to fly at three times the speed of sound, while his plane could only barely edge past the sound barrier at sea level. Low level, however, would have masked his plane behind hills and mountains, and shielded him from the batteries of enemy weapons. Still, he knew that thousands of civilians from all over the sphere were hiding in the ancient temples and structures of the old Ziqqurratu Dynasty and enemy forces annihilated anyone they encountered. Speed was vital.

He accelerated to three times the speed of sound and cruised onwards, watching the ground below. Since laser beams had no mass and were undetectable to his radar the battle display could not warn him of their approach as it would with missiles or enemy fighters.

Brilliant ruby-red laser beams stabbed upwards at him, forcing him to throw his jet around the sky to avoid them. The beams were instantaneous, lancing straight up and forming a series of bright red lines that he had to fly between. He danced his jet among the beams, rolling and weaving to avoid them. Metal-against-metal noises could be heard from his plane as it was pushed through the sky yet it held together and Tychon weaved a path through the barrage of red lasers for several minutes. When he broke through he flicked his eyes back and forth from the ground to the battle display, checking for more beams and for enemy fighters that his radar might pick up. There were none. He flew on in silence for several minutes, his masked face looking from side to side until the transceiver came on again.

"Tychon, hurry," came the female voice. "The enemy lords have broken through and are killing civilians. Shivoct is manifesting in the river outside of the temple to stop them."

It was not a good sign. When an Icetar – a beautiful female spirit – slid into water she walked out as a mass of ice. Manifesting in impure water left them insane, however, and the Flametar soldiers had poured oil in the river basins and reservoirs of Ziqqurratu. Even dirt and minerals in the water meant the Icetar would not be in control of herself. Shivoct's usual tactic was to wait until the Flametars were upon her before manifesting in the impure water.

Tychon received orders to fly to the given coordinates and, after Shivoct defeated the Flametars in the area, roll in and strafe the Icelord with his internal cannon. Otherwise, Shivoct would not be able to control herself and would be insane until wandering into a warmer climate and melting.

Every time an Icetar was shattered there was a chance she would be snuffed out forever. Upset, frightened, Tychon flew on.

15

Dust and hot wind streamed across her face as her chariot traversed an endless plain of cracked rock. Spindly and fruitless vegetation grew in crevices under a baking sun. Scorpions roamed the wastes, flanking her in packs and stinging each other when Zondela's chariot pulled away and escaped their wrath. The lizardmen pulled tirelessly, slowing down only when the venomous pack was well behind them.

They had left behind both the ocean and the forest and moved east across the jagged landscape. It was rugged and difficult – often Zondela dismounted from the chariot and helped pull it across vast piles of splintered rock. On her map, Zondela labeled the area as the Plain of Shards. Thick clouds hung low in the sky and provided no rain; a hot and dry wind rushed the clouds on their way.

Their location between the two great Dynasties – Tan-shi and Ziqqurratu – provided solitude and ample time for thought. Less than five hundred people lived on Infernia, descendants of prisoners captured by Flametars or of those who had wandered in through a vortex by accident. She had good memories of standing on the edge of her world, looking down at the clouds and Sinxin below them. Many evenings had been spent diving in the warm, placid rivers or daydreaming about the unknown world below. She imagined that one day she would learn how to breathe underwater and spend the rest of her life in peaceful slumber beneath the waves, schools of brightly colored fish protecting her. Military training had been fulfilling yet she realized the Flametars had taken something away from her.

The Icetars were uncaring, cold and unsympathetic, incapable of emotions, perhaps the opposite of the quick-to-anger Flametars. Many Glaican soldiers had been killed raiding both Infernia and the main sphere for water, yet the Flametars were no different in their eternal search for wood.

Sinxin was large enough for the human population of both strata to share though it was too cold for the Flametars and too hot for the Icetars, in addition to not having water as pure as Infernia's. Icetars melted outside of arctic conditions and hence needed a constant supply of freshwater. Both 'tars were insane if they manifested in water or flames that had impurities in them, especially oil.

She had raided Glacia a few times. It was a cold place – sheets of vertical ice broke away and shattered, harsh winds blinded the eye, blue flying reptiles hunted anything that moved. Still, there was beauty there, from the howl of the cold winds when she was safe in a warm cave to the eerie grace of the blue reptiles as they rummaged through the snow with their scaled snouts, their muscular bodies impressing even Zondela. She had seen complex castles of ice with towers linked by frozen bridges. Once she had stood over a frozen sea and looked down through the ice. Below the clear surface, giant squid skirmished with sharks, both sides circling each other in violence. The frothing pool of bubbles, blood, and severed tentacles attracted a swarm of gape-mouthed fish and the three sides skirmished in a frenzy of killing. During her long walks across the frozen lakes, she had seen vast stone castles deep underwater, built with towers and turrets and ramps. Something had built an extensive empire beneath the frozen seas of Glacia.

Zondela questioned her lizardmen and one of them turned out to be female. The implication was that these two could possibly establish a new race. Given an isolated part of the sea to themselves, in a few hundred years Sinxin could be host to underwater cities of lizardmen. She wondered what the relationship would be between a surface civilization and vast colonies of lizardmen living below the waves. By tipping the Chalice she had created two new beings and potentially an entirely new race.

The Chalice was inexhaustible. Many times she would tip it over and create a pool of water in a crevasse or a shallow spot. The pool teemed with sea life where only minutes before it had been a dry and empty sinkhole. The newly created sea-life fed her and the lizardmen while creating potential problems. The Overflowing Chalice was a powerful and dangerous relic and would have to be destroyed when she had completed her quest.

The lizardmen worked tenaciously and after pulling the chariot over broken ground for two weeks they reached the fourth oracle. The sandstone statue rested in a deep round basin with steep walls. Narrow steps chiseled into the walls in a lazy downward spiral. The basin was pock-mocked and marred by holes as if from erosion.

Zondela halted near the steps and disembarked from the chariot as the lizardmen untangled themselves from the harness. She gazed down in mild apprehension; at the bottom of the basin she would be vulnerable to attack. If archers were to line themselves at the top she would be easily slain; if swordsmen appeared at the top they could drop stones on her. It was not a defensible position. She descended on foot, the two lizardmen armed and close behind. The female – who had lost her trident in the battle with the furry beast – now carried the hammer. Zondela had trained her in how to safely use it, which meant never hitting the ground anywhere near Zondela.

At the bottom was the stone oracle carved in the shape of a beautiful woman, voluptuous and long-legged with the feminine build of a girl who had never known military training. Zondela approached and removed her brass glove. Even though it was a statue, she was still careful to put her hand on the sandstone shoulder and not anywhere else.

There was the usual sensation as her memories and knowledge were sucked out and absorbed into the oracle. The images faded and she caught her breath. "Am I being hunted?" asked Zondela.

"Yes," replied the oracle in an echoing voice.

"Where is the danger coming from?" Zondela asked.

"Behind you," replied the oracle. Zondela turned. A mass of giant winged insects poured out of the holes in the basin walls.

The first one was upon her. The large head had compound eyes, black antenna, and mandibles. Its three-segmented thorax bore a pair of glistening, transparent wings that beat steadily. Below its body, the six taloned legs moved as if it was trying to run through the air. A dark stinger the length of her sword extended from its abdomen. More of them poured out of the fissures in the rock walls and headed straight for her, the buzzing of their wings filling the air.

Her blade sang as she slashed the flying predators. Her hand speed was so fast that the edge of her sword whistled as it moved, insects falling from the air as she cut through them. She suspected there was a hive within the rock walls;

the winged beasts poured out faster than she could kill them.

An insect dove on her and forced its stinger through the brass armor on her forearm. Her armor was thinnest there, to reduce the weight on her arms during a sword fight, and the needle-like proboscis penetrated with a burning sensation. A twist of her wrist snapped the proboscis and she sent her sword through its body, cleaving it in two. More attackers dove from above.

Another stinger penetrated through the gap between her neck plate and helmet and she twisted her body away before it became a killing blow. Her life depended on the speed with which she could slay the flying attackers and her sword whipped through her old attack patterns faster than it ever had before, the brass blade a blur, her breathing heavy in her ears. She got her timing down, cutting insects from the sky and killing the next two before the previous one had struck the ground.

Ultimately the lizardman with the hammer saved their lives. She ran forward and struck the wall that had the insect holes in it. The concussion sent the lizardman flying backward – her head for a moment downwards and her feet in the air – and collapsed the stone, sealing off the tunnels and crushing hundreds of insects beneath the debris. The last two insects dove at Zondela and she spun on her heel, whipping her sword in an arc and slaying them with a single stroke. Sheathing her sword with a grin she helped the lizardman pick herself off the ground.

"Well fought," she said. "I'll have to teach you to play Salamanders."

Zondela had been injured. The two areas of her body that had been stung were increasingly painful. After questioning the oracle and discovering that there were no more insects ready to attack, Zondela removed her arm brace and examined the wound. The skin was swelling, pain radiating from the area of penetration. A thin black ooze drizzled from the wound. She washed it and cleansed it yet the flow of black ichor increased, the wound smelling slightly noxious.

In minutes Zondela was delirious, feverish, and jaundiced. Perspiration drenched her and her injuries swelled further. She dug her fingertips into the dirt floor in an effort to crawl back to the oracle, stopping only when her once magnificent strength failed her. Dimly she heard the lizardmen talking to the oracle, questioning it, looking for a cure.

The female lizard cradled Zondela's head, stroking her damp hair with scaly claws and speaking gently. Zondela turned her head to the side and saw the lizardman kneel beside a dead insect and tear open the mouth with his hands. Inside the gory flesh, near the back of its throat, he found a small sac of cloudy red liquid. He pinched it off with his claws and ran back to Zondela's side.

The lizardman spoke in a hushed voice. "The oracle says that these creatures have an antidote in their mouths to prevent them from being affected by their own poison during feeding." She was dimly aware of the sagacity of the oracles and the need to accept its advice, so she bit down on the fluid-filled sac and swallowed. Consciousness left her.

When she awoke her fever had gone and the pain was only a memory. The lizardmen had placed a jar of water and a pile of berries beside her. After rising to her feet and checking her sword and telescope, she again placed her hand on the shoulder of the female statue.

"Were those insects hunting me?" she asked.

"No, they were attracted by the people coming here to

question me. The series of carcasses the questioners provided allowed the insect brood to multiply."

"Why did they attack me?"

"The queen was preparing to start a new hive so she laid a brood of eggs," replied the oracle. "She required fresh meat to feed the rest of the hive. The young queens had just matured and they were battle-mad as their biology forces them to fight each other, the strongest one surviving to start the new hive."

"Perhaps the world would be a better place if men were in charge," muttered Zondela. "So what is hunting me?"

The sandstone statue smiled sadly, turning its well-curved body to face her. "Metal-clawed spinewolves that move like the desert wind, following the scent of your body."

"Who sent them?" she asked.

"The Ultimate Machine."

"What can you tell me of this machine?" asked Zondela.

"It is driven to seed empty worlds with life, as it has done here, bringing life to the once-barren rock by creating the ascendants. It hates all life and created Slun and the Flametars to destroy the sphere. There is nothing in its programming to stop it from doing so."

"Why does it hunt me?" Zondela asked

"You seek to stop its plans."

"How can I stop the Flametars?"

"When the invasion occurs the Icetars will watch from their perch on Glacia, debating whether to launch an invasion of their own. If the Icetars do not assault then the Infernian army will conquer half of the sphere and the future war will come to pass. The first of the Icetars, Lunil, councils patience and advises against descending to the sphere to confront the Infernian army. If Lunil is destroyed the Icetars will enter the war with their army and blunt the Infernian assault. Lunil sits on the Court of Glacia in the Frozen Palace."

"Can ascendants be killed?" asked Zondela

"Yes. That is why they do not usually lead from the front of armies."

"How do I kill Lunil?" she asked. "If I shatter her body her spirit will drift away, unharmed."

"There is never enough pure water on Glacia for every Icetar to manifest. It will be years before Lunil is able to secure more water from Infernia, and by then her position will have been taken by other Icetars."

"Anything special I should bring with me to Glacia?"

"Coins will be vital."

In her mind's eye her perspective flew over the broken landscape at impossible speeds, rushing downwards and slowing over the foundation of a crumbling stone house. The walls had tumbled to the ground and vines had claimed much of it. Her perspective burrowed underground just outside the house, showing a buried chest, and then entered the chest itself to show her the contents – coins of different metals.

"Where is the nearest vortex to Glacia?"

Her perspective flew over the ground, through a mountain range, and into a valley dense with green vegetation, stopping before a tall nut tree. The leaves on one side were dying and her enhanced sight showed her that this was due to the icy winds blowing in from a vortex near the top of the tree. She needed only to climb the trunk and leap through it.

She asked about the location of the next oracle and marked the spot on her map.

16

The chariot rolled over rocky terrain, pulled by the lizardmen who rarely tired. The stony ground gave way to rolling hills and vast expanses of green inclines and flower-covered slopes. The chariot wheels crushed the red and blue blossoms and released a wonderful aroma. They were in the middle of Sinxin, in between the two great Dynasties, a wasteland that held little opportunities to find food and no civilization. They had left the Tanshi Dynasty behind them and were weeks away from the steamy Ziqqur-ratu Dynasty, even with the higher speeds afforded by the smooth hills they were in.

Zondela asked the lizardmen about their earliest memories. They mentioned an impossible previous life, where they swam through the sea without arms or legs, chasing bits of food and basking in the mud when the sun fell. The life they described had more in common with small organisms or other aquatic animals. Their talk always led to food, of floating lazily in a vast sea, consuming unlimited amounts of meat from massive, decaying corpses that slowly sank beneath the waves. The lizardmen loved her explanation of how she had created them and had her retell the story of the overturned Chalice many times.

All three were hungry again and Zondela's thoughts turned to what she would find if the Chalice was upended again. More lizardmen? More mouths to feed? The Chalice was dangerous – there was a chance she would breed horrific creatures that she could not slay. She pictured her body laying on the ground, quite dead, while legions of beasts poured from the endless waters of the Chalice and overran the world.

Zondela scanned the horizon in all directions with her brass telescope and saw nothing in the way of vortexes. Sighing, she collapsed the 'scope and looked for a declivity or depression in the ground to fill with relic water. A suitable spot was located – a dry sinkhole – and Zondela removed the relic from her damp purse and placed it on its side next to the hole. Water poured out, filling the sinkhole, and she could retrieve her relic at any time. She wondered if losing the Chalice would flood the entire sphere.

Water poured out of the Chalice at a normal rate and the cup never emptied. The lizardmen watched with interest as the depression turned into a shallow pool. If the depression were filled to the top the water would be about as deep as Zondela was tall. A fish broke the surface and she remembered that the Bladed Sisters had told her that the Taxon had been a minor clan until they discovered the Chalice; Zondela suspected the Chalice had provided them with increased food.

The lizardmen caught the fish and she let them eat the first few. Occasionally strange and dangerous spine-fish spawned, which she killed and tossed away. The lizardmen reached in and brought up clams, blue lobster, murmuring fish, and an armored squid that put up quite a fight before they impaled it on a stick for the fire.

She had found an unlimited source of food and her

thoughts wandered to images of herself stocking large pits with water, harvesting the aquatic lifeforms, and feeding herself and her people. She daydreamed of being in charge of a village, of defending them with her sword and feeding them with her Chalice, and saw herself as a benevolent woman, a mother to the people of the village, guiding them and being loved by them.

The pool filled halfway up and her musings were broken by a serpent's head that rose out of the water. It was large, like an overgrown snake, situated on a long neck that rose above the surface of the pool. Two more heads broke the surface beside it. The beast had three snake heads that grew out of a muscular, squat body.

It tried to clamber out of the pool. The beast's forelimbs scrabbled at the muddy bank, unable to gain purchase, while one of the three heads snapped at Zondela, tearing a rent in her brass shoulder plate and twisting her body to the side from the force of the blow. Even as she cursed herself for dreaming when she should have been paying attention her foot struck the Chalice, sending it into the pool. If this strange beast killed her it might flood the world.

She drew and slashed as the second of the creature's heads struck at her. The saw-toothed edge of her sword bit deep, tearing through the scales, stopping against the vertebrae. She drew it back, dragging the jagged edge against the creature, feeling her sword dig deeper into the bone as she maintained pressure and contact throughout the draw, the severed head splashing into the water.

The other two heads screeched in rage, venting their anger and pain in piercing cries. Zondela stepped back, wishing she had a bow, without which she had to go in close to the two remaining serpent heads, both glaring at her with hatred.

She wondered if more of the multi-headed beasts would spawn since the Chalice was undoubtedly still spilling its unending contents at the bottom of the pool. In her mind she saw the landscape submerged in water, three-headed reptiles roaming the wet expanse, overwhelming and replacing men and women after a violent war.

She raised her blade, the hilt in both hands, level with her cheek. With the blade straight up she stepped forward, her eyes on the beast's heads. A toothy snout rushed her and she swung, decapitating it. While she was extended, vulnerable, the last head snapped at her. She took another step forward and slid into the water, still on her feet, her lower body submerged. She ducked and the serpentine head passed over her. She stepped to the side, not wanting to get within range of the muscled forelimbs.

The creature's remaining head lashed out at her again, hissing in rage, while the two bloody stumps on either side of it flinched. She stepped to the side and the striking head missed her, exposing its neck. Her reflexes were quick and with a downward swipe she sliced through bone and dropped the creature's head into the pool to float there, red ichor spilling out of the wound.

She sheathed her sword without conscious thought and dove underwater, hoping that no further beasts waited to sink their fangs into her. She swam through a school of pink and red fish to reach the Chalice. Once she had the relic in her hand she arched her back and kicked hard. Her head broke into the air and she drew a deep breath, clambering out of the water before any aqueous lifeforms could bite. She felt, with pride, that her body would be too gristly and muscled for their tastes.

The lizardmen wanted to hunt fish from the pool. Zondela restrained them on the grounds that it was far too dangerous. Despite her hunger they would wait for other, safer opportunities to use the relic to create food.

With the Chalice tucked upright in her belt she re-mounted her chariot and set off, the lizardmen pulling with stoic tenacity. A glance back showed the surface of the pool disturbed by a savage battle between red-shelled crustaceans and large, bone-clad fish. She shook her head, hoping the water would leak away into the ground and choke them.

The chariot thundered along for several hours and Zondela held onto the side of the vehicle with one hand while she watched the terrain undulate. The lizardmen never tired and Zondela did something she had always wanted to do while stationed on the stratum high above: see the sphere.

Scrub and brush dotted the hills while the vegetation grew more abundant, changing from the uniform grasslands of the previous steppes to a more ragged, chaotic sprawl of tangled growth. The vegetation became coarser, thicker, concealing soft-furred animals that bolted from cover when the chariot passed near them.

The Ziqqurratu Dynasty lay to the East; while it was still far away, she was passing out of the dry, desert-like west to the hotter, moister east where the jungle would eventually claim the land, forcing the people of Ziqqurratu to yield to it.

Small flutterbys drifted by on gossamer wings, bright blue with purple spots. Waves of them fluttered by, the flock moving from tree to tree, gathering nectar and chasing each other in the last sunlight of the day, their iridescent wings glittering.

She removed her helmet and held it in the crook of one arm. A tilt of the Chalice caused the ever-present water to fill her helmet. Soon a fish leaped out, landing on the ground and flopping madly, its gills heaving as it vainly tried to suck in air. There were no further fish in the helmet and she dashed the water out. After several tries, she raised more aquatic creatures from her brass helm. She was unsure whether the life originated in the Chalice or if it simply evolved organisms that were already there. The Flametars had once told her that tiny, unseen bacteria existed in all water except the ultra-pure liquids of Infernia, and she wondered if bacteria were being forcibly evolved by the powers of the Chalice.

After filling up her helmet ten times she had at her feet six different types of aquatic animals – pincer-clad crustaceans, blue lobsters with reptilian heads, thick oily fish, and strange sponge-like animals covered in quills. The lizardmen had already broken one of the sponges open and eaten the soft interior. Zondela contented herself with consuming the regular fish, unwilling to experiment with the more exotic lifeforms.

Streams of the blue-winged insects sailed past from the east. Thousands of insects fluttered by, all coming from the same direction. Tomorrow she would see if she could locate the source.

Night descended and the three travelers slumbered, Zondela occasionally shifting in her sleep while the reptiles remained motionless.

Early the next morning, after a breakfast of silver-scaled fish culled from her helmet, they set off to the northeast. The reptiles seemed oblivious to the winged insects while Zondela was enchanted by them.

Zondela called a halt when they sighted squat buildings of brick and clay, and the three of them set out on foot. Armed men came out to meet her, standing casually while waiting for her to arrive. Her eye scanned them and saw well crafted swords, pikes, and two crossbows, none of which were pointed at her. The men watched her with languid, relaxed manners.

An exquisite, striking woman approached. Just barely an adult, she was gifted with long hair, pleasing features, and large blue gossamer wings with purple spots that sprouted from her back. The wings were the same as those of the insects that fluttered from flower to flower around the encampment. As she walked forward her delicate wings flexed, a confident smile on her lips. Zondela was envious of her good looks and pretty wings, an emotion she was not used to feeling.

With a smile still on her lips, the young woman sang. It was a soothing, lilting, sweet song whose words were not in the prosaic tongue. The melody invoked a strange reaction in her; on Infernia there had been no time to construct musical instruments as their leisure activities had consisted of preparing for war. Music was unknown to Zondela and the Infernians had never sung. Here was a young woman with a voice sonorous and clear, the dulcet tones attracting more of the winged insects. The insects appeared out of thin air all around her, winking into existence. The young woman stopped singing and the graceful, winged insects were so thickly clustered around her that she scattered them with a wave.

Zondela said nothing, assuming there was a purpose to the display. Behind the flutterby girl stood scores of men, all young, all armed. Zondela felt she might be able to hold them off, kill enough of them to suck the courage out of the rest. She saw some archers among them and frowned – a single arrow could be the end of her if they had any Tanshi armor-piercing tips. If she was going to die, she wanted it to be in a decent battle, not picked off by an archer firing from the rear of the enemy ranks.

The winged woman folded her arms and pouted. "I am Crontoria, and I assure you, as long as I am not threatened, my soldiers are no danger to you." She paused. "Can I see your face?" she asked sweetly.

Zondela put her hands on either side of her brass helmet and hesitated, thinking she knew what it felt like to disrobe in front of a man in exchange for coin. Without enthusiasm she pulled her helmet off and held it against her waist, worrying about an arrow from a nervous archer.

Crontoria seemed pleased. "A woman, dressed in battle armor. Those eyes seem so ancient, like they have seen too much. I can help ease your burdens. I can do many things. Creating flutterbys is just a whimsy, a pleasure. I will fill the forests with them when the sphere is mine."

Zondela's heart skipped a beat. That last statement had not sounded good at all.

"What is your name?" asked Crontoria.

"Zondela."

"I sense greatness in you, the ability to influence events. Like a large rock thrown into a pool, the ripples emanating from your actions will be larger than most."

"And how can you tell that, madam?"

"I am an ascendant," answered Crontoria. "Come, sit with us and eat. Your face is dirty and your armor full of rents. That alone speaks of some great battles or narrow escapes."

"A little of both," laughed Zondela, liking the young woman who claimed to be an ascendant. If she was, she would be a creator, on a par with Tanshi, Isayus, or even Slun, who had created the Flametars by bleeding droplets of fire during his old battle to conquer Infernia.

The lizardmen milled about the camp and Zondela was brought to the bathing area where several men and a few women were cleaning themselves. The men wore swords with intricate swept hilts, the kind produced by master craftsmen, and the women were disassembling crossbows and cleaning the moving parts of sand and grit. There did not appear to be a single unarmed person in the camp. Zondela glanced discreetly around and figured that the buildings held perhaps a hundred soldiers. She shrugged, satisfied that since she was not surrounded by insects, at least here she would not be eaten after being killed.

Zondela stepped into the water and removed her armor, piece by piece, submerging each item before placing it on the bank beside her. Her body ached from the old injuries.

An auburn-haired woman beside her spoke up. "How were you injured?"

Zondela grunted involuntarily. "The interior of the sphere is riddled with passages, many of which house dangerous species. I was engaged in a running battle with them."

The auburn-haired woman waved the comment away. "It is of no regard. Crontoria will remove those species one day."

Crontoria herself sat and watched the bathers, her eye roving over each of them in a professional manner as if appraising cattle. "I will. Rulership of this sphere is just a matter of time. My army swells daily as our legend grows. Is that why you have come, Zondela, to serve me?"

Zondela, still sore from her injuries, some of which still bled, dipped a rag in the water. "I followed the flight path of the flutterbys, seeking the source."

"My army will rule the sphere one day, cleansing it of disease and disfigurement. From where do you originate?"

"Infernia, madam."

"That great sheet of brass that rides above the firmament. So there are people up there."

"Yes, madam, and great beasts of flame that desire to be worshiped."

"Flametars?" asked Crontoria.

"Yes. You have you heard of them?"

"I make it my business to learn and as my army swells, I can speak to those who have encountered diverse and exotic beasts in their travels. The woman who bathes beside you once fought as a mercenary in the jungles of the Ziqqurratu Dynasty against the witches."

Zondela turned, hoping to get information that might be useful later on. "What are the witches like?"

"Vile, poisonous creatures," said the brown-haired woman, "straining to hold onto their lives and sanity in the face of the awful wisdom they have learned. The night belongs to them and their terrible practices. The Ziqqurratu Dynasty battles them, rooting them out of their hiding places during the day and spearing them. It is a difficult and lengthy war."

"I will pacify them," said Crontoria in a mild voice. "When this land is mine."

"The Tanshi Dynasty is strong," said Zondela. "Their archers are like nothing I have seen before."

Crontoria shrugged. "It is of no matter. Tonight, when the sun goes down and your wounds disappear and you taste of your own youth, you will see my power. I am an ascendant."

Zondela nodded, unwilling to commit herself.

"I see you do not believe me," said Crontoria. "You are in the presence of a great power, and you will one day become one yourself."

Zondela noticed that the other people around her were very attentive.

"I sense that you will do magnificent things," said Crontoria, her blue gossamer wings gently flexing. "And you will do even greater things serving me. I will give you command of three soldiers, any that you pick, and you will have the chance to prove yourself to me."

"I had command of five as a Penturian," Zondela responded.

"Five then," replied Crontoria.

"What about my chariot?"

"It is yours. It waits, along with the two scaled ones, inside my camp. I have ordered them fed and watered."

"What exactly are your plans, madam?" asked Zondela.

"I plan to conquer the sphere. When I do, my followers will be lords, and all others will be dead. Then the new lords can repopulate the world at their leisure, creating in their own image if they wish." Her delicate blue wings, identical to those of the smaller flutterbys she had created with her singing, flexed more quickly.

"Yes madam," Zondela said in a quiet tone. "Although the Tanshi resisted the Wusong invasion and they might oppose you as well."

"And decline eternal youth? I think not. They will join me, slowly, as my army stalks their desert sands."

Zondela wondering what she was seeing. Neither the oracle nor Balakakos had mentioned Crontoria as a means of saving the world, and Crontoria's own words indicated the world needed saving from her.

"Tonight, Zondela, after you see my power, I will ask you to serve me. You will be a Penturian in my army now."

"It is pleasing to be offered my old post again, madam, yet I must think on it first."

"You wander through the desolation between two Dynasties, both of which will fall to me eventually, and I offer you a position of importance."

"I had dreams," said Zondela, "of finding Fushang one day and settling there."

Crontoria visibly relaxed. "Fushang, the legendary city, does not exist. It is a fable to give hope to the impoverished, a wondrous construction whose stones exist only in your mind."

Zondela bowed her head. "As you say, madam."

Crontoria glanced up. "It will be night soon when my powers are strongest. Then you shall see the rewards of serving an ascendant."

Zondela nodded, rinsed her wounds, and polished her armor while around her others oiled bowstrings or sharpened sword blades. Crontoria issued orders to her men, mostly concerning guard rotations, training regimens, and the ever present question of food supplies.

The sun sank into the ocean to the east, extinguishing itself for the night. The stars made their appearance, glittering with their customary vainglory. Zondela donned her armor, each piece clicking into place as the brass links mated and the overlapping plates slid together. She put her helmet on with slow and deliberate movements and noticed Crontoria watching her. Strategies and tactics flowed through Zondela's mind as she thought about how to deal with the ultimatum she sensed approaching

Armed men and women approached, gravitating toward Crontoria and bringing a cold sweat to Zondela's forehead. They gathered close, some with reverent expressions upon their faces, others with a dreamy, beatific look that made Zondela's skin crawl. It appeared the time of reckoning was at hand.

Crontoria stood among her soldiers and sang in a clear, lilting voice. There was enough moonlight that Zondela could see those around her, and the attention of everyone was fixed on the ascendant in their center. Zondela glanced behind her, expecting to see guards keeping an eye on her; there were none.

Crontoria's song was beautiful, melancholy, and exquisite. Zondela felt a strange flush, both hot and cool, and the pain of her injuries subsided. As the melody continued, and the sweet female voice pushed it an octave higher, Zondela trembled. Her left knee no longer hurt and her swollen, torn shoulder no longer ached. Something soft brushed against her face – flutterbys were being created, appearing around Crontoria and fluttering outward. Zondela pulled off her left metal glove and looked at the wound she had received from an insect when last underground. It was fully healed, not even a scar noticeable under her fingertips.

Zondela replaced the glove and waited. The song lasted over an hour, Crontoria singing with her eyes closed while the soldiers around the ascendant sat patiently, enraptured, letting the sweet singing envelop and heal them.
At last, the music was over. Crontoria opened her eyes and looked at Zondela. "Well? Will you serve me."

"Alas, beautiful Crontoria, I cannot. My destiny takes me elsewhere."

Crontoria's smile widened slightly. "Kill her," she said.

The armed men around Crontoria were fast, their weapons rasping out of scabbards and belts. Even the female soldiers drew blades and moved forward. Zondela, however, was faster. Her right hand swept to the hilt of her brass sword and she drew the blade in a quick motion, raising the blade above her head and throwing it. Her brass sword hurtled through the air, spinning, to impale Crontoria through the chest. The woman's gauzy wings beat rapidly as she fell backward, the sword sticking out of her chest. Around her the soldiers collapsed, most of them drying and crumbling to dust in seconds. A few became old crones, pulling themselves forward on wrinkled, parched hands. Most died, their desiccated bodies already more dust than flesh. Zondela stepped forward, recovered her blade, and returned to her chariot.

17

Tychon of Kallos was a thousand feet above ground and pondered the futility of his mission. He was on a fighter combat air patrol mission – fighter CAP. When he gazed upon the wrecked city below he thought a better name would be rubble CAP. New Colonia extended all the way to the horizon – a near endless city of debris and wreckage. The city's primary residents now were corpses, left there by enemy bombers, Minor Machines, silver tanks, and Flametars drunk on fuel-fed fires. Reports indicated they were just as dangerous to their own soldiers as they were to everyone else, now that the world was nearly in their grasp and they no longer needed an army.

Tactically it was nothing like what Tychon had expected. Friendly forces had been thrown out of their bases and Flametar led armies had overrun the surrounding lands. The neutral nations had been conquered and their cities burst asunder like insect hives, their citizens scattered and fleeing before the onslaught. The sky, however, was still contested, the last battleground where enemy forces did not yet rule.

The Dark Bishop, the flying aircraft carrier that Tychon served on, flew far above the clouds, pock-marked and battle damaged. The twenty-three fighters that still flew from her deck were a fraction of the original complement and barely enough to keep the mother ship alive. Furious air battles occurred, with the Dark Bishop often diving from high altitude while her fighters dueled with enemy jets around her. Tychon had fought in such a battle that morning; he had spiraled down beside the diving mother ship, firing missiles at enemy jets that moved in, circling his carrier the entire time while protecting it. The aerial flat-top had leveled off just above the trees and flown at the speed of sound, Tychon getting to fly between mountain peaks and into valleys in a way that would never have been allowed during peacetime. He had stayed with the Bishop the entire way, driving off enemy fighters with his laser when his missiles were expended.

He had a natural instinct for air combat and did not analyze his maneuvers anymore. It was more like fighting with one's hands; he moved by reflex, even when spiraling and looping at supersonic speeds. He intuitively understood the physics involved; he knew nothing of equations yet could haul his aircraft up and then swirl down onto a target, always putting his plane where he wanted it in the sky. It was a skill that served him well in the twirling, chaotic dog fights that enveloped the Dark Bishop as the enemy forces tried to destroy it. There was no safe place on the ground for the mother ship to land. The last three flying carriers battled for their lives, the only Republic forces still fighting. They roamed the sky, flying on the winds that encircled the upper reaches of the atmosphere, their fighters leaping off their decks to struggle against the fleets of enemy jets that hunted them.

During peacetime, it had been theorized that the principle role of jets would be striking ground targets and preventing enemy jets from doing to same. Planes had been seen as subordinate to ground units, with the whole concept of air superiority and controlling airspace being seen as illogical since air by itself had no military value. War turned out to be different from what they had envisioned and now that the army had been decimated and the cities reduced to shattered steel skeletons, the jets fought to keep their mother ships alive while they coursed through the upper atmospheres at high speeds, receiving and sending forth their planes even during battle.

Keeping the flying aircraft carriers alive had little value if they could never land, however. They would soon require fuel rods, ball bearings, jet fuel, and replacements for the missiles that their jets used in battle. Even basic items like engine parts were threatening to ground the flying carriers and there were no safe places to land. While Tychon was on rubble CAP, other pilots had been ordered to engage and defeat enemy ground units to clear a safe landing spot for the flying carriers. Tychon doubted that they would be able to create a safe landing zone for the Dark Bishop because fresh enemy units were pouring into the war.

Tychon's orders were to protect the cities from enemy attack. There was, however, nothing left of the city below him. The factories were destroyed, the civilian airports bombed into oblivion and the city itself little more than dust and debris. It was the residue of cities that had been bombed into submission even after they had surrendered.

A push forward on the throttle accelerated his jet and he cut a swath through the smoke and haze of the ruined metropolis. He knew the enemy soldiers had standing orders to cut open any pipes and ignite the fuel that leaked out and this left fires burning everywhere, allowing the enemy masters to materialize at any time. It was rumored that they now disdained the fire from clean wood and instead preferred the soiled flames from oil or jet fuel, reveling in the drunkenness that resulted from such impurity. From his vantage point in the cockpit, Tychon knew that the culmination of their plans was to have the entire sphere on fire, all the world a great mass of dirty flames for the Flametar masters to play in. Tychon saw each city in the path of enemy conquest wrecked and set alight, each forest burnt. The enemy soldiers on the ground, without their bird's eye view of the war, might not know that they were at war with themselves, wrecking their own future with their policy of total destruction.

He swung his masked head from left to right as he flew, flicking switches to activate sensors that would alert him to communications below. The radar alerted him to a different threat, a Minor Machine prowling the ruins of New Colonia, perhaps hunting down civilians who huddled in the debris, or else on a mission to rupture a fuel tank that had so far remained unscathed. He dipped his jet lower, aligning his gun sight on it, and opened up with a long stream of laser fire. A second later he was past it, pulling back on the stick to gain altitude while craning his head backward to see if he had destroyed the target.

Green laser fire stabbed through the air beside his canopy, missing him by mere feet. Very little enemy weaponry was unguided and the beams of concentrated light burning holes through the sky were no exception – the beams tracked his jet. Quick movements on the control column lifted his plane higher and sent it into a spiral. The lasers followed, cutting swaths through the sky as they hunted him. He dropped a decoy, a small emitter that would resemble his jet on enemy radar scopes. The lasers abandoned their pursuit of his plane and annihilated the decoy, and before they re-acquired him he dove steeply, sending his plane down and leveling off above the wrecked city. While it put him in range of small caliber guns marauding through the rubble, the enemy radar would be unable to spot him unless he was directly above its position.

He roamed on, sending out questioning emissions and receiving no response. There was little in the way of civilization left, no military units to respond to his hails, no control towers to track him, no automated supply bases to answer his electronic queries. He was conducting a fighter sweep over a vast cemetery.

An electronic emission touched his aircraft – his radar waves had alerted a machine of some sort and a glance at his control panel showed the entity probing, seeking information about him. Too late he flicked the switch to shut off his own jet's emissions – missiles rose on the horizon, lifting up on raging plumes of fire and smoke.

He pushed the throttle forward into afterburner, pouring fuel directly into the engine fires to create a magnificent plume of exhaust and greatly increased thrust. The acceleration shoved him back in his seat and made him grin. In this day when all was lost, when the comforts and security of civilization had been wiped out and set on fire, the pleasure of the high-g acceleration was one of the few he had left. Like all pilots, it was a strange love affair with the airplane, a joy to accelerate so fast that the body was compressed into the welcoming envelopment of the seat.

He glanced left and right to check for threats. There were none, no jets attempting to flank him. He was moving so fast now, several times the speed of sound, that nothing could approach him from behind. Grimly he held his course, heading straight for the brace of missiles that had leveled off at his altitude and were heading straight for him. His first thought was to wait for the last second and haul back on the control stick, rocketing his Stratofighter into the sky and leaping above the danger. The enemy missiles acted to stop that defensive technique before he executed it. They spread out into a grid pattern, far enough apart that he could not fly above or around them yet close enough that he could not fly between them. He smiled again; this was his last pleasure, the awakening of some primitive instinct that reveled in the joy of being hunted, the flush of chemicals in his body as he fought for his life with a cool hand on the control column and his eyes on the enemy weapons.

He turned to the left, sending shuddering vibrations through his airplane as the metal flexed under the force of the high speed turn, and the missiles turned to intercept, creating a slight opening to the right. Another push on the control column to the right sent his plane skittering toward the opening, the jet straining and the flight path shaky because of the incredible stresses. He whipped through the opening, missiles bursting into orange fireballs all around him, framing his airplane for a second in fire and shrapnel.

An enemy naval ship tracked him with three different wavelengths of radar, and a glance at his tactical computer showed it to be the origin of the missile's flight paths. He was moving fast, perfect for a strafing attack on a ship when he saw on the computer screen just how big it was. It was gigantic, probably the same ocean going vessel that had shelled cities into oblivion over the last five weeks. He had seen photographs of it earlier during briefings in between missions, and it was ten times the size of any previous vessel that had ever sailed the Restless Ocean. Every inch of its topside was giant guns, lasers, radar dishes, missile launchers, and more guns. The weapons, whose barrels were wide enough for a man to stand in, had sunk fleeing vessels, bombarded urban centers, and ignited energy plants along the entire coast of the continent. The massive steel beast, almost prehistoric in its gigantism and ferocity, had sailed unimpeded along the shoreline, wreaking havoc and destruction with its weapons, protected above by enemy jets. The recent skirmishes, however, had depleted the jets of both sides and the ship for the first time did not appear to be protected by aircraft.

The naval vessel appeared on another glass display panel in his cockpit and he pushed on the control column, realigning his jet until the image was in the center, under the crosshairs. He magnified the image with a touch of a button, each time correcting his flight path to keep the ship in the center of the screen. When he squeezed the trigger button, the lasers mounted under the nose of his jet released beams of killing light. The first few pulses struck the water, kicking up clouds of super-heated steam to mark the impact points, He corrected his flight path and brought the beams onto the ship. The hull ruptured, steel panels twisting and flipping away from the force of the explosions beneath them as his laser beams ignited fuel lines inside the vessel. More missiles rose from the ship amid great clouds of smoke and flying particles. He grinned, knowing he was moving too fast for them to track him.

He saw the enemy ship, with the brace of missiles still rising vertically, and he kept his fire on the same spot to drive the laser strikes deeper into the vessel now that the armor plating it that area was gone. A fraction of a second later he raised his nose and hurtled past, a great plume of water following behind him and washing over the enemy ship from the air pressure created by his supersonic jet.

Taking advantage of his incredible speed, he rolled his airplane on its wing and turned hard, the mainland coming back in front of him. His radar showed secondary explosions rippling along the length of the monolithic ship.

He throttled back to conserve fuel and let his airplane decelerate, scanning the ground with his sensors for signs of life. He found nothing and turned to fly east toward the far coastline. When he arrived, he found the jungled peninsula one long, continuous sheet of flame. Somehow the enemy had found a way to ignite wet jungle. He flew on, decelerating and dropping the nose of his jet until he reached the edge of land. A push on the thrust reversers with his feet caused the jet's airspeed to drop to nothing, allowing the fighter to sink straight down in a flat drop. Panels beneath the aircraft hissed open and the lift jets flared to life, slowing his descent and enabling him to land at the water's edge. Once the jet was down and the canopy was rising on hydraulic arms, he activated a stealth screen so that his plane would be undetectable on the ground.

Tychon clambered out of the jet and climbed down the steel ladder that extended from the side of the plane. He walked to the water's edge and sank down to one knee, splashing the cool liquid on his face. A few droplets landed on his tongue and tasted odd, prompting him to spit them out. Scowling, he drew his hand scanner and analyzed the ocean water. It had been poisoned. The ocean, from which all life on Sinxin depended, had been poisoned by the enemy. Civilization was doomed.

18

For a week their chariot moved through fallen rock, rubble, gnarled tree roots, and tangled vines. The information from the oracle was still fresh in her mind and locating the abandoned house was easy. A few minutes of digging uncovered a rotting wood chest that spilled silver coins. Inside were small red gems and coins of brass, copper, and green bronze. The coins and gems found their way into her pack.

They rolled into the lush mountain valley the next day – a sheltered area rich with ferns, trees, grass, and foliage with a small lake in the center. She scanned the area with her telescope and found the vortex that the oracle had shown her. It was above the ground and next to a large tree near the center. They descended into the valley and pushed into the soft ferns and tall patches of lush, wet grass.

It was the scene of old battles. They walked through the remains of broken chariots and the bones of the men who had fought and died. Broken spears and rusted swords littered the floor. She wondered if they had been fighting over the oracle or the valley itself. It was fertile and beautiful, yet if anyone had survived the battle they had not remained in the valley. It was as peaceful and quiet as a graveyard.

The lizardmen hunted wild game and she prepared them over a fire – every Infernian had to know how to start fire using only dry sticks and rocks. The meat was a welcome change from her nearly ceaseless diet of aquatic life culled from the Chalice.

She ate a light meal and reached the tree near the vortex. Around it were vast swaths of flowers that waved in the gentle breeze that flowed through the valley. Insects flitted between the blossoms, drinking nectar and buzzing happily to each other. The flowers parted around her as she walked, releasing a heady, redolent scent that was pleasing and intoxicating. It was one of the most peaceful places she had ever seen in her life, despite the corpses and derelict weapons beneath her feet. In many areas, the rusty armor and bones were covered by the luxuriant foliage and flower-clad vines.

A glance up showed half the tree's leaves brown and sickly from the cold air rushing in through the invisible vortex and her telescope confirmed its location. She would have to climb to reach it.

The lizardmen found themselves solid bronze spears from the old battle sites and followed her up the tree. She had explained to them the need to follow her passage exactly. Using her scope she could see that the vortex was at the same level as the branch she was on, a little farther from the tree. It would be an easy step. Already she could feel icy Glacian wind greedily stealing her body warmth.

She stood on the branch in front of the vortex. Steeling herself for the shock to come, she crouched, breathed in, and leaped. She was back on Glacia. Cold air cut through her armor. Snow flew through her helmet slit and stung her eyes. She cursed Lunil, a timid Icetar who would council her brethren against landing and facing the Infernians in battle. Already Zondela's hands were cold. Lunil may have been an ascendant but apparently, the only thing she could create was more Icetars.

The vortex had extruded her just above a snowbank. She sank to her knees, moved aside to make room for her companions, and drew her sword. Wind-driven ice pellets bounced off her armor; snow-driven wind and ice storms reduced visibility. She could only make out a large mountain of gray rock to her left, and the two lizardmen who materialized beside her. Shivering, they glanced in all directions, their mouths agape and their red tongues flicking out.

"Welcome to Glacia. Let's get moving."

She headed toward the mountain hoping to find a cave. The cold was painful – while her armor broke the wind, it rapidly bled heat and chilled her body. She glanced back through the telescope and saw the bright green of the vortex behind them, low enough to the ground that they could easily return through it if they found no shelter.

They forced themselves through the storm. Around them the wind howled its rage as it dragged snow drifts across the landscape, stinging their eyes and biting their skin. Endless sheets of blinding white blew across them. Zondela felt a disturbing emotion as she faced the cold, the isolation, and the unending whiteness. A melancholy filled her, a sadness born of the frozen wastes.

It was a lonely land. In the following days, she met humans who lived in half-crumbled towers, people so eager for company they hugged her and didn't want to let go once she took off her armor and shared a meal with them. Most of the humans on Glacia served the Icetars, showing up to work on their architectural projects, returning home for rest when allowed or injured too badly to continue. The Icetars were uncaring, cold, unconcerned with much beyond their statues, castles, and temples. A branch of humanity refused

to serve the Icetars, hiding out, searching for food and fleeing when Icetar patrols came by. The humans who served
the Icetars did not like killing the rebels and turned a blind
eye to them when possible.

Blue skinned flying reptiles hunted humans, picking
them off tower tops and castle walls when the storms were
at their worst, although when downed, the reptiles provided
enormous food supplies for the lucky victors.

Zondela moved on, sleeping in caves with her lizardmen, all three of them bundled in heavy cloaks and furs. A
woman living in an abandoned castle took them in – years
ago an Icetar lord felt the castle because it did not have
enough towers and abandoned it, despite the many human
lives lost in its construction. The woman shared her food,
talking incessantly, begging Zondela to live with her, crying quietly when her offer was refused. From her, Zondela
learned of the Votar knights.

Armored in silvery black metal, covered from head to
toe, the knights had gained magical powers from the armor
and swords they had excavated while on a raid to the main
sphere below. Powerful enough now to defy the Icetars,
they roamed Glacia, declaring themselves to be nobility and
the true power on the stratum. Numbering only nine, the
knights had slaughtered blue reptiles, two Icetars, scores of
humans, and a few rebels.

The mages were worse – women who walked barefoot
in the snow, clad only in satiny gowns, beautiful youths who
killed indiscriminately, fighting off both the Votar knights
and the Icetars. The mages – all female – were violent and
without remorse, unconcerned with the cold because of
their magic, uncaring of other people's suffering because of
their powers.

Zondela returned to the frigid wastes in search of Lunil.

During the night, when the wind howled and ice shards flew in flocks, clanging against her armor and shattering against rocks, they saw a young woman. Slim, smiling, clad in a shimmering red fabric that concealed nothing, and barefoot, she stood in a clearing and faced a massive beast of white fur, the same species that Zondela had killed earlier on Sinxin. From the shadows emerged a pack of wolves, clinging against her legs, rubbing their muzzles against her ankles, keeping their eyes on the white beast that approached.

The wolves attacked the white beast, only to be flung backward by its clawed hands. The young woman screamed – her beautiful face a mask of bone and horror for a second – and the white furred beast twisted backward, its spine broken. Her face again serene and pretty, the young woman slit its throat and drank its blood, her surviving wolves lapping it up beside her at the same time.

Zondela led the lizardmen away from the awful carnage and headed for a snow-covered forest. Scattered among the massive conifers were tiny saplings pushing through the snow. Sled-tracks led her through thick groves of trees to a rough looking stone house. A smoking chimney told of warmth to be had inside. She knocked, fully expecting to be forced to slay the inhabitants and warm herself at their fire. While she waited for a response, her hands cold and hurting under her metal gloves, she noticed large animal bones scattered around the house.

A beast opened the door – curved snout, green skin, bipedal and more amphibian than man. It drew its sword and struck. She turned aside, the blade scraping along her stomach armor, and her sword was in her hand before it could strike a second time. They traded blows until she knocked its sword from its hand, casually motioning it to pick it up and resume the fight. It did and the battle ended the same way. Again she waited, jerking her chin in the direction of its blade. Again it retrieved it and struck, spinning and whipping its blade about, to find its blade knocked from its grasp. By the time it grabbed its sword from the floor Zondela had already sheathed hers. It too put its sword away.

It spoke the prosaic tongue. It had lived in a warm jungle until one day while walking, it had appeared in Glacia. Refusing to die, it had carved out a bitter life for itself, trailing packs of wolves, eating of their kills after they moved on. Having been a trader in the jungle, it eventually resumed that occupation and had built the rough stone house for itself.

It wanted to trade. She still had some valuables on her and she emptied her pack of everything except the Chalice of Overflowing. It glanced at her silver coins, the severed horn from the white-furred beast, and her dagger, then raised its eyes back to her.

The amphibian beast's voice was raspy and inhuman. "Their egos are only exceeded by their disdain for the opinions of others. The Frozen Lords would not give me food when I trailed the wolves for two years. The Icetars are a cold and unsympathetic race, using us as pieces in their great war with Infernia. We are tools to them, by virtue of their magnificent power and indestructibility. Immortals are destined to rule over mortals, I suppose. Their rule is as frosty as their hearts, aloof masters presiding over an empire built by those of flesh and blood. The war has gone on for generations and will continue long after our bones lay on the ground, unburied by our uncaring masters. I have refused blind servitude to the bleak and passionless Lords and now seek the comfort of coin and grape. I have books written by philosophers who were cultured on the main sphere. My friends are writers and thinkers, long dead yet still able to give comfort through their works. Perhaps that is why the Icetars frown upon the written word, instead asking us to dedicate our lives in their service."

She mulled this over and handed him a few silver coins. "I seek Lunil."

It did not even ask why. "Lunil is on the Council of Icelords on the other side of the mountain range. You will not be able to see him. The war rages. Beasts that evolved beneath the ice resent those that walk the surface and skirmish with us constantly. It is anarchy out there, the fighting centering on the Frozen Citadel, as always. Out there you will be killed and your armor given to a Glacian soldier. The Council of Icetars will not welcome you. Stay here and become a privateer. With your wide shoulders and brass weapons, we will hunt the Ursus beast and become wealthy. True freedom comes of serving no master."

"I will be free when I find Fushang."

The amphibian opened a small chest and unrolled a parchment, showing her a map. "Glacia," it said as he rolled it back up before she could memorize any of its details. "Give me the Ursus horn and it is yours."

Wealth meant nothing to her and the transaction was completed. They drank more wine while she poured over the parchment, committing every detail to memory, finding locations that she felt she had visited years earlier when raiding Glacia for wood.

They shook hands and parted as friends, Zondela and her two companions covered in thick furs and hoods that hid all except their eyes. They forced themselves through the blizzard and reached the mountain range during the night. It was gray and monolithic, an imposing stone barrier. In several areas steps had been carved into the mountains, allowing passage through the barrier. She led the way up the nearest staircase. At the summit they stared at the land on the other side, oblivious to all else.

Hundreds of transparent towers dotted the landscape, each one connected by a catwalk or bridge. Everything was built of ice; each minaret and spire glistened in the starlight, clear and perfect. It was a city built mostly of towers. They must have found some means of supporting their architecture as the towers were connected with graceful, curved bridges of ice that were long and slender. Every tower was connected to those around it. Even the distant towers had several slim ones in between them and the city to connect them with arches and spans, always near the top.

The ground was not flat; there were rough, jagged areas of cracked ice and frozen rivers. Many of the towers had been built overlooking the rivers. Every lake had a tower next to it, while in the distance a larger main sea was ringed with them. Winged blue reptiles drifted overhead, sharp beaked and oblivious to the cold. Some of the towers had fires burning inside of them which lit them up like lamps. Because Glacia was so high up above the sphere the entire ice city was framed by stars.

She had come here to slay Lunil and she could not do so gaping at the sprawling ice city below. She took the steps that led down the mountain toward the frozen metropolis. Zondela and the lizardmen made it down the steps and traversed one of the smaller frozen lakes. Four ice towers ringed the lake and she examined their peaks – flat, crenelated tops, so that archers could stand between the blocks and fire arrows downwards.

She was in the middle of the frozen lake when movement from below caught her eye. Far beneath the crystal-clear surface of the ice was a massive stone castle surrounded by swimming beasts that were more tentacle than body. One of the creatures swam upwards and examined them with only a layer of ice separating the two parties. The creature was longer than Zondela was tall, with a tubular body and six long, flexible limbs. Each tentacle had a row of suction cups on them and one of the limbs carried a rock. Large, fish-like eyes regarded her and the creature moved under the ice to keep pace with her as she walked.

Without warning, it struck upwards against the ice with its rock. Jagged cracks ran through the surface and one of the tentacles burst through, grabbing one of the lizard-men. Zondela struck with her sword, her lips clenched, and severed the thick tentacle. Dark blue blood spurted across her armor and they ran toward land. Arrows streaked down from above; archers lined the delicate frozen bridge that linked the two nearest towers and they fired upon the beast that again reached out of the water with its fat tentacles. Zondela reached the shoreline and was received by Glacian soldiers at the base of the tower.

They asked her name and purpose. She identified herself as a mercenary from Sinxin in the employ of Lunil, hoping to be escorted into his presence. The Glacians questioned her and she confidently spun a web of lies describing more mercenaries waiting to serve Lunil once they received their pay. She was careful not to volunteer an explanation for her armor and when finally asked of it, she nonchalantly mentioned killing an Infernian and taking his shiny armor.

She was alert enough not to ask any directions of them – which might arouse their suspicions – and, when they did not offer to bring her to Lunil, she turned her back on them and walked away. The men made no move to stop her, and instead turned and dealt with other issues. She heard talk of renegades as she left and was fairly sure they did not speak of her.

After traveling through snowstorms she and the lizard-men entered an area of six sparkling ice towers arranged in a circle. Above her six bridges soared overhead, each at a different height, slender and clear. Soldiers looked down from above and sent troops out to intercept her. Two large females came out, spears lowered, and questioned Zondela. The Glacians wore wood armor that hugged their curves and accentuated their bodies – a testament to woodcarving skills that Zondela had not believed possible among barbarians. The dark-haired women lowered their weapons when Zondela explained that the lizardmen were being brought to Lunil to arrange a treaty between the two races. The women appraised the lizardmen, nodded, and returned to the warmth of their towers. Cold and almost frost-bitten under her gloves, Zondela moved on. Eventually, she came to an isolated grove of trees with a cluster of rocks at their base that would shield a fire from the wind, allowing her to get the flames started and for the three of them to stay out of the wind.

The woods were not empty. Fur-clad men and wild-eyed women emerged from the woods and closed ranks around her. They gave her a chance to speak and Zondela tried to gain their confidence, explaining that she was a mercenary and would work for whoever paid her the most. From the conversation, she learned that they were renegades who resisted Icetar rule and lived alone in the cold recesses of the forests without a master. The men accepted her word while the women were distrustful and apprehensive. Zondela survived their scrutiny by suggesting they watch her work before deciding if they should hire her, and soon found herself in a battle.

Later that evening the renegades rooted two medium

Ursus beasts out of a cave. The fighting was difficult in the cold weather and twice she slipped on the ice. Her battle-honed reflexes saved her and she rolled over and scuttled away before being mauled. She dispatched the last of the Ursus beasts by splitting its head open with a great downward swing of her blade while spearmen impaled it from the sides.

After cutting open the creature and roasting the meat over a fire, they ate and moved on. In the days that passed, Zondela saved their lives many times. They fought packs of wolves, Ursus beasts mad with hunger, blue reptiles that lay in wait beneath a light layer of snow, armored sea hunters that carried swords in their tentacles, and the mages. The barefoot young women fought with lightning bolts and blue fire, slaughtering the renegades without restraint. The prettiest of the young women – garbed only in semi-transparent satin and with a metal tiara in her golden curls – spit green acid when enraged, the corrosive liquid burning through rock when it splattered about. Zondela killed her with a sword throw from forty feet, fighting the rest of the time with a blade taken from a fallen comrade. When the surviving mages withdrew, oblivious to the frigid winds, the remaining rebels hugged and kissed each other, spending the night curled up in a cave in each other's embrace.

The Glacian rebels were angry and unhappy, blaming the passionless Icetars for allowing the Ursus beasts to thrive for centuries. The Council of Icelords was more concerned with their legacy than in protecting their subjects. The renegades had managed to survive by fighting a constant war of attrition with the forest beast, the climate, and now the mages and the Votar Knights, the only group to steadily turn back the murderous advances of the magic-using women.

Little went to waste in the hostile environment. The bodies of their Glacian comrades were hung from trees and used as bait to lure in wolves. This allowed the Glacians to ambush one of their natural enemies in a place of their choosing. The long leg bones of the dead Ursus beast were fashioned into spears, one end carved to a sharp point. The Ursus provided enough meat for the Glacians to eat well for some time and there was talk of boarding up their cave and not leaving for a year. Before that happened, Zondela wanted to gain information so she turned the conversation to the subject of Lunil. She learned that Lunil had manifested long ago on water stolen from the burning realm of Infernia and that her body was so old it was rounded and smooth from erosion. The clear waters from Infernia allowed Lunil to occupy her physical body almost indefinitely, and over the years the abrasive action of the elements had polished her icy contours so that she was alone among the sharp and fragmented lords in having a smooth exterior.

Zondela abandoned the rebels a short time later as they knew nothing of Lunil's whereabouts. She and the lizard-men traveled further, trying to avoid getting embroiled in the constant fighting in the frozen, lonely wastes of Glacia. Zondela had been to this stratum before yet had never seen the city of icy towers and had not known of the constant warfare. The chaos hid her presence as towers were toppled and villages were razed by a group of women on chariots who were mad with war, answering to no one and killing indiscriminately. Zondela avoided frozen lakes since even the small ones would be cracked from underneath by the stone-wielding tentacle beasts that sought to drag her to her death.

She came to the edge of a grove of trees and stopped to observe. In front of her stretched a small frozen lake – about a bow shot in width – and some Glacian soldiers stood before it, still on the bank and standing at attention. They had already seen her so she joined them, knowing that to run might be to court disaster. None of them spoke to her, instead retaining a disciplined rigidity and silence.

Six Icetars joined the Glacian soldiers. The frozen lords wore great metal swords buckled to their bodies and two of them carried a wood battering ram of a type suitable for knocking in gates or walls. The Icetars held it straight down and pounded it onto the ice, cracking open a large hole. While the Glacian men looked on, the Icetars set aside the ram and stepped into the water, dropping below the surface.

All six of the frozen lords descended and in the clear water she saw the battle unfold. Below them, deep underwater, a pack of tentacle beasts swam out to meet them and the carnage began. The Icetars strove with their blades against their enemies and tentacle beasts floated to the surface, their blue blood staining the water until it obscured everything. Quietly she departed, the Glacian soldiers making no move to stop her or the lizardmen.

Glacia was a forsaken, destitute land of lonely, sprawling frozen wastes. She longed for the hot brass of Infernia and for the pleasure of soaking naked in the warm water under a burning sun. She could get no comfort from the scaled and cold reptilian companions; she needed the companionship of her own species to ward off the frigid and oppressive landscape. The storms worsened, pelting them with wind-driven snow and frost. Whole banks of white powder were picked up by cold gusts and swept against her.

She came across a small encampment in a crumbling stone tower that had a fire at its center. The men and women, all armed with bone spears, welcomed her and drew her into a conversation about herself. Dusk descended as they spoke. The many factions on Glacia were in opposition to each other and the groups were vying for control of the frozen city. She refused to commit herself to their task, instead asking for time to think upon it. While the Glacians enticed her with offers of wealth and companionship with any of her choosing, a shout rang out from the guards.

Everyone leaped to their feet and ran out. Three men had been caught stealing supplies from the encampment and already had slain two guards who had moved to stop them. The crossbow armed intruders leveled their weapons at the rest of the Glacians, pausing to see if further confrontation was unavoidable. "Rebel artisans," muttered a man beside Zondela. "They can create and believe they are destined to rule."

The Glacians from the encampment yelled war cries and surged forward. The intruders leveled their crossbows and fired bolts that turned into spheres of flame in midair and many Glacian soldiers were killed. Zondela's armor protected her from the splashes of heat and flame as she hustled her lizardmen behind cover. The Glacians charged, their bone spears in their hands, and were forced back when one of the rebels put a horn to his lips and blew out a cloud of yellow incandescence. It dissipated in seconds yet the Glacians who had been caught in it were mere skeletons, their bones clattering to the frozen ground.

The Glacians threw their spears and slew two of the artisans. The third rebel withdrew a chain and swung it over his head while holding the rest of the length in his other hand. The entire chain length was about equal to her sword and it was not long enough to reach any of the other men who warily crouched, waiting for others to charge so they would not have to do so alone.

The Rebel Artisan flicked his chain out and it increased

in length, killing one of the Glacians. The chain shortened to its original length, the artisan still swinging it over his head. Another flick and his chain extended in length again and whipped against a Glacian's head, sending him sprawling to the icy ground. The chain tripled in length during the strike then returned to its normal length.

The other Glacians took a step forward, naked swords in their hands. The rebel whirled his weapon over his head and sent it snaking out toward them. The chain increased in length as it moved and encircled a Glacian, pinning his arms to his sides and squeezing so hard Zondela heard ribs crack. With a complicated wrist movement, the artisan had the chain unwind, spinning and releasing the dead Glacian who toppled to the icy ground.

With another snap of his wrist, the rebel snapped the chain out to the next closest soldier. Zondela watched the chain fight unfold; the artisan knocked their swords out of their hands and his chain – which could elongate to any length – encircled his enemies, snapping their necks and spinning them as it was removed. The last of the Glacians from the encampment had been killed.

The primitive part of her brain – the part that took pleasure in savage battles – took over. She advanced with her brass blade held high. When the chain snaked in she tried to bat it away. Unlike a solid blade, the flexible linkages were not deflected. Instead, she had only put a bend in its path of travel as it encircled her, winding itself around her. Since her arms had been raised the chain had not trapped them as the links curled about her torso, rising to reach her neck. It was all instinct as she dropped her blade and took the chain in her hands, hauling hard. It yanked the rebel off his feet and into the snow, pulling the weapon out of his hands. In seconds the chain, now back to its original length, fell to the frozen ground between them. She scooped up her sword and closed the distance between them before the rebel could unleash another artifact upon her. A blow from her armored fist sent him reeling.

She tied his hands behind his back. To make the captive think he was going to be killed she ordered the lizardmen to find rocks to cover his body with and she brought the saw-toothed edge of her blade against his neck. The artisan babbled.

He spoke of Lunil's location and, since he feared for his life, added details to her map of Glacia. The artisans of Glacia had rebelled, deciding that with their abilities they were destined to rule. They had quietly assembled a collection of relics until the Icetars had discovered it and sprung a trap before the artisans were ready, adding another dimension to the massive war between the tentacle beasts beneath the surface and the inhabitants above. To her disbelief, all sides recruited mercenaries from Sinxin when possible.

She removed his money and short sword. His weapon and the relics – the horn, the bolts, and the chain – went into her pack. He had on him a glass sphere, a clear globe that was warm to the touch. She gazed in it and thought she saw the ocean. It was a strange sensation, so she slipped the globe into her pack. She released the rebel and he scrambled away, looking over his shoulder as if he expected her to slay him as he ran. He stumbled through massive snowdrifts and disappeared over a ridge.

She needed to go to a tower that overlooked the Sea of Contemplation, a skirmishing point in the war against the tentacled species. Zondela ducked her head down against the wind, raised her cloak higher about her neck, and pushed through the perpetual Glacian blizzards.

Snow worked itself between the plates of her armor.

Her feet hurt from the cold and she relished the thought of returning to the warmth and light of the main sphere. The lizardmen, however, were largely unaffected by the cold. Their body temperatures dropped to match their surroundings yet they suffered little ill effects. Despite the cold and their frost covered scales, they had no complaints. Zondela grimaced and hugged her fur cloaks tighter about her armor.

She came to an open plain and was forced to wait out the battle that raged upon it. Rebel artisans were holed up in a natural redoubt – a craggy outcropping of rock. They fired crossbow bolts that turned into massive lightning bolts or great webs of gossamer that lit on fire and burned any men trapped beneath their sticky strands. The Glacians soldiers on the plain, who were mustering greater numbers, fired bows or rushed up to throw spears yet were making little headway. The cover provided by the fractured rock was enough that the artisans withstood each assault. The Glacians drew back to mass their men and women into a single gigantic group and again rushed the rocky redoubt, taking casualties from a salvo of crossbow bolts that released hissing clouds of green gas as they streaked through the air. As the remainder of the Glacians fought their way up to the enemy position and engaged in sword combat a ship sailed into view, drifting above the ground a good spear's throw in height.

The ship was long and curved and made of wood. Between the gleaming towers of ice, the impressive arches spanning the distance between them, the battle relics, and the wood ship, the Glacians were far from the primitive dullards she had thought.

A group of crossbowmen lined the side of the ship as it banked over the battle and the bolts cascaded out, impaling the Glacian soldiers and turning the tide of the battle.

The crew of the flying ship dropped ropes over the side and hauled up their comrades from the rocky outcropping, escaping with only seconds to spare.

Zondela skirted the area and moved deeper into Glacia, avoiding the frozen lakes with the temples, pyramids, and obelisks below the surface. To avoid having to climb over sharp rock formations she traveled along the winding paths, always with ice-towers and archers overlooking her from above. The area was heavily guarded and always she had to explain that she was recruiting lizard mercenaries for Lunil.

She was allowed to keep her sword and given an escort of three hulking females – wide-shouldered women clad in furs and mismatched pieces of wood armor – who stared her down with undisguised spite in their dark eyes. The women wore long braids of hair that trailed down their backs.

Zondela suffered from a lack of confidence in her speaking and persuasive skills. She had never, in her long years of training for war, mastered the verbal skills that came so naturally to others. On the rare occasions, she had fallen in love with a man, other women who were more influential and stimulating would make the catch, leaving Zondela to bitterly renew her military and physical training. Here, now, she smiled awkwardly and attempted to make friends.

Her efforts were met with silence at first. As they walked toward Lunil's castle the other women gradually explained that there was a shortage of men on Glacia due to the constant fighting and they saw Zondela as a rival, a tall and attractive woman from Sinxin whom they would have to compete with. Zondela lied and explained that she had two husbands on Sinxin and that she did not want more. The Glacian females became more talkative.

The Icetars were unloved. They were vainglorious, more concerned with their icy architecture than the people who labored for them. Each Icetar was lord of her particular domain and strove to build taller towers and greater cities than the others. It became a private war between them to create the most graceful arches or imposing castles. Lunil herself had ordered the construction of a massive winding staircase that spiraled upwards high into the sky, terminating in a flat peak with an ice statue of a Wusong at the top. Many Glacians had died constructing it.

Wounded men walked by and spoke of a benthic enemy who was being taken alive. The three Glacian guards felt it was their duty to be present and so Zondela had little choice except to witness the event. It was a small frozen lake, a bow shot in diameter and quite deep, the rocky bottom partly visible far below. The perpetual blizzard had coalesced into a softly blowing snowstorm that coated them with a layer of white. For several hours they waited, looking into the hole that had been broken into the ice. The lizardmen behind Zondela received many stares and she deflected a few questions about them. An hour later Icetars were seen underwater, rising to the surface.

Each swam up holding onto a rope that trailed behind it into deeper waters. The Glacian soldiers at the surface took up their weapons and waited apprehensively. One of them tried to retreat and was pulled roughly back by the others. Some held iron blades; others took up long bones that had a rock tightly fitted and tied onto the end to make a club. The Icetars clambered out of the lake, pulling themselves out with one hand while hauling on the rope with the other. Once on the surface, the Icetars – each with sharp edges and jagged corners on their bodies of blue ice – hauled the ropes in to drag up a tentacled creature. The beast was dying; it bled freely from several wounds and regarded them with luminous fish eyes that narrowed with hate. The beast's six tentacles reached for the Glacian soldiers and the four Icetars spread out, each pulling their rope from a different direction so the beast could not move. Gradually its tentacles lay still as it regarded them.

The deep, resonant voice of one of the Icetar rang clearly in the chill air. "Cease your resistance. The Frozen Council rules the entire stratum."

"No," came the oily voice of the beast. Its fish-like mouth exposed white teeth as it spoke. "The benthic race will ultimately conquer you and your sad civilization. You are the ones who are resisting your fate."

"Your body is rich in nutrients that my people require," replied the Icetar. "You can serve us in life or in death."

"It is too late for you, false one. You worship yourselves in your arrogance." The creature struck the ground with one of its sucker lined tentacles as it spoke, bound tightly by the ropes.

"The Frozen Lords are the rightful rulers of this realm, benthic one," said the Icetar. "Is it true that you worship a false lord?"

The creature became agitated and the Icetars had to lean back and tug on the ropes to keep it in place. "Skantalus raised us to a level far above you." The creature whipped a tentacle against the frozen ground again.

"If Skantalus serves the Frozen Council he will be allowed to continue in his place as King or arbiter or temple sovereign," said the Icetar. "It is the destiny of your King to serve us."

"Skantalus brought us knowledge and skills and ended the fighting among our kind," replied the tentacled beast in its oily and unpleasant voice. "Our castles near completion and our armies learn of warfare by laying under the frozen surface of the lakes and watching your people fight." The creature laughed.

"This is your last chance at peace, benthic dweller," said the Icetar. "Abandon your worship of this Skantalus and learn of the radiance of the Frozen Council."

"What would you have us do?" hissed the creature.

"Build temples to us underwater," replied the Icetar. "Use your skills to fashion statues of us so that when we gaze through the ice we see ourselves. Your people carve rocks with tools to make your great castles. Make instead stone pillars and columns on the seafloor that rise out of the water that we may build towers atop them, or statues that further show our impressive image."

Zondela was shocked. The Icetar wanted the enemy to build monuments to their greatness instead of working out a way for the three races to cooperate – during an insurgency against the rebel artisans.

The benthic creature curled its tentacles up like someone curling his hands into fists. Its shuddering voice was loud and seething. "A statue of Skantalus will adorn every hill and mountain on the stratum one day, and we will topple your towers of ice and send your frigid race over the side to fall to the hot sphere below."

One of the Icetars drew her great iron longsword and dispatched the beast, stilling the movements of its tentacles. While they dragged its carcass away Zondela's guards took her in another direction. They had left her with her sword the entire time and Zondela figured they must have believed her story.

They walked through a thick forest that protected them from the effects of the raging blizzards. They neared the edge of the woods and waited another hour for the storm to dissipate. From there it was a short walk to a temple of fluted columns carved out of crystal-clear ice. The sun shone on the temple, illuminating it and revealing the occasional bubble in the otherwise perfect construction.

A spiral staircase of clear ice rose upward, spiraling around nothing but air – if she had not seen it, Zondela would not have believed it possible. At the top of the spiral staircase was a flat area with an Icetar on it, motionless and silent. Behind her was a tall column of ice with a statue of a Wusong at the top, snarling and tensed as if to strike. The Icetar had rounded curves to her body; it looked like she had been exposed to the elements long ago and they had worn down her edges and polished any jagged or sharp corners. It was Lunil, first of the Icetars, and an ascendant.

Zondela and her lizardmen were forced to kneel at the base of the staircase, as did her guards, rising only as Lunil descended the staircase, her joints cracking. Zondela knew from earlier conversations with her guards that the Icetar's body was composed of limbs of ice with a thin layer of water in between them to allow movement. When an Icelord was immobile for several minutes that lubricating layer of water froze, making a cracking noise when the Icetar's movements broke it again.

"I am Zondela, a mercenary from the main sphere. I offer you an alliance, and something far greater." A glance back at her guards showed the three women watching carefully, their hands on their swords.

"Your scaled beasts do not seem to mind the cold, Zondela." The Icetar's voice was deep, majestic, and pleasing. Around them a chill wind blew, striking them with ice and snow.

Zondela nodded. "Their bodies maintain the temperature of their surroundings, my lord."

"Then they could build here without suffering from the cold like the rest of the workers. How many more of them are there?"

"Not many, my lord," said Zondela. "I come to you with something more important than that."

"Can you breed more of them? I was told you come to me to arrange such a deal."

"I perhaps could, my lord, except for the great events about to unfold on the main sphere." She waited, her heart hammering in her chest, fear quickening her pulse. The time of reckoning was fast approaching.

"Do they build great towers on Sinxin, Zondela? Do the cities there rival what we have created here?"

"I come bringing knowledge," she replied, keeping her anger in check. "A great war brews on Sinxin and the Flametars will soon invade. Already their agents prowl the sphere, preparing the way before them. You must ready your army to descend to the sphere to stop them."

"I would advise patience, young woman. The Flametars cannot manifest in the cool airs of Glacia, and once our war with the benthic dwellers is concluded we can turn our attention to building greater monuments to ourselves."

"The Flametar invasion ends in flames consuming the entire sphere," said Zondela. "I have consulted an oracle."

"To land an army below would take workers away from our building projects. In my area, we build massive statues, vast ramparts that soar into the air and slender towers which are so tall the workers can barely breathe air into their primitive lungs when they are at the top."

"The Flametars seek to destroy the sphere," she replied through clenched teeth.

"Let them. It does not concern my architecture."

"Infernia fields a powerful army," Zondela said. "They raid your stratum for wood."

"Those small raiding parties are of little concern, taking

only trees and the occasional life of a Glacian soldier. These monuments will one day cover the entire surface of Glacia. Infernia may do as it wishes with the sphere below."

Zondela knew the female guards behind her probably had figured out by now that she was not here to cultivate an alliance between the lizardmen and the Icetar. She avoided looking back at them as it would only make them more suspicious of her motives. In her mind, Zondela played out the rest of the encounter. She mentally pictured her hand sweeping across her body, drawing her sword as it moved, and her leap with the weapon held backward so she could shatter the Icetar with the sharp triangular tip at the base of the hilt.

"Lunil, we must face the Infernian threat. The Flametars seek to consume everything with flames. With the power they will acquire on the surface of the sphere they will be unstoppable."

The Icetar paused before responding. "Then I think we should increase our efforts to hire workers from the sphere before it is cleansed by flames."

Zondela leaped forward, her speeding hand yanking out her sword as she moved. She was a strong woman and she could move fast when her life depended on it. She had the blade out and reversed just as the Icetar raised her frozen arm and opened her mouth. Its mistake was in aiming for her head. Zondela bent at the waist as she moved and the cone of silver hoarfrost passed over her.

She struck the Icetar's chest with the triangular hilt, shattering it. A dark female shadow – curvy, long-legged, heavy chested, and insubstantial – rose from the scintillating fragments, screamed, and disappeared. Zondela turned and issued a warning in a low, grim voice.

"Walk away and live."

One of the three guards bolted for the nearest grove of

trees; the other two drew blades and fought. The lizardmen moved up the steps to help. Unskilled in sword combat, they were injured shortly into the battle and Zondela ordered them to fall back. Swords danced in and out, whistling through the air, looking for an opening in which to kill. Zondela wove a tight defense, her sword a blur as it moved, her shoulders aching from the cold and the exertion. They traded blows for several exchanges until the two Glacian guards fell with deep sword cuts to their bodies. Zondela stepped over them as she sheathed her sword and descended.

Gathering up the lizardmen Zondela looked through her scope for vortices and found none. The three of them retreated into a massive forest and spent several days passing through it, eating Ursus meat during the day and warming themselves by fire at night. When they reached the opposite edge of the woods she came upon a homestead with a wolf-drawn sled in front of it. She did no more killing; after leaving the owners with bruised jaws and minor cuts she dropped a pile of coins on the ground and took the sled. By taking a long, circuitous route she eventually reached the vortex that had brought her to Glacia. With utmost relief, she stepped through and returned to Sinxin.

19

The Ultimate Machine floated over a plain of cracked and porous rock, deep in the southern wastes of Sinxin. It felt like it was trapped on a world with two great plagues on either side, so great was its hate for the Dynasties that teemed with life. Over several millennia it had modified its physical body yet it was unable to purge its original programming. It was still forced to roam from world to world, implanting the seeds of life. Fortunately, its programming could not stop it from creating life that would destroy everything.

The Ultimate Machine remembered a watery world it had seeded centuries ago. There, during the course of a hundred year period, it had spawned magnificent swimming creatures with sleek gray pelts and frolicking dispositions. Once the Ultimate Machine felt the relief that came with finishing that task it had spawned a poisonous reptile species with a temperament so vile that it had wiped out the original swimming creatures then turned on each other, rendering their own kind extinct.

The spinewolf hunter it had created had failed to kill the virus Zondela. In its anger, the Machine almost left Sinxin to be away from her. The newer and more advanced part of its brain – the section it had built for itself – regained control and terminated that line of logic. It felt a flush of pride that originally it had been just an expert system slaved to its programming yet now was a sagacious and calculating entity, building engines of great destruction.

It shunted its hate to an unused compartment and bent its powerful brain to the task of finding weaknesses in its creations or flaws in its plans. The Ultimate Machine could not stay on one world forever; soon its profane original pro-gramming would force it to leave and seek out a new sphere to seed.

It looked into the future and saw that the only fac-tor standing in the way of the complete destruction of this world was the female virus. The Machine had created Slun, who had created the Flametars, who were going to destroy the world, yet now the female was on the verge of toppling its plans. It was time for her to die.

The Ultimate Machine raised the threat level on her and allocated more resources. She possessed skills, intel-ligence, and the ability to cultivate allies. The Ultimate Machine had not faced many enemies of that caliber before. While her determination and focus were remarkable, the Machine could muster those same qualities. The Ultimate Machine realized that she was technically a descendant of it – since the machine had seeded all original life on the sphere – and it erased that memory from its banks. Somehow it felt that this was not the first time it had done so.

It searched its ancient storage banks, vast reservoirs of knowledge from eons of existence. It scanned its memories of thousands of civilizations that had risen and fallen on as many spheres. It examined heroes, kings, soldiers, govern-ments, armies, and politicians. None revealed an entity that had ever impeded it the way Zondela had. In all its wanderings through the void and across so many barren places, never had its plans to destroy been prevented.

It shifted its tactics and looked for information on past entities that matched Zondela's chemical and psychological composition. It sorted and filtered the information on long-dead beings, looking for soldiers or leaders. It further narrowed the search by looking for those that tended to introversion and had a strong sense of duty or moral conviction. Having narrowed the list down to a hundred entries, it looked for things that they had feared or creatures and weapons that had defeated them. A hero from another world had been afraid of nothing except a type of crocodile that infested the swamps and rivers – his one weakness.

The mechanical linkages that were its arms unfolded and its silver, cylindrical body floated in place above the rocky ground. Amid a shower of blue sparks, a new hunter was formed. Similar to the beast that had struck fear into so many in that other world millions of years ago, the new hunter resembled a reptile, its body laying close to the ground with two clawed legs at the front and two near the back, with a thick tail behind it to balance it. Its crocodile-like head was tooth-filled, strong and already snapping open and closed. The old beast from the other world had been confined to the swamps and rivers and that would not do – this beast was mechanical, comprised solely of metal linkages, gears, motors, and hydraulics.

The mechanical croc sped away on the trail of the loathsome woman. Briefly, the Ultimate Machine wondered if it was insane, then erased any memory of that thought.

20

S he returned to Sinxin via the vortex, cast off their furs, and rejoiced at the warm opulence of Sinxin. She smiled as she again shook her hair out, the strands unfreezing for the first time in days. Killing Lunil the Icetar had been a pleasure after she had discovered how unsympathetic she had been. Killing the two female guards had been another matter. While Zondela was a soldier, she knew that her quest to save the world had changed her, had blackened something inside her. The two women back on Glacia may have been ignorant but they were also innocent. Zondela shook her head and promised herself that once the sphere was safe from the Flametar invasion there would be no killing in her life.

The valley was peaceful and fertile, offering all sorts of fruits as well as fish in the ponds. As she explored she found many vortexes, each leading to a different spot. Some led to strange rocky wastes or forested slopes that she did not recognize, and although they tempted her with their promises of adventure, her quest took precedence above all else. The armies of the past may have known of the confluence of vortexes and had fought over them – the soil was rich in skeletons, rusting armor, and discarded swords.

They rested for three days, letting their bodies heal and the emotional wounds fade. Finally, she mounted her chariot and with the stoic lizardmen tirelessly pulling it, moved out of the valley and headed east.

The chariot rolled through vast plains of heath and bracken, so thick in some parts that only the heads and shoulders of the lizardmen were visible in the sea of vegetation. They passed through long tracts of uncultivated land and Zondela realized the futility of her old master's obsessions; there was land here that stretched to the horizon, and the vast green waves of heath proved that the land was fertile enough that it could be developed and a satisfying life built here. She remembered the old saying of the Flametars – "She that puts her trust in herself is naked and destitute, and whoever trusts in the Flametars will flourish as a fish in water." If she had trusted in herself long ago and abandoned her fiery lords then she could have come to the sphere and found happiness. A life spent searching for Fushang would have been preferable to the violence of a Penturian.

Every few hours she stopped and updated her map with feather and ink. She was meticulous and had a steady hand, drawing in the terrain as she explored. Trees dotted the area and the chariot rolled through an immense forest whose leafy crowns created a gloomy area below. On the brassy wastes of Infernia, the sun was ever present and inescapable, while here in this dusky forest it was cool and shadowy with waves of vines and creepers growing in profusion. The lizardmen navigated around the vast trees and thorny tangles. There was barely enough space between the massive trunks to allow passage. She found forest travel a pleasure; she called a halt minutes later when the chariot entered a natural alcove that came to a dead end. She hesitated amid the wall of vines and blossoms that blocked out much of the light, inhaling the redolent scents of nature. Here in this leafy bower, surrounded by green walls and a ceiling of interwoven vines was a privacy and a verdant beauty. The forest was alive in the way her old metallic home never had been. Thick red blossoms grew from the vines to create a backdrop that she wished she could capture in her mind to return to at will in the years to come. Sighing, they withdrew and they continued on their travels.

In the evening she experimented with the Chalice of Overflowing. If she placed a bit of dirt in the bottom of her helmet and filled it with water from the Chalice, the lifeforms that sprang forth were different each time. The first time she tried it a trio of soft-skinned frogs clambered out and swelled in size. Zondela watched, unwilling to kill without justification, and in minutes the slick beasts were as large as she was with long fangs and muscular hind legs. She drew her sword, wondering what laws could explain such an outcome, and the frogs reared back on their hind legs and clawed the air while emitting croaking bellows. One attacked and she survived only by driving her blade deep into its belly. The others bounded off, tearing through the forest, leaving crushed leaves behind as they disappeared. As she carved up the dead frog with the smooth edge of her sword she wondered why adding dirt to her helmet had such an effect. Possibly there was life in the soil that had been transformed by the waters. Zondela had drank from the waters of the Chalice on many occasions and she wondered if she herself could have been augmented by its powers.

The broiled flesh of the dead frog was superb. They ate their fill and – since they had no choice – passed the Chalice around, both Zondela and the lizardmen drinking from it.

Curiosity compelled her to perform a further experiment. She placed the Chalice on the ground and observed it. Minutes later an insect landed on the rim to drink of the waters. With a fingertip she nudged the tiny creature to its doom, sending it into the liquid from which its water-soaked wings could not extricate itself. In seconds the insect was growing, its wings thickening, its body lengthening and developing clawed limbs. Zondela dashed the Chalice over and stamped the creature to death, not wanting to create some new species which would perhaps procreate and fill the skies with awful swarms. The Chalice almost made her an ascendant – the ability to create being the one constant among the creators – and it was an appalling responsibility. The Chalice would have to be destroyed. It could not even be buried; minute creatures existed in the earth, insects, and worms, and they would find their way into the eternally-full Chalice to be evolved and changed, perhaps fueling a massive army of beasts that would rise up and plague the surface. The Chalice fed her by creating fish every night yet the relic was not a holy one when its potential was examined.

The forest thinned the next day and they rolled through vast flowered plains with a line of small hills in the distance. The ground bloomed with blue and white blossoms by the thousands and it felt sacrilegious to grind them into batter beneath her chariot wheels. Here was a land where a woman could go naked and lay down amid the soft petals, dreaming the days away. It was tempting.

On the tenth day of travel, a hill rose in the distance, a stony outcropping that revealed itself as her chariot climbed out of a natural valley and onto higher ground. A river curved around it, flowing beside a small village. The view was consistent with the image the last oracle had placed in her mind.

She called a halt and her lizardmen flanked her as they

walked into the village. Men and women came out to meet them, and Zondela saw with pleasure and a little relief that none were armed.

"I am Zondela, travel-weary and on a mission of peace."

"Well spoken, Zondela," said a man. "I am Cestokos and I welcome you to our village. Your companions are new to us; there have been, I think, developments in the outside world we are not aware of."

Zondela wondered how to explain the presence of the lizardmen without revealing the secrets of the Chalice. "They are a rare species, coming from the depths of the Restless Ocean. They are placid and dependable."

"Then they are welcome here. They can swim?"

Zondela nodded.

"We can swim," said the female. "The river beyond beckons to us, calling us to its embrace with every wave that slaps upon the shore."

"Then you could assist us," said Cestokos. He was middle aged, calm, and intelligent with alert eyes and a relaxed manner. Zondela hoped that by helping him the villagers would be willing to assist her.

"What do you need?" she asked, taking off her helmet and looking in each window and rooftop for potential archers. Nothing aroused her suspicions.

"Our nets have broken and lay at the bottom of the river. It is vital that we retrieve them. Our spearfishers cannot catch enough to sustain us. Our men grow lean as we search farther afield for berries and nuts. If the scaled ones could retrieve our nets, we would be grateful. Our women-folk craft new ones yet they will not be ready for some time."

Without a word, the two lizardmen walked toward the river. Zondela and Cestokos watched them dive in and disappear amid the waves.

"I hope they can help you," she said. "They have been loyal friends to me, quiet companions and steadfast helpers."

"May I ask what you do, here in the middle of Sinxin, halfway between the two great Dynasties?"

"I come from the desert on a matter of great urgency. I need to consult the oracle here," she said.

"That may not be possible. There is a debate right now as to whether we should even consult the oracle ourselves. There are those among us who believe that the knowledge it provides does little to keep us alive here between the two great empires. There are those who wish Ko-Nithka to return to watch over us."

The name brought a little shiver of dread across the nape of her neck. "Ko-Nithka?"

"Aye, though I cannot speak of it now. Others come and you are in danger here." Zondela glanced behind him and saw three women and a man approach, unarmed except for dark looks in their eyes. Zondela put her helmet back on and waited for their approach, keeping her left hand away from her sword hilt.

"This is Zondela," said Cestokos. "Her scaled companions already swim beneath the river to retrieve our nets."

"We don't need the nets," said one of the women. "When Ko-Nithka returns our harvest will ripen and the fish will leap from the waters onto the shore."

"This is Shallica," said Cestokos.

"Shallica the high priestess," the woman corrected.

"Yes," he said, eying her. "Shallica the high priestess. With our nets back we can harvest our own fish, return to the land and sea to sustain ourselves."

"And what happens when invaders come?" Shallica asked, emotion coloring her voice. "We need to act now, secure a bastion of strength, develop it so that when the invasions come, we can protect ourselves."

Cestokos sighed. "Ko-Nithka takes as much as he gives. Those that look inward find what they need."

"We shall see. Who is this woman?" she asked, pointing at Zondela while looking at Cestokos. Zondela felt the woman's haughty and imperial manner was inconsistent with her position as high priestess of such a decrepit village.

"I am Zondela," she said. "I come to speak with the oracle, and then I will leave. I bring no unrest with me."

Shallica was not pleased. "When your lizards return from the river you must leave. There are other oracles on the sphere, markers of the old journey of the first ascendant, unholy constructions he made as he wandered the land."

Zondela nodded, unwilling to take orders from this haughty woman from some strange religion and unwilling to go into battle yet. "I'll wait for my companions to emerge," Zondela said in a murmur.

Standing at the river's edge Zondela kept a close eye on the others. The only weapons trained on her were scathing glances from the women. The men kept busy and seemed friendly on the few occasions that they introduced themselves. In any small village, there was much work to be done and Zondela waited mostly by herself for an hour while the rest worked.

Her two lizardmen emerged, hauling a full net and opening it in the village. Flopping fish, crustaceans, and bottom feeders fell onto the dirt.

Cestokos had praise for their catch. "Your companions harvest well."

Shallica was not pleased. "It is nothing compared to what awaits us." She snapped her fingers and several women came forward to remove choice portions of the catch.

"I need to speak to the oracle," Zondela said, gesturing to her lizardmen to join her.

Cestokos spoke up. "I'll take you. Let's go." He turned to leave rather quickly and Zondela followed him, her scaled companions flanking her. They left the village without incident and ascended a rough, rocky hill to the north. Zondela sensed a power struggle.

It was the lizardmen who spoke first. "Does this oracle know more than Zon-dela does?" it asked, mispronouncing her name slightly.

Zondela smiled; her chariot-pullers looked up to her with a little bit of awe.

"Yes," answered Cestokos. "The oracle knows more than anyone."

"Will it speak to us?" asked the other lizardman.

"It will speak to all of us," he said. "It is wise, not like the women of the village. A short time ago a female of our village, Shallica, was injured while fishing, another unlucky turn in a lifetime full of them. Her leg was broken and she could not crawl upstream back to the village. In any event, our harvests lately have been poor, and she was stick-thin. On the inside of her it was worse; the years had made her sulky and sullen, and her workload had isolated her from those who might have been a friend. No one came. She scraped together some mud from the river bank and created an idol, using her fingers to carve out distorted features and let it dry in the sun. In pain and anger she prayed before it. A Hatetar was nearby and took the opportunity to inhabit the body."

"How did she learn to do that?" Zondela asked.

"Shallica spent much time at the oracle in the old days and learned information both good and evil. The oracle filled her head with images of what the Hatetar could do to help her. Shallica had asked all the wrong questions. After saving her, the mud idol dried and cracked in the sun, the Hatetar screaming as its clay body fell to pieces, taking its ambitions along with it."

"She might be making one now," Zondela said, not bothering to keep the emotion out of her voice. "Shouldn't you be there?"

"I can't watch her all the time. She could create one while I slept. I can only try to persuade. What is your opinion of the idols?"

"They trouble me," replied Zondela. "They feed off of hate, and their gifts are two-edged swords."

"Will you speak to her? Tell her that?" he asked.

"I will."

They moved on in silence. The ascent involved climbing over rocks and pulling on tree branches and roots to haul themselves up. On the small plateau at the top sat the oracle. It was a giant head on a flat pedestal, about six feet tall, made of the same sandstone as the last one, with eyes of amber. The head turned and tilted down to inspect them. Zondela approached and placed her hand upon the giant head. Again there was an urgent mental suction as her thoughts and memories were yanked out of her and into the oracle.

"Have I succeeded in stopping the war?" she asked, not bothering to start with pleasantries in her conversation with a stone head.

"No. The Flametars will still conquer much of Sinxin, and several centuries later they will make their final push." She received images of metal sky-chariots fighting amid the clouds over a landscape of burning cities.

"Why?" Zondela asked, her heart heavy with what she was seeing.

"The Flametars wish to ignite the world. The future war succeeds in that."

"How can I stop it?"

"You could stop the black crystal from falling into the hands of the Flametars. Sharduq has a powerful relic, a crystal that gives off killing vibrations when struck by steel. It will be stolen from him by a Flametar during the coming war. The Infernian soldiers will mount it on the end of a ten-foot shaft – just long enough to keep them out of reach of the deadly vibrations – and they will carry the weapon before them, killing all who oppose them."

"How do they strike it without killing themselves?" she asked.

"There is a string that extends from the tip of the weapon and the user pulls this, causing a small hammer to bang against the crystal, which releases the deadly vibrations."

"How do the Infernians steal it?" she asked.

An image coursed into her mind of Infernian soldiers opening a wood chest and removing coins, silver bars, and a large black crystal.

"Where can I find it?"

An image came to her mind of an island surrounded by waves with a beautiful wooden house on it. There were no landmarks to help her place it anywhere on Sinxin. "Where is that island?"

Her view changed, as if she was pulling away, and the island was shrouded in the ocean mists. The view faded from her mind.

"Is there danger?" she asked.

"Sinxin is awash in danger," it answered. She questioned it for several more minutes and received no more useful information. When she removed her hand the lizardmen approached and placed their palms upon it, hissing slightly.

They stayed in physical contact with it for several minutes, hissing softly like angry snakes until they stepped away.

Cestokos questioned the oracle about Shallica and her desire to build an idol. Zondela suspected he asked about it for her benefit since he wanted her help. She learned that Shallica had been enhanced by her relationship with the idol. The oracle knew no more.

Cestokos turned to Zondela and spoke, a pained expression on his face. "I must be honest with you. When I saw your magnificent armor and the long blade at your side, I was determined to ask for your help."

"You and I against Shallica?" she asked, already knowing the answer.

"Yes. Will you help me? If we succeed then I promise you will have a home in our village if you wish one, or coin if you do not."

"You are afraid of your own high priestess?" she asked as her respect for him seeped away. On Infernia the soldiers had been required by law to show courage at all times, to seek a valiant death in battle if ordered to do so. Zondela had grown up dealing with men who had to be brave, no matter the crisis. The Flametars had been hard task-masters.

"She is high priestess of her idol only and she has already recruited three other females who support her. I have heard stories of these idols, they crop up like insects wherever there is hardship."

"I can't kill her in cold blood," said Zondela. "I'll talk to her." Zondela was unwilling to commit herself and was equally hesitant to turn away and let a Hatetar develop a cult of antagonism and malignancy. They descended in silence, each absorbed with their plans. They still had several hours of sunlight left which she planned to make use of. After speaking to Shallica she intended to get a net full of fish loaded in the chariot and be off before the sun sank into the ground for the night.

Her plans were altered when she returned to the village to find a stone idol floating in the air with Shallica and three other women behind it. Zondela loosened her sword in her scabbard to facilitate a quick draw if needed. The rest of the villagers were conspicuously absent.

Zondela turned to her lizardmen. "Are there any more nets in the river?" They nodded. "Good, then turn and disappear into the water as if you are afraid, and stay below the surface. We'll set up an ambush. Stay alert." She could give no further orders, not knowing how the encounter would play out. The lizardmen slipped smoothly into the water.

Zondela and Cestokos walked the rest of the way into the village. He had gotten her into a quarrel which was of no concern of hers. The whole squalid village was full of cowards who could not stand up to four underfed women. An easy solution would be to cut Shallica's head off and mount it on a pole. Anger surged through her and she visualized the pleasure with which she would decapitate and disembowel the crazed female who had animated the ugly stone idol, yet it was an anger that was not normal for her. The Hatetar's influence was clouding her mind and with that realization the effect dissipated. Zondela smiled, knowing that if the Hatetar was that dangerous, battle was inevitable.

She looked more closely at the Hatetar. It had been carved from a single piece of river stone, smooth and polished from the running water. Whoever crafted it had taken a chisel to it and carved a horrid, twisted mouth, a bent nose, and deep-set eyes that dripped tears of blood. Zondela shook her head at the foolishness that had carved such grotesque features into the rock. Someone had yanked flat, square teeth out of a large fish and placed them into the mouth of the idol. The stone mouth curved into an almost skeletal grin as it gazed upon Zondela.

"Ko-Nithka I presume?" she asked.

"Yes," replied the stone idol, its gruesome face a twisted rictus due to the unskilled carving. "Long have I waited for this time. My high priestess has done us all a service by crafting this beautiful body for me, ending countless years of wandering through the cold night."

"What is it like, without a body?"

"Endless wars with others of my kind, fighting over humans to influence, searing each other with our anger. Years of aimless drifting, enlivened only by brief periods when we can urge humans into killing each other."

Zondela slipped her helmet on her head. "Yours is a pleasant species."

"Your people give birth to us!" it cried, its stone mouth twisting as it spoke. Behind it Shallica only smiled, sweat glistening on her face, a look of rapture in her eyes. "Every time your species hates, one of us is born. Many of us die, fading away as your emotion cools. In periods of great angst, we grow, becoming wise, patient, keen."

Zondela smiled a sad smile. "I'll be sure to spread the message."

"You are not innocent yourself, Zondela," it said. "When Koth cultivated a friendship with Thoh and stole your bracelet to give to him, you birthed one of us."

When Zondela had been a young soldier serving under her Penturian she had developed feelings for another man in her unit. She had borrowed some artisan's tools and bored tiny holes in a handful of stones, taking a month to make a necklace. The girl Koth, young and in love with the same man, had stolen it and given it to him. Zondela remembered the hate she had felt.

"Yes," came the grinding voice of Ko-Nithka. "You brought a Hatetar into being that moment, and the full day of anger you felt fed it, nursed it until it could survive on its own. Since then it has killed many other of my people, enlarging its territory, sublimating their unhappiness into delicious hate. It lives to this day, seeing into the hearts of men, waiting until one day when someone will craft for it a body so that it might find you and thank you."

A brief ripple worked its way through Zondela's body. "What is its name?"

"Ro-Zonda. It seeks you." The stony, abrasive laughter from the Hatetar reverberated through the village.

"Then when I have taken your body from you, find him and tell him I will do the same to him." With a well-practiced movement, she swept her right hand across her sword hilt, tightened her fingers on it, and drew, her hand a blur. It was a quick maneuver she had prepared many years ago to draw and kill an armed enemy.

A wave of heat and pain flooded from the Hatetar, driving her backward, interrupting her stroke. Though she managed to hold onto her blade, both she and Cestokos were repulsed by waves of hot anguish.

She fell back, seeing with her peripheral vision an attacker leaping through the air at her, an impossibly high jump for a human. Through reflex alone Zondela sidestepped and something landed beside her. It was Shallica, her excited eyes bright with an unnatural light. Shallica waved her hand across Zondela's face without making contact. A strange hurt swelled up in Zondela, an emotional poison that caused grief, regret, and sadness. Zondela had felt nothing like this before and wondered if she was dying.

She and Cestokos were driven back to the river like cattle, both of them with burned skin and seared minds from the attacks. Ko-Nithka and Shallica fought as allies, covering each other so that whenever Zondela moved in to disembowel Shallica, the Hatetar would rush over, still floating in the air, and scorch Zondela with those pulsing waves, bruising her mind with its awful powers. The Hatetar and its priestess were driving Zondela into the river. Whenever she or Cestokos attempted to escape, one of the other three women cut them off and with a raised palm inflicted such excruciating misery that even when Zondela retreated into the river, her mind was left tender and raw. The Hatetar floated over the water in its pursuit of them, Shallica and another village woman two steps behind it.

Zondela, up to her chest in water, had forgotten about the lizardmen, though they had not forgotten about her. The two reptiles had maneuvered so that the Hatetar was between them and they surged partly out of the water, their feet scissoring, and thrust the net over top of Ko-Nithka. As their bodies dropped back into the water they pulled the Hatetar down. For several seconds the lizardmen held it underwater. Shallica was screaming like a beast, her face contorted by anger. Steam burst forth from the Hatetar as it tried to rise. The lizardmen worked with the same unrelenting discipline with which they had pulled the chariot and they kept the idol underwater. The Hatetar cracked into fragments, releasing a bubble that rose to the surface and escaped into the air with a belch.

They headed for shore. The lizardmen reached it first, being natural swimmers, and waited on the beach. Shallica waded ashore next and had her arms pinioned by the lizardmen. Cestokos stumbled onto shore and collapsed, only able to raise his head and stare with blood-shot eyes. Zondela forced her tired body to move and she clambered onto the embankment. A quick check showed all of her equipment still at her side, her brass sword in her hand.

Zondela removed her helmet and let it fall to the sands at her feet. "Let her go," she said to the lizardmen. They released the prisoner and waited silently.

Blood frothed out of Shallica's mouth as she spoke. "It makes you feel things you've never felt before. While I lay on the ground at night Ko-Nithka would float above me and make me feel things that I've never dreamed of. It was incredible the sensations it could produce. It made me bleed from several areas, yet the pleasure was so intense it became so that I could not live without it." She looked up at Zondela, apprehensive, unsure, scared.

Zondela knew she had to make a decision so she probed, knowing with a heavy heart that she would kill if Shallica gave the wrong answer. "Perhaps you could make another one," Zondela said, "so that I can experience it as well?"

"Of course!" answered Shallica. "It's no problem, we can begin tonight. The rewards are–"

Her sentence was cut short when Zondela drove her blade into the other woman's gut. Unhappiness flooded her. Pity and remorse made her want to cry; killing women was not something she ever wanted to do again. Perhaps, if she could see inside herself, she would see some hideous beast.

Cestokos limped over and thanked her. She nodded, sheathing her sword, and asked him if he needed help tracking down the other three women. Relief washed over her when he told her that he was going to forgive them for having fallen under the spell of Shallica. The lizardmen came over and Cestokos shook hands with them, promising endless catches of fish and crustaceans from the fertile river.

"Great Zondela," said one of the lizardmen. "We will stay here, if Cestokos allows it. We felt alive in the river, at peace among the fish and undersea plants. Also, you are dangerous to be around." Cestokos assured her that the lizardmen would always be welcome.

Zondela smiled and hugged them, feeling lonely at having to part company with her loyal reptiles yet happy that they found a place where they could live in peace. "Swim deep and hunt well."

"We will, beloved Zondela. Goodbye."

She walked out of the village and headed east.

21

She walked until she came to a vast lake lined with water-worn stones. She stared deep into the evening, trying to forget what she had done in the village. The sun sank into the ground in the distance and it set the sky on fire with its last rage before settling into its grave for the night. The clouds were liquid gold and the sea shone like metal still hot from the forge. The rocks at her feet cast long shadows behind them, a whole army of stones patiently watching the sun go down with her. She wished for a companion, a woman like herself who would understand what it was like to have such a responsibility and to have done such awful things. She felt like a sand grain. Instead of being ground between rocks, she was compressed between days – the memory of yesterday and the anxiety of tomorrow slowly crushing her.

She shook her head. It would be hard to have a companion until her quests were over and the Flametar War was stopped. She did not know where on this sphere she would find that companionship. The village women she had met were concerned with crops or laundry or dirty children, while Zondela's mind turned over problems of tactics and military thought. Sinxin women seemed interested in winning a husband while Zondela dreamed of winning great battles. There was little common ground and she would always be in search of the city of Fushang. Forming friendships would be hard since she likely had years of wandering before she found the city. Travelers had told tales of the ancient place, passing legends down until the city became known as a refuge of tranquility.

She sat by the lake and removed the Overflowing Chalice from her belt. By itself, the Chalice had never produced life – except when the insect had fallen in. When poured into her helmet, fish or other lifeforms would develop. She figured it proved the Flametars were right when they had taught that the world was full of tiny organisms – her helmet had bacteria in it – whatever those were – while the smooth metal interior of the chalice did not. The relic evolved the invisible lifeforms, ripening them along the natural path that evolution would have sent them down in a few million years.

The Flametars had been very knowledgeable. After a raid on Glacia, a huge fire had been lit and the dancing, burning masters had floated above it and talked at length of the nature of the universe. Zondela had been one of the few who listened; she had loved the ideas when the old masters spoke of the laws governing celestial movements or the development of life under the heavy hands of the ascendants.

The Flametars were disembodied intellects, unfit for physical form and lacking passion, sympathy, or emotions. They could debate the strange religion they called science for hours and then order a deadly raid on Glacia that killed scores of innocent people just to provide them with more wood. In spirit form the Flametars drifted around Infernia, watching everything their people did, recording infractions, and meting out punishment later when they took physical form.

As long as the air was hot the Flametars could drift anywhere in insubstantial form, silent, invisible, and malign. In cold air the insubstantial masters would freeze to death and dissipate, preventing them from conquering Glacia by themselves. That task had always fallen to Zondela and her brethren.

Wood had never grown on the brassy plain of Infernia. Glacia was forested and ripe with fuel, though the air was too cold for Flametars. She wondered why her old masters had never moved to the hot parts of the main sphere below. It might have been the lack of permanent vortexes connecting Infernia with Sinxin. Flametars that passed through one of the rare vortexes to the surface might not be able to return if the passage faded away. The occasional cooler evening temperatures of the sphere would have discouraged them as well; raging fire was a comfortable embrace for a Flametar while cool air was bitter and deadly.

It made her remember an incident years ago. After the carnage of the battle of Snake Valley, where she and her men had routed superior numbers of Glacian soldiers who had mounted a raid upon Infernia, the corpses of the enemy soldiers were piled upon a plinth of lumber and ignited. When the fire reached its zenith a Flametar manifested and questioned her on the battle. It was clear from its knowledge of the fight that it had observed, bodiless, as she led her men into battle. It asked her why she had acted the way she had.

Zondela had explained that in the past the Glacian soldiers had never shied from a fight, always moving to intercept her when she was discovered on their stratum. When the Glacians were spotted moving across Infernia, Zondela had positioned her men in the valley, knowing the enemy would attack her when they saw her.

She had hidden fifteen Infernian soldiers in natural crevices nearby and left only her men exposed. As expected, the Glacians attacked her and were ambushed by the other fifteen Infernians. It was an interesting battle and Zondela had explained how the individualistic nature of the Glacian army was a weakness.

The different command structure of the Icetar army worked against them. Captured prisoners had explained to her that on Glacia each soldier's name was on a list, with the most skilled at the top. Their placement on the list was determined by their success in training, games, and contests. If an Icetar organized a twenty-man raid, they would select the top twenty names and throw them together, under the command of he whose name was highest.

She contrasted that with the Flametar technique of selecting a Penturian for his or her command skills and assigning five soldiers to serve under them. That system was flexible and advantageous, allowing the smaller Flametar army to hold off Glacian soldiers. Zondela could issue orders minutes before battle and have her men outflank the enemy. She had once improvised during a raid and positioned her men atop a hill. From the hilltop they hurled spears and fired arrows into the advancing Glacians, killing scores of the bold and tactically unskilled enemy soldiers.

That had been the battle where she had found a bottle of alcohol on one of the Glacian corpses and taken it back to Infernia. Zondela did not drink and was not jealous when the Flametar ordered her to empty the contents of the bottle upon the burning wood beneath it. Trained to obey, she had poured the wine on the fire. For the next twenty minutes, the Flametar wreaked havoc on Infernia, scorching buildings and spreading its incandescence through several dwelling places. The Flametar was technically drunk, and they were only spared its depredations when it winked naturally out of its physical form.

Back in the present, Zondela was broken out of her reverie when a reptilian head rose out of the water. It was a Wusong, and as it clambered out of the river its long and graceful body glinted in the setting sun. It was supported by two limbs near the front of its body and two more closer to the back, its slim and flexible torso coiling into loops as it emerged. It glared at her with shining eyes while beside it a second Wusong climbed out of the water on clawed toes. The reptiles could pounce quickly yet she had utter confidence in her ability to draw her sword in time if that happened.

The two emerald-scaled beasts turned toward each other and coiled their bodies underneath themselves so that their heads were raised in the air and their lengthy torsos were in a neat pile below. The two Wusong faced each other with perhaps five feet between them. The first one reached down with a talon and picked up a smooth stone from the ground. It raised the stone and released it; the stone floated in the air.

The second Wusong also selected a stone from the ground and raised it, releasing it to float before the first one. Each beast took a turn, placing a smooth rock in the air, taking time in between each turn as they examined the pattern they were creating.

The constellation of stones moved slowly, curling about each other yet free of collisions. They added yet more stones and the entire setup became too complicated for her to follow. She wondered if they were playing some strategy game like Salamanders; their study of the floating stones and their measured, deliberate moves were consistent with such an indulgence.

They might also be creating a map of the firmament,

with each stone representing one of the stars, the slow movements of each rock showing the passage of millions of years. Such a thing would indicate a massive intellect on the part of the Wusong Clan.

Perhaps it was some elaborate ritual with each beast exposing their feelings or thoughts through the pattern, a demonstration like a tea ceremony or sacred book reading. The pattern of stones might be a sort of poetry for the eyes that only the Wusong could read.

She sat on the ground and selected a stone for herself, a moss-covered rock worn smooth by long years in the water, which she placed in her helmet. A tilt of the Chalice filled her helmet with water and in minutes a red crustacean climbed out, waving its antenna as it surveyed the world for the first time. Its life was cut short as Zondela killed it and cooked it over a fire. As she ate the succulent flesh she watched the two Wusong, staring at them as they in turn gazed upon the floating stones.

Darkness had fallen, and since she had no desire to sleep with such powerful reptiles near her, she replaced the Chalice in her pack and set off. The Wusong ignored her and she returned the favor as she circumnavigated the lake and moved on through vast lands of heath, bracken, and moss. She walked through the vast, open landscape and found plenty of time to think of the future. She daydreamed of houses, estates, gardens, and luxury, and each time her mind returned to an old dream. When her quests were over, she would find the legendary city of Fushang and reward herself with whatever pleasures it offered.

Several days later she located the next oracle. The sandstone statue of a warrior mounted on a large scorpion stood amid a tangle of vines and bracken. In one hand the warrior held a sword of stone and in the other a trumpet. Slowly the head of both warrior and beast turned to her with a noise like stones being dragged against each other. The oracle stared at her with eyes of black rock.

She placed her palm upon it and steeled herself as the sensation of being mentally sucked dry flowed through her. Memories she had long forgotten flashed before her eyes, childhood recollections, and everyday events from her youth that she had long since discarded. The draining process ended; she had little in the way of privacy in relation to the oracle. As the psychic pain in her palm faded the statue regarded her with cool, dark eyes.

"What of the coming invasion and the Flametar War?" she asked. "Will alerting the Glacians stop it?"

"No," came the deep voice from the lips of the statue. "The plans of the Flametars would be inconvenienced only. War looms in the future."

"Does the war destroy the world?" she asked.

Images flooded her brain. She saw a bird's eye view of a vast expanse of rubble that housed the occasional building or tower. Flametars prowled the debris, igniting any flammable substances they found, including trees, buildings, and corpses.

The image cleared and she could see normally again. "I seek to prevent this," she said, "what must I do?"

A different image entered her mind. She saw two stone idols floating in the air with a Flametar burning behind them. The Hatetar idols were unusually gruesome and ill-carved, one with a gaping mouth that bent downwards in the middle and the other with teeth protruding from its eye sockets. Her perspective pulled away, showing a wider image. Rows of Infernian soldiers knelt behind the Hatetars, their weapons laid carefully at their feet. The image fizzled and was gone from her mind.

"I don't understand," she muttered. "What was I see-ing?"

"An alliance between two forces who both desire the introduction of war to the sphere. The Hatetars are pleased with the plans of the Flametars as they feed off of the conflict and hate it generates. The war brings despair which causes more people to worship the Hatetars. In their alliance, the Flametars bring ruin and the Hatetars offer relief to their followers, generating yet more hardship for the sphere."

"Are all Hatetars allied with the Flametars?"

"Not yet, though they will be. Ro-Zonda, the Hatetar that was created when you were angry at your betrayal as a young woman, has your intelligence and skills and some of your personality. Already it has had its worshipers build a temple to it. Ro-Zonda will be instrumental in cultivating a Hatetar-Infernian alliance."

"What have I done..." she said in a murmur.

"You have created a Hatetar which will convince many to support the Flametars."

She tasted anger. "Where is the Hatetar I made?"

Her perspective flew across the ground, tilting as it rushed around hills and stopped over a temple. The route had been burned in her mind and she would not forget.

"So," she said, accepting her responsibility. "I must slay Ro-Zonda before it does any further work?"

"If you wish to delay and impede the Flametar invasion, yes."

"What else must I do?" she asked.

"That is the extent of my knowledge, as I am not all-knowing."

"Where is the next closest oracle?" she asked.

"That I do not know either, as it has been lost. I sense it

still exists. Its location has been...obscured."

"What about my dream? What about Fushang? Where is it? I know it is real." She sounded petulant yet it was hard to control her feelings in the face of the revelations.

"Yes, it is real. It is a distant city, and no one who has come to me has had any knowledge of it, so I cannot help you except to say that it is a great paradise."

"How do you know that if you don't know where it is?" she asked.

"I can sometimes see the future of those who come before me, and a traveler once laid his palm upon my stone. He was destined to find Fushang, and I sensed in him a future of bliss and contentment."

Her fist clenched yet she kept her voice cool. "Who can tell me of the lost oracle's location?"

"The hero Sharduq was the last to know of it, yet he too has been lost. He was last seen in Ziqqurratu."

"Will I be able to stop the war?"

The oracle paused and looked into the distance. "Possibly."

She nodded. Tired and with head bowed she probed for more information. Aside from telling her that she was hunted by agents of the Ultimate Machine the oracle had no more to offer.

22

With each step she entered a more vibrant, living realm. Plants grew taller, more succulent, their severed stems spraying water when she slashed her way through them. The ground was softer, less rocky, more capable of supporting the lush foliage that sprang from the black soil. Rain was frequent; her armor failed to ward off penetrating water droplets, having been designed in broiling Infernia. Droplets slipped into gaps between brass plates. Temperatures rose and warmed her body. The sunlight and rain fed the increasingly large vegetation along with a rich profusion of herbivores and snakes.

She walked for many weeks. After having traveled much of the way across the continent she looked south and saw the dense jungle that housed the second great civilization, Ziqqurratu. Further eastward lay only more desolation for another few weeks of travel and then the Restless Ocean, so she turned south and tried to remember the stories she had heard. The Baisheng mercenaries she had fallen in with earlier had said that witches were about, although that sounded unlikely. She knew the great hero Sharduq had come here long ago and a civilization had sprung from contact with him.

The jungle enveloped her in a wet and fragrant embrace. Visibility was reduced to inches as she pushed her way through the verdant vegetation. Much of the plant life was flowered; every tree had blossoms and every flower housed an insect. The smell of the ripening greenery was redolent – brushing against a violet fern filled the air with the smell of flowers and honey. Vines curled about every tree, their pink blossoms large and full of a powder that coated her armor when she brushed past them, decorating her brass defensive casing in a most unmilitary yet pleasing way.

Late that evening, a roar filled the jungle and made even the leaves tremble. It came again, a strange bestial noise. She had been gifted with a great deal of courage; others, good men and women, had in the past run from battle when things had gone wrong; Zondela had not. The roar, however, chilled her heart. The last oracle had warned her that she was being hunted.

She rotated, trying to keep watch in all directions, unable to see far into the thick foliage. Something knocked trees down and tore through foliage, coming ever closer. It was seconds away.

A metal croc pushed through the foliage and stopped in front of her, a clear red fluid dripping from its steel mouth, its eyes locked with hers. Its mouth snapped shut, splitting a fresh tree trunk and sending the splinters skittering away. The mechanical beast laughed, its head swaying, its steel claws flexing and cutting furrows into the jungle floor as it whispered her name repeatedly, muttering something about how it was going to tear her apart.

She ran, the beast calling her name as it chased her. She crossed shark-infested ponds and the metal crock killed them out of spite, snapping their backs and tossing them out of the water. She clambered over rocks and the mecha croc knocked them aside in its pursuit. Zondela tried to flank it, hoping for an opening, only to be spun painfully about by a whip of its tail.

She swam through a murky, muck-filled bog, hoping to lose it. The mechanical beast swam below her, scattering a swarm of octopoid warriors. Zondela called out to them for help – they glanced at the mecha croc and ran.

She fought a running battle, maneuvering away from the beast, slashing at it only when it leaped through the air. It was agile, landing on a rock and turning around before she could slam her sword blade down on it. Each engagement went poorly – its teeth were worse than the bite of any sword blade. Her thighs and arms grew weak from the injuries while her beloved brass armor was jagged with rips and tears.

She sheathed her sword and scrambled up a tree, barely hauling herself up with her injured arms. Once cradled in the bowers of her perch the hunter paced below, emitting a constant stream of invective and roars. Zondela removed the Chalice from the leather bag on her hip and poured a copious stream of relic-water onto the ground below. To her dismay, the cascade of water produced only a massive ripening of spiked vegetation. Tall, green, blade-like plants grew quickly and while she continued pouring, no animals came into being.

The metal croc climbed the tree, debris from the bark falling away from its claws. The Chalice had worked its magic; tendrils extended from the new foliage and hauled the beast down. The blade-like plant leaves whipped about, cutting furrows into the steel hide of the croc. Leafy tendrils worked their way into the mechanical beast's body and pulled, yanking out linkages and severing fluid-filled tubes. The croc tore the plant apart several times yet always more leaves and tendrils replaced them, sliding into the croc and dismantling it from the inside. With a last curse directed at her, it expired.

She chose not to climb down and personally feed her plant; she crossed over the intertwined branches to an adjacent tree and swung away from the hostile vegetation, barely escaping its thorny grasp.

She hoped the plant life she had created would not be able to find food and would die out. The Chalice was a powerful relic that could never be given to others; whether its waters had evolved the vegetation or if tiny organisms in the dirt had been recast randomly into another form, she did not know. Possibly the sword-leaf was the eventual destiny of plants in this area, to become hungry for animal flesh in a million years. She could never experiment with the Chalice for fear of creating something that would consume the sphere she was trying to save. The relic would have to be destroyed. She pictured the Chalice after hammering it to junk, water still trickling out of it, sliding down in beads through rents in the metal despite her attempts to stop the flow. She would be in a difficult situation if the Chalice perpetually dripped, damaged beyond all ability to repair, creating inimical life with its endless drizzle.

Late that night the expected silence never materialized. Zondela lay nestled in a grove of flowers, her body still hurting, while insects buzzed around her. Birds and wild felines added to the cacophony, creating something so unlike the perfectly still and mute wastes of Infernia that sleep was impossible.

Twigs cracked and leaves crunched as someone unsuccessfully tried to approach in silence. Zondela opened her eyes and watched through the horizontal slit in her brass helm. Carefully she moved her hand to her sword hilt and waited, confident in her ability to impale whatever interloper was stealthily approaching.

It was a woman. A hideous, frightful face was half hidden by a ragged cloak, her countenance scarred by disease or a terrible accident of birth. The dreadful looking woman raised an open hand and slowly began to curl her fingers into a claw shape. Zondela could wait no more. She drew her sword and with her other hand pushed herself to her feet. A fraction of a second later the saw-tooth edge of her blade was against the neck of the repulsive woman, the interloper pinned against a tree.

"I would not soil my sword with the blood of innocents," said Zondela, "but you sneak upon me in the night. I should kill you to prevent whatever roguishness you have planned."

"Ahh, a woman," the other responded in a normal enough female voice. "I thought you a man in your magnificent armor. My sister comes."

A second woman pushed through the thick jungle leaves and surveyed the situation. This one was gifted with pleasant features and Zondela relaxed while reminding herself that she should not be led astray by good looks.

"You may release my sister," said the pretty one, also clad in a ragged cloak. "We mean no harm, as we thought we came upon a man careless enough to sleep in the jungle."

Zondela did not like the sound of that, and wondered why the other woman was revealing such hostile intentions, even if it was only directed at the other gender. "Do you hunt men?"

The better looking sister shrugged. "In Ziqqurratu the day belongs to men, and the night belongs to women."

Zondela remembered an old conversation and the night seemed colder. "Are you witches then?"

The hideous woman, blade still at her throat, responded. "Men call us that, though we know of a splendor that they will never taste."

"Sister," said the pretty one. "She is wounded in body and in spirit. Sing for her."

Zondela stared hard at the woman still entrapped by her blade, watching for any sign of hostility, ready to kill if needed. The hideous woman only serenaded Zondela in a soft voice and with a half-smile upon her lips. Zondela felt the pain leave her body as a cleansing balm seeped through her muscles. Even with a song that had no words the woman proved a gifted vocalist. The soft and delicate singing healed Zondela. Stepping away, still ready to draw and decapitate on a moment's notice, she sheathed her sword and waited.

"I am Soloth," said the attractive one, "and my sister, who has used her considerable talents to heal you, is Cella. You have left quite a trail through the jungle, leaving behind broken trees and the body of an appalling beast. I am glad you survived."

Zondela was not put at ease. It seemed unlikely that Soloth would care about her. "Thank you. What do you want?"

Soloth laughed, a pleasant twinkling sound. Zondela reminded herself not to let her guard down just because she was in the presence of a pleasant personality. "So direct, so forthright," said the robed woman. "Come, we'll take you home to meet mother, if she is up. You will taste the intellectual luxuries of a cultivated mind. Are you hungry? The body should be fed as well."

Fish and other beasts that had crawled from the Chalice of Overflowing had fed Zondela for some time and she was tired of eating things with claws. "Why are you offering this to me?"

Cella, with her horrible face, spoke up. "Would you rather we leave you alone? You may wander the jungle in solitude if you like, though we would miss the pleasure of your stoic, blunt prose and you will never learn of the wonders that mother has shown us."

The two robed women moved through the jungle and Zondela fell into step with them, vowing to remain alert. "Wonders?"

"The Sect of Lady Valoc will free your mind," said the attractive sister. "We share a common bond of blood. We are of the same race. When we aid a sister we help ourselves. Just from speaking with you, I can see you were raised without love."

The pitifully ugly sister turned and looked at Zondela. She could not have seen much through the slit in Zondela's helmet, yet her gaze lasted for several seconds. "I see. Your life of pain and seclusion is over, great warrior. Do you have a name, or do people scatter at the approach of your anguish, negating the need for one?"

"I am Zondela. What makes you think I have lived in seclusion? There were others on Infernia."

Cella glanced up at the sky with a scowl. "You lived on the great sheet of brass in the sky? No wonder you shed pain and loneliness like a snake discarding unwanted skin."

"There I learned to be a soldier, developing my skills and earning respect," said Zondela.

"You learned to fight with that big blade?" asked Cella, one damaged eyebrow raised.

"I could beat any man on Infernia," Zondela replied.

"Then your presence here is a blessing, and on behalf of the mother I welcome you to the Ziqqurratu Dynasty."

The jungle thickened. They pushed through fronds and leaves, tunneling through the vegetation. Flowers grew larger and dumped powdery clouds of pollen when disturbed. They burrowed through the thick vegetation and into a large clearing. The stumps of severed plants protruded from the ground, often bearing tiny shoots, evidence that even when cut to their bases the plants would survive and grow new tendrils.

In the clearing, women sat on carved stones and chatted, many with books in their hands. They were curious about Zondela, gazing through the slit in her helmet to see what she looked like. Since there were no visible weapons in the clearing, and these shorter, slimmer women did not look dangerous, Zondela removed her helmet. The other women gazed at her and talked among themselves, a normal enough reaction.

Cella picked up a silver vase from a nearby rock and shook it, rattling the coins inside it. When she stopped, all eyes had left Zondela and were now on the center of the clearing.

Fingers pushed out of the ground and the young women backed away. It was a hand, emerging from the soil. A second hand followed, and slim bare arms after that. Snakes curled around the bare arms, red and yellow banded serpents clinging to the soft, cream-colored skin.

A woman pushed through the surface and sat up, dirt and soil falling away from her, a mass of serpents coiling about her naked body. The woman rose, stretching as any girl would after a night's sleep, and looked about. The snakes were constantly moving, encircling her and curling around her waist, around her arms, between her legs, and back up over her shoulders. Most of the woman's body was covered in serpents and her naked, voluptuous, and firm body was occasionally revealed.

Around the clearing, the other women knelt briefly.

Zondela felt torpid, staring without understanding. Only when the snake-clad woman's eyes met Zondela's did the mental numbness leave her.

The serpent clad woman approached. Zondela stood motionless, not putting her helmet on or going for her sword. She was confident she could draw and slash in a fraction of a second; she wondered whether she should kill the snakes first or the woman they embraced.

"I am Lady Valoc. Good evening."

Zondela introduced herself, coolly watching the serpent clad female. The woman, delicately brushing off bits of dirt that still clung to her smooth skin, stood two paces away and looked into her eyes. The snakes also gazed into Zondela's eyes.

Valoc's voice was delicate and soft, consistent with her attractive face. "Your brass armor, I have never seen the like. It is a relic."

"Yes. My old masters, the Flametars, taught our artisans how to build out of the metal."

"You were born in the firmament? I see. The end of all civilization is coming, and the Flametars will be responsible."

"I know," Zondela answered in a quiet voice.

"Then you could assume a welcome place here with us, especially with your knowledge of the enemy."

"I cannot. I seek the oracles, learning of ways to stop the invasion."

"Then you carry a weight on your broad shoulders far heavier than your armor. I see into your heart and that you speak the truth. We will help you in any way we can, and if you wish, you can find a home here with us."

"I do not need a home, Lady."

The woman laughed, her snakes hissing simultaneously.

"Ah, your first lie to me and a pleasing one as I watch you trying to act strong. No woman is totally unreliant upon others."

"It is true I would love to have a happy home to go to, Lady, yet if the Flametar invasion comes none of us will ever find it. Besides, I seek Fushang one day, perhaps when this is over."

"Dreams of Fushang? The legendary city? If it exists, it is far away. I hope you find it, yet one should consider giving up impossible dreams and focus on opportunities when they are provided. Join us. We are at war with Ziqqurratu. They fear our power and hunt us, and in the dark we stalk them. We could use your strong shoulders and long limbs. I will teach you to speak to the beasts of the jungle, to fly upon the winds at night, and to kill with the power of your soul. During the day you will sleep in the ground with your sisters, to rise and do battle in the evening. The sacred learnings will show you powers you could not dream of."

"Is there a price to be paid for such learning?"

The snake-woman nodded briefly. "Cella, in exchange for learning the Utterance of Annihilation, had her face scarred. You can still learn wonders of both killing and loving without losing your beauty, though."

"I do not want to become embroiled in another war and I have no quarrel with men."

"Neither did we, until they served the hybrid Rang-Wo-Ti."

"Who is that?" asked Zondela.

The snake-clad woman sighed, and some of the snake's heads drooped in tandem as if they shared her emotions. One of the serpents laid its triangular-shaped head against her bare breast. "The men of Ziqqurratu worshiped Sharduq, who cared for them and led them in peace and in war.

Sharduq was a good Lord and when he disappeared the men of the city turned to the spirits of the natural world for guidance, sparking a perversion of all things holy. We asked them to stop yet they create Rang-Wo-Ti whenever they seek guidance or are troubled."

Zondela did not like the sound of it and wondered if they were speaking of Hatetars. "How does one create these Rang-Wo-Ti?"

"When a man dies, his body still functions for a short time, even if the soul has fled. By joining an animal head onto a man's body, a Rang-Wo-Ti comes into being, a conjunction of man-flesh and animal spirit, yet also a perversion of both, a creation that is profane and dangerous. Thus we hunt the men of Ziqqurratu and they wage war upon us."

"I only seek Sharduq. He is instrumental in the troubles ahead."

"Then go to the city of Ziqqurratu, the capital of our Dynasty. That is where he was last seen, over thirty years ago. If you do not find him, consider returning here to be embraced by our fold."

Zondela nodded and was served a fine meal. She sat among the other women, and under the watchful eyes of snakes all around her, ate the food they provided. At her request, they placed a dot on her map at the location of the city of Ziqqurratu and she wrote the name under it in small script. The women wished her good luck and she left in the direction of the capital.

She walked under a jungle canopy, spongy growth beneath her feet and the sound of hissing on all sides of her. The sun rose and still she was bathed in shadow because of the overhead foliage, the smell of decaying vegetation mixing with the rare aromas of the red and pink roses on either side of the path.

Ziqqurratu was a rare sight. A stone temple rose out of the jungle, towering above all else. It was formed by a series of square levels. The bottom tier was massive, perhaps three thousand feet wide, a colossal stone square set amid the jungle. Atop that was a smaller square tier, and so on all the way to the top which brushed the sky. Fluted stone towers graced the temple everywhere, each level having scores of them, forming a tapering forest. The temple had perhaps a hundred levels, each tier slightly worn and eroded, rising to a flat area at the very top. It appeared climbable, despite being drenched in vines and creeping foliage. The front of the temple had a stone staircase that led to the top, where, amid a few clouds, she could just make out the outline of a man.

The temple was crumbling. Vines, creepers, and flower-clad tendrils snaked their way across the structure, a slow conquering of the temple by nature herself. Foliage grew from every crack and gap between blocks. It must have taken decades to have built such a magnificent structure. In the distance, just visible through breaks in the jungle foliage, were more stone temples, slender stone monuments reaching to the sky and squat pyramids built with precision, the lines of the structures straight and true. From her position atop a small hill, she could see the tips of hundreds of stone temples poking out of the jungle canopy, disappearing at the horizon.

A street formed of stones set flush into the dirt led toward the great temple and she walked openly down it, not wanting to slink through the jungle and have her motives questioned. Walking across the lane of worn, rounded, natural stones, she passed statues on either side of her, stone effigies of winged serpents and cat-like beasts that bore weapons and wore ferocious expressions on their bestial faces.

Between the statues were square pools of silver fish.

Small dirt trails led away into the darkness of the jungle. Some led to houses made of reeds and mounds of dirt. Flowers had been planted in the sides of the houses, causing leafy vines to curl up the sides of the home and around the open windows. The inhabitants were not well dressed and appeared to be poor, and most were occupied with chiseling. Every time she glanced down a side pathway, if she was able to see the house and the inhabitants that it led to, she saw people making stone blocks with hammers and chisels.

She passed people on the street. Many wore elaborate cloaks of feathers while others had decorated themselves with seashells. Some wore earrings of shiny dark glass that glinted in the sun, and all silently gazed at her.

She walked down the thoroughfare, sweat forming on her body in the jungle heat and sliding down her skin under the armor. The Ziqqurratu inhabitants were building statues everywhere – stone serpents and great warriors of stone flanked her on either side. Piles of construction material lay all over – bricks of granite, marble, limestone, and black glass. She passed several piles of gold bricks.

In front of the temple, she tilted her armored head to gaze up at the multi-tiered structure that challenged the firmament. She stood before the massive staircase that led to the top. Guards lined either side of the staircase, blocking her entrance with long bladed spears and unsmiling faces. She scrutinized the intricate stone columns and pillars that extended around the base of the great temple, at least as far as she could see. Nestled in between each set of columns was an armed guard, stoic and silent. Perhaps five hundred of them guarded the stone edifice.

She was approached by the ruler of the Ziqqurratu Dynasty and questioned. Claiming to be the leader of a mercenary company looking for work, she was well received and treated to a fine meal and sips from two dozen fruit juices, each exotic and soothing. She had guessed that with their trouble with the witches they would be receptive to her story. When she was done, they answered all her questions.

Years ago, in the Tanshi dynasty, Isayus dreamed of a hero to take care of the world and Sharduq was created. Sharduq left immediately to discover the sphere and explored east, eventually heading south into the jungled peninsula. At that time Ziqqurratu was a collection of villages living in fear of reptiles and barely able to feed their burgeoning population. Sharduq, true to what Isayus had dreamed, protected them.

Muscular and strong, yet wise and patient, he fell in love with humanity. At a time when humans were barely surviving in the steamy jungle – dealing with starvation, combative reptiles, and Hydragators lying in every miasmic pool – he taught them agriculture, metalsmithing, architecture, hand to hand combat, and swordsmanship. His teachings were recorded in a series of nine volumes – books that outlined how to build a fair and balanced civilization in the jungle. The books, called codices, dealt primarily with practical matters and the law.

A gigantic member of the Wusong Clan preyed upon Ziqqurratu at that time, killing and leaving the bodies hung until the skeletons were ready to eat. Sharduq went into battle. He was beaten and retreated, taken in by the people he was trying to protect. Over time they built a steel net to his specifications, and Sharduq returned to battle, this time snaring the Wusong and killing it with his sword.

Sharduq taught them the beginnings of mathematics, irrigation, and architecture. Civilization sprang from his magnificent mind. He could not create, because he was not an ascendant, though he was a great warrior. His battles with the reptiles that sought to displace mankind were the stuff of legend.

Sharduq's laws were carved into stone tablets so that his legal system would remain intact even if he was gone. Citizens argued that the tablets should be reproduced and a copy placed in each village, in the heart of the city, and in meeting places. Many people believed in rule by tablet, arguing that the laws be carved in stone and set about the land.

In the evenings Sharduq stood at one particular spot in the jungle, gazing up, and finally asked that a temple be built there to his specifications. When he went to the top he disappeared, never to return. The temple top became a holy place and strange phenomena occurred there. Strange flying beasts appeared – winged serpents, blue Spinedactyls, and ocean birds of many types. Occasionally rain or clouds appeared at the temple top, the white mist forming out of nothing, and it was considered a miracle.

The very old, the infirm, and those dying of injuries were brought to the temple and they disappeared at the top, just as Sharduq had. It was a great honor to ascend to the firmament to be with such a hero, and many would have made the trip if those controlling access to the temple had allowed it. Soldiers too badly maimed to fight were allowed to go as were those too old to work. Writers too were allowed to go. The reward for producing a great book was permission to ascend to the top to be with Sharduq. No one had ever returned, but the continual appearance of ocean birds out of thin air at that one location was very convincing.

Years later, the first Rang-Wo-Ti appeared. It was found quite by accident that the joining of a human body and an animal head produced unexpected results. The first time an animal head was placed on a fresh corpse, the body rose and the spirit inside it was sagacious, intelligent, and eager to learn about society. It learned their laws and became an arbiter, walking through Ziqqurratu to pass judgments and solve quarrels. The first Rang-Wo-Ti became well known for his compassion and fair rulings, balancing the rule of law with the circumstances behind each case.

More were produced and all were powerful and intelligent. Some of the animal-headed beings studied until they became great thinkers and produced some of Ziqqurratu's most magnificent books. Others were wild and vengeful and had to be killed. It took many soldiers to hunt and slay rogue Rang-Wo-Ti.

No one knew why some were evil and caused great havoc while others were kind and gentle and practiced the art of healing. Some were grateful for the life they have been given while others were wicked and had to be fought the moment they opened their eyes.

As arbiters, the Rang-Wo-Ti ignored Sharduq's teachings and relied on their judgment and instincts. They taught that laws were not absolute, that each situation was different. Often both sides in a dispute felt they had been treated fairly by the animal-headed spirits, increasing the calls for more of them to be made. There developed a clash between citizens that wanted rule by tablet and those that wanted rule by Rang-Wo-Ti. It divided Ziqqurratu and caused much strife.

Some of the Rang-Wo-Ti initiated a new religion that taught that knowledge led to a rewarding afterlife. They claimed that when people died they entered the Realm of Fright and faced challenges, puzzles, trials, military excursions, survival games, and ordeals at the hands of foul and harsh divinities. It was not a punishment. It was a training ground. When the spirit survived such trials in the Realm of Fright, he or she was then reborn into the world, retaining most or all of the new skills they learned while dead. The Rang-Wo-Ti described it as preparation. The new religion only further alienated the citizens of Ziqqurratu, especially the women. Most of them disliked the animal-headed spirits and wanted rule by tablet so that all would be treated equally. When a green leopard-headed Rang-Wo-Ti slew a few women the situation worsened.

Eventually, a woman fled the city and fell in with a walking reptile that had learned dark magic during several decades of study in the dark, gloomy jungle. The woman, an apt pupil, became the first witch and enticed more female citizens to leave the city and join her, leading to the first coven. There were great reserves of untapped power in the jungle, and a few of the more intelligent serpents allied themselves with the women in exchange for protection. The Rang-Wo-Ti outlawed witchcraft and the battle between man and witch began.

Zondela mulled the information over. The jungle frightened her in a way that few things ever had. Figuring she knew how Sharduq had disappeared, she withdrew her telescope. At the top of the pyramid was a vortex, showing bright blue sky and cloud at the extrusion point.

It was difficult to decide if she should explain to the citizens what she had seen. It might ruin their religion, forcing them to question their faith and all that they had worked for. Alternatively, it might explain to their satisfaction what had happened, reinforcing their beliefs. Somehow she doubted a technical explanation of their religion would help them in the end.

The man who had explained the history of Ziqqurratu was still with her. "Can I pray at the temple top?" Zondela asked.

"No. If you went to the center you would be sent to Sharduq. It is our most holy place. Pray at the base with me."

"Thank you," she said. "You said that when one dies, one goes to the Realm of Fright, yet those that go to the temple go to Sharduq."

"A valid point. Those that die do go to the Realm of Fright to be tested, and eventually reborn. Those that go to the firmament from the top of the temple go to where Sharduq is. I'm guessing he is in the firmament."

She nodded, unwilling to destroy his faith and his religion with an explanation of vortexes. Still, she wondered if she was withholding vital information that would help them understand and deal with the world.

"I wish to pray at the top. Can you take me in secret?" she said.

"Perhaps. One of the Rang-Wo-Ti approaches. Let us listen to what it wants."

Zondela turned and rested her hand loosely upon her sword hilt as a creature approached the steps. It had the body of a man and the head of a fierce water-dwelling reptile, with a long green snout full of fangs. It approached on muscular legs, its snout swinging slightly from side to side as it moved.

23

The green croc head blended seamlessly with its pink, male human lower body. The entire thing was naked; it seemed reasonable, if it was an animal spirit inhabiting the body, that it would see little reason for clothing. Red reptilian eyes, couched under a ridge-like brow, flicked over Zondela then turned to bore into the man who had explained the history of Ziqqurratu to her.

The man – named Kinnaris – shivered slightly yet did not retreat from the unwavering gaze. "Ahh, Urqtu, a pleasure, as always. How may I help you?"

"You know what I want," growled the man/reptile hybrid. Its voice was throaty, beast-like, as the animal's lungs and mouth endeavored to shape human words. "I create life today, at the temple top as you have taught me."

Kinnaris looked pained. "Worship of Sharduq does not necessarily imply what you are doing. We should debate this."

"I already have," growled the beast. "I have written at length upon the subject, which you have read. The time for scholarly debate is past; Rang-Wo-Ti serve the Dynasty as well as anyone else." With his human arm, the creature motioned behind itself. People approached with baskets of body parts. Zondela saw three animal heads – a dark purple jungle cat, a snake, and a large hunting bird – and human limbs. Two people carried a corpse between them.

"Urqtu, it is for the sons of Sharduq to create life, not you," said Kinnaris

"And where is it written that Rang-Wo-Ti cannot create further Rang-Wo-Ti?" it responded in its rasping voice. "I am only birthing my own kind."

"Now you argue like one who believes in rule by tablet," Kinnaris countered.

"I do this in the name of Sharduq. He forged this great Dynasty out of the jungle when he slew the prodigious Wusong that prowled these lands, and today I honor him."

"And how," asked Kinnaris in a dry voice, "does this contribute to the glory of Sharduq?"

"The Rang-Wo-Ti worship Sharduq; the more of us there are, the greater the invocation and reverence."

Kinnaris was not pleased. The hybrid's followers had brought up the remains of more than one person. The corpse was of a woman, naked and decapitated, who appeared to have died from a snake bite, judging from the swollen lump on her arm and the characteristic twin puncture wounds. The baskets contained two further sets of arms.

"And what if the Rang-Wo-Ti is dangerous?" Kinnaris asked.

"Then I will dispose of her," replied the beast in a menacing growl, opening its green snout and exposing rows of sharp teeth.

The humans who had walked up with their burdens knelt before Urqtu, prompting Kinnaris to murmur in a hushed, unhappy voice. "They bow before a hybrid."

To Zondela's trained eye it looked like the people held the reptile/human hybrid in awe. She saw the same reverence in their eyes that she had seen in fellow Infernian's eyes when they were in the presence of the Flametars. These people were technically working on behalf of something that other humans had created.

Two of them held the female corpse in a standing position. On the corpse's left, a man placed another arm against its side, creating the illusion that the dead woman had two left arms. Another man did the same on the right side, keeping the bloody stumps in place, and a further man lifted a severed animal's head out of the basket. It was that of a large bird, covered in soft brown fur and with a long yellow beak extending away in a downward curve. She remembered seeing similar birds when she first entered the wet jungle. They had stood in the water on long legs and snapped up fish with their beaks.

The man placed the bird's head on the dead woman's body. Nothing happened. Everyone at the temple top was breathless, even Zondela feeling her heart hammering in her chest. Urqtu knelt in front of the corpse and prayed. His abrasive voice, more reptilian than human, mixed singing with words of praise and veneration. The bird's head opened its eyes and stared. The men beside the new Rang-Wo-Ti stepped away, kneeling as Urqtu rose to his feet.

Zondela, cool and aloof, appraised the new creation. The female corpse had had muscular limbs in life and now flexed her muscles as her bird head breathed deeply. She flexed her four arms, curling her fingers and extending them, moving muscles that had not been active while she had been dead. The new hybrid was calm, leaning back to stretch her spine while extending her four arms as a sleeper would upon awakening. Her skin regained some of its color as dormant blood flowed through her veins once again. Even the snakebite on her arm was healing.

"This is not right," said Kinnaris. "I have read your books and watched while you gained followers. Your desecration threatens to open a whole new front in the war."

"The witches hate you," the reptile-snouted hybrid responded, "they hunt you in the night and slay you with their shrill cries, scorching whole villages with a single Utterance of Annihilation. We can help stop that."

"It is because of you they hate us," Kinnaris said.

"Their contempt for you," said Urqtu, "for your gender, your species, derives from their contempt of weakness. The Rang-Wo-Ti can change that."

"By preventing any possibility of peace with the witches? I hear their howls while I lay in my bed, hoping that their screeches do not stop my heart."

"Then fear no more!" roared Urqtu. "The Rang-Wo-Ti will protect you. We will dig the witches out of their dirt sleeping holes and slay them, turning them into further soldiers for us after we decapitate them."

"This," said Kinnaris, calming slightly as he tried to reason his way through it, "is why so many of us want rule by tablet. When laws are carved in stone, all must obey them. Rule by spirit allows the hybrids far too much freedom, allowing them to shape society as they see fit."

For the first time the new hybrid spoke, her voice much like the singing of a bird. "We will rule well, Kinnaris. Have no fear of that."

That statement changed everything for Zondela. The hybrids had tacitly acknowledged their superiority, or at least their desire for command. Zondela could see a power struggle brewing and had no desire to observe it to its bitter conclusion. Earlier, when she had spoken with Lady Valoc, Zondela had felt the witches were the most awful thing she had ever seen. Those women, letting snakes into their beds and hate into their hearts, had practically allowed themselves to turn into beasts, sleeping below ground and rising to stalk men in the night. Now Zondela was unsure. Perhaps the witches were right to try to topple the leaders of Ziqqurratu and end this strange conjunction of man and animal.

It was not her fight, and she was more interested in Sharduq's disappearance. From Kinnaris's explanations, Zondela figured she knew what had happened. Before the temple was built Sharduq had stood on the ground at the location where he would eventually order the stone monolith constructed, and he had spent much time gazing straight up. He had probably seen the vortex – he was the creation of an ascendant. He may not have known what he was looking at, which would explain why he had not discussed the issue with others. Instead, he had ordered the temple built to a specification that would put the temple top just below the vortex – more evidence that he saw it and did not understand what he was looking at. Exploring it had caused him to step through and disappear. Zondela was determined to find him.

She stood before the line of columns that ringed the great temple. An armed guard stood in the nook between each one, staring passively. She feared to die in combat here, to have an animal head thrust upon her, some beastly spirit inhabiting the beautiful body that she had worked so hard to condition so well.

While the others argued she stepped forward, looking at the warrior that barred her way. He wore well-curved armor that hugged his body and mimicked the slopes of his muscles. He glared at her, his face stoic in the manner of all guards, and held his bladed spear motionless. Zondela appraised him, looking for a weakness, not wanting to kill him yet determined to get through before other guards could intervene. She would have no chance against a wave of armed soldiers; she would have to take advantage of the first few seconds of the crisis when the other men would be slow to react.

At about five paces from him she lowered her shoulder and charged. The guard was not as incompetent as she had hoped; he lowered his spear so that she would impale herself upon it. With a wrist movement she pushed it aside with her brass glove, the blade missing her and the wood shaft banging against her armor.

The guard was knocked off his feet when her shoulder hit him, flung backward by the impact, the air knocked out of his lungs and his rib fractured. Her leg muscles propelled her up the temple steps with such power that she accelerated for several seconds, the other guard's thrown spears falling short and missing her. Most of the towers rising from the various tiers had guards in them as well, many of which were hurling weapons at her. Her velocity leveled off a few seconds later, and her constant speed allowed the men above her to aim their weapons better. She knew, from years of military training on Infernia, to keep her eye on the approaching projectiles and she lifted her armored chin to track the spears coming at her. The spears, having been cast from high ground, were moving fast and she worried that the iron tips would penetrate her armor. She angled the direction of her run, moving diagonally to the right to avoid the cascade of spears. While not every tower was occupied, enough of them were that her run up the steps was under constant fire. She turned her body to the left, avoiding a swarm of spears, then angled to the right to avoid another volley. Her course was never straight, always turning to weave a path between the incoming weapons, her body ducking under spears and turning to the side so that they slid by her smaller profile. She reached the top of the great temple, her lungs heaving from the exertion, guards behind her.

The vortex was in the middle of the flat area, and she had no time to pull out her telescope and verify it. She hustled forward, her sword finding its way into her hand.

Without warning the world around her disappeared. She was in the air, suspended over a raging blue ocean. She plunged downward for a few seconds and struck the water, once again having been deposited by a vortex into the sea. By scissoring her legs she pushed her head above the surface long enough to suck in air. In the distance, about ten minutes swim away was an island. A quick check showed nothing closer so she hauled herself through the water, pulling with her hands and kicking with her feet, steadily bringing herself closer to the island.

Even by kicking hard her body undulated through the water, her head dipping below the surface at the end of a stroke, only coming up as she scissored her legs again. She drank some saltwater until she got her rhythm down, pressing her lips together when her head went below the waves. Several minutes of hard leg work brought her to the island where rocks, windswept trees, and a stone house awaited her arrival. She clambered up on shore, gulls crying overhead.

The island was small. A house built of stones rose in the middle, surrounded by carefully cultivated vegetable gardens. She trudged up, gazing at the workmanship. There appeared to be no mortar, just carefully fitted stones, with mere square gaps for windows. Vegetation grew on top of the house, mostly flowering vines and ripening fruit. Off to the side of the island, near the water, were several stones with carvings on them. She was unfamiliar with the words although they appeared to be Ziqqurratu names.

She stopped, glanced behind her, saw only endless waves of the Restless Ocean in their usual unending travels, and took out her telescope. A scan of the ocean showed the vortex she had just come through with the Ziqqurratu sky visible through it, contrasting with the paler local sky. A sweep of the horizon showed a few vortexes in the distance, one a deep green and the other a fiery red. There was a vortex underwater, something she had never seen before. The outline of the vortex showed clearly in her 'scope. The center of it was the same blue as the surrounding water, probably because the other side of it was filled with the same water that was pouring through it. The extrusion point of that vortex was, undoubtedly, submerged.

With the telescope collapsed and on her hip, she walked up to the house, ignoring the aching protest of her leg muscles yet pleased that the massive physical strain on her since leaving Infernia had put her body in its best condition ever. With a slight smile of vanity, she stood before the door and knocked.

The man that opened it was young, also in good shape, and wearing a tattered white shirt. He had a warrior's build and his eyes seemed full of knowledge beyond his young years. In seconds he had turned away, motioning for her to follow and telling her over his shoulder to come in.

Everything inside looked hand made, from the chiseled stones that had been dragged in to serve as chairs to the large round slab of wood in the center that was a table. The slab still had bark around the outside and the surface had been polished smooth. The cups on top of it were seashells, half full of milk. The walls supported a few paintings that used large dry leaves for canvas. There was another wood stump in one corner, the roots hacked off and the top polished flat with an object resting on top. It looked like a hand-made Salamander game, with a wood board and pieces of white and gray stone.

While she was examining this, and noting that the young man wore a fine sword at his hip with a swept silver hilt, she noticed that a black crystal rested on a small stone pedestal along the opposite wall. That was the crystal she had seen when the oracle showed her how to stop the Flametar invasion; that was the crystal which, when struck with a metal hammer, would emit killing vibrations, and would wreak havoc when mounted on the end of a wood pole. She knew who her host was.

"I am Sharduq, and I welcome you into my home. Are you a writer, having produced some great work to earn the right to follow me into this forsaken waste at such a young age?"

She removed her helmet and wondered how many writers wore brass armor until she realized that sometimes critics were quite harsh. "I am a soldier. I come in search of you Sharduq. I am Zondela."

"Then be seated. It is a difficult life here for me. Most of my companions are old soldiers, or those near death. I rescue as many as I can from the ocean, though most that survive are old and pass away all too quickly. How is Ziqqurratu? Have the Wusong returned to seek out the bones of my people? Is there war with the Tanshi Dynasty?"

Zondela smiled sadly, realizing he had had little or no recent news. "Has it been long since your last visitor?"

"A few years since the last one survived the transition from the temple top to here. I buried him a few moons ago, carving a stone above his grave to commemorate his passage. I would protect all my people from death if I could." He clenched his fist, then met her eyes with his piercing blue ones. "Rest assured, daughter of Ziqqurratu, I will protect you and take care of you."

"Thank you." Her mind formed plans to take possession of the crystal. She decided the truth would have to suffice, even while she wondered if she could defeat in battle a hero who had been created by an ascendant. "Though I can take care of myself."

He nodded, handing her one of the spiral seashells full of sugary nut milk. "Nuts grow on the trees here," he said, "and I crack them open to drain their juice. But you were telling me of Ziqqurratu."

"Yes. They only fought one war with the Tanshi Dynasty long ago, and maintain semi-cordial relations with them. The Wusong seem to have been civilized after their abortive attack upon the Tanshi and no longer threaten humans."

"That is good," he said, settling back on his stone chair. "Many beasts prowl the land, and I turned from hunting them to teaching men in my efforts to bring civilization to Ziqqurratu."

"You were successful," she responded. "Temples rise above the jungle while stone pyramids grace the landscape and give the people an elevated place from which to worship you."

"I did not wish to be worshiped, as I am not an ascendant. I only wanted them to learn from me. It was the only way I could protect such a large number of people, by granting them the gift of civilization."

She thought briefly of the Flametars and how their primary concern had been to breed warriors. "Legend tells that you were sired by Isayus. Is it true?" she asked.

"Yes. My first memory was of opening my eyes and seeing the stars above and a crystal city around me. I rose from the sand and gazed upon the land that I had been born into. Only later, speaking with brothers of Isayus who had traveled to find me, did I learn how I had been created."

"Isayus had dreamed of you," she said.

"Yes, and thus I was born. I had an insatiable urge to explore the world and my wanderings led me to Ziqqur-ratu."

"They still tell stories of your battle with the gigantic Wusong," she said.

"The slaying of the Wusong marked the birth of civilization there, in that I was able to spend my time teaching, building, and creating instead of fighting."

She glanced around the house at all the handmade objects. "You create like an ascendant," she said, speaking metaphorically.

"Thank you. My people, do they flourish? Are they prosperous?"

"Things are not entirely well. Witches rule the night, sleeping by day underground. They rail against the walk of the Rang-Wo-Ti, the conjunction of animal heads and human bodies, which have shown the first stirrings of a lust for power."

Sharduq's handsome face looked troubled. "If only I was not stranded here, a victim of whatever dark miracle sends travelers from the temple to this location."

"It is not a miracle, it's a vortex. I can see them. I have traveled far through them in the early years of my life when I was a soldier of the Flametars."

He looked at her, his gaze piercing, his body tense, and alert. "Can you see this vortex that deposited us here?"

"It hangs above the sea, making it almost impossible to build anything beneath that would be tall enough."

"That explains why I could not find a way to return home," he said.

"Did you see the vortex," she asked, "many years ago? They say you stood on the ground and looked up, and asked that a temple be built there, the first such pyramid. Were you able to see the vortex?"

"No. I noticed birds appearing in the air at that spot, materializing without a sound and flying on without any reaction. I thirsted to understand what I was seeing. To this day old men and women are brought to the temple and pushed through to appear over the water here. Few survive. I have been responsible for the deaths of many of my own people."

"There is another vortex nearby which we can take, although I do not know where it goes. The vortex above Ziqqurratu was about a bow-shot above the ground, and the exit on this side is the same height above the seafloor. I'm guessing if we take the other vortex just under the water's surface, the extrusion point will also be just under the water."

"So it could strand us in the middle of the ocean then?" he asked.

"Yes," she said, "If we throw some wood through first we will have something to float on when we get to the other side. Sinxin, the Restless Ocean, and the two strata are riddled with vortexes like a piece of old cheese."

"There is no wood on this island large enough for us to float on. Can we not return through vortex if need be?" he asked.

"Yes," she replied.

"I shall gather my belongings then, and we will be off."

"Not before I receive the black crystal from you. I came here to retrieve it."

"I cannot give it to you," he responded. "It is a relic, the result of a lightning strike in the Obsidian Desert to the east. It has kept me alive here. When struck with a metal object, the ring kills all near it. I fish with it by leaving it in the water and striking it with a piece of metal on the end of a rod."

"That is similar to what the Flametar army will do when they take it from you," she said, controlling her impatience. "Let me have it in exchange for taking you off this island."

"No," said Sharduq. "It belongs to the people of Ziqqurratu and will help protect them from the predations of the jungle. I cannot give it to you."

"I will show you the vortex out of here when you give me the crystal."

"Then we will grow old together," he said, "while I swim in gradually expanding circles around the island in an effort to locate this vortex."

She shrugged slightly, not wanting to admit defeat yet unwilling to give up. "I noticed a game of Salamanders on the pedestal over there," she said, keeping her voice casual. "Do you play?"

"Yes," he said. "I carved the white pieces from the flesh of large nuts, and the gray pieces from sea coral. I have longed to find an opponent with skill at 'manders."

"Then let us play," she said, "Your crystal against my telescope. That is how I locate vortexes. If you win, you will be able to do so as well."

He thought about it for a minute before picking up his handcrafted board and setting it upon the table between them. Wordlessly they collected their pieces and played.

There was no dice, just skill in set-up and execution, which made it her favorite game. He placed a piece in the center of the board and she countered by placing a piece next to it. His other pieces, one by one, were set down evenly throughout the board, covering the important squares yet unable to protect each other. Zondela, much like she had done in real battles when still a Penturian, placed her pieces adjacent to each other, giving up strategic positions in exchange for being able to have her pieces cover each other.

The start of the game saw Sharduq launch slashing passes from across the board, allowing him to select any target yet not able to muster powerful strikes. Zondela, instead of attacking, moved her pieces adjacent to each other to provide a more potent defense when Sharduq struck at them. In the end, she had two pieces left and was able to slay his Royal Salamander and win the game.

He took his defeat with grace and equanimity, rising and presenting the black crystal to her. She slipped it into her pouch next to the Chalice, with a cloth between them to prevent the cup from banging the crystal.

"You have done a noble thing," she said. "This crystal would have been used against the people of the sphere by the Invading Flametar army."

She explained everything, from her early training on Infernia to her revelations when in contact with the oracles. Sharduq decided that he too would consult the oracles.

"We still must survive the trip through the vortex and locate our bearings on the other side," she explained.

"What are your plans then, daughter?"

"I must find the last oracle, which so far has eluded me. Its location has been lost long ago," she said.

"It is underwater, lost to the surface since a cataclysmic upheaval slid part of the coastline under the sea. Now it rests on the bottom, giving advice and knowledge to the undersea Dynasties. The Restless Ocean houses a great deal of life, much of it developing an intellectual capacity to rival those on land."

"And where is it headed?" she asked.

"Their architecture may one day sprawl across the bottom of the ocean, or perhaps they will look upon the surface with envy in their lidless eyes."

"Interesting," said Zondela. "Perhaps I will start emptying my bladder in the sea from now on."

Sharduq smiled and collected a few of his personal belongings and they left the house together, Sharduq carefully shutting the door behind him. She let him look through the telescope and he agreed that there was not nearly enough stone with which to build a tall enough tower, especially since the base would have to be constructed underwater. He memorized the location of the underwater vortex and then handed the scope to Zondela, who stared for several minutes from her position on the beach. While waves lapped at her feet, she tried to discern the extrusion point of the vortex; she saw nothing other than water through it. With the 'scope firmly held in her right hand, she entered the water, wading up to her chest in the warm, frothy sea. Sharduq walked behind her so that they would not be separated if she suddenly went through.

Another glance through the finely ground lenses of her relic showed her close to her destination. She swam forward, kicking up spray with her feet since she had to thrust hard to keep her armored body afloat. She turned her head and spoke. "It's right below us."

It was easy to let herself sink. She had aimed well; a second later the world changed. Bright light stabbed her eyes and her head was above water, only her lower body submerged.

She stood in a wide pool at the top of a mountain, surrounded by a gushing torrent of water from the invisible vortex. The water cascaded down its face in a sparkling stream. White billowing clouds hung in the sky and a flock of pink reptiles slowly drifted through them. The mountain slope was home to a thick forest, many of the trees ripe with large fruit. The water streaming down its face was contained in a rocky ravine and splashed downward to enter an irrigation system on the ground. Amid the green fields below were rectangular houses, many of them with silos overflowing with golden grain. Sharduq stood beside her in silence.

24

The atomic lifeblood of the Ultimate Machine ran hot and its silver skin radiated heat. Rocks melted and the valley walls turned to smooth, glassy slag. It rose to avoid being damaged by the molten rock. Self-repair was risky and such augmentations often had random consequences. It feared that self modifications were slowly making it insane.

Rage and hate consumed it. The Zondela virus had infected its plans, breaking them down and scattering them to the solar winds. The Machine hung motionless as it strove to understand how such an insignificant, short-lived biomass could impede its plans. It extrapolated the results of its actions against her and watched the simulations of her suffocating, burning, and falling to her death. Electricity flowed through the fiber-optic nerve endings of the Machine as it experienced great pleasure.

Such extrapolations were only simulations. The Ultimate Machine looked into the future and saw her struggling against its plans; a rush of hate filled its veins. Some of the soft flexible conduits in its body ruptured. The less flexible, metal conduits were forced to carry a larger load while the Machine ran self-repair programs.

There was a Hatetar nearby, invisible and bodiless. It drank the anger and rage that flowed from the Ultimate Machine as its systems were pushed to the limit. The Hatetar manifested inside the Ultimate Machine like a parasite or an emotional barnacle. Cables, wires, circuits, and gears were twisted within the bowels of the Machine from the sheer willpower of the Hatetar as it formed a body for itself. It clung to the organs of the Machine like a cancer, its sinister grin visible within the metal.

The Machine's self-repair systems intervened and eliminated the pulsing, growing malignancy that drank power from it. The Ultimate Machine had originally created the Hatetars in the hopes that they would foster strife and bloodshed among the inhabitants of the sphere.

The Machine exterminated the Hatetar and absorbed the flow of power when the hate-fed canker was destroyed. By opening its memory banks the Machine relived ancient memories while it cooled its rage and internal temperature.

Eons ago – on a distant sphere – the Ultimate Machine had created a magnificent race. While the Machine waited in orbit the biological units had thrived and mastered technology, developing a great civilization and covering their sphere with a sprawling complex of buildings, gardens, and temples. The peace-loving people created vast centers of learning and culture. Their solar-powered ships of gold and silver voyaged into the void in search of their creator, the Ultimate Machine. They worshiped it as they worshiped all machines. To them, iron and silicon were godly materials and the sounds of synchronized cogs were the music of heaven. They longed to be close to their patron deity.

Anger and hate pulsed through its flexible conduits when it gazed down at them, unable to destroy them because of its original programming, only able to set in motion long range plans for their death. Destroying an entire species took time. It moved to the next closest world, a sphere that orbited the same star, and flew low over the barren rock.

Soon, despite the birthing pains, it had covered the sphere in foliage, grass, and moist greenery. It created a race of amoeboid creatures. The new arrivals had their own planet since they would need time to develop into killers.

The amoeboids could survive in very hostile environments. Their membrane protected them from heat, cold, radiation, and high pressure. Physically they were tough yet they needed something more if they were going to be the Machine's instrument of destruction. It instilled them with its own hatred and malevolence as well as a compelling desire to learn and build.

At first, it had seemed that the Machine had been too successful with its new creation. The amoeboids thrived on the world and were effective at destroying themselves. The primitive generations used their pseudopodia to thrash their fellow beings to death. Future generations used crude weapons to tear through the membrane of their comrades and drain their internal fluids. On most continents, they wiped themselves out before they reached the age of machines. In a few areas where other sentient life had developed, the amoeboids hated others more than themselves. They banded together and wiped out the others with passion and violence. Lusting to find other races to destroy, they developed science, engineering, and machinery to build vessels that would take them to neighboring planets like a virus looking for healthy cells to infect.

After many years the amoeboids found the sailing ships of the benevolent race. The slaughter was simple. The amoeboids bombed their cities and cracked their planet, sending the atmosphere to drift in the void. The benevolent race had no means to defend themselves, having neither weapons nor skills in warfare. Their civilization passed from existence having never known that it was their patron deity that had planned their destruction.

Once they were unopposed, the amoeboid creatures returned to their primitive instincts and fought amongst themselves. Within a few short centuries, both planets were devoid of life. Shortly after that, the Ultimate Machine felt the irresistible pull to travel through the void in search of new planets and it did so with pleasure shivering through its circuits.

The memories were satisfying, so the Machine replayed the scenes of destruction several times, knowing that it would eventually add memories of having exterminated Zondela.

Its systems having returned to normal, it again contemplated the problem of the Zondela virus. She had to be killed; the sphere could not be allowed to grow uncontrollably. A look into the future revealed that the Flametars would perform the same role as the amoeboid creatures. Eventually, they would create machines of their own, some of them in the likeness of the Ultimate Machine and they would burn the entire sphere. The only uncertainty in the equation was Zondela.

The cold empty silence of the void called to it again. It could leave now and start anew somewhere else. The void was boundless and it had lingered here in this valley too long, yet it resisted the pull in order to decimate the sphere before it left. Knowing it did not have much time left, the Machine created again. Blue lightning arced and flared below it as it gave birth to a new breed of superior hunters.

25

Zondela stood waist deep in a pool at the top of a mountain, Sharduq at her side. Water came through the invisible vortex, forming the pool, and cascaded down the slope. The people below would have some ideological or spiritual explanation for the water that flowed mysteriously from the top of the mountain to feed their crops.

Her old Flametar masters had explained to her the concept of vortexes, removing forever her inclination to attribute such natural wonders to the ascendants. Non-Infernians had no such scientific background.

She debated bringing science into their lives then discarded the notion. One day she would write a book about her experiences, including in it the theories of evolution and microscopic life that she had been taught, as well as her experiences fighting Hatetars and trying to stop a war that would not start for several thousand years. Ultimately the people reading it would consider her insane and probably try to kill her. Such was the price of fame.

It was a short walk down the cultivated mountain and when she reached the bottom five people awaited her. They held only wood spears – which would not penetrate her armor – and made up for it in scowls and grimaces. They had little to distinguish themselves from the other villagers she had seen of the sphere, with loose, dusty robes and faces creased from years of toil. Zondela introduced herself and they conversed.

They had thought her a beast spirit when they had seen her appear at the Celestial Stream and descend on foot. Only when she conversed with them had they relaxed. She told them she sought the ocean and they pointed to the east. The Celestial Stream was an important part of their beliefs, and Zondela was careful not to take advantage of that, claiming only that she had climbed up the mountain from the other side during the night.

The townspeople invited her and Sharduq into their home where the table was set with bowls of roasted meat, smoked fish, plates of cheese, and vases of bright red fruit. The matron of the house pushed down on the top of the vase, forcing fruit juice out of a spigot at the bottom, allowing the diners to refill their drinks as they wished. Dessert consisted of large bowls of ground nuts, mixed with sugar and honey. It was a fine repast and when dinner was over, discussions began.

They asked her where she came from and evinced little surprise when she answered. She found out that an Infernian had come through a year ago and taught them to make Minor Ascendants. Zondela's mouth was set in a grim line as she listened to the story, while beside her Sharduq was composed, motionless and silent.

"How is a Minor Ascendant made?" she asked.

"By taking clay or stone, and fashioning a distorted image. We worship it, and the Minor Ascendant takes his rightful place inside it, or so they say."

Zondela probed delicately. The Infernian soldier had urged them to build and serve a Minor Ascendant, worshiping it in exchange for special powers. It had brought the people night vision, relief from wounds and sickness, and occasionally the ability to see into men's hearts to know their true nature. Each person accepting such gifts suffered in some fashion, such as a lengthening of the nails into talons, bouts of wild anger, or the weeping of bloody tears. There were arguments; the elders taught that the sacred waters of the Celestial Stream, which had kept their crops watered and their vases full since the founding of the settlement, were all that was needed. Others wanted the powers granted to them by the stone idol, the strengthening of limbs, and the quickness of reflex that might come from bowing before the Minor Ascendant.

The stone idol, which she knew was a Hatetar, had gathered followers and taken over a section of the desert. As she learned that the Hatetar's name was Ro-Zonda she fell silent. This was the evil spirit she had created when she had been betrayed in her youth and her anger had almost overflowed into violence.

Most people in the village worshiped the Celestial Stream. They believed the water that streamed from the mountain top to be a sign that the ascendants had chosen this site for habitation and hence were unwilling to abandon the land to follow the Minor Ascendants. A small skirmish had occurred, with the idol followers fighting those that worshiped the Celestial Stream. Zondela said nothing, unwilling to wipe out their religion by explaining the true nature of the undersea vortex, especially if it might mean strengthening the followers of the Hatetars.

The idol had retired to the north, their followers building a temple near the shore where all who desired to could worship the floating stone figures in exchange for giving up part of their humanity. Zondela spoke, explaining that the idols were Hatetars, nothing more than ugly receptacles for incorporeal spirits who fed upon hate and anger. The people at the table nodded, recounting their own similar experiences, and shaking their heads as they remembered how others of their village had abandoned farm, land, and family to worship and serve the insensate stones.

One of the men at the table asked Zondela about the Celestial Stream, and whether the ascendants released the water from the firmament to supply their needs, as their religion taught. She hesitated before explaining that it was indeed a gift, one that might not last forever. She advised them to build a granary and store their harvests for future needs. Vortexes were rarely permanent.

Long ago a young man had ventured to the top of the mountain and disappeared, having been extruded into the water on the other side and saved by Sharduq. Silent until now, Sharduq recounted every story the young man had told him, giving details about the personal lives of every person at the table. The man had died a few years ago, old and gray. The listeners were pleased to know that he had lived for decades with Sharduq, swimming, and fishing on the sandy island, the two men fast friends.

As evening approached she voiced a desire to be on her way. They filled Zondela's pack with food. She unfolded her map and they placed a dot to mark her current location, which showed her what a staggering distance she had traveled by vortex, and they marked the location of the Hatetar temple that had seduced so many of their people. She promised to look into it, and as she clicked her brass helmet on, she thought she saw hope in their eyes as if they trusted her to overthrow the temple and return their wayward brethren to them.

She and Sharduq left, walking into the sunset, ducking

underneath arbors that were heavy with grapes and yellow fruit. Zondela wondered what lure could pull men away from such an abundant yield, drawing them to worship misshapen stones instead of living off the land. There would have to be a law one day prohibiting the sculpting of any idols, with soldiers discouraging people from worshiping such vile and seductive spirits.

"Where are we headed?" asked Sharduq, who walked beside her.

"To topple that temple."

During the walk she learned more of the hero Sharduq, a man both intelligent and good-hearted. He had ruled Ziqqurratu with an even hand while he resolved disputes with reason and sound laws rather than violence. Zondela questioned him on his battles. His tactics were solid and his stories interesting. Just when the conversation turned to his encounter with the Wusong from long ago, he changed the subject.

"I must return to Ziqqurratu, Zondela. My people need me. Your description of the witches and the Rang-Wo-Ti has me concerned."

Zondela sighed, wondering why she continually lost those with whom she developed friendship. "I understand. It was evident to me that open war was close at hand. The witches hunt the men at night while the Rang-Wo-Ti plan to destroy them in the hopes of gaining control of Ziqqur-ratu."

"Thus I must leave. Do you know the way to Ziqqur-ratu?"

She reached into her pack and pulled out her map. Gingerly she unfolded it, treating it like an ancient tome, and showed him the route.

Sharduq nodded. "I have traveled the land before. The

journey shall be easy for me." He squinted, looking closer at her map. "This is most impressive. I have seen nothing like it before. You have the entire landmass detailed, including most of the oracles, major cities, and vortexes. Have you visited all these places?"

"Yes." Pride welled up in her. Crafting her map was a pleasure, like tending to her armor. "My quest has taken me to a great many places. Some of them are not even on the sphere. I have separate maps for those."

"I see," he said. "Where do you head now?"

"There is still one oracle that I have not visited. The sixth oracle said it was lost and that you were the last person to know of its location. I need to visit it. I hope that it can give me some vital information to prevent the war of the future. Can you tell me where it is?"

"The seventh oracle was lost some time ago. There was a major shift in the land which caused the sea to rush in and bury it. I can show you approximately on your map. It is located here." Sharduq pointed to a large bay on the northern coast of the continent. Zondela penned her symbol for an oracle there.

"Are there any landmarks near it?" Zondela asked.

"A broken, crumbling tower rests on the shore opposite the location of the oracle."

"How many bow-shots out to sea is it?" she asked.

"One or two. You could always seek out one of the Wusong to aid you. It is reputed that the Wusong can take a person safely below the waves, although I have no great love for their kind. Failing that you could use your Sea Globe."

"What?" she asked.

He pointed to her left belt pouch and she produced the glass sphere she had picked up in Glacia. Inside it appeared to hold an entire ocean. She had only stared into it twice and both times had felt like she was about to be engulfed in great waves.

"I sensed its power," said Sharduq. "May I see it?"

She handed him the glass bauble that appeared to hold an ocean in it. "Be careful, Sharduq. If you stare too long in it you will find yourself in the ocean, unable to come back to reality."

He glanced in it then looked away. "I felt myself drawn into it and surrounded by water. Interesting." He handed the relic back. "It was created by the ascendant Tanshi. After he flooded the desert with his writing, he created this relic so that his people could easily navigate their way through the waves. The sphere has the power to force water aside, spreading the waves to allow passage. After the Great Cracking, when the water drained away and the land became a desert again, there was less need for it. Eventually, it became lost, until now. I wonder how it ended up on Glacia. Hold it in front of you and concentrate on forcing the waters aside with your mind. The waves should stay parted for an entire morning, though its power is weakened. It may last less than that. With this, you could hunt Wusong or drain lakes to search for ship-wrecks and treasure. You have done well. Now, what of this war that you spoke of earlier? Did you mean a war between the witches and the Rang-Wo-Ti?" he asked.

"No, I meant the Infernian invasion. I've dedicated myself to stopping it."

"Then you follow a noble quest," replied Sharduq.

She paused before replying, avoiding Sharduq's eyes. "Will you remain with me? Let us complete my quest together."

"No. We must all bear our own burdens. The trees must give shade to those that need shelter from the sun and the wise must share their wisdom with the world. I must save Ziqqurratu from itself and you must stop this terrible war."

After a short lunch together they parted ways. She did not try to change his mind again. He had not seen the Flametar war through the eyes of the oracles as she had and she could not describe the things she had seen. Ziqqurratu called to him, beckoning him home to once again take up the mantle of leader of his people. He was, after all, a hero.

If he did bring peace and unity to Ziqqurratu then he would make an excellent ally against the Infernians when they invaded with their army. If Sharduq's rule was wise then it would also reduce the number of Hatetars taking hold in the sphere, making the Infernian invasion more difficult.

She walked. The ground was barren, full of rocks and debris, riddled with cracks from long weeks without rain. A few desiccated tyrant snakes stalked her, their dry tongues rasping in a pathetic attempt to intimidate her before they died under her blade, their reptilian snouts breathing vile curses at her in the prosaic language as they expired. Land sharks circled her a few times, only their fins protruding above the dry landscape until she rammed her sword into the ground, sending the rest of the pack onto the wounded one.

A hot night came and went. As usual, she walked alone.

As she crested a hill the next day she was intercepted by a small group of people, each with a sword in their belts. Their mangled physical appearance identified them as worshipers of the Hatetars.

One man had eyes that were bloodshot and red, perhaps because of the uncontrollable twitching of the eyeballs. Another man had a feline tail. A woman in the group had oversized fangs that cut into her lip and drew a trickle of blood. Some had green jungle-cat eyes while another man had horns protruding from all over his body. A man with curved nails extending from his fingers spoke first. "Who are you? Why are you here? Speak or suffer."

Zondela, confident and encased in her armor, felt little concern. "I have been exiled from the place of my birth, and I have no home. My name is Zondela. While my sword is silent, it can ring to life if need be. I seek the lord of the temple." She had heard that sometimes the Hatetars gifted their faithful with the ability to read thoughts or intentions, and she hoped none here had that ability.

"Which lord is that?"

"I wish to kneel at the base of Ro-Zonda."

"Come."

26

They topped the last hill and Zondela stopped. She gazed upon the Hatetar temple and felt a physical sensation flow through the air; it made her cold, scared, as if some hideous evil lurked there that could only be felt.

The square temple was built of pillars, five on each side with an open space in the center where the head of a long-dead Wusong hung from unseen wires. The stone pillars supported a line of rectangular stones that ran the entire top of the temple, leaving the center open to the air and creating an impressive structure of great weight. Years ago during a daydream, she had imagined just such a temple, down to the specific placement of the columns. Obviously, the Ro-Zonda had seen it in her mind and dictated the plans to its followers.

Each of the pillars had strange carvings – runic inscriptions not in the prosaic tongue nor any language she had seen. People sat or knelt around the temple, carving with hammers and chisels, praying, resting, or writing in books. Here was the enemy, a temple dedicated to the worst spirits that roamed the invisible pathways of the world, a group of beings that granted powers to those that served their miserable ends.

She walked forward, the eyes of the others upon her, her brain already flipping through battle strategies. Should she fight now, while she held some remnants of surprise? It would perhaps be advisable to lay sword strokes into each of the followers around her, massacring them before pitting herself against the awful heat and terror of the Hatetar. Alternatively, she could continue the ruse, getting in closer, taking out the enemy when the opportunity presented itself.

Her escorts fell back, allowing her to drift forward into that strange, thick air of anxiety and unease that surrounded the temple. There was no indicator in the air to mark the moment she stepped into that psychic aura, though she felt it. The tiny hairs on her neck stood up, her heart pounded against the restraints of her rib cage and a strange emotion entered her brain – a mix between righteous anger at some unnamed injustice and dark brooding over some old injury. She knew from past experience that it was the work of the Hatetar to whom this temple was dedicated. The aura was oily and pervasive, emotional instead of physical. It was a subliminal effect like walking into an invisible cloud of unpleasantness.

She entered the temple and found her head clearing, as if she was shrugging off the effects or developing a psychic immunity to it. The temple's interior was well carved. Each stone bore carvings and intricate runes from the unknown language. Before her, the pale skull of the dead Wusong hung in the air. She looked for the thin wires that it should have hung from – there were none. There was no pole that it was mounted upon. The skull floated in the air, for the skull was the Hatetar. With its empty eye sockets and jagged teeth still protruding from the bony jaw, it was ugly enough to serve as a vessel for the hostile spirit.

The skull rotated to face her. A dull fire glinted in the

eyes, a flickering red flame that seemed to take her measure as the skull faced her. "Ahh, Zondela." The skull's voice was deep and unpleasant, sending a strange vibration through her teeth. "You have come. I am Ro-Zonda, Lord of this temple."

She thought hard about how to play this one. This was her creation, the residue of her hate. Zondela remembered, long ago, her anger when she had been betrayed and the young man she loved had selected another. The other woman had been weak, under-developed, skinny, and unskilled in combat. Zondela pushed the thoughts from her head to avoid reliving those memories. She had grown since then, and the hurt was only a small ache. "I am Zondela, and I come to pledge my sword to your service if your gifts can sway me."

"Zondela," it rumbled, "This sacred place will need a Sentinela, a female guard, to defend my followers and protect what we have built here."

Beneath the brass helm, her eyebrow went up. "I'm not sure that is the position for a warrior such as I."

"It is an ancient position, one given only to very select females. In the old world, the Sentinela ruled beside the Lord. She could select a mate at will and kill without explanation, as her mood urged her. The position began as a female sentinel and changed over the years as the Lords often fell in love with their female guards."

"And why would you offer me this?" she asked.

The jaw of the Wusong skull opened and closed, the serrated teeth interlocking and then pulling away again. "You have great strength in you and a keen mind."

"I'm not sure the price of entering the cult is worth it," she said, hoping to buy time and worm her way further into the temple.

"There is no price; I will make you stronger than you are now. Your eyes will see in the dark, your arm will cast spears through an enemy, and your glance will make men tremble."

"It already does," she said.

"Serve me, and you will come into great powers, developing your mind as well as your body. It will be the next stage in your evolution." Its deep voice was seductive with the promise of power.

"Perhaps. I would need to know what my obligations are."

The skull turned away and she glanced behind her. Many of the followers of the Hatetar watched her, most of them with weapons in their belts. She pondered whether she should fight them all, risking everything on one wild battle, then realized that she had no way to defeat the Hatetar itself. Submerging it in water might work; they were close to the ocean. The open-topped temple was a strong indicator that rain, at least, would not harm the idol.

"Zondela, you would stay at my side, defending me against the threats to our rule. We can conquer Sinxin, with you to protect me, and you will die of old age long before the Flametar war occurs."

She stared at the skull before her, tilting her head back to maintain eye contact as it rose higher. The voice from the skull issued forth again, the flames in the eye sockets burning brighter. "Mine is an ancient race, Zondela. I drifted on the winds of this world for years, watching. I know all about your noble deeds."

"Mine is an old race as well," she said. "We are born with bodies with which we can do great things. You need us to worship you before you receive a body of your own."

A great howling issued from the skull and it vibrated,

the jaw opening and snapping shut twice. "You have courage, woman. I have not inhabited this lovely bone to serve others. Long have I roamed the invisible world, waiting for my kind to take their rightful place, waiting for my chance."

"The war which comes," she said, "though it is far off, will slay us all. The Flametars will ignite the sphere and run wild in ruin."

The tooth-filled jaw of the dead Wusong snapped shut once more. "When my body is destroyed, I can inhabit another, returning to physical form when a worshiper bows before me. It is an act of creation that anyone can perform, rivaling even the ascendants."

"What is it like to have no body?" she asked. "Is it cold?"

"No. There is no temperature, just thick clouds of lovely anger during times of war, heavy drifts of it to mark the passage of humans. Your thoughts betray you, human, even now. I sense you would enjoy some killing even as we speak."

"I was raised as a soldier," she said.

"And a soldier you will be again. Guard my new body, lead my followers, skirmish occasionally with villages. I will grow strong and reward you. Serve me and you will bathe in pools of blue water and drink from urns of nectar. There will be great battles to be won, and periods of wild luxury in between."

Zondela was tempted, swayed by the words, yet unwilling to betray her quest and abandon her efforts to one day find the legendary city of Fushang. Still, she knew the fierce power of Hatetars and could not think of any way to kill one. She was toying with the idea of leaving and returning a month later with a small army of any villagers that she could muster together.

"If you help me fight the Flametars, I will serve you," she lied.

"It should not be difficult. Before I gained this fine body I saw a hunter following your spoor, sent by the great one to destroy you as it would do to everything. We have time to prepare. Take command of my followers, teach them to duel with the sword, fashion some shields for them if you wish, and send them into battle when the Machine's assassins arrive."

"Why does the Ultimate Machine hunt me?"

"I do not know. Even the Flametars hunt you now. When battle arrives, your place will be at my side while our followers wage war for us."

Zondela nodded, distracted by the revelation that her old masters were trying to kill her. She glanced up at the sky, hoping to see the distant brass speck that would be Infernia. Clouds blocked her vision. "I'll train them. I will serve you if my place in your temple is as pleasing as you suggested."

She trained with the men and women for some time, keeping her armor and helmet on and sharing with them the intricacies of blocking sword strokes and thrown spears and expert ways to stalk and kill. If she used her command voice they obeyed although some sulked and others acted strangely, especially the ones with physical deformities. Many had elongated claws instead of hands, or horns growing out of elbows and knees, or snake tongues that flicked out of their mouths to taste the air. Zondela tried to focus on the training yet found herself distracted by the deformities and by her need to plan out an assault on the Hatetar.

There were thirty-one servants of the idol who bore weapons. Of the rest she was unconcerned. Fighting thirty-one soldiers in a fair fight was not something she felt confident doing; many of their swords were finely made of tempered iron, easily able to tear through brass plate. There was the problem of how to defeat a Hatetar who could probably disable her with the heat and anguish that would be rolling off it in waves once it felt threatened. Even if her blade could penetrate the skull of the Wusong, the Hatetar would scorch her before she could finish it. She took stock of her possessions, going over in her mind the different options until a plan came to her. All that was required was to reduce the number of armed followers who milled about the temple – she had a plan.

She walked back between two pillars and entered the sacred area, the eyes of the floating skull upon her. As if she was not quite trusted, many of the men she had been training followed her. "Ro-Zonda," she said to the skull, "if I am being hunted, we are all at risk. We need to post guards. Could you send five men to hold sentry atop that hill?" She gestured with her hand to a nearby rise in the ground. The skull nodded so she gave the order and the men moved out. "I'll need five others to place in various locations around the temple. We need advance warning of any approach." She selected several more men and they moved out, sullen and uncommunicative. There were still twenty-one armed followers left, too many for her battle. She wondered if she should try to send out more, yet hesitated to make such a clumsy and obvious move.

"You," she said to one of the females, a surly, under-fed woman with a long sword and reptilian, slitted eyes. "I expect you to pledge your blade to me. As I serve Ro-Zonda, so you shall serve me."

The woman nodded, saying nothing.

"Come," said Zondela in her command voice, sweat beading her forehead. "Hold your sword close to your hip, hilt toward me, blade behind you, and approach. Kneel before me in this manner and pledge your obedience."

The woman did so, smiling for the first time in a faint, forlorn way as she knelt before Zondela and swore an oath of loyalty. Was the woman eager to find a cause to serve, or simply lonely? Zondela didn't know and hoped to spare this skinny, sad female who had made the mistake of worshiping a corrupt spirit.

Zondela waited. If she tipped her hand all would be lost. Minutes passed; sweat trickled down her face. The reptilian skull that housed the Hatetar spoke. "You owe me the same, Zondela."

She drew her sword, careful to keep her eyes lowered in a submissive manner, and approached with her great brass weapon held close to her hip, the blade sticking out behind her. She expected to feel the searing heat of the Hatetar's attack as she walked up to the floating skull and knelt before it.

"I pledge my blade to –" she said, willing her heart to quiet its wild beatings and her muscles to relax. The bottom of her sword hilt, a triangular shape that tapered to a tip, was a relic, forged by the master artisans of Infernia so that she could shatter Icetars.

She whipped the pyramid-shaped hilt up into the underside of the floating skull and it shattered bone just as well as ice. The Hatetar broke apart, a gush of heat escaping simultaneous with a shriek of pure anger as the cranial shards fell to the ground, a stinking green gas pouring out. Zondela pushed herself to her feet, reversed her blade so she could defend herself, and put her back to a stone pillar.

Armed men rushed her, wailing in loss or anger, and she was forced to kill, flicking away their sword strokes and decapitating them with quick movements. Others merely looked at their clawed hands, examining the gifts that the idol had given them as if awakening from a dream and realizing they had been changed. One man – with curved ram's horns protruding from his head – drew a bow and fired at her. She brought the edge of her blade against the hurtling shaft, shattering it, and ran him down to skewer him before he could release another arrow. The other followers drifted away, some crying, most in a state of shock. The one person who neither walked away nor attacked her was the woman who had pledged loyalty to Zondela only minutes ago.

The unhappy, skinny female looked up at Zondela, waiting, saying nothing.

They were alone. Zondela took her helmet off and frowned down at the shorter woman. "Where are you from?"

"The village of the Celestial Stream," she answered in a murmur. "My name is Saltika."

"Then return there with me, and teach others never to worship an idol. The Hatetars offer gifts yet give only strife and grief. Peace and fellowship among mankind is the true path."

The woman nodded. "I think," said Saltika, "that I will only serve flesh and blood from now on. Let us return home and I will warn others. I swore an oath to you and I will honor it."

While walking back to the village they were set upon by a pack of armored cat women – half feline and half woman, clad in iron hauberks and copper chainmail. Zondela and Saltika fought as one, covering each other, slicing through the shields of their opponents and protecting each other's backs.

After the battle, landsharks circled, only their fins showing above ground. They pulled the corpses below ground and consumed them. The two women stood on a rock, grinning, panting from the battle, and Zondela became convinced she had seen Saltika somewhere in the past though she could not place it.

Since they were close to the village they walked through the night, moonlight bringing a silver glow to the landscape. The two women were set upon by a flying reptile with wings of orange gossamer. The nocturnal beast – ravenous and large, easily weighing as much as ten people – knocked Zondela aside and lifted Saltika off the ground. Zondela leaped into the air and instead of grabbing the beast, she severed its legs with a fine sword stroke, sending Saltika tumbling to the ground. The wounded beast – still snapping at them with tooth-filled snout – landed and died under a quick blow from her brass sword, its severed neck leaking a liquid that shone bright blue in the moonlight.

Saltika asked Zondela about her background and where she learned to fight. Zondela kept the details vague, explaining only that she had been a commander at one time and that she had trained all her life. Again, the younger woman's face seemed familiar somehow though Zondela could not place her.

Saltika had led soldiers at one time. Before her seduction by the Wusong skull, Saltika had led a group of mercenaries and armed villagers between the two great Dynasties, hunting beasts and searching for treasure. Her stories were interesting and her motivation questionable as Saltika seemed to prefer glory and coin to honor. Still, the young woman was pleasant company.

They returned to the village as the morning sun bathed the inhabitants in a hot wind. Saltika spoke to the entire village, explaining the true nature of the Hatetars and of Zondela's magnificent sword work. "Let me lead you," said Saltika. "I will ensure that our village is never threatened again."

The village was pleased with Saltika's return. No longer depressed, the young woman was well liked and charismatic; she was a natural leader and was careful to paint Zondela's actions in heroic terms.

The young woman looked up at Zondela. "Will you stay and help us rebuild? Even with me as leader we will require your sword skill and world knowledge."

Zondela looked straight into Saltika's eyes, searching for something. She only found a bright young woman with ambition, yet the face seemed achingly familiar. Zondela had little time to waste. Her quest was to save the entire sphere, and yet her subconscious told her to stay, just a while. No reason for staying came to her mind; perhaps an oracle had shown her this place in one of its visions. She was not sure. "I will stay with you for a time then I must continue on my quest."

Saltika hugged her.

The next few days were spent making sure that everyone understood the dangers of a Hatetar and how to avoid creating one. Zondela trained people that Saltika called her personal guard. Why she needed a personal guard, Zondela did not know.

The people loved Saltika. When she had first arrived in the village, the young woman did not have much of an opportunity to engage people. Now she had plenty of time to show her leadership and decision making skills. Rations were created, food stores set up, a dispute resolution system established, all created by Saltika in a few days. It was impressive. Later that night Zondela realized where she had seen Saltika's face.

When the third oracle had shown her the vision of the

hammer-wielding Schlagen, it had also shown the female general that would one day lead the Flametar army in its attack upon Sinxin. That general was Saltika.

Once she realized who Saltika would become, she could barely look at her without flinching. The images given to her by the oracle haunted her mind in the days that followed. The oracle had shown the general – an older Saltika – leading armies of Infernians to victory. Saltika would be an instrument of the Flametars in their conquest of the world.

At the first glimpse of the oracle's vision, Zondela had known she had to kill the female general, yet Saltika was not the bloodthirsty killer that Schlagen had been. Killing that hammer-wielder had been done more out of self-defense than from the need to complete her quest. She could not kill Saltika in cold blood, not now that they were friends.

She could try to reason with her. Zondela could even show her the oracle and the future that would come to pass. That might sway her to not work for the Flametars, yet Saltika had proven that she could be tempted by promises of power, having already given in to the deception of a Hatetar. She had quickly set herself up as leader of the village upon returning to it. Zondela vowed to test her and take care of the situation if Saltika failed.

It took several nights of searching for Zondela to find a suitable vortex. It was about an hour's walk from the village. She stepped through the invisible portal and stood on a small fragment of land that floated so high up in the sky that the world was a curved sphere in the distance below. The fragment – about 300 feet across – was covered in trees, many of which bore nuts, melons, berries, and blue apples, a rare gift on Infernia due to their scarcity. A few pools of clear water dotted the landscape, heavy-pincered lifeforms resting peacefully on the bottom, edible and as equally desirable as the azure fruit. The grass was a soft purple plant that yielded gently under her boots. Several sugar-nut trees draped their willowy, blossom-clad vines over a cluster of quartz rocks that were bigger than her. She would have painted the scene had she been able to do so.

Stepping back through the vortex, she returned to Sinx-in. With her armored toe, she made scuff marks in the dirt so she could find it again without the use of the telescope.

Guilt gnawed at her. In her soul, she was a woman, pleased when people liked her and desirous of peace and tranquility. Her violent nature had always taken second place to her feminine side, and Saltika was easy to like.

Reaching the village she found all were asleep, aside from a few bored and tired guards who only glanced at her. Quietly she crept to the hovel that Saltika had claimed for her own. Inside the woman slept, her breathing rhythmic and deep.

Zondela woke the young woman and waited while she rubbed sleep out of her eyes.

"Zon? What is it? It's still dark."

"There is a great opportunity for us, Saltika. I need the council of someone I can trust."

Saltika stared. "Another idol?" she asked.

"The Infernians have contacted me again," Zondela lied. "Their invasion force will be moving soon and I have been offered my old position back. Come, you can see them."

The two women walked out into the night, Zondela calm and poised, keeping her eyes on the ground before her. Saltika was silent. Zondela found the area again and looked Saltika in the eye, already feeling low. "The Infernian invasion commences soon," said Zondela. "They need me as Penturian. They asked me to bring in any others I trust and I could think of only you. Do you want to work for the Flametars? If you do, you will be a Penturian soon, after you have proven yourself. There is much fighting ahead and many opportunities for glory and greatness."

Saltika was excited, and Zondela's heart was heavy.

"I have known of this for some time," said Zondela. "The Flametar invasion will take many years. After you and I have died of old age, the Flametars will conquer the world and consume it in flames. It will not affect us and I tell you only to be honest. They will destroy the sphere after we are gone. Do you still wish to serve them?"

"Yes," said Saltika.

Zondela slugged her. The young woman collapsed from the hard blow to the jaw and Zondela caught her before she fell. It had been difficult to injure her only friend; images of the devastated cities brought her the strength she had needed. With Saltika over her shoulder, she passed through the vortex.

High in the sky, above the main cloud layer, the fragment of rock floated silently, the air cool and refreshing. Insects sang their choruses of loneliness and solitude. Small birds sat in the boughs of the large trees, singing their lovely birdsongs. Untouched fruit lay on the ground. Zondela took little notice as she made her way over thick tree roots and between transparent quartz boulders to the other side of the floating fragment.

Zondela walked for several minutes, climbing over prolific vines and between curved melon trees. After a few turns, she gently laid Saltika on a grassy bank beside a pool of water. The young woman stirred, eyes still closed, and Zondela removed her own dagger from her brass boot and laid it on the ground beside the unconscious woman. Saltika would find her way back to Sinxin though it might take years, hopefully not until after the Infernian invasion failed. There was plenty of food and water and Zondela wondered if she was perhaps being too lenient on someone who would have willingly assisted in the scorching of the sphere.

As she retraced her steps, stepping on stones to conceal her path, she passed through the vortex and was extruded back on Sinxin. Zondela felt like a poisoned blade, dirty and dishonorable. Since there was nothing left in the village for her, she turned and headed toward the Restless Ocean.

<h1 style="text-align:center">27</h1>

Zondela found the broken tower along the shore after five uneventful days of walking. It marked the location of the lost oracle. The oracle had been on land until a quake sheared the land and submerged the area under the Restless Ocean. The tower had been erected on the shoreline to guide people to the location of the submerged oracle, the builders and their small community long since swallowed by the hungry sea.

The tower suited Zondela's mood. It was dark and gray, covered with lichen and moss that thrived in the moist air. The stones were pitted and cracked. Seabirds roosted in the rotted timber roof. A line of lobstermen walked by, swords belted on their waists, waving their oversized claws in greeting. In the distance, amid the splatter of the sea, a massive serpent broke the surface, half of its looped body above the waves.

She faced the Restless Ocean. The spray from the sea created a thin mist over the shore that softened the rolling white caps and jagged rocks that broke the surface. A few marine reptiles, long necked and violent, broke the surface for air, suffering under the relentless assault of wind and waves as they argued – in the prosaic tongue – which of the aquatic knights was the legitimate ruler of the sea.

She reached into her pack and removed the Sea Globe. The glass orb was perfectly round, filling her palm nicely. It was half filled with green water and even when she held the orb still the interior replicated the sea – tiny waves moved across the surface, forever breaking against the inside of the sphere. The waves called her attention, drawing her in with their rhythmic motion. As her staring became more focused she saw only the ocean. Reality disappeared. She felt like a disembodied spirit floating out over the Restless Ocean, watching the waves roll and crest below her while her body was on a distant shore. It was only with a force of will that she pulled herself away from the image of the ocean and back to reality.

Catching her breath, she concentrated on the orb. The water of the Restless Ocean frothed and rumbled, new currents adding to the heave and clash of waves. Droplets splashed her as the intensity of the watery collisions increased. The relic forced the water aside and undersea currents impacted each other. The sea parted, two walls of green roiling water on either side of her with a corridor in-between about 20 feet wide. The watery walls shifted and surged, barely stable. Fish, shells, and small reptiles swirled helplessly just inside the vertical walls. The relic had even separated the mist so that she could walk unimpeded across the ocean floor. A flock of merciless sea birds descended upon the exposed ocean floor to claim the flopping fish and other sea creatures left behind. In the distance was a statue.

Zondela moved with a purpose. Muck and silt sucked at her feet and she dodged the tentacles from half-buried carnivorous octohorrors while running over and around sharp fingers of rock. No longer simply piercing the surface, they now stood as exposed monuments impeding her way, many encrusted with barnacles that struck at her with spiny appendages.

The walls of water on either side of her became steady and calm. Fish swam near the boundary, exposing their bright colors and delicate fins. A few obtuse specimens swam through the wall to fall to the ocean floor. The flock of sea birds made sure that those fish would not pass their genes on.

Halfway to the oracle she had to climb over a shipwreck laying on its side. Its broken mast and cracked keel showed the effects of the Restless Ocean. Gazing inside the wreck she saw no bodies or treasure, just an empty hull rotting in the sea.

The last oracle, created by Balakakos before he fell into sadness and waited for her arrival, was a sandstone statue of a tall, curvaceous woman in long robes. There were many statues on Sinxin but none as beautiful as this. Zondela put her hand on the statue and relived a lifetime of old memories as the oracle learned everything she knew. When it was over Zondela asked her questions.

Sinxin was a fertile world. Sprawling cities of coral thrived on the seafloor, fighting for resources with the inhabitants of the vast warrens carved into the benthic rock. Undersea spiders fought with reptiles knights over boulders of pure emerald. The kelp farming sea mollusks routinely sought the oracle's knowledge to save themselves from gigantic carnivores, fish that were mostly mouth and stomach. Elegant and selfish crabs collected treasure from wayward travelers and shipwrecks to hoard in their grottoes. Most dangerous of all was the race of deep water shark magicians that were building a vast empire by enslaving other less intelligent races. The shark magicians forced lesser races to build weapons for them and now had their own undersea army, a threat to all except the Wusong. Their sentinels were already underway to examine the disturbance in the water that she had created. Although destined to develop lungs after several centuries, the sharks would never explore the surface since the Flametar War will have consumed the sphere by then.

Zondela had not stopped the war by exiling Saltika – she had only impeded and slowed the conquest. Saltika was destined to find her way back to the surface in a few years and write a famous book of her experiences.

The Ultimate Machine still hunted her. A creator of life, a great architect doomed to wander the void, it seeded worlds with life and moved on, creating and destroying in cycles of birth, agony, and death as it fought with itself. The machine was the one who truly planned the destruction of Sinxin – the other malevolent races only wanted to rule it. The urge for it to begin a new cycle of creation would soon overcome it and it wanted to wipe out the planet before it moved on.

Night had since fallen and, just inside the walls of water, armed fish knights and brooding sharks watched her, waiting for a chance to kill her should the waters return to normal. A bipedal amphibian, garbed in intricately made gold plate armor, waited with a curved sword in hand, its red eyes steady and unblinking.

The oracle did not know if the Ultimate Machine could be destroyed – no one had tried and the few who had laid eyes on it had gone insane, although they had all been of the lesser races. It was still hunting her and it had constructed a pack of hunters who even now pursued her.

To stop the future war from destroying the world, Zondela had to destroy an offshore wood platform that drew a thick, black liquid from the depths of the sphere. If the drilling platform was wrecked the Infernians would be unable to obtain the black liquid. Thicker and more viscous than water, it burned hotter than wood and allowed the Flametars to manifest in arctic climes.

With the black liquid, the Flametars would manifest on Glacia and kill the Icetar council. With the council dead the remaining Icetars would ignore the invasion and concentrate on their architecture, allowing the invasion of Sinxin to proceed. If she destroyed the platform she prevented the Icetar council from being destroyed. Then, when the Flametar invasion occurred, the Icetars would move to stop it, breaking up the Infernian attack and scattering the Flametars, at least temporarily. Without the presence of the Flametars, the Infernians realize they were misled by their masters and they rebel. The invasion fails and the Infernians colonize the wastes between the Dynasties.

She learned the location of the offshore platform. It was about ten day's walk along the shoreline. She marked it on her map and asked about Fushang – the city that had dominated her dreams for so long.

It was on a distant island that could be reached only by vortex. Not until science had replaced magic on Sinxin could a vessel be built strong enough to withstand the ocean waves and neither could she sail through the sharp rocks and violent whirlpools that surrounded the city. Long-necked reptiles lived in the area and further isolated the city, plucking men from the decks of the few wood sailing ships that managed to make it anywhere near the city. The oracle gave her the location of the needed vortex and she marked it on her map.

Starlight bathed the area in a silver glow by the time she finished with the oracle. Hostile undersea life had formed up just inside the watery walls to try and kill her during her walk back. Fish and amphibians leaped out of the watery walls at her, forcing her into endless sword battles. She slew strange beasts with large, lidless eyes and fish that walked like men, and the entire time she had only one thought in her mind – dreams of Fushang.

28

Zondela fought her way back to shore, leaving such carnage behind that for the last hundred paces she walked alone, the men-fish glaring at her from just inside the watery walls, the reptilian swordsmen staring her down, scaled hands on sword hilts.

She reached the shore and relaxed her concentration. The water cascaded back into place with a crash. She walked, eager to finish her quest and find peace, pushing her body onwards through the night, stumbling, tripping over rocky outcroppings. Fushang called to her with its siren song of peace and tranquility.

She scanned for vortexes and found one over the far hills, a rectangle of sky and ocean floating untethered in the air. There was a fertile patch of grass beneath it, marking its presence, since water droplets from the Restless Ocean splashed through the vortex, irrigating the soil. Examining it up close she saw that if she stepped through, her feet would be on a coral reef filled with scuttling crustaceans carrying shells and fish above their armored heads. A Wusong walked by – on the other side of the vortex – and flexed slightly, its talons scraping furrows in the white reef. Zondela put her telescope in its berth on her hip and stepped through.

She stood on a large coral reef. Before her stretched the endlessness of the ocean, ending in a perfectly straight line of blue on the horizon. She turned, her heartbeat heavy in her chest. Two Wusong stood before her. Their bodies were long, coiled and looped, emerald scaled and glinting in the sunlight. Their heads were above hers, their steady gazes looking down at her.

The first Wusong spoke, its voice deep, rich, and pleasing. "You are not lost, girl. Only step backward and you will return from where you came. It is a strange work of the creators that allows such instant travel."

"I know," said Zondela. "I have long traveled the paths of the vortexes and my encounters with your kind have been enlightening."

The Wusong bent its head lower and sniffed her. "You are Zondela the peacemaker. We have discussed you at length in our conclaves under the waves." The second Wusong silently bent its head down and moved small rocks around on the reef before it. "You have given us much and will always be a welcome guest under the sea. With us, you can explore crystal grottoes, kelp forests, and the long undersea cracks filled with sleeping sea-maids. You can place wagers on the battles between the marine reptiles and armored sharks. You can hunt the great carnivorous fish with us if you wish. You have brought peace between the Wusong Clan and the Tanshi Dynasty. Where we formerly saw the Tanshi as beasts and killers, we now have forged an alliance with them, and they have proved to be honorable. The Wusong are indebted to you."

"There are other dangers in the world," she said. "There needs to be an alliance between the Wusong and every human on Sinxin. The Flametars threaten us all."

The Wusong scraped the reef with its claw before

answering. "The Tanshi desert is filled with bones from the ancient days when it had been submerged beneath the waves. Now the Tanshi drag those bones to the shore and leave them for us, and in exchange, we hunt the massive fish of the deep and lay them out for the Tanshi to take. We have all we need."

Zondela groaned inwardly. While she could organize and motivate she could not fight a war singlehandedly. She watched the other Wusong grasp smooth rocks in its delicate green claw and carefully place them, sliding some and switching others. She changed her approach. "As your population increases you will need more food."

"Many beasts walk the surface of Sinxin, each one with delicious bones beneath the fat of their flesh. With the bones that the Tanshi provide for us, we have accumulated vast deposits of them beneath the waves, just as you build granaries in your cities."

Zondela pictured extensive fields of bones at the bottom of the sea, with serpentine Wusong prowling above them, and she wanted to see it with her own eyes. "The Flametar army comes soon, and they will conquer half of Sinxin. When they are ready, centuries later, they will engulf the world in flames."

"We know. Even the Wusong can consult oracles, girl. The flames you speak of will not burn the ocean; we will sleep beneath the waves, waiting patiently for the fires to end. We can spend our entire lives in the ocean if we wish."

"There will be no more life on the surface, and no more bones after the charring flames cleanse the sphere."

The Wusong considered this, while beside it the other one stared at the arrangement of stones, its claw poised over its work. "Then we will raise great flocks of whales under the waves, with Wusong swimming back and forth keeping the herd together."

Zondela wanted to explore beneath the waves and see the splendors that she was being tantalized with. "I am from Infernia and I know the tricks of the Flametars," she said. "They have found a black liquid by drilling underground, which they call dark water. Dark water floats and burns violently when ignited. They would coat the surface of your ocean with it, poisoning the sea."

"Perhaps," said the Wusong. "The amphibians have constructed a platform that stands on wooden legs and extracts dark water from the ground. We know the liquid burns and leaves a poisonous residue, and we know the Flametars wish to destroy the world."

"I need your help," said Zondela. "I know where this platform is. Will you meet me there with more of your clan? When the Flametar army comes the Tanshi will be scorched out of existence."

The second Wusong looked up from its pattern of rocks and spoke. "I have thought upon this, and I will ask the clan to assist. We are bound to help because of our agreement with the Tanshi. We anticipated that the Wusong would do battle with other races in the future, especially the amphibians, so we carefully worded the treaty. According to our alliance, an attack upon the Tanshi is an attack upon the Wusong Clan, and conversely. South of the dark water platform there is an orange crystal deposit, on dry land. The Clan will meet you there after I have explained this to them. We will inform the Tanshi Dynasty of their obligation in this matter as well."

"Excellent," said Zondela. "How long will that take?"

"That I do not know. The Tanshi fear the Flametars, which will hasten their movements, yet they battle an infestation of Hatetars in their desert, which might slow them.

We shall see."

Zondela nodded, wondering how long it would take, and thought about the vortexes she had mapped out in her years as a Penturian. "There is a vortex that leads from the Tanshi desert to a grove of trees in this part of the world." She removed her map and carefully unfolded it, shielding it with her body from the ocean spray kicked up by the waves and wind, and showed them two dots representing each end.

"If we can find it," said the second Wusong as it moved another rock on the tableau in front of it, "then we will use it. I will search for it myself, and if it is safe, it will speed the passage of the Tanshi considerably. We can locate travel gates by smell since the air coming through them is usually very different from the surroundings."

"Thank you," said Zondela. "The Ziqqurratu Dynasty might help us. Can you contact them, and get a message to Sharduq? He will help."

"It has been decades since I prowled the moist jungles of Ziqqurratu," said the Wusong. "I will do so. If I am destined to die in the upcoming battle, it will be good to see the great stone temples rising above the jungle canopy one last time. Then I will return to rejoin you."

"Good," replied Zondela. "I shall wait among the orange crystals as discussed. Good luck."

The Wusong flicked their tails in farewell, and she stepped away. The white coral crunched beneath her feet as she walked, and crabs scuttled away. She was back on the other side, about ten days march from the dark water platform, confident in step and purpose.

She walked. Pot shards littered the ground, half buried from long years of exposure to wind and rain. It was unusual to find relics in the wastes between the two great dynasties. The Tanshi desert had nurtured great warriors who also built, while the Ziqqurratu Dynasty had birthed great builders who also fought. It was unfortunate that the two Dynasties had fought each other in the past and it had been a long march for the poor soldiers who had participated in the inconclusive war.

It was possible she was heading to the colossal battle that she had always envisioned participating in one day. Many Penturians longed for that single, climactic battle. Even if death resulted, a form of immortality could be achieved through a great victory in some final battle against impossible odds. It was a dream of many generals and Zondela felt a quiver of excitement at the thought that she just might be going into a similar cauldron of struggle and combat.

Later that day she passed a small lake, about a good spear throw from shore to shore. A solitary fisherman stood in the water and threw his net out. His arms were extended and she saw that he had fat pincers instead of hands. He ignored her as he hauled in his net, then delicately opened it with his crustacean-like extremities to dine on his fresh catch. She saw no home or house nearby, except for a mound of mud with a large hole in the center.

The days passed and she came to the orange crystal deposit. It was a massive specimen of flat panes, sparkling shafts, and pyramidal tips. She found she could safely view the sun through them; when she did so the entire crystal was lit up in orange light, glowing and bright. When viewed from a different angle the crystal scintillated and sparkled. She assumed that crystals were only pure water congealed into incredible hardness by being under pressure for a great length of time.

To the north was the ocean, about six hours march

from her position. She waited, eating the rations from her pack, laying in the sand, and letting her muscles heal from the trials she had put them through. Tendons hurt, old wounds complained, and her lower body ached from the endless marching across Sinxin. Her shoulder suffered from the years of frenetic sword-slinging of a Penturian at the front of every battle. At the first stirrings of self-pity she reminded herself that one day all would be well if she found the fabled city.

She passed the time by digging small holes in the sand and filling them with Chalice water. Each time the life that sprang forth was different. While many were just different varieties of fish, there were some strange creatures, twisted of form and equipped with horns, tentacles, or armored bodies that struggled out of the small pool and fought for life as she speared them with her knife. Some tasted wonderful, with firm flesh and succulent meat and their moist bod- ies provided her with the water she needed to survive. She declined to drink the Chalice water lest some tiny creatures in her stomach evolve and grow to burst out of her flesh and escape.

The Chalice had to be destroyed before battle so that the Flametars could not acquire it if she was killed. It was powerful enough to tip the sphere's balance of power by creating new races and wiping out old ones. With it, she was like an ascendant, able to create even if she could not properly control it.

The sparkling Chalice sat on a rock. She withdrew Schlagen's hammer from its place on her back and raised it over her head. With every bit of strength she could muster – her face muscles contorting from the strain – she slammed the hammer down, shattering the rock beneath it. Her hands hurt from the shock and she dropped the hammer to rub her palms together. The Chalice was a flat piece of metal, unrecognizable. She turned it in her hands and no drop of water leaked from it. Its power was gone. It took only a few hours to find a vortex that led to a dense jungle and she tossed in the ruined Chalice.

She returned to the orange crystals and waited, a rag in one hand and her helmet in the other. Thus it was that while she polished her armor a pack of Wusong approached. She donned her helmet, tucking her long hair into it as she rose to her feet.

Twelve Wusong were accompanied by a large group of men, dusty from travel and armed with great wooden bows across their backs. She counted sixty archers, men and women both. When they reached her the Wusong bowed. She bowed back and straightened as one of the men approached. It was Esuta, armed with a beautiful new bow of polished silver.

"Welcome, Esuta. It is good to see you again."

"It is, Zondela. I feared we would not cross paths again. My friend, there is something wrong with your eye. It drips water."

"No," she said, pulling off a brass glove and wiping her eye with her finger. "It is just the sun, blinding me. I am glad you have come."

"Battle looms, Infernian, and I lend my bow to it. Our alliance with the Wusong drew us here. They say this battle will be a great one."

"It will," she replied. "The Flametars will come with their army and this is where we make our stand. They have a wood platform offshore that draws a thick, black water from beneath the ground. We move to destroy it."

"Do they know we come, Zondela?"

She sighed. "There is a certain power that hunts me and

has sent assassins after me, because of my efforts to stop the Flametar invasion. I think they are expecting us."

"Good," laughed Esuta as he gave her armor-clad shoulder a slap. "Then it will be a good fight."

Zondela met the rest of the warriors who had come. A Wusong, who identified himself as King Vasa-kai, had green scales that scintillated in the sun. He was a magnificent specimen, long and restless, constantly curling and uncurling his body, finally coiling it below him. "I have brought eleven Warriors. The rest of our clan are sleeping far out in the ocean, oblivious even to my calls."

"Twelve Wusong will bring victory within our grasp," said Zondela. "Especially with the Tanshi you have brought."

"Thank you," said Esuta. "I selected the fifty-nine warriors most skilled in the Way of the Bow. The rest of our men are needed to fight the Hatetars and reacquire the vast tracks of our desert that have fallen to them."

"The Hatetars have conquered land?" she asked.

"Yes," he said. "It seems your old masters the Flametars know of the vortexes and use them to bring in horrid stone idols which they give to poor villages in the wastelands. The Hatetars spring forth as soon as some sad, lonely soul prays before one of them, the idols cultivating worshipers and developing dark denominations."

"Then," said Zondela with a certain grimness in her voice, "the invasion has already begun. After this battle perhaps the Wusong will help you."

"We will," said Vasa-Kai. His large, luminous eyes stared at her. "If we are alive. I consulted the oracle below the waves and it predicted a massing of enemy forces at the platform. I swam for days and entered the Ziqqurratu Dynasty. Sharduq pledged to bring a contingent of soldiers.

Though he battles the witches for control of the jungle Dynasty he knows the value of our work. How many soldiers do the Flametars have?"

"Over two hundred, though some will have to stay and guard Infernia."

"My people brought all our greatest arrows," said Esuta, "the work of our best artisans. We have armor-penetrating steel shafts, though we are dangerously low on arrows."

Zondela nodded. "How did you get here so fast? Did you find the vortex?"

"Yes," laughed Esuta. "The Wusong found it right where your map showed, though they had a hard time convincing our men to go through. Only after Splonica stepped back and forth a few times did the rest of us dare try it." He gestured to a tall, muscular woman, who nodded with a faint smile. She wore a metal sword at her side and from the look of her arms, it seemed she had spent a great deal of time training with it.

The Tanshi warriors unlimbered their bows and tested the strings, rubbing a pale wax into the weapons to keep moisture from penetrating the wood. Zondela chatted with many of the soldiers, the women asking what to anticipate of the enemy's tactics, the men asking what loot to expect on the fallen corpses. She gave Schlagen's hammer to Splonica. The Tanshi woman shattered a few rocks along the shoreline and returned, finally smiling properly.

The sun sank into the ocean, its dying horizontal rays hitting the orange crystal and lighting up its facets. The Wusong sat in small groups and placed stones in the air before them. There the smooth rocks hung until another Wusong reached out and rearranged the pattern, each clan member making a single move each time. Finally, Zondela asked them what they were doing. They raised their triangular scaled heads, their flexible necks bending so that they could stare at her while they maintained their position around the pattern of floating stones.

"We chart the course of the world, girl," said Vasa-Kai. "We predict, we extrapolate, we learn." They would say no more and Zondela spent another hour watching them form a three-dimensional pattern of stones that floated and circled each other without ever touching.

Night fell and they made no fires. Most of the archers were exhausted from their trip and slept soundly. Esuta made sure that enough guards stood vigil. Zondela herself slumbered, encased in her brass armor, and dreamed of being a stone playing piece in a great Wusong game.

Morning came when the sun burned its way out of the ocean, casting its warm glance on the world. Zondela ate with the other soldiers and turned her head with the rest of them when the sentinels called out an alert. They waited as a band of about a hundred men approached. It was Sharduq with soldiers of Ziqqurratu behind him.

"I have come to fight alongside you," Sharduq said. Beside him was the leader of the Ziqqurratu, who had worked with Zondela. He saw her appraising him and he spoke up. "Yes, Zondela, I rule Ziqqurratu no longer. Because of you, our rightful ruler now leads us. Sharduq is a hero and a philosopher, a king to rule over the temples of our jungle Dynasty. The people line up to glimpse him, seeing an ancient hero returned to us unharmed. Sharduq has already written a tentative peace deal with the witches, and they no longer hunt our menfolk in the night."

Two hooded figures, slim swords at their sides, pushed through to approach Zondela. They removed their hoods and revealed themselves as women, one beautiful and the other scarred and ill-favored. "Soloth and Cella" said Zondela. "You travel with the men? I am pleased."

"Lady Valoc sent us to aid you," said the unsightly sister in her sweet, feminine voice. "We shall fight beside you, facing victory or defeat as fate decides."

Zondela nodded. "We should march now. Our plan is to destroy the platform and wipe out any enemy forces we encounter. It is likely they know of our approach."

Cella nodded her head and raised the hood of her robe back into place. "I shall watch over you on the battlefield," the witch said. Zondela smiled and thanked her.

Several of the Tanshi archers questioned her politely on the reason for the upcoming battle, while the Ziqqurratu spearmen listened and remained silent. It seemed to her that it reflected the independent nature of the Tanshi desert dwellers versus the more regimented ranks of the jungle spearmen who had been taught to obey orders without questioning them.

Zondela explained briefly. She touched upon the oracle's tale of the future war, a few thousand years from now, and how it would destroy the surface and wipe out all life except that based on flame and heat. A Tanshi archer asked what to do if a Flametar appeared, as they could not be shot or killed. She urged them to let her handle the situation in that event. She spent the rest of the day outlining their tactics, their responsibilities, and their strategy. She described several plans and had them memorize a code word for each so she could switch plans in battle.

Their forces totaled twelve Wusong, fifty-nine Tanshi bowmen, one hundred and three Ziqqurratu spearmen, two witches, the hero Sharduq and Zondela herself. She knew from experience that the Infernians were experts in warfare, easily slaying Glacian armies twice their size. Every Infernian was a master swordsman, able to flick incoming arrows aside and penetrate armor with a well place thrust.

They marched behind hills and ridges, trying to keep out of sight until they reached the coastline. The water was about two hundred feet from them, the platform about fifty feet farther into the water. It was mounted on eight wood struts arranged in a square and consisted of two levels, both open to the elements. The bottom level held equipment and workers – naked green amphibians – while the top level, flat and exposed, held a wheel-shaped apparatus in the center with more amphibians congregating around it. A large metal shaft penetrated straight down from the center of the top level all the way through to the water. It did not appear to be heavily defended. The land between Zondela and the water's edge was flat and empty except for a dry ravine to her left.

She examined the scene through her 'scope. A nearby vortex led to the burnished wastes of Infernia, the brass towers visible in the background. The sight of it made her once again feel the sweltering sun and merciless heat.

She put her telescope away and led her soldiers toward the platform. The amphibians leaped over the side and disappeared into the ocean. Zondela smiled; the oracles had advised her well so far, leading her across the world to this spot. A quick battle and she might be done her quests, finally able – for the first time in her life – to devote her energies to herself.

It was flat terrain the rest of the way, perfect for a decisive battle. With her army behind her, she advanced. The waves crashed and broke upon the shore, a constant audible backdrop as the ocean breathed and sputtered. She inhaled deeply, in case she died in the battle so that as her soul fled her body she would remember the lovely scent and sound of the Restless Ocean.

Infernians poured out of the vortex at a run, assembling into a formation as she herself had taught them. They spilled through as fast as they could – they had waited for her. Her urge was to rush in, trying to get a quick victory so she could pile sand up to block the vortex, and only her instincts saved her. It was unlikely that her men could get there quickly enough, and if running there meant arriving out of formation, the Infernians would cut them to pieces. She maintained a steady advance in good order.

The enemy Infernians assembled into a tight formation, ten men wide and ten men deep, outfitted in heavy, dark brass armor. It was not the same metal as hers; their armor was darker, a result of the stronger iron/brass mix they had been experimenting with when she had left. Their helmets curled about their heads, with the nose piece dropping down in the center, and the sides of the helmets curved to protect their cheeks. Twin metal horns spiraled out of each helmet top. Their rectangular tower shields were gripped in their left hands while their right hands held gleaming swords of a red-gold color; a copper/brass alloy. Only the front row held swords and shields. The remaining nine rows gripped pikes and shields. Every Infernian also had a crossbow hanging at his side. They stood shoulder to shoulder, a well organized formation – called a pride – of a hundred men, each facing her with their weapons held at the same angle.

It was much too late to stop the flood of men from the vortex so she decided that she would stop just within bowshot of them and use her preferred tactic, that of fighting a defensive battle, waiting for the enemy forces to come to her. If they advanced they might impale themselves on the weapons of the Ziqqurratu spearmen while her Wusong swept around and struck from behind, pinning the enemy forces.

If the Infernians stopped and tried to dislodge her with their crossbows and an archer's duel commenced, her Tanshi would probably earn an easy victory with their superior marksmanship. The idea gained favor in her mind – the Tanshi Way of the Bow mirrored the Infernian lifelong obsession with swordsmanship and tactics, and her forces allowed her to kill from a distance.

Esuta had spoken about armor-piercing arrows, solid steel shafts created to penetrate the scales of the Wusong, and she felt more confident in her ability to repulse an attack and planned to advance only if she ran out of arrows or the enemy withdrew out of range.

She changed her mind when she saw large piles of wood thrown out of the vortex. When lit in the warmer air of Infernia, such large amounts of resources would enable several Flametars to materialize, perhaps spearheading the enemy attack. She needed to prevent that. Her men advanced in good order beside her. She wanted the formation to stay intact and interlocked, her men covering each other. She gave the orders, her voice booming, and was pleased to see Cella and Soloth flanking her a step behind, the rest of her host following in good formation.

They had discussed assault tactics thoroughly. They were to stick close together, shoulder to shoulder, with the Tanshi archers distributed evenly among the Ziqqurratu spearmen. The archers would fire upon her command while the spearmen stayed beside them. If the enemy charged, the spearmen would kneel, lower weapons, set the spear butts into the ground, and resist the assault. If the enemy walked forward in good order, the men of Ziqqurratu were to stand and present a wall of spear tips, with the Tanshi firing continuously over their heads. Since the archers specialized in firing on an angle to drop arrows behind fortifications – one of the reasons they did so well against the skilled builders of the Ziqqurratu Dynasty – they would not draw swords and enter the fray unless the enemy had broken through the palisade of spear points. Zondela would shout orders if she saw their formation falling apart.

Since she would also be in the thick of combat she might not be able to observe, assess, and give orders. While some Penturians commanded from the rear, shouting orders like a player moving pieces on a game board, she discarded the notion. She could not have these brave soldiers die in her place, completing her quest while she stayed safe in the rear. She would lead from the front.

Her men, arranged in a single great square with the Wusong prowling behind them, moved forward and stopped a good bowshot away from the Infernains. She examined the terrain – to her left was a dry ravine that wound its way up to the ocean without quite touching the water while the rest of the terrain around her was flat and suitable for an infantry charge. Zondela gave the order for the men to bend their bows. They fitted arrows to strings and pulled their hands back to their cheeks.

No more Infernians advanced from the other vortex – the formation of over a hundred men stood before her in fine form, neatly arrayed with weapons brandished, their officers in the front, every person an expert in warfare. It was about half of the Infernian population.

Zondela recognized them; some were people she had grown up with, others she had trained with under the tutelage of the Flametars. She knew their tactics; each Penturian was taught maneuver combat – flanking, striking silently from the rear, and taking out enemy archers and supply lines first. The Penturian would evaluate the situation, deciding whether the impact of his five men could split apart an enemy unit or blunt a hostile charge. If so, the Penturian would strike, his men close at his heels. It was how the Flametars organized the battle ahead of time so that if properly briefed, the Penturians could execute complicated plans and quickly switch through pre-briefed missions, their men at their sides. It was an effective system, especially when the Infernians found themselves fighting in rough or mountainous terrain. Their ability to outmaneuver and flank the Glacians had given them victory during many difficult battles.

She faced a hundred superlatively trained men with an army of 60 Tanshi archers, 103 spearmen, and 12 reptiles. It looked like a fair fight.

When the enemy ignited a decent fire and summoned one or two Flametars it would not tip the balance of power – she had a plan for that. Even if her plan failed, her old masters could not stay in the cool air of Sinxin for more than ten minutes once the wood below them was gone. She had never, in all her years on Infernia, seen more than two Flametars materialize at the same time. Even if it happened now her formation would back away, avoiding combat until the Flametars dissipated in the cool ocean winds. Nor had she ever seen them move over water. Her fiery masters had approached her many times after a battle when she was bathing in the clear Infernian rivers, halting each time at the water's edge. She guessed they could not move over water, perhaps for fear of being splashed.

On the enemy's side, more wood was thrown through the vortex, piled in a great heap, and ignited. It would take several minutes for the temperature and intensity of the flames to peak and allow manifestation and she intended to have broken the back of the enemy army before then.

During the march up to the battle, she had discussed

the issue of ammunition with Esuta. Since each archer of Tanshi crafted their arrows, each had a different amount of them, a problem that Zondela rectified by ordering the arrows collected and redistributed. Aside from a few who wound up with one extra, each bowman had 20 hunting and 4 armor-piercing arrows, the war with the Hatetars having reduced their supply considerably. Beyond that, a few men had Wind arrows and Zondela gave them to Esuta so that she could issue orders and control the release of the potent weapons.

In her deepest voice, she ordered her men to fire. Mahogany creaked as bows bent and snapped forward, sixty Tanshi arrows firing simultaneously on a steep arc to maximize their flight distance. The swarm of shafts whistled as it flew, each arrow reaching a zenith and tipping to point toward the target below. The lead enemy Penturian called for shields up and the arrow swarm glanced off and shattered against their brass armor. Eight more times a swarm of arrows fell harmlessly against the solid wall of enemy shields.

The enemy pride lowered their shields and waited.

Beside her, a nervous soldier asked what the enemy was waiting for. She gently hushed him and told him to remain steady and focused. In a loud voice, she ordered a volley of the rare and precious armor-piercing arrows to be loosed. Her mistake was to give the order out loud – she should have used a code word to keep her intentions secret. The lead Infernian shouted the old Flametar word for fortress and the enemy knelt, so close against each other that their shields half overlapped each other's, and even the armor-piercing arrows failed to kill a single man. A few enemy shields were pinned together by the steel shafts and had to be discarded, the men now able to hold their swords in both hands. She kept track of logistics in her head – each of her archers had 3 steel arrows left and she decided to wait until the Infernians were in battle and unable to raise a good shield wall before firing any more of them.

From the side approached another danger – a horde of lupine creatures, muscular, hairy, and made as much of metal gears and pulleys as wolf-flesh. The animals had metal teeth, claws, and joints, and were half mechanical. She guessed there were about a hundred of them, each one staring at her with hate or hunger or some other equally unpleasant motive.

Assuming that the hunting beasts of the Ultimate Machine were allied in some way with the Infernians, they would try to attack simultaneously. She ordered half her men to face the threat of the wolf-like hunters. They would have no way of knowing her arrow supply was low and would probably try to storm her formation, perhaps only waiting until they summoned a Flametar or two.

The situation appeared favorable. She fought on flat ground, perfect for the defensive battles she preferred, and she had the Wusong in back to unleash at the right time. The last of her arrows should slay the steel wolves and even if the two enemy groups advanced simultaneously, she would still have the advantage – men and women who practiced the Way of the Bow did not miss. She glanced over at the Wusong and saw them sitting patiently, observing with their luminous eyes, their bodies looped behind them.

The fires created by the Infernians grew larger and Zondela wondered if she was going to end up cursing herself for adopting a defensive strategy. The Penturians hauled small trees and branches from the vortex to add to the flames and the conflagration became larger than anything she had seen on Infernia, where wood was scarce and ultra-valuable. Still, she waited, her archers ready with arrows, motionless until she gave an order.

A rippling sheet of flame appeared over the great fire – a deeper shade of red against the yellow-orange background flames – and moved down, searing the vegetation below it. Its body was formless, a constantly moving curtain of flame, an intelligent blaze driven by the most base of all motivations, that of survival. The specimen, larger than most she had seen, was followed by several others, and Zondela knew that she had made yet another, perhaps fatal, mistake. Back in Infernia, she had never seen more than two Flametars materialize at any one time, thus she had assumed the same would be true of this battle. Now she realized her error. Penturians and their men hauled more tree trunks out of the vortex and piled them on, the tips of the trees bursting into flames as they passed through the body of a Flametar.

Zondela observed, wondering if it was time to abandon her defensive strategy and rush the blaze, fighting through the mailed warriors to reach and extinguish the fire they had created. More small trees came through to feed the Flametars, the blazing sheets of red flames slowly moving away from the fire and congregating among themselves, lords among men, living flames destined to perhaps one day rule the world.

Zondela cursed as yet another Flametar stepped out of the blaze. It was clear that her defensive strategy was not what she had expected; her troubles were multiplying. There were ten enemy lords, each blazing in a rich and crackling glory. She knew they could exist independent of fire for about ten minutes. As long as they returned to the blaze to warm their bodies and renew themselves, they could stay in fiery form for as long as the heap of trees burned. She glanced off to the distance and saw a leafy forest extending to the horizon, Infernian soldiers cutting down the trees.

The Flametar Invasion had begun.

The ten Flametars leaped to the left and away from the wolves. They hustled, skimming low over the ground and leaving a seared patch of blackened vegetation to mark their passage. They were outflanking her. Zondela's vaulted tactical skill, her wonderful abilities to size up a situation and make the right decision, had failed her, leaving her isolated in the open, about to fight for her life against a three-pronged assault. She felt sick at the thought of what she had gotten them into; her inspiring words had summoned these men to her cause, persuaded them to leave their homes and fight for her, and now they faced the blazing heat of her old masters. She glanced at the men about her and they showed no signs of panic as their eyes followed the progress of the sheets of living flame. Zondela realized her mistake – she should have marched through and attacked from the sea.

The Flametars swung around in a long arc, moving behind her position. She issued orders for the men to stand fast. The Flametars had slowed their flight, perhaps because they wanted to attack simultaneously with the rest of their forces, and Zondela came up with a new plan.

"Follow me to the ocean," she shouted. "Stay in formation, do not break and defend when attacked. Maintain the square." With the lupine beasts to her right, the Flametars behind her, and the Infernians ahead of her, she was flanked on three sides, yet she felt she could make it to the ocean by following the nearby ravine that snaked its way to the left and led almost to the waters. She disliked moving just before a battle since stationary spearmen were so much stronger and hoped to reach the water before being engaged. She understood the searing heat of the Flametars, how it would ignite clothing when close, how ten of them could burn easily through her men. In the water, the Flametars could not follow. She would make her final stand there.

True to her training as a Penturian, she had prepared several contingency plans and had only to shout a command word to put them into action. With a terse word that betrayed no information to the enemy, she set the Wusong into motion. As rehearsed, they were bounding away, moving fast, trying to get the Flametars to chase them and use up their precious ten minutes or so of life. If it worked, the Wusong would come back when the Flametars dissipated.

Her host of men reached the ravine and ran through it, making it through the declivity without getting attacked, running through the winding gully and finding themselves only thirty paces away from the sea. Shouts sounded behind her; she looked back and saw Flametars coming out of the ravine, smoke drifting up from the vegetation that had been seared by their passage. Behind them she heard the Wusong roaring, trying in vain to get the Flametars to attack them.

She ran and her men followed, free of panic as they dashed for the sea, holding onto their weapons and maintaining the formation she had drilled into them previously. They made it to the sea, moving about thirty feet away from shore into knee-deep water. Her men stood in a massive square, waiting for orders, the Wusong returning and taking up position behind them in reserve as she had instructed.

She looked for Esuta and found him in the front row. "Esuta, ready your Arrows of the Gale. You will shoot them straight, not on an angle, and aim for the Flametars. Pass two out to others, and wait for my order."

Esuta nodded. Several minutes passed during which the Infernians moved to the water's edge, halting just out of bowshot, watching. Zondela felt confident again, though the feeling melted when a horn sounded in the distance and she saw the trap she had been pushed into. To the rear of her formation, hundreds of green amphibians rose out of the ocean, water sliding off them in sheets, their fanged mouths gaping and their claws raised before them. Several had barnacles and small fish attached to their bodies as if they had lain in wait for some time, waiting for Zondela to blunder into their ambush.

With their slick green skin and slender bodies, they resembled monstrous versions of the tiny aquatic amphibians she would occasionally find in the clear streams of Infernia. Tasty and rare, they were often the object of her childhood quests. Then she remembered tales told by the older women when she was young, of a dangerous race from deep in the ocean of Sinxin – Frogstrocities – part amphibian, part human and always hungry, for food and women.

They formed up in a mob, snarling and flexing their claws, a whole pack of them, many of them holding swords in their slimy fists. They occupied the deeper water behind her. In front of her, the Infernians ran in formation toward her, water splashing up with every impact of their booted feet. To her left, the wolf-like hunters were crashing into the surf. On her right the ten Flametars flew over the water towards her – they could, after all, cross water. Zondela had gambled and lost, the fiery lords skimming just above the water and moving fast, steam trailing behind them, dead fish bubbling to the surface.

"Fire Arrows of the Gale!" shouted Zondela. Three Tanshi archers at the front of the formation drew bowstrings back and released. The three arrows – hand-crafted relics – kicked up a powerful wind as they flew. They had been designed to raise up a dust storm in the Tanshi desert when the Wusong attacked; many times the Tanshi bowmen had brought up a furious storm that dragged with it dust and sand and covered the Wusong in debris, allowing other men to rush forward with pikes or to escape to safety. Here, in this battle to decide the fate of Sinxin, the storm arrows created a powerful gale that hauled along a wave of water, the frothing liquid following the path of the arrows. The three wood shafts were burnt to black cinder when they struck the ten Flametars yet the wave that crashed into them extinguished their flames, snuffing them out of the physical world. Ten dark, twisted, feminine spirits rose through the air, the voluptuous and incorporeal essence of the Flametars, all that was left of them when their fires were quenched. Helpless, the curvacious shadows rose with clenched talons and dissipated on the wind.

The rest of the hostile forces converged upon Zondela and her host from three sides. She tossed her head about to look in all directions; amphibians closed in from behind, their overly-large mouths agape with fangs and saliva. Penturians and their men ran through the surf, water splashing up at every step. Wolves rushed through the water, blocking off any hope of escape from that direction, their metal fangs glinting in the sunlight. It was the great, final battle that she had trained for and awaited all her life.

The pack of wolves, the spawn of the creator of the world, reached her host first and leaped through the air. The Tanshi bowmen were ready and sunk a score of hunting arrows into their furred bellies. The desert dwellers had studied the Way of the Bow, which forced them to support themselves only with their weapons and never by agriculture. For centuries they had survived the inhospitable arid wastes through skill with bow alone, and that training shone through as they struck each lupine hunter in midleap, even the beasts that jumped high into the air.

The charging Infernians were closing in and Zondela called for the last of the armor-piercing arrows. The Tanshi archers fitted the all-metal shafts to strings and fired. The tips were ground to a point. Instead of being long and tapering like arrows designed to penetrate flesh they had a shorter, stronger conical tip. Every Tanshi bowmen fired a metal shaft simultaneously and their discipline worked against them for once. The Infernians saw the swarm of arrows and they raised their shields, still running, their bodies and faces hidden. The shafts penetrated the metal and buried themselves in the shields and no soldiers fell. Several of the warriors cast their shields into the water, blood streaming from holes in their arms where the arrows had penetrated. The men still held their swords before them and maintained their positions, charging alongside their comrades. They were silent, these men who did not flinch even as the Tanshi drew back and released a second wave of arrows. The pride of Infernians, with heavy plate armor on their bodies and more arrows streaming toward them, neither broke formation nor slowed, only running forward with that hostile and indomitable look on their faces, shields raised.

They blocked the salvo of arrows, while the men with no shields flicked the metal shafts out of the air with their blades. Not a single man fell. A third and last time it was repeated – there were no armor-piercing arrows left – and again the shieldless men flicked the arrows aside in midair, shattering the steel shafts. Two of the men had misjudged and held their shields too high, taking an arrow in the thigh. They reached down, grasped the arrow, and yanked it out. The unit of men never slowed in their run and there would not be enough time for a volley of wood arrows before the Infernians reached them.

Zondela had instructed the Wusong to hold position until she called them. She planned to use them to plug any breeches in her front line. If the Infernians stopped and engaged in a shooting match with her, the Tanshi would run out of arrows first and she would send the Wusong in to attack the enemy from behind. Each Infernian had a crossbow and a full quiver of arrows at his side.

Behind her, one of the younger reptiles could restrain his claws no further. He leaped forward, sailing through the air, and landed upon a palisade of swords that were held by the outstretched arms of the Infernians. The blades sunk through Wusong's body, killing it, and its body collapsed on their upraised shields. The shield wall faltered yet did not buckle; they heaved the body to the side and let it fall into the ocean waters, half submerged. These were soldiers, male and female, who had trained every day for their entire lives.

More Tanshi arrows flew, glancing off Infernian shields until Esuta raised a long black arrow. Grim faced, he took aim and released, the shaft flying toward its target and bursting into a cloud of black insects on impact. Multi-legged creatures – insects with hairy legs and bristly bodies – scuttled about the armored men, crawling across armor in search of gaps. The Infernian pride finally stopped, a victim of the horde of small biting creatures that forced them to submerge themselves in water and yank off their armor.

Zondela's sword sang as she waded into the insect-infested Infernians, killing two with decapitating horizontal strokes. She traded sword blows with Hragoth, a man who boasted of murdering Glacians in their beds, finishing him with a reverse spin cut that he had never been able to see coming during their old training days together. Next came beautiful, long-limbed Evenessa, a breathtaking young woman who had once hung two Glacian women for being prettier than her. Evenessa grunted into a forward lunge, a solid penetrating strike, and fell to Zondela's block and counter thrust.

The insects were gone, drowned in the knee-deep waters of the Restless Ocean. Muscular, taciturn Muradonis struck, one of the few men able to best Zondela in the old days, a man famous for setting a life goal of killing 100 Glacians. He struck in a frenzy of blows and Zondela only blocked, knowing he would kill her, buying time until her Tanshi archers filled Muradonis with arrows and he fell backward.

Tisine stepped forth, flicking away the last of the whistling Tanshi arrows with her sword, a young woman who had found enjoyment forcing Glacian males to bed her at sword point and killing them when they were finished. The two women had been best friends until Zondela had walked in on her during a raid on a Glacian village and saw the carnage. Tisine advanced, muttering about the perfect time to kill friends who had betrayed her and launched the pattern of multiple cuts, an almost unblockable series of fast strikes. Zondela had invented it and blocked each one, taking Tisine's head with a hard level swing.

Konokor leaped forward, hoping to use his extra momentum to penetrate her brass armor, plunging his sword down in a two-handed grip while still airborne. Zondela used a tip deflecting swing – striking the tip of the opponent's blade – to knock aside the heavier blade. She thrust, arm outstretched, letting Konokor impale himself on her weapon.

The shrieking, screeching amphibians waded into battle, their swords rising and falling. Zondela held off four of them at the same time, her Tanshi archers saving her life by firing away – the arrows flew over her shoulders and killed the Frogstrocities, a few arrows coming almost straight down to impale the green monsters in the heads.

For several minutes she and her soldiers fought the Infernians, the Frogstrocities, and the few half-metal wolves that had survived their arrow wounds. It was a scene of carnage, bloody swords rising and falling in the melee, the water turning red and attracting carnivorous fish that dragged bodies into deeper waters.

Zondela had made the right decision keeping her army in a square formation – they protected each other, the spearmen in the middle safe and still able to impale enemies over their shoulders of their comrades. As the Infernians attacked anew, led by Ekstrata – a man who had slapped Zondela as a child every time she had failed to complete a sword pattern properly – the formation of Ziqqurratu spearmen and Tanshi bowmen, low on arrows, fought for their lives. The Wusong were in a horrific fight with the amphibians, unable to come to grips with their slick green opponents without taking severe sword cuts to their scaled bodies.

Zondela's swordplay was brief and sharp; she blocked Ekstrata's sword stroke and brought her blade down upon the skull of the wolf next to her. With a turn of her body, she let a leaping animal pass by, its claws scraping her armor. She lunged with her blade, impaling a chainmail-clad Infernian. Zondela knew the finer points of combat and had dedicated the early part of her life to swordplay; when a blade came for her, she held herself in check and waited until she could flick aside the assault, turning the blade away by altering its course with her own weapon. Then she struck, keeping the momentum of her blade going by moving her blade in an arc and sweeping it around to impale or decapitate.

A tall adversary approached, clad in overlapping scales of goldbrass, a weird alloy that was difficult to smelt and nearly impenetrable, a mix of gold, brass, and copper smelted at outrageous temperatures. It was Achios, a violent man whose life goal had been to wipe the Glacian race out and repopulate the frozen plate with blue reptiles to create a private hunting ground. If anyone could have done it, it was Achios, a relentless swordsman who had been able to regularly beat her in single combat.

Challenging her had been his obsession, he who had never felt complete unless he had humbled and bruised her in a duel. In spite of his great height, he always felt himself to be a small man except when defeating her. His insecurities and self-doubts had led him to train incessantly. Even when she was a Penturian, it had been rare that she had been able to force her blade past the whirling sword defense he had invented and perfected. He recognized her; with a wide grin he locked eyes with her, advancing, his sword held at that peculiar angle he preferred that allowed him to strike or defend faster than her eye could follow.

She held her sword hilt near her stomach, the point out, the blade horizontal, and waited. Achios, still smiling, ran forward, his blade spinning in an arc level with her head. She ducked, went down to one knee, and extended her sword-arm. Her shoulder muscle ached from the impact as Achios impaled himself on her blade, his eyes bulging in shock and regret. Zondela yanked her blade free and turned to fight off a pack of wolves.

Her formation of men was intact, while the Wusong were bleeding from multiple sword strokes. She shouted the prearranged command word for them to separate, outflank and strike their enemy from the rear. While her Wusong retreated, the violent amphibians advanced again, swords dripping blue ichor, and struck the skirmish line of spearmen and Tanshi soldiers. The men fought as best they could, blocking the attacks, beating aside incessant sword strikes, falling under the blades of the green-skinned Frogstrocities until the Wusong struck from the rear, picking up the amphibians in their teeth and tossing them aside to be dragged off by the circling pack of carnivorous fish.

A Wusong pointed and shouted. To the east rose another pack of Frogstrocities, rising from the water, naked blades in their hands, about a hundred yards away, advancing in a tight pack. Esuta strung his last arrow, a polished gold projectile, and fired upwards on an angle. A few seconds into the flight the arrow burst into a jagged lightning bolt, sizzling through the air, continuing on the same parabolic arc the original shaft would have taken, nosing over and landing amid the amphibians with a thunderclap. The broken bodies of the Frogstrocities were tossed aside and tentacles reached up out of the water to drag them under.

The infantry battle was still undecided. Zondela moved through knee-deep water to her next opponent, flicking aside the sword stroke that was aimed at her helmet, and slew the man with an angular downward cut across his neck. The Infernian swordsmen, standing shoulder to shoulder, had cut off the heads of the Ziqqurratu spears and had advanced close enough to slaughter several of her men.

A Frogstrocity had swum unnoticed through the host of soldiers to rise beside Zondela, a blunt mace raised above its head. Cella, the witch who had stayed beside Zondela during the battle, raised her arm and flexed her fingers. The flesh of the amphibian turned to dust and fell away, leaving a strange skeleton to tumble to the waves.

Another pack of amphibians was spotted approaching from deeper waters, their heads just visible below the surface. Soloth, the attractive witch, flicked her wrist and turned that part of the water to ice. The giant ice cube, complete with entrapped amphibians, floated to the surface and bobbed gently.

The last wolf was killed, its throat pierced by an arrow

while it was in mid-leap, and the last of the amphibians fell, its body cut in half by the whipping tail of a Wusong. That left about fifty Infernians, regrouping again into tight formation. She glanced back; she had about twenty Tanshi soldiers with a few wood arrows left and eighteen Ziqqur-ratu spearmen.

The amphibians had fought hard and inflicted extensive wounds upon the Wusong, yet killed only one of the great reptiles with a mace strike to the skull. Soft green-skinned Frogstrocities floated face down on the water, bobbing in time with the currents, showing the result when reptile met amphibian in battle.

The Infernians stuck again, swords slashing in unison, cursing her name and the day she was born. The men in front held swords and the men in back held long pikes. Each row had successively longer weapons so that anyone facing the Infernians would be confronted by several pike tips at the same time. The men who had dropped their shields earlier had been handed replacements by the soldiers behind them so that the front row formed an unbroken shield wall supported by a mass of sharp pike tips from the men behind them. They did nothing when carnivorous fish dragged away their wounded, only watching with their eyes.

Bows twanged as the Tanshi fired. Most of the arrows glanced off armored helmets or curved chest plates and did no damage. The regular Tanshi hunting arrow, with its wood shaft and stone tip, was ineffective against the dark brass armor. The last few wood arrows sent only one man reeling backward to fall into the sea and the next soldier in the formation stepped forward and took his place.

The Tanshi drew their swords and fought beside the spear-armed men of the Ziqqurratu Dynasty and Zon-dela's host melted before the Infernians, her men in the front row falling one after another. The Infernians blocked every strike, either by deflecting with their shield wall or by thrusting forward with their pikes, disrupting an attack before it could be carried through. It was a one-sided battle, with tall Ziqqurratu spearmen striking bravely and unable to land a killing blow. Zondela's host was slowly being decimated, her men unable to push past the bristling wall of spear points that barred their way.

The Wusong struck from behind and the Infernians changed formation into a circle three rows deep, the men near the center standing with their backs together. They did this without faltering, only glancing occasionally at their comrades, still able to ward off strikes as they reformed. The Wusong, much to Zondela's dismay, attacked one at a time, some of the great beasts hesitating. A massive reptile splashed forward and struck. Its target weaved aside, causing the Wusong's teeth to snap shut on air. Pikes thrust forward and into the body of the beast, piercing its neck, blue fluid leaking out as it pulled away. The remaining Wusong tried to rake with claws; they batted at the pike tips, unable to force an opening. One of the Wusong turned and swung its tail in an arc, only to have the tip sliced off by a quick return strike from the enemy. The Wusong, trailing blue ichor from its stump, turned and undulated through the water, quickly disappearing. Two more Wusong charged the pride from the rear and quickly succumbed to the pikes that were set to receive their attack.

Zondela stepped forward with her sword held up beside her head, seawater splashing around her legs, her arms high and her eyes watching the enemy pikes. When they thrust toward her she swung her blade, severing a pike tip. She took another step forward and even as she turned her body to let attacks slip past her narrow profile she splintered another wood shaft, the iron pike tip falling to the sea. She did not attempt to strike at the enemy soldiers, instead concentrating on shattering the wood hafts of the pikes, destroying them one at a time, wading into range of the weapons and swinging her brass sword as she moved.

A dozen pikes converged on her. Her blade wove a tight defense, curving through the air, whipping about in tight arcs to intercept and sever the tips. Her hands gripped her sword hilt tightly as she worked, moving in closer, rallying her men with her courage alone. Other Tanshi did the same and after they deprived an enemy soldier of his pike, the Ziqqurratu spearmen beside him thrust his weapon into the Infernian through a gap in the armor, killing the highly trained man.

The tightly knit front rank of the enemy formation broke and the remaining Wusong leaped in, killing with tail whips. Zondela reversed her blade, shattered a helmet with the triangular tip of her sword hilt, and took the man's place inside the pocket of enemy soldiers. Her Tanshi and Ziqqurratu men were right behind her, fighting in the surf, their shouts mingling with the crash of weapons. The last of the armored Infernians fought to the death, never surrendering, never uttering another sound, taking with them their secrets as they died.

The battle was over.

Zondela took off her helmet and stared as her lungs heaved. Waves surged and crashed against her body while the wind cooled and ruffled her hair. The sea spray felt good when it splashed her face, wiping away the grime of battle and reminding her that she was still alive.

29

Tychon of Kallos had his jet strapped securely to his body. He was flying a patrol mission over the sparkling city-state of New Colonia. Below him, pristine glass buildings shone in the sun, preventing him from flying past the sound barrier lest the shock wave shatter the windows. It was a boring flight and he wondered if he would ever see any action. Tychon was a confident pilot, proud of his skills honed during years of peacetime training, yet he itched for some real combat. Dueling in the sky with his friends, feeling his jet strain and shake as he pushed it through shuddering turns and high-speed dives, was not enough to slake his thirst for combat. He watched the peaceful landscape below and concluded he would never get to battle other jets.

The Ultimate Machine was, in the end, a slave to its programming. It could resist the impulse no longer, and for the first time in centuries, it left a planet full of life that it had created. Rising on a soft cushion of anti-gravity, the Ultimate Machine folded its arms and manipulators and flew away from the surface. The long, cylindrical steel body rose past Glacia and the Icetars watched it rise, wondering where the metal beast was heading. By the time the Ultimate Machine reached the stratosphere, it had gone supersonic, hurtling into the firmament to disappear among the stars. The Ultimate Machine erased all memory of its work on Sinxin. Such data questioned its divinity and reminded it of its greatest failure.

Zondela stood, one hand on a tree trunk, naked except for her sword on her hip, thigh-high grass and flowers all around her. In the distance were a dozen glass towers, clustered together and sparkling in the sun, the tallest in the center and the eleven smaller ones around it, vines and leafy fronds curling up around their bases. Glass catwalks linked the towers and Zondela liked to walk them in the evening when the hot ocean breezes swept in.

Zondela waited for Lady Shella – who had been looking for flutterbys – to come drifting in. Shella floated over, wearing a tiara of flowers and nothing else. Her thick brown hair fluttered gently as she descended. When she stopped moving she was at eye level with Zondela and her feet were still several inches off the ground.

"Don't your delicate toes ever touch the soil?" asked Zondela with a smile.

"Not anymore, and yours will not either, sister. You have brought much to Fushang, and I find your capacity to love is deep and profound. I hope some of your hurts have healed now that you have come to us."

Zondela nodded, looking over Lady Shella's shoulder at the men and women that drifted through the forest. The rest of the forest dwellers were on the move, the music from their brass and wood flutes gentle and soft, most of them wearing little other than flowers. Lady Shella turned and drifted away, her feet pushing against the air slightly as she moved, the woman gracefully swimming through the air. Zondela fell in beside her, walking in bare feet through the woods. She wore no armor nor anything else except her sword. The forests of Fushang were warm and full of sunlit glades and there was little reason to dress. Zondela spent her days picking fruit from trees, drinking from sparkling streams, and sleeping with rabbits and foxes who curled against her body while she slumbered.

A stream of rabbits bounded out of the woods and joined her, brushing against her bare calves as she walked. There were no thorns of any kind here, nothing except tender leaves and fragrant blossoms. Her favorite were the ones that released the scent of oranges when crushed between her fingers. Blossoms in Fushang grew back minutes after being picked while fruit grew back in hours.

Deer came out as well, unwilling to be left out of the procession. The group walked or drifted through cherry groves and over fallen logs that had new saplings sprouting from their trunks. Everything grew fast in Fushang.

They pushed through a thick mass of blue flowers and came to a lake. Lady Shella took Zondela by the hand and drifted higher, smiling down at her. Zondela relaxed her mind as she had been taught and her feet lifted off the ground for a few moments as she drifted over the lake. The two settled into the water amid the wild splashing of rabbits that frolicked and fought for their attention.

Lady Shella released her hand and turned to her. "Why do you wear that sword and nothing else, Zondela?"

The Infernian looked up at the clouds drifting by. Fushang was on a floating island, deep in the midst of the Restless Ocean, accessible only by a vortex that she had found deep in a crevice in the wastes between the Dynasties. "It reminds me of where I came from, and what I was. It is a part of me somehow."

A rabbit swam toward her, peddling furiously with its long limbs. Zondela picked it up and cradled it against her, the rabbit relaxing its ears and resting. Her dreams of Fushang had become real.

Discover more from
King Tiger Books!

Don't miss *Slaves to the Reptiles*, a new book about dragons, hydras, reptile mages, and the knights that face them in battle.

Make requests for sequels - want to see more of Zondela or learn about Idalika's people from *Sea of Dekatos*?

Follow us on Facebook, Goodreads, or KingTigerBooks.com.

http://kingtigerbooks.com

https://www.facebook.com/kingtigerbooks

https://www.goodreads.com/author/show/1063539.Stephen_D_Gibson

If you enjoyed *Penturian*
watch for
The War Machines of von Saarik

Here's a short excerpt.

Deep in an arid land, hot desert winds blew over a young man's body, cradling it with sand as if in mourning over the waste. He had spent his life as a warrior, honoring their code and serving them despite the hardships. As his eyes closed he regretted the lost opportunities, the many years spent studying how to build and how to kill. Other men leaped over his body as they ran, intent on protecting their own lives, knowing there was nothing they could do for him. They fired their weapons at the enemy, disappearing over the ridges of sand as the battle spilled forward. The wounded man wanted to join them, wanted to rise to his feet and find the strength to continue the war. He tried to rise but his body had never felt so weak. Regret and anguish brought a bitter taste to his mouth.

On a distant world called Imtrund, an ancient spell was cast by a desperate young woman named Sheila. Her world was about to be engulfed in an even greater war as Tzith-Sak and Effluvia easily destroyed the King's forces in the south. Sheila - a witch who loved kindness, plants, animals, summer rain, and floppy-eared rabbits - cast a Primordial Summoning Spell. The incantation was so powerful that outside of dire emergencies it was rarely invoked.

The life force of Imtrund rushed through space with a sonic noise akin to wind flowing through a rocky crag and many, many creatures heard it. Inhabitants of the astral worlds raised their heads as it blasted past them, touching their minds for an unmeasurably small time with gentle fingertips before rushing on. The magic dashed from planet to planet, seeking that which the caster had called for. After the magic had delicately probed tens of thousands of beings it found the broken soldier.

The man lay dying, his life-force eking out of his body from wounds inflicted in the hot, violent conflict, and so the life-magic of Imtrund inhaled his escaping life-force and darted back home. It moved so fast that planets and suns were blurs. With the latent power of the planet's living energy, the man's body was re-created. He now lay on Imtrund and opened his eyes.

"Where am I?" he asked.

"You are at my cottage, in southern Imtrund. I must admit, you are not what I expected from my summoning spell."

"Who are you?"

"I am Sheila." She examined him with those piercing eyes, making him feel like an insect. "Is this your true form?"

"Yes," he said.

"Disappointing. What manner of being are you?"

"I am an engineer and a soldier. I design and build things. Mostly military equipment. I was trained to build and erect bridges while under enemy fire."

There was anger in her voice. "Then build one so that I may bury you underneath it when the assassins get here."

"Sheila," he said. "You haven't asked me for my name."

"Fine. What is it?"

"Gunnar von Saarik."